In the Aftermath

In the Aftermath

A Novel

Jane Ward

She Writes Press, a BookSparks imprint
A Division of SparkPointStudio, LLC.

Published 2021

Printed in the United States of America

Print ISBN: 978-1-64742-193-9
E-ISBN: 978-1-64742-194-6
Library of Congress Control Number: [LOCCN]

For information, address:
She Writes Press
1569 Solano Ave #546
Berkeley, CA 94707

She Writes Press is a division of SparkPoint Studio, LLC.

"'I will die and be reborn in my own child. He will bury my remains here and carry on in my place.' The Benu Bird turned and soared into the sky, vanishing into the light of Re."

—from *Cry of the Benu Bird*,
by C. Shana Greger

He checks his watch. The friend he waits for is twenty minutes late for their meeting at the café, maybe held up at work or in traffic, maybe dead on the side of the road, for all he knows. He does know for sure that his cell phone is dead. He made too many long calls earlier in the morning and ran down the battery: the one to his friend, arranging to meet; earlier, a call to his father, leaving a voicemail, begging; to the bank, begging some more. Wasting precious minutes pleading, pleading. And the phone charger that plugs into the cigarette lighter is in his wife's car. Nothing is going right this morning, not one thing.

April 2008

1

Jules Herron stepped out of her tub onto the looped cotton rug and reached for a bath towel. The morning's shower had been brief, taken as much to wake her up as it was to wash. Her long soak would come later in the day, after her shift at the bakery, when she really needed it. She had long ago accepted the lot of the baker: reeking of browned butter and sugar. The same homey aromas that customers breathed in deeply and exclaimed over once they crossed the threshold of the bakery weren't as pleasant to the person trapped in the small, hot kitchen day after day. Cooking and baking smells settled into a baker's hair, her skin, and got trapped in the woven fibers of cotton T-shirts and aprons. Twice a year, every piece of her work wardrobe had to be tossed and exchanged for new.

Still, Jules loved her job. Opening the shop with her husband, David, ten years earlier had been a risky venture. David had left his lucrative but stressful job at a powerhouse accounting firm, she had given up her safe head baker position at another bakery, and they'd sunk all their money and then some into renovating the rundown downtown property. But taking their shot at becoming business owners had paid off. Their small family had strengthened as their venture took off, and as a bonus, the bakery had bound them to their community, had in short order become one of the most inviting anchor shops in the downtown landscape of storefronts, a familiar and popular sight on the main street with their sparkling plate glass windows and seasonal displays.

The years showed on her body a little less kindly than they did on the bakery. One glance down over herself confirmed what she knew to be true: she looked good enough for her forties, but not as vibrant as she used to. Her bath-towel fluffed-up hair was still good and thick but was no longer glossy. Her gaze passed over thighs that jiggled a little when she walked, a small swell of belly below her navel, a few silvery stretch marks, buttocks that firmed up nicely only when tucked into a good pair of jeans, and arms that, despite the constant lifting of buckets of batter and mixer bowls heavy with bread dough, displayed that dreaded swing of flesh when she raised them. She was not at all fat, but she wasn't exactly toned either. She could use some real exercise, but between work and Rennie's school and after-school activities, there wasn't much time left at the end of the day.

At the beginning, she and David had imagined a more balanced life, with them taking turns baking in the wee hours and poring over the books together at tax time, but that hadn't quite panned out. After the excitement of the first year wore off, Jules had proven to be an impatient teacher with David and his inexperience with pastry, and she'd reclaimed the kitchen as her territory. He, in turn, had rolled his eyes when she couldn't grasp what he thought were the simplest of business terms, concepts like balance sheets and profit margins. Sometimes she wished David had caught on to the craft of baking or that she had given him more time to catch on, and that he had given her time to master the bookkeeping and financials. They might have split both the full-time physical job and the managerial headaches between them, giving each other breaks from their individual stresses. But that door had closed years ago. Through some negotiating and tweaking of schedules, however, they had at least arrived at an agreement that worked to move the busy days forward: Jules opened the bakery and David brought Rennie to school; he got the extra sleep he needed in the morning and she went to bed early; she stayed in the back of the house crafting the pastries and breads she loved to make, and David concentrated on keeping the business finances on track.

Maybe it was time to cut back her responsibilities and give her full-time position to someone younger and less prone to aching knees and a stiff lower back after hours on her feet. Sandy, the other full-time baker, would be the logical candidate for taking over the head baker job. She might like the raise and the title, and Jules already knew and trusted her skills. With the extra time for herself, Jules thought, she could get more rest, get back onto a normal sleep schedule, maybe even hit their friend Charlie's gym to address all the aches and stiff joints and lack of muscle tone. At the very least, she thought as she reached around her back to hook her bra, she should start stretching before she became permanently stiff and inflexible.

The movement annoyed something in her right shoulder, some muscle or tendon, so she slowed down and took her time pulling on one of the few T-shirts in her collection that had some life left in it. Carefully, nursing her arm, she reached for her jeans.

She should discuss both the gym idea and any potential staffing changes with David, she considered as she dressed in the quiet of the steamy bathroom. But when would they find the time? The normal pace of work alone kept them comfortably busy. On top of that was Rennie's homework, chorus rehearsals, after-school clubs, and pleas for more play dates with friends. And now David was caught up in managing a bakery expansion.

Over the course of the past six months of construction, he had grown as distracted and testy as he had been in his last two years as senior vice president for the accounting firm. The upheavals in their workplace were getting to Jules and the staff as well, but some people found better ways to cope. Their counter help made jokes about the ripped up and unfinished unit next door, calling it "the abyss." When they nicknamed the plastic sheeting that hung in the passage between the two spaces "Swayze" for its ghostly rustling every time the bakery's front door opened or closed, Jules had to laugh. But David, much more invested than any of the counter help, had bristled at the silly joke.

"Relax, it's not a criticism of you," Jules had told him when he heard the nickname for the first time. "Joking lightens the atmosphere. They're blowing off steam. You have to admit, 'Swayze' is pretty funny."

But he hadn't agreed. The renovation project was his baby—his idea, his goal. And it had all happened so fast at first, a whirlwind of activity—until, almost as abruptly, the work had come to a standstill.

Jules pulled on her jeans, buttoned them, and threaded her wide leather belt through the belt loops. She paused in the middle of dressing, the two belt ends in her hands, as she caught her reflection in the mirror. There, she noted some new laugh lines around her eyes, and puffy half-moon circles underneath. Joining these was a vertical crease at the bridge of her nose, likely a permanent result of drawing her brows together so often. She leaned in close to the mirror, let go of the belt buckle, and used her index finger to draw back the skin near her eyes, then turned her head from one side to the other, assessing the wrinkles and the elasticity of her skin. *I need some rest; we both need some rest*, she thought as she took her hands from her face and watched the skin take its time settling. *We also need to reconnect.*

Like the renovation work, their sex life had come to a standstill. They hadn't made love since breaking ground on their new space. The day the work started, David had been giddy with the prospect of taking the bakery in a new direction, and his words had bubbled over faster than the champagne they'd opened in haste for celebration. Before long, fueled by excitement and alcohol, two pairs of hands were grabbing at clothes, unbuttoning, unzipping, undressing.

Jules remembered giggling, the champagne making her lightheaded in the middle of the day. "We're naughty," she'd said as she slid a warm hand across his chest.

Since then, in the few quiet moments when their schedules had coincided and she had tried to initiate sex, David had put her off with excuses. He was tired or not relaxed enough. Twice, he'd claimed he had a headache.

"I thought that was supposed to be my line," Jules had said after the second time. Then she'd rolled over onto her side, her back to him.

The rejections depressed her.

Stop it, she told herself. *David says the builder will be back soon. This time there's a real end in sight.*

To make herself feel better, she made a mental list of tasks she could accomplish over the next day or two: *I'll talk to David, and then to Sandy. It's time to pass the reins. If I'm home more, I can even take on some of David's responsibilities. I can make the calls to the contractor and shuttle Rennie around to her activities.* "And get some damn rest," she said aloud to her reflection. "Both of us."

Jules brought the belt end and buckle together and cinched. *It's nothing, nothing we haven't already weathered. Tough it out*, she added, and then she flexed her bicep, mugging for the mirror. The reflection lifted her mood for a few seconds.

As she turned to grab the sweater she needed for cool mornings while she waited for the bakery to heat up, she realized it wasn't hanging in the bathroom and hadn't made it onto the clothes hook with the rest of her clothes. She looked behind her. Not on the floor either. She cracked the bathroom door and flipped up the hall light switch. Ah, yes, there it was, a puddle of midnight blue in the middle of the runner rug. Mystery solved.

She grabbed the sweater and reached for Rennie's doorknob, wanting to check on her sleeping child and blow a kiss before leaving, but was interrupted by the creak of her own bedroom door opening. David stood inside the doorframe, squinting and shielding his eyes with one hand.

"Oh, shoot," Jules whispered. "I'm so sorry."

"Can you turn off the light, please?" he said. "It woke me up."

"Again, I'm sorry. I dropped my sweater and I needed the light."

"It's fine." David lifted a hand in a tired wave and took a couple of steps backward into the bedroom. He started to swing the door closed.

"Wait," Jules said before the dark bedroom swallowed him up. She wasn't ready to let him go.

David turned his head to look back at the clock on the nightstand. "You're running at least ten minutes late. If you're any later, I'll be doing crowd control during rush hour."

Looking beyond him into the darkened bedroom, Jules could see the red glow emanating from the digital clock's face. "I'll catch up on the work, I always do." She walked the few steps toward David and reached out to touch his shoulder. The muscle cap on his upper arm felt cushioned and doughy as she began massaging it. She smiled, thinking of her own promise to make more time for the gym. She should get David's sedentary ass to the gym as well. She would call Charlie after her shift; he would help.

David let go of the doorknob. He reached up and removed Jules's hand. "That feels good, but—"

"I know, I know. The light. My husband, the vampire. Or is it werewolves who are sensitive to the light?"

"Both, maybe?" He shook his head. "I really have no idea."

"So, I was thinking in the shower—"

"Usually dangerous."

"Don't tease. Let me finish." She didn't want to let him go without making her offer. David gave a slight nod and she continued, "I've been thinking about the expansion. How about if I make some calls when I get home and see if I can find us a new builder?"

David blinked. "I told you I don't want to start from scratch. It makes no sense."

"I know you said that, but—"

"But it still makes no sense," David said. "Christ, you're beginning to sound like my mother, finding fault in everything I do. Can you, for once, let me handle it?"

Stunned, Jules's mouth dropped open. "That's not fair," she said when she found her voice again. "I only want to help. I think this project might be less stressful if we help each other."

David sighed and slouched against the doorframe. "Look, I'm tired. I just want to go back to bed."

"And I woke you up."

"You didn't. The light did."

Jules looked at her husband, noticing for the first time some new lines around his eyes. His skin was pale and had a gray cast to it, and there was white in the stubble of his beard. His hair was also turning gray. She recalled her own face in the mirror, her body under the bath towel. *Suddenly, we're old.*

She stepped closer, reached for his hand, squeezed it. "Can we call a truce for now? Maybe we can talk more tonight?"

"Sure, a truce."

Jules gripped his hand once more and then let go.

"Don't forget the light behind you," David said as he retreated back into their dark bedroom. "Also, don't forget what we discussed the other day, about the sugar cookies."

Jules suppressed an urge to roll her eyes. "I won't," she answered, but David had already closed the door behind him.

She gave one last look at the closed bedroom door and then walked carefully down the unlit staircase. Outside, she dashed through steady but gentle rain to her car, reminded that a storm had been predicted for later that morning. With luck, she would be at the bakery before the wind picked up.

She was halfway to work before she realized she had never opened Rennie's door to check on her. She was running too late to turn around and remedy that mistake, so she promised herself she would give her daughter an extra hug later in the day and continued on downtown.

When she arrived at the bakery, she flipped the switches to turn on the lights, the ovens, and the vents. Within seconds, the bakery kitchen was bright and noisy. As the convection ovens heated up, she put on a small pot of strong coffee for the jolt of caffeine she needed to get her through the first few hours of baking. While she could probably do the job in her sleep, she didn't want to. Coffee was essential.

She waited by the machine for the first few drips of coffee to hit the pot. As soon as there was enough for a serving, she filled a tall paper cup and brought it, along with a clean apron, to her workbench. Most days, she savored the first few minutes at work alone as she brewed and sipped her cup of coffee. With her back resting against the broad oak worktable set in the middle of the kitchen, she would look out onto the dark and empty main street, letting the coffee do its work. This morning, though, she knew she shouldn't linger.

Still—*"Christ, you're beginning to sound like my mother."* She winced; the comparison to her mother-in-law stung. She was nothing like Miriam, with her skill for focusing on failure. The woman was negative, a person with impossibly high standards who poked and prodded at other people's shortcomings. At Jules's most generous, she described her mother-in-law as chronically disappointed.

She sipped more coffee and recalled the night she and David had announced to his parents that he was quitting his job and they were buying a building to open a bakery downtown, the same night she'd vowed she would see her mother-in-law as little as possible in the months leading up to the opening.

David had warned her the evening might get ugly; he hadn't wanted to tell his parents at all.

"So how does that work?" she had asked him. "We open a business and we swear everyone we know to secrecy?"

"Something like that, yes."

She'd smiled at him then, and suggested they invite his parents to dinner to make the announcement on comfortable turf. "We eat, we tell them, they leave."

David had relented. The invitation had been issued and accepted. Between the main course and dessert, he'd dropped the news.

It was met with his mother's stunned stare.

During the awkward lull, David had offered coffee and had risen to make it. Jules remembered the looks that had passed between mother and son, and how she'd waved him back into his seat, knowing he would want the time alone with his parents to get them on board with the news.

"Let me," she'd said, and she'd disappeared into the kitchen to start the drip machine. As soon as she left, their voices had risen.

"Why in the world would you do this? Turn your back on all your education for something so reckless?"

"Nothing's 'reckless.' We wrote a business plan, and the bank approved it."

"For a bakery?"

"For a bakery. It's what we want to do."

"I have a hard time believing you want to do this. Someone like Julia, who couldn't even finish college? Yes. But not you."

"Jeez, that's—"

Later Jules had told him how, alone in the kitchen, she'd tried to drown out the rest of the argument by running cold water full blast. "But it would have taken a tsunami to drown her out."

He had reached for her then, told her they would keep their distance from his parents. That they would create their own world, one where no one and nothing negative could interfere. But now, in the quiet of the bakery, that morning's sharp words came back to her.

Stop it, she told herself, and she shook her head to clear it. They were both overwrought, and she was being a drama queen. The only thing to do was throw herself into work. She set down her coffee cup, tied the crisp apron at her waist, and walked over to the refrigerators to gather the ingredients she needed to make the first round of pastries.

She checked the production list David left taped to the fridge door and then lifted a wrapped package of butter-rich dough from the shelf where it had been chilling overnight. She looked it over for problems or irregularities, but there were none: numerous alternating layers of butter and yeast dough, a perfect tri-fold, nice squared off edges, and a good height. Sandy had prepped it well yesterday afternoon.

David had been reminding them lately to eliminate as much waste as possible, so Sandy's meticulous prep work mattered. The Danish and croissant dough couldn't be rolled more than once, and this rectangle would feed into the rollers of the Rondo and come out the other end in a mostly neat sheet, meaning nothing much to be trimmed and tossed. If this had been sugar cookie dough, though, given David's latest protocol change, she would have had to gather up the scraps and re-roll them at least twice.

"The cookie that gets cut from a re-roll is a tougher cookie," Jules had argued the previous week when they'd discussed changing the practice.

"Crisper," David had answered, "not tougher. And still acceptable," he'd added, pointing out that the decorated sugar cookies often went to children. "A five-year-old won't be able to tell if the cookie is crisper than you'd like it to be. They are into the sugary frosting and biting the ears off the Easter bunnies. Besides, I don't feel right tossing scraps in this day and age."

Making less-than-perfect baked goods bothered Jules, even for undiscriminating children. But David was right: throwing away good food was a bad habit, especially now, when food costs were so high. From her vendors, from the invoices she occasionally had to sign when accepting deliveries, she knew flour prices had risen sharply. Prices of all her ingredients had, really. At least he wasn't asking her to scoop less muffin batter into the tins. Not yet, anyway. Although it was probably only a matter of time before she had that conversation with him.

Jules frowned as she anticipated arguments about portion control. Customers loved her oversize muffins. The way their plump domes glistened with crystals of sanding sugar prompted people to head home with more treats than they had intended to buy. She was convinced of it.

She began feeding the Danish dough into the Rondo. *Thunk, thunk*—the gears engaged as she operated the handle and sent the dough rolling down the belt and then back. "Think of my muffins as a loss leader," she would tell David if they had another cost control conversation. "Economizing can't be our only goal."

Unless he dismissed that conversation, too, as yet another not worth having and made the decision without consulting her.

Jules frowned but kept dialing down the settings on the rolling machine and sending the dough up and down the belt until the sheet had reached her desired thickness. Up and down, up and down. When the dough looked just right, her hands went to work—running the rolling cutter down the length and cutting the sheet into long ribbons, twisting each one into a corkscrew spiral, coiling each long twist like a snail's shell, tucking in the ends before placing the sweet rolls, ready for their fruit fillings, on the waiting baking trays. She barely needed to think about the movements anymore. Before she knew it, her first few trays were full and ready for the proofing box. She racked them for their rise and turned to the muffins, scooping into buckets of batter lifted from the fridge, filling tin after tin.

As she was sliding the pan of muffins into the oven, she was hit with a blast of cold air pushing its way in through the front door. Jules turned. Sandy had arrived for her shift on a gust of wind.

"Quick, Sandy, close the door. It's freezing."

"Sorry. The storm's blowing in. Temperature dropped at least 15 degrees on my drive over. But the rain has stopped. For now." Sandy pulled the door shut behind her and turned the lock, causing the tarp they called Swayze to rustle back and forth a little before settling back into place. Jules noticed that the once-clear plastic sheet was cloudy and marked all over with white wrinkles and its bottom edge was tattered, despite the fact no one had pushed it aside or crossed through it in days.

"Sorry I'm late," Sandy said as she detoured to the coffee pot. "I'm glad there's coffee. You're a peach, boss."

"No problem. I got a late start, too—just now catching up." Jules returned to her bench for another muffin tin.

Sandy reached for an extra-large paper cup and held it up to Jules. Jules shook her head. Her coffee had gone cold, but she would wait until she had more baking underway before accepting a refill.

Sandy poured the last of the coffee for herself, took a sip, and groaned with pleasure. "Coffee, you are my first true love." As she shrugged out of her coat, she looked over at the tarp.

"Swayze looks a little worse for wear." She tipped her chin in its direction. "When did that happen? What does it say about me that I hardly notice it anymore?"

"I actively avoid noticing it," Jules said.

"What's going on with the construction?" Sandy looked over the rim of her cup at Jules. "You know yet?"

Jules frowned. Sandy was uncharacteristically chatty this morning. Most days, they maintained a relationship that both appreciated: companionable and cooperative, but separate. The two barely said more than good morning until much of the baking was done and the shop was priming to open. Jules was scrambling today and wanted to stay focused on work. They both needed to.

Without looking up from her bench, she said, "David told me the builder had to start another job or lose the bid. But he hopes to be back once he frees up guys from that other job. Next week, maybe."

"Maybe? So, no guaranteed return date?"

Although annoyed with Sandy for pressing for answers, Jules paused and tried to recall David's exact words: "I don't want you to worry about it, too, okay? It's not ideal but I talk to him often enough that he remembers we're waiting. They'll be back in a week or so, I predict."

Predict. That was the word he'd used, she remembered now. David's guess, not the builder's guarantee. At the time, she had let his vagueness slide and had gone right back to her job of putting food in the display cases.

"Next week. Or the week after," she said to Sandy with more conviction than she felt, and then she set the timer, subtracting a minute to make up for the time she had wasted talking.

"That's good," Sandy said. "My boyfriend says this sometimes happens when someone commissions a job but can't pay their bills. I told him he was off base." Sandy made no move to start her work. Instead, she took a big sip of coffee.

"Yes, he's off base." Jules spoke more sharply than she intended but she felt irked that a guy she barely knew would weigh in at all, especially with his suggestion that money was somehow at the root of the problems. Their bank loan had been secured months ago, through the same bank they had been doing business with for years.

"I shouldn't have said anything. He's anxious, is all. He's been trying to sell his condo and his agent's telling him it's worth less than his mortgage. At this point, he'd be better off holding on until the market improves, but he really wants to move closer to his work. It's getting to him, I think."

Jules nodded. "It's fine. Everyone's anxious about something lately."

"They're calling this housing market a bubble, like everything was inflated and it's now about to burst. For once, I'm kind of glad I lost out on that that condo I made an offer on last year."

Housing bubbles? This really was all news to Jules. Talk about a bubble; she'd been in her own, working and sleeping, driving her daughter here and there, for months seeing no one except the people who passed through the bakery's doors. "If it helps, I remember the same thing happening about twenty years ago and the banks adjusted their lending. At least, that's what our loan officer said at the time. I don't really follow this much. But I'm sure things will straighten out again. Then maybe you can look for another condo. It's nice to own." She cleared her throat. "Hey, my muffins are all in and I'm going to clean up," she said, putting an end to the talk about Sandy's boyfriend's anxieties and the stalled renovation in the café space. She walked over to the sink and mixed up a weak bleach and water solution that she took back to her bench and, head down, used to clean up the sticky worktop.

As much as she wanted to put these thoughts out of her mind, something about the boyfriend's observations nagged at her, and for the first time Jules wondered about Nancy from the arts and crafts shop next door. One day, she'd been complaining that no one was shopping for art project kits anymore; everything they needed they could find online, delivered right to their doorsteps. The next day, there had been brown paper on the windows. At the time, Jules had given Nancy's comment little thought. David's excitement about the extra space finally opening up to them had eclipsed everything. She smiled, thinking about how infectious his enthusiasm had been. Just as quickly, though, an image of David popped into her head: David on the sidewalk outside the bakery, arms outstretched, palms up, exchanging words with the project boss, who only shook his head.

The timer rang and interrupted her wandering thoughts. Startled, she looked down at the rag in her hands and the bench. Eleven minutes had passed, it was time to rotate the muffin tins, and she had been scrubbing the same square foot of the table's surface over and over. She felt her face flush with embarrassment and looked up to make sure Sandy hadn't noticed her distraction. She set down the cloth and wiped her hands on her apron.

The top shelf of the oven was a stretch for Jules without the stepstool, but she didn't want to waste any more time crossing the kitchen to retrieve it. She grabbed a set of potholders and stood on her toes to reach for the uppermost tin like she had done a million times before. This time, both her forearms hit the hot oven rack.

Jules had been burned so many times over the past twenty years—her hands bore many scars—but she'd never grown accustomed to the first moments of searing pain.

"Shit!"

She rotated the muffin pan the rest of the way around, slid it onto the shelf, and shut the door. She had managed to save the half-baked muffins from the floor, but now the skin on her forearms stung and red stripes were emerging—one on each arm, almost identical twins—a few inches up from her wrists. When she lifted them up closer to her face, she could feel the heat radiating off her skin.

Sandy came up behind her. "I've got the first aid kit."

"I'm fine. Maybe just some cold water."

"You're not fine." Sandy took one of Jules's hands in her own and looked closely at the puckering skin. "These are already starting to blister. Let's get some ointment and bandages on there."

Jules nodded. "Actually, I could use some ice first. My skin feels so hot."

"Ice. Sure," Sandy said. "Go sit in the bathroom, I'll meet you there."

She handed the red metal box to Jules and hustled over to the freezer. Jules walked with the kit to the back of the kitchen, into the staff bathroom. She hit the light switch and was greeted by her reflection in the mirror. The fluorescent bulb made her skin look sallow. She set the first aid kit down on the sink vanity and looked away.

"What a rookie mistake," she said when Sandy walked through the door. "Rookie and stupid."

"Sit down," Sandy told her.

Jules obeyed, took a seat on the toilet lid. Sandy had filled two bread bags with ice cubes, and she applied these to the burns once Jules was settled with her arms resting on her thighs.

"Happens, boss."

"It shouldn't happen when we are already running behind schedule."

"That's when it always happens." Sandy smiled. "Murphy's law."

"But still."

"Meh, so we're behind. So what? It's not the end of the world."

Jules smiled at Sandy's steadiness. She had been right, Sandy would make a fine leader.

"No, it's not the end of the world," she agreed. *Things could be worse*, she thought as Sandy made quick work of the bandaging.

They could always be worse.

Jules measured white and wheat flours and a whole grain and seed blend and poured them all into the proofed yeast waiting in the bowl of her big Hobart mixer. She added some salt and a good amount of honey and turned on the machine. Soon, the Hobart whined and scraped and groaned, its dough hook making slow circles, gathering the ingredients together in a shaggy mass. This was her second batch of bread dough, multigrain. The muffins were completely cooled, the oatmeal bread dough was in its first rise, and they would open the doors soon; her morning was in full swing.

A couple of times since the accident, Sandy had sidled over to the back bench to ask how she was feeling. She'd also offered to wash all the dishes that had accumulated, an offer that would double her chores.

Jules couldn't meet Sandy's eyes. She dipped her chin to hide the blush of embarrassment and kept her eyes on her work. "Thanks," she said to the offer. "And I'm fine."

But she wasn't fine, not really. The accident had shaken her. As had Sandy's annoying boyfriend's questions, and getting such a late start, and bickering with David. These didn't add up to anything more than just a bad day, and yet something about the morning poked and poked at her like the pointed end of a stick.

Jules stood at the mixer and watched her dough go from

shaggy to cohesive and springy. Losing concentration led to mishaps, and she had to fight her tendency to go through the motions, her mind elsewhere. There were potential dangers in any kitchen: finding a sharp knife at the bottom of a sink full of dishes, wearing jewelry that could get caught in mixer gears, touching hot things. She had lost focus earlier, and now her body was paying the price. Her arms throbbed in a steady pulse.

Once the dough had formed a ball, Jules increased the speed, set the timer, and left the mixer to do the heavy kneading. She stepped over to the sink to wash her hands, taking care to avoid wetting the bandages. As she scrubbed her hands together to remove the flour and sticky honey residue, she felt a hand on her shoulder and jumped, splashing drops of water onto the front of her apron. Jules turned to see that Florence, the morning's counter help, had arrived to open the store.

"Oh, sweetheart, I didn't mean to startle you," Florence said. "I only wanted to say good morning. I thought you must have heard me come in earlier, I made such a racket at the front door. The wind is wild outside! I think it's going to rain any minute."

Jules shook her head. "I hope I didn't scare you either." She wiped her hands on the towel at her waist and swapped all her soiled linens for clean ones. She tied on the new apron on her way back to her bench.

"It'll take more than a little fright to do me in." Florence stepped around her and grabbed some clean metal trays, along with parchment sheets, from the storage shelves. She took the trays to the far end of the bench and started lining them with the paper. "Muffins look good, as usual."

"The Danish is done. Sandy's scones, too." Jules slid the cooled baking sheets down to Florence's end of the table. "Here you go."

"So many of everything," Florence noted. "On the couple of

days I did the afternoon shifts last week, we didn't sell out. David told me he planned to cut back."

"Cut back?" Jules asked. "Cut back on production levels?" Perplexed, she drew her brows together. Then, remembering the deep crease on the bridge of her nose, she tried to relax her face. "First I've heard of that."

"Really? I thought that after—well, never mind." Florence waved off the unfinished thought. "What do I know? I'm sure I misunderstood. Three trays of muffins okay for now?" she asked. Without waiting for an answer, she began arranging the different types in their neat rows between the three trays.

Jules walked over to the Hobart and switched it off several seconds before the timer sounded. The machine wound down with a defeated whine and then stopped. "Florence," she said.

"Mm-hmm?" The older woman didn't look up from her work.

"Stop working for a sec and look at me. 'You thought after' . . . what?"

Florence stopped placing muffins in neat rows but continued to square the display trays with the corners of the bench, as if stalling for time.

"Florence?"

"I'm not comfortable being in the middle of this."

"If you know something I don't, then I'm sorry, but in the middle is exactly where you are. Fill me in on what happened last week."

"There wasn't waste, not really," Florence said. "It's not as if David's throwing food away. The food pantry took all the extras. And like I said, this was only on those two days I worked late because of the conflict with my morning doctor appointments."

"The food pantry?" Florence's explanations weren't helping to clear up any confusion. If anything, Jules was more confused than ever. "If we had leftovers, why not start using the day-old shelves again?" she asked. Before they'd even opened their doors for the first time, she had convinced David to install a day-old rack right inside the front door to hold the stock that was left over as they worked to get production levels right. As they'd improved their calculations and customer traffic had increased, they'd rarely had leftovers, save for a few loaves of bread, at the end of the day. When the bakery expansion began, David had tucked the rarely used shelves behind the counter.

"The food pantry needs donations. Haven't you seen their pleas in the local paper?"

Jules shook her head.

"Trust me," Florence said, "there's lots of need." She picked up the tray of muffins she had been arranging and walked with it to the front of the shop.

Jules followed. She caught Sandy's eye and registered her concern in the moment she passed by her, but she kept going, following in Florence's wake.

"Donating food is not even the point. The point is, I asked you about something David shared with you that he didn't share with me. What exactly did he say to you about the production levels?"

Florence set the tray of muffins down in the case and sighed heavily. When she turned to face Jules, she looked upset. "I said I didn't want to get involved in disagreements between you two, but . . . David told me you wouldn't listen to him about cutting back, that you insisted on making the same amounts of food even though business has slowed down. No offense, Jules"—Florence took a step closer to her and laid a hand on her shoulder—"but you can be stubborn when it comes to getting your own way with the baking."

"He said I wouldn't listen to him?"

"It's okay, dear. Most of the time it's a good thing you're such a stickler." Florence patted Jules just below the meat of her shoulder. For the first time, she noticed the bandages farther down on Jules's arms and reached for her hand to get a closer look. "Oh, what happened?"

"Nothing." Jules drew her arm back. "Minor burn, it's fine."

"Well, if you're done with the questions, I'm going to finish getting the cases filled and put fresh coffee on." Florence bustled back for another tray, leaving Jules standing by herself at the open cases.

She couldn't move as she tried to make sense of the conversation. David had not discussed any of this with her; of this, she was certain. She stared out the large window into the morning's darkness. The sun showed no sign of rising; it would be a gloomy day. Still, the main street was coming to life. A few buses lumbered by and stopped at the traffic lights. In a little less than an hour, the corner would be crowded with workers on their way to offices, waiting for transportation, and buses would come more frequently.

One of their neighbors, a man who spent most of his day out-of-doors, usually smoking on his front stoop, now strolled up and down the block. Both Jules and David had scolded him in the past for littering their length of the sidewalk with the black filters of his nasty-looking brown cigarettes. Scolding had made no difference, though, and neither had an offer of a free cup of morning coffee. The man had gladly accepted the brew but the littering had continued. Unhappy but resigned, David took out the broom three times a day and swept up after him. Jules wondered if the man was now passing the time, waiting for her doors to open so he could get his coffee.

She wondered, too, where David was now or if he was even up. He liked to stay under the covers until the last possible moment. She thought of calling the house with the pretext of saying good morning to Rennie but decided not to. She feared she would launch into another argument, unwise with only the information from Florence to go on. Why would David place the blame for overage on her? And why, if there were substantial amounts of leftovers—whoever's fault that was—why weren't they selling the pastries at half price, as agreed? Even the decision to donate should have been made together. The burns started to throb, and Jules relaxed her arms to reduce the pressure on the wounds. She closed her eyes. She was tired of asking questions, tired of thinking.

"Hey, boss." Sandy had made her way over and was standing at Jules's side. "Want me to finish the bread?"

"Oh, brother. I completely forgot."

"Let me finish it. You look like you could use a break."

"Did you hear any of the conversation with Florence?"

Sandy nodded. The two bakers looked away from each other and toward the pastry cases. Florence was in front, affixing the product signs onto the trays. A new pot of coffee perked.

"While you were talking, I checked the production book. I looked at all the sheets going back to last year. David hasn't made any changes at all. Not even minor adjustments. Don't be angry that I looked. I didn't doubt you. But I wanted to be sure we hadn't missed something."

"And?"

Sandy shook her head. "Nope."

"So what's this all about, then? We're baking more than we sell, and David gives away the extra without discussing it with me? Why? And why blame me?"

Sandy's face screwed up in concentration. "It makes no sense. He's a bottom-line guy. If he wanted you to stop baking, he'd tell you, right? Like with the cookies you've been fighting about, rerolling the sugar cookie scraps? He's been telling us for weeks."

The two women fell silent again. Several feet away, Florence reached for her keys in the handbag she kept stuffed in the cabinet underneath the cash register. The jingle of the key ring meant it was almost opening time. In under fifteen minutes, she would unlock the front door.

"Let me get the bread shaped and in the proofer for you," Sandy offered again. "Give your arms a break." She nodded at Jules's bandages.

"I won't say no. Actually, if you don't mind, I think I'll take a walk. Fifteen minutes, tops. And Sandy," Jules said as she grabbed her cardigan from the peg where she had hung it earlier, "thanks for the sanity check."

Jules stepped outside. There was a damp chill in the air, and the forceful wind pushed back at her as she walked into it. She could have used more than the light sweater she was wearing but made do, pulling it tight against her body and wrapping her arms around her front. If she went back into the bakery to borrow a jacket, some piece of work, some glitch in operations would surely derail her. Right now, she needed out of the close, overheated space. She needed fresh air to clear her head. She needed, above all, to think.

She stood on the sidewalk, contemplating which way to turn. Seeing her aimless neighbor to her left and headed her way prompted her to turn right, away from him and away from the center of town.

She walked past the last of the storefronts and into the warren of residential streets, went past them and then turned right again, intending to make a big loop behind Main Street that would eventually circle back to work. She picked up her pace and listened to the sound of her clog heels hitting the pavement. The foot strikes, hard sole on stone, sounded angry. Anyone who saw her approaching would almost certainly sidestep out of her way. Inside, however, she felt the anger and embarrassment subsiding. She no longer feared she would throttle her husband the minute he showed up at work. If he had kept something from her, there would be a reason. And he would tell her what that was when she asked.

She stopped before she reached the corner of Main Street. She leaned against a stone wall surrounding a large, brick-fronted, two-family home, settled back, and wrapped her arms around herself again. Under her sleeves, the first aid tape yanked the hairs on her arms, but she ignored the pain.

The bakery was just around the corner. She wasn't wearing a watch and had no idea of the time, but she must have been gone fifteen minutes already. Florence would have unlocked the doors by now, and the first early bird customers were likely trickling in. She shivered and thought of the blasting heat of the ovens. It was time to head back and throw herself once again into her work. She sighed and pushed herself off the wall.

At the corner of Main Street, she saw a familiar figure crossing at the lights of the intersection. Mai owned the restaurant across the street with her husband, Leo, and they did regular business with the bakery, buying multigrain rolls for their dinner service. Mai wore a long coat sweater, both chic and snug, and, seeing her, Jules felt colder and dowdier than ever in her plain T-shirt and stretched out mom cardigan. She lifted her hand in a wave as Mai walked her way.

"Perfect timing," Mai called. "I was on my way to see you."

"You're up and out early," Jules said as they met at the corner.

"I had a few minutes before I have to take the kids to school, and I thought I'd run in to see you about our roll order. You walking back to work? I'll walk with you."

The two set off together. Jules slowed her pace to match Mai's, relaxing a bit in the even-tempered presence of her slightly older acquaintance.

"You wanted to talk about your order? I hope it's not a quality issue."

"Oh gosh, no. Everyone loves your bread. But . . ." They had already almost reached the bakery's front door, and Mai stopped. "It might be better to do this out here rather than inside."

Jules felt a prickle of anxiety. She had expected an order change, loaves of bread instead of rolls. But this felt like a prelude to more bad news.

"Believe me," Mai said quickly, "this has nothing to do with your bread. Oh heck, I'll just get right to it. Listen, we have to cut back on our order. By half." Mai cringed but continued, the words spilling from her mouth. "I wish I could be doing the exact opposite and ordering twice as much. You guys have been good to us. But Leo and I—well, business is down. Not scarily so, yet, but noticeable. Enough to make us pay attention to news about a recession. We hope to weather it, if it comes. We have to—we own the building like you do, only we live in ours. We can't lose it. Right now we're cutting where it makes sense to cut—starting with less bread, since we have fewer customers."

Jules struggled to draw a breath. She remembered a time when, as a child, she had sledded down a snowy hill straight into a pine tree and had the wind knocked out of her. For several seconds after, she had thought she was dying.

Mai noticed her struggle. "Oh my God, I'm so sorry. I rehearsed that much more calmly and then nerves got the best of me. It's nothing I wanted to tell you, I hope you—"

"No," Jules said, finding her voice. "It's fine, I understand. It's just that, I guess I didn't know things were so bad. Recession. I mean, wow."

"You and David haven't felt the pinch, then?"

Florence's conversation replayed in her head: left-over food, food pantry, production cut back. Too much food, too much, too much, too much. That could only mean one thing: too few people were buying. How had she not noticed? For starters, David had kept much from her. And she had been content not noticing, getting lost in her thoughts while her hands went through the motions she knew so well. Blood pounded in her ears and when she spoke again, she could barely hear her own voice. "I haven't felt it. I didn't know."

Mai reached out a hand and touched Jules on the upper arm. "That's good, then. That makes me hopeful. Maybe this will turn out to be nothing more than a blip." She smiled. "Again, I'm sorry for doing this, and so badly, too, but now I have to run. My two are waiting for their ride to school. Let's try and have coffee soon. Or better, a glass of wine and a nice long talk."

"Sure," Jules croaked but her mind was back inside, checking the clock. It was zeroing in on the moment when the work stopped on the space next door. It was traveling back over the last several weeks, assessing crowds and orders and receipts. It was taking stock of details she should have noticed and asked about months ago.

She lifted her hand in a wave and left Mai at the corner, waiting for the walk signal. Before reentering the bakery, she paused for another minute and took measure of the morning. Clouds hung in the sky. People were up. Cars moved. Nothing unusual. Despite the wind and threat of rain, it was an ordinary sort of day, one where she would expect to feel the steady pace of the early-morning baking give way to the rush of ordering and sales, just as it always did, the sleigh bell on the front door jangling every few seconds. She lifted her nose like a dog catching a faint scent. Was the day actually quieter? she asked herself. Was there nothing of the usual buzz in the air? Was this about to be another ordinary day, or were things about to change?

Or had something changed already?

2

"Daddy?" Rennie lifted her head from the table and blinked to get rid of the last of the sleep from her eyes. "I mean Dad," she corrected. More and more lately, she fought her impulses to be childish. One of the boys in her class had called her a big baby at the beginning of the school year when he heard her squeal "Daddy!" as she spotted her father standing outside of his car at the school pick-up lane.

Some days she forgot she was in the seventh grade, where it was a mistake to act anything but cool. "Dad-dy, Dad-dy," the bullying bigger boy had mimicked the day after, following her around the playground at recess and hounding her with his taunts. Her cheeks had burned with embarrassment when some other boys, friends of the jerk, had laughed along with him. Boys were stupid.

But from that moment on, she'd decided to copy some of the eighth-grade girls she sometimes watched walk in the hallways, the ones who sneered at all the boys. Maybe if she did that, she would become a cool person that no one would make fun of ever again.

"We'll never be cool," her friend Gigi had said when Rennie had suggested they could change.

"Maybe not. But we can try." And she did. But reading all the right celebrity websites, keeping up-to-date on song lyrics, and practicing her sneer and arched eyebrow in the mirror was a tiring business. Between the late-night web surfing and her homework, she often had trouble waking in the morning.

"Am I late?" Rennie felt disoriented after dozing off at the kitchen table and she wondered if she had wasted all the time she had for breakfast. Not such a bad thing, she considered, thinking of her friends' older siblings and how they ran out the door for school with empty stomachs along with their backpacks full of textbooks. Maybe skipping meals was cool, too. Her dad wouldn't notice. He had barely acknowledged her presence when she rolled into the kitchen, still bleary-eyed from bed, and he wasn't answering her question now. She pushed her chair away from the table.

The noise got his attention. "Where do you think you're going?"

Rennie was close to both her parents, but in particular her father. He had been the one to introduce her to books and reading aloud, and their bond was strong after hours spent curled up in the big armchair in the den, sharing stories about spunky dragons and spunkier princesses and a host of forest animals who went into battles dressed as if they were human warriors. When they weren't reading together, they simply hung out, enjoying each other's company. But not so much anymore. Her father, usually so patient with her, was quick to snap lately. This morning, he seemed more on edge than ever. She decided this wasn't the best day to stop eating breakfast.

"I need to finish packing," she said. "I have to bring in my diorama today. I'll take the toast with me in the car, I promise." She reached for a napkin as she spoke, sandwiched the two pieces of buttered bread together, and wrapped them up.

Her dad nodded, and just as quickly the dark mood that had crossed his face vanished. Letting her leave, he went back to his laptop, hunting and pecking at the keyboard with his index fingers.

The atmosphere in the house had felt weird lately. Both of her parents spoke to her as if she were an annoyance: *Clean your room. Pick up your shoes. Finish your homework. No, we can't host a sleepover this weekend, or next.* Orders issued, no discussion. Gone was the gentle teasing from her mother when she encountered a stray pair of gym shoes discarded in the front hall. Gone, too, were the offers of ice cream cones or a chapter of their favorite read-aloud, rewards from her father in exchange for finishing homework.

They must think I don't notice, Rennie thought once she closed the bedroom door behind her. She crossed the room and reached her bed. There, she dropped to her knees at the side and slid a hand between the mattress and box spring. She really had needed to collect her diorama, but it was on her desk, already packed up and secured. This gave her a few extra minutes to write in her diary, the latest in a series of bound books she had written in since she entered the third grade.

Her fingers brushed the soft leather cover as she sat down on the edge of her bed, and she felt calmer almost immediately. Her favorite pen was tucked between pages, marking the place where she had left off. This would have to be a quick entry. Even though her dad was caught up in his computer, she knew he would start hollering up the stairwell if she was too slow. She paused and listened for his footsteps on the stairs, but she heard none. She thought she heard a voice; maybe he was watching a news video online or talking on the phone. Either way, it would keep him busy for a while. She picked up her pen.

Everyone here is grumpy, she wrote, underlining the adjective with three thick black lines. *I am too. But no one seems to care how I feel. They don't ask anyway. Mom wants me to get my chores done without complaining and Dad makes excuses for not taking me anywhere. They've been weird since . . .*

Rennie paused in her writing to flip back several pages in her diary. There. October 16, the date she first noted the changes in her parents.

She lifted her pen from the page and tapped her bottom lip as she reread the October entry: *Mom was tired after work today. Acted like a B.I.T.C.H. Dad even told her to stop acting so bitchy. I heard him. And he never swears. Mom shushed him and she told him he wasn't being fair. She'd had a hard day at the shop with part of the bakery ripped up. They probably think I didn't hear but I did, and whispering can still sound angry.*

Rennie looked up from the old entry, chewed on the end of her pen, and thought about all the tension and what it meant. She flipped forward to the page she'd started only moments before and resumed writing. *They've been weird since October, and most of the time they're grumpy with me. Sometimes I wish everyone would just disappear.*

"Rennie!"

She jumped at her father's voice. He wasn't angry yet, and if she hurried, she might make it to the stairs before he hollered again. She slammed the book shut and jammed it back into its hiding spot. There was no time to do much more to the bed then pull the covers up and smooth the wrinkles. It would have to do. With luck, she would avoid another tidiness lecture from her mother later in the day.

Rennie grabbed the cold toast, her backpack, and the diorama, and ran out the bedroom door without a look behind her.

The ride to school was a quiet one. Rennie laid her arm along the crook of the passenger's side window and propped her chin on her hand. Out the window were the same houses and storefronts they passed every single weekday on this ride to school, familiar landmarks that her dad usually pointed out while giving her some history of the town. The new neighborhood that had been built on filled-in marshland. The buildings that sat empty and derelict before businesspeople, like him and her mom, invested in them to revive the downtown. She must have heard a million times that the bakery's windows had all been broken on that first day he brought her mom to see the space he wanted to buy, how hard he'd had to work to convince her the store and the main street both had potential. Rennie also knew that her grandparents had disapproved of opening a bakery. She had heard that a million times, too. More so lately, when her parents argued.

Today, though, her father barely acknowledged her, let alone the landmarks. This man who usually drove like some crotchety old person sped by it all and held his tongue.

"Dad, can you slow down? I feel sick."

"Can't," he said. "I have a meeting later and I'm in a hurry. It might help if you stop looking out the window and close your eyes."

Rennie stifled a groan and slid farther down the passenger's seat. Her father settled back into his silence, eyes on the road. *I might as well not be here*. She tried his suggestion and shut her eyes, but sightless she felt the speed more, not less.

"Dad," she said again.

No answer.

"Dad, I'm going to be sick."

"Open the window and get some fresh air. We're almost there." He pressed the gas and the car lurched forward, making her stomach plummet like it did when she lifted into the sky on a Ferris wheel.

"No, really, I think I have to—" Rennie broke off when she saw her father's nostrils flare, his jaw tighten.

"Open the window!" he yelled.

Rennie flinched. *Fine, be that way*, she thought. She couldn't wait to get out of the car. To tune out, she began writing tonight's diary entry in her head: *My dad is acting like a jerk.*

Her dad finally slowed down as he turned into the side street flanking her school. He took a left into the driveway and immediately had to brake. As it was every day, the traffic was start-and-stop as each car complied with the maddening rule of letting students out of cars only at the front door.

Her dad tapped his fingers on the steering wheel, his face grim, as if he couldn't wait to be rid of her and this responsibility. "Come on," he urged the drivers in front of them.

As if that will help, Rennie thought.

When they were two car lengths from the front door, he said, "Start getting your things together. I'll need you to hop right out." As Rennie began to sit up straight, he snapped his fingers. "Let's go. We're up next."

She stared at his profile but he never looked at her, not once. Tears stung her eyes and blurred her vision. She fumbled with the seatbelt release.

"Okay, finally," her dad said. He rolled forward a few feet and then came to a full stop. Rennie slid an arm through her backpack strap, opened the door, and hurried out of the car.

"Are you forgetting something? No 'Bye, Dad'?"

Rennie turned and bent slightly so she could glare at her father through the half-opened window. He had taken his eyes from a point on the horizon and was now looking at her. She said nothing.

"Rennie, I told you I'm in a hurry."

"You've said that a million times already." Rennie saw hurt and confusion in his eyes, but also something else. A flash of something hot. Their eyes locked and neither moved or said another word. The car behind them interrupted their silence with a second blast of the horn. Her dad looked in his rearview mirror. Rennie looked, too, and saw that the large black Escalade behind them was hanging on the rear bumper, its driver impatient to drop off her own child.

Ignoring the blast, her father said, "Fine, be that way. I drive you around every single day. Every. Single. Day. Do I ever complain? Not at all. But the one day I ask you to accommodate me, all you can do is act like a spoiled brat."

While he hadn't raised his voice, Rennie heard such disappointment in his tone that she wished he had yelled. Anything would be better than this. All she had wanted this morning was a little attention from him after months of being shooed out of rooms or bossed around or flat-out ignored. She had wanted space in which she might share her fears about her parents' arguments, about their changed moods. But he wasn't getting it. He wasn't even present.

Rennie didn't try to hide the tears now. "Go. Just go. I don't care. I hate you!"

"For God's sake, Rennie!" her dad yelled, but he was too late. She slammed the door and ran toward the entrance to the school.

Soon, she was up the steps and swallowed into the throng of students, swept up with them and through the front doors.

Charlie sat stuck in traffic, the Bob Seger CD in the disc drive turned up loud. He drummed his fingers on the steering wheel to pass the time. There wasn't much else to do but wait out the backed-up traffic and continue to inch his way up the highway to his exit. He had left his condo thirty-seven minutes ago to make what, at certain times of the day, was a twenty-minute drive to work. This morning, though, the highway was choked with traffic. Not unusual. The road had been engineered years back, when there weren't so many commuters, and it couldn't handle the number of cars headed to the office buildings that had shot up all along the suburban Boston corridor.

Things could be worse; at least he had remembered to grab his CD case on the way out the door and didn't have to resort to FM radio. He tried to stay focused on the hard-driving beat of "Hollywood Nights" but his mind wandered instead to Lift, his gym, and the uncertainty of the workday ahead of him. Being late wouldn't affect opening; he never opened anymore. His trainers did everything necessary to get the place ready for the day's first clients. But Charlie liked to arrive well before seven thirty to get some exercising in before he started the business portion of his day. This morning's workout would have to be curtailed. A shame, since the combination of workplace problems and the morning's bad drive called out for an extra hard session spent between the bench press and the heavy bag.

At least the exit sign was in sight now, the off-ramp itself about a mile down the road. Charlie signaled a right turn to move into the first lane and waited for a small gap in between cars before starting to nose his way over. Safely situated, he thought briefly about switching from Seger to the radio for a road and traffic update but decided against it. Knowing if the tie-up was due to an accident or roadwork or simply the heavy winds gusting across the highway wouldn't change anything, wouldn't make him get to his exit any faster. So, instead, he turned up the volume a couple of clicks. He regretted this immediately; the way the guitar licks buzzed through the speakers was a reminder of his dissatisfaction with the car's sound system. It had been an expensive after-market addition, and yet the sound was crap. Calling the stereo installer today meant one more difficult conversation to add to an already difficult day. That call could wait. He dialed the volume back down.

"Hollywood Nights" segued into "Old Time Rock and Roll" and the seconds and the inches ticked away, counted off by the tapping and releasing of the brake pedal. Charlie heard more buzzing and thought it was the speakers again, but he soon realized that the noise wasn't coming from the mount at the back of the car—it was his phone, set to vibrate and buried in the kangaroo pocket of the hoodie draped across the passenger seat.

Luckily, traffic ground to a halt again, giving him a free hand to grope around for the BlackBerry.

If it was Lexi calling from the gym, checking up on his whereabouts, he would let the call go to voicemail. She called more often now that they spent almost every night together, a shift in her behavior since they had gone from occasionally hooking up to practically living together. The relationship was new enough that he still found the calls, the ones in which she told him how she would greet him next time they were alone, exciting. Lexi was one of his best trainers and an all-around fun and physical girl, uninhibited and playfully resistant to drawing lines between work and personal conversations. That was okay by him, sometimes more than okay, like when she cornered him in his office behind the closed door.

But Charlie felt uncomfortable knowing she might be calling him and speaking in her sexy way from the large, open workout floor or the reception desk at work, in earshot of his customers and other employees. He was fine for now keeping the extent of their relationship under wraps.

He was fine, too, keeping their relationship just hot, plain and simple, and not moving into hot and heavy. After some failed long-term relationships, Charlie was wary of heavy. He had a habit of falling into heavy very easily, dating exclusively and moving in with women too quickly. He didn't like being alone, and his loneliness got him into trouble with women he was attracted to but had little in common with. His best friend's wife had told him after the last breakup that he should take his time and examine his tendencies and impulses. He liked Jules, she was sensible, and so he'd listened to her. With Lexi, he was taking things slow.

By the time Charlie had the phone in his hand, the vibrations had ceased. He gave the screen a quick glance to see if the missed call merited a call back. Not Lexi at all, he was relieved to see. It was David—husband of Jules and his best friend, someone he would always talk to. His parents and David's had met playing in bridge tournaments but later broke off from the larger social group to form a weekly pinochle foursome, alternating between houses to play. Thrown together, the two nine-year-old boys, both only children, had found playmates in each other and eventually became as close as brothers.

Charlie held a pair of tickets for tonight's Celtics game against Atlanta, and he hoped his friend was calling to confirm their plans and not cancel them. David wasn't a natural sports fan, but they hadn't gotten together in a while. Of late, David had begged off plans at the last minute more than once, claiming work fatigue. More so as his bakery renovation intensified and consumed his time and energy. A game, Charlie had insisted when he first offered a ticket to his reluctant friend, would be just the thing for relaxing and letting off some steam over a couple of beers.

Charlie hit redial and after a few rings, David answered.

"Charlie? I just called."

"I know, man. I couldn't get to my phone in time. Driving. Or trying to, anyway. I'm stuck on 128, but what else is new? You calling about tonight?" he asked, shifting away from traffic talk.

"Tonight?"

Charlie sighed. "Jeez, the Celtics. Did you forget?"

"Sorry," David said. "My mind's on other things, I wasn't thinking about tonight. But sure, I'm looking forward to the game. The Celtics. Against the . . ."

"Hawks. Eastern conference quarterfinals. We're going all the way this year, my friend. Hey, hold on a sec, my exit's up and I have to merge." Charlie took the phone from his ear and used the heel of his hand to steer through the on-ramp traffic crisscrossing his path to reach the off-ramp.

Safely off the highway and on the town road, he returned to the conversation. "Anyway, I'd like to decide where we're meeting now, before the day gets away from me. I have a ton of stuff to do once I get to the gym, most of it I'd rather not have to do, quite frankly."

"Listen, Charlie, the reason I called—"

Charlie gave a wry laugh. "I forgot for a minute that *you* called *me*. Sorry, man, too much going on. What's up?"

"I need some advice. It's the bakery expansion. The project isn't coming together, I've run into . . . some trouble."

"Your guy stopped working a few weeks back, right?" Charlie racked his brain to recall the exact conversation he'd had with David not long ago. "He started another job and left you hanging?"

"Yeah," David replied. "That's only part of it, though."

"I hear you. These projects never cost what you think they're gonna cost, that's the only guarantee in construction. And things feel a little rocky out there in the real world right now, even at the gym, my friend. We're trying to get the second place up and running. Meanwhile there are a bunch of machines in the original gym that need to be replaced. I've got regular customers signing up month by month because they don't want to lay out the cash for a whole year. I've got trainers who sit on their asses instead of bringing in new business." Charlie felt himself getting worked up again. *Damn traffic*, he thought. It put him in a mood that was proving hard to shake. Maybe he should work out anyway, burn off this negativity and to hell with getting a late start.

"Charlie."

"Right. Sorry. I'll give you my contractor's contact info tonight. You can mention my name when you call him."

"Charlie, please. I don't need a new builder. I need you to listen. I need some help."

In all the years they had spent as friends, as near-brothers, David had rarely come to him looking for advice. For approval, yes, like when he brought Jules to dinner for the first time, clearly eager for his best friend and the woman he wanted to marry to like each other. But for counsel, it was always Charlie who went to David: *"My parents' fighting is driving me out of the house; can I stay with you?" "I'm dropping out of college to work in a gym and my dad says I'm a loser; what do you think?" "My relationship is tanking; what should I do?"* Charlie had never thought of himself as someone with advice worth seeking. He was a good friend, no question; he would defend his friends, especially David and Jules, to the death. But he wouldn't call himself wise, not at all. Too often, he flew by the seat of his pants. Still, the edge of anxiety he heard in his friend's voice made him want to help.

"I'll listen," he said. "I don't know what kind of help I can be, but I'll try. Over a couple of beers before the game, maybe?"

"I was thinking more like now. Could you meet in, say, fifteen minutes? I can be at a coffee shop not too far from here by eight o'clock. I just need a few minutes with you." David named the spot. "I wouldn't ask except it's . . . I've got this deadline to meet. Sooner is better than later, if you can."

Charlie took a deep breath and exhaled. This sounded heavy, and he didn't always do so well with heavy. He had seen his share when he was younger as his parents fought, made up, cheated on each other, and fought again before splitting for good. Through it all, David had been his steady mooring, always the anchor in turbulence and never the source of it; this shift unsettled Charlie. As he considered this, he approached the gym parking lot.

"Hold on a sec, I'm pulling into the lot." He set the phone on his lap, took a right turn, and drove to an empty row at the far end of the lot, where he backed into a space.

After he killed the engine, he sat in the car and looked around him at all the other parked cars. By now the crowds had thinned out, as the nine-to-fivers finished showering, dressed, and sped off to work. A quieter gym meant he had time. He could focus on David, his problems. His workout could wait. Firing trainers could as well. He took the cell phone from his lap and returned to his friend.

"Hey, David, I'm at the gym and it looks slow enough here. I think I can get away. Let me get inside and let them know I'll be gone for a bit. If there's a problem, I'll call you. Otherwise, I'll be at the coffee shop at . . ." He checked his watch; it was already seven-forty-five. "Eight's a little too early. I'll shoot for eight fifteen."

"Charlie, that would be great." David's relief was hard to miss.

"Hang in there, man. I'll see you in a few."

3

Jules opened the front door and stepped into the bakery, letting its steamy warmth revive her cold limbs. While she stood, she looked up at the wall clock. She had been outside for close to half an hour, and she would be behind in her work once again, but she didn't care, didn't feel that rush of nerves and adrenaline that usually motivated her to get the job done. When a customer excused himself to get around her to reach the coffee urns, Jules apologized and moved, but reluctantly. Finishing the day seemed almost pointless.

As she slipped into a clean apron, Sandy acknowledged her return with a slight nod. The bakery's routines had gone on in her absence, and Sandy was tackling Mai's roll order. What irony, Jules thought, returning in the middle of production of the damned multigrain rolls that they now would have too many of. *Maybe those can make up the bulk of David's donation to the food pantry today*, she thought, a poor attempt at sarcasm that only left her feeling sick to her stomach. David would be here sometime soon, and she no longer felt calm enough to keep her temper in check.

But for now, there was work that had been started, work that had to be finished, regardless of David or Mai or even her own apathy. Jules squared her shoulders and pushed herself to join Sandy at the back bench. "I'll take over," she said, pointing to the last round of dough waiting to be divided into rolls.

Sandy wiped her hands free of flour and moved aside. "Good walk?" she asked.

"Fine." Unexpected tears welled in Jules's eyes and she kept her eyes down. The last thing she wanted was for Sandy to see her cry. She reached for the dough and drew the mound toward herself. Once she had patted the dough into a circle, she took the bench knife to it, cutting the large round into wedges. Sandy had banged out all but this last two dozen of the batch earmarked for the restaurant. Short of throwing the unbaked mass into the trash, Jules wondered what she could do with all the excess product. She smacked each small wedge of dough on the table before gathering the ends and pinching them together to form a ball. These she arranged into concentric circles, edges barely touching, inside a deep, round baking pan.

What might have seemed a pointless exercise in frustration began to soothe her; the smacking noise of dough hitting wood made her feel slightly better.

Sandy left the sink with dripping hands and grabbed a clean towel to drape over the apron string tied around her waist. She wiped her hands dry and returned to Jules's side. "I'm scheduled to do cookies right about now but we're behind with the cakes. What do you think? Should I switch the production order so the cakes have time to cool before we decorate?"

Jules stopped working and bit her bottom lip. David would want the cookies in the oven by the time he arrived, and she had promised him early this morning they would follow his new cookie protocol starting today. She thought of the rolling and rerolling he demanded and felt overwhelmed by how much time it would add to Sandy's morning. "You know what? Let's skip cookies altogether for now. Doing the cakes is a great idea. We have some orders, and we'll need extra for the case."

Sandy nodded. "It's a plan. If there's time I can throw in a few pans of brownies along with the cake layers, then at least we'll have something for the after-school crowd."

Jules felt like crying again, but this time with gratitude. If she got through this day in one piece, it would be largely due to Sandy's common sense and her ability to stay calm under pressure. "Awesome, Sandy, that's a great idea."

The sleigh bells on the front door jingled. Jules and Sandy turned and looked across the bakery to see Rachel, one of their counter clerks, coming through the door, scowling. Inside, she gave the door a shove with her palm, closing it behind her with a bang. The leather strap of small jingle bells swung back and forth, the bells ringing furiously.

"God!" Rachel retreated a few steps to grab and halt the sleigh bells. Once she silenced them, she stomped across the floor, her wet umbrella spraying customers as she pushed her way past. The business of ordering and filling orders came to a standstill. A few customers lingering to chat at the coffee urns put lids on their cups and left. Rachel grabbed an apron from the shelf and said to Jules in a loud voice, "This was the worst possible day for David to call me at the last minute."

"Could you lower your voice, please?" Jules asked.

Rachel took a deep breath and exhaled slowly. "Sorry, but I'm completely frazzled. I never mind coming in, you know that, especially when David's in a bind, but I need more lead time than a few minutes. You're lucky he called before my next-door neighbor was leaving on the school run. At least I didn't have to chase her down the street to ask her if I could put my kids in her car."

"Wait. How is David in a bind?"

Rachel shrugged. "Who knows? He sounded stressed out and told me he was going to be late. I figured you would know what was up."

"No," Jules admitted. "I don't know." Was it something to do with Rennie, she wondered, some problem with the diorama due today for her social studies class?

Lost in thought, she missed something Rachel said to her.

"I'm sorry, what?"

Rachel stepped across to the sink and washed her hands. As she dried them, she looked over Jules's shoulder and out at the customers. "I said, it's not even that busy. Florence can probably handle everything until David gets here."

Jules took a look around. The coffee drinkers had slunk out, leaving one person being waited on at the counter and two more people in line behind her. No, not busy at all. She returned her attention to Rachel.

"Can you stay until then anyway? I'm going to call him to find out what's up."

"I can stay. I'm just not sure you need me. Things aren't exactly jumping lately."

Jules frowned. Why was she the only one who hadn't noticed? She shook off the irritation and tried to stay focused on getting through the short-term tasks. "I actually have a job for you. We have too many rolls today, and we need to be creative with the extra. Box up half for the restaurant and call Mai for pickup. When the rest have cooled completely, bag them in half-dozens. Price them at, I don't know, three dollars a bag? Five twenty-five for a dozen? Okay?"

"Okay," Rachel agreed with a shrug, calmed down for the moment.

"And while you're waiting for the bread to cool, help Florence with the customers."

As Jules stepped away from Rachel, she withdrew from everything—the people hanging around the counter, the hum of the ovens and the fans, the work Sandy was doing, the bulk of the work still to be done. All the activity felt far away and incapable of affecting her, as if she had stepped into an isolation chamber. In this quiet space, doubt crept in; checking up on David felt unnecessary, silly, even. Traffic and Rennie dragging her feet and impromptu errands had held him up in the past. Perhaps today the electricity had gone out or a fuse had blown or French toast burning in the skillet had triggered the smoke detector. David would likely walk in at any minute, incredulous that his tardiness would have sparked such concern.

His tardiness was nothing, it had to be nothing, and later, after she vented her frustration to him, he would fill in the missing pieces and explain himself. They would clear the air, and they would go to bed, pull the covers up, and start fresh in the morning. This awful day would go down in the books as a total loser. All he had to do was walk through the front door.

Jules shook her head, tried to rid herself of the funk that had invaded her thoughts. She looked around to assess the morning's progress. Rachel had thrown herself into bagging rolls, was even adorning the bags with long, curled strands of colored ribbon. Busy work, but the packages would be eye-catching.

Jules touched her on the elbow as she walked by and smiled. "Looking fantastic, thanks."

Sandy had cakes going in and had remembered to remove several pounds of butter from the walk-in. These blocks now rested on the corner of the workbench, softening. It had been a while since Jules had made buttercream, but why not get it started? She caught Sandy's eye and pointed to herself, the butter, and the mixer.

"Wish you would," Sandy agreed. "I made the simple syrup already; it's cooling off the heat. The whites are ready, too." She gestured to the bowl of viscous egg whites on the counter.

Jules found the pan of sugary liquid resting, still warm but no longer lava-hot, on the back burner and grabbed it. She would start with the meringue that elevated their buttercream from the standard fare found in other bakeries.

She took a second to attach the bowl to the mixer, and she started whipping. As the egg whites frothed, she added the syrup to the bowl in a slow stream. The noise emanating from the mixer didn't quite drown out the ring of the telephone, and she watched as Florence, waiting on a customer, picked up the cordless.

"The Welcome Home Bakery, can you hold a minute please?" Florence asked, but instead of laying the receiver on the counter, she kept it wedged between her shoulder and her ear. Her forehead wrinkled into the deep worry lines she sometimes joked about eradicating one day with Botox or collagen injections.

Although the meringue was at a delicate stage, Jules cut the machine and walked to the counter. "Florence, is it David? Florence?" She held out her hand for the cordless and Florence extended the phone to her.

"It's Rennie, calling from school. But there's so much noise there and here that I can't tell half of what she's saying."

"From school?"

"Either school or Grand Central Station during rush hour. Actually, she's asking for her dad."

"Give me that." Jules took the receiver. "Rennie?"

"Mom! I left my diorama in Dad's car and I need it in about an hour. He said he had a meeting this morning, but has he gotten to work yet?"

"What?"

"Mom," she wailed, "I really, really need someone to drive my project to the school or I'll get an F. Can Dad bring it? *Please?*"

Before Jules had a chance to reply, she heard the first-period bell sounding.

"Mom, the bell. I have to go before I'm late. Please ask Dad.

The diorama's on the backseat. Or it should be. Maybe I put it on the floor."

"But Rennie—"

"Gotta go, Mom."

A second later, Jules heard nothing but dead air.

No David, no car, no diorama, and now, a mystery meeting.

"Great," she muttered to herself. "Now all I need to do is find you, David."

As Charlie stepped through the front doors of Lift, he walked into the gym's familiar din, the clang of metal weights and the whir of machinery competing with loud music videos and the rise and fall of many voices in conversation.

"Hey, Charlie!" Ashley, the cheerful receptionist, greeted him with a smile.

"Hey." He smiled back. "Can you do me a favor?" He wanted to get a jump on his work so he could turn his focus to arranging a time to meet David. Enlisting Ashley's help would save time. "Look up something on the master schedule for me, will you?"

"Sure." She tapped the computer keyboard to return to the home screen. "I'm ready."

"I need to see Jen and Stu later. They working today?"

Ashley scrolled through the shift calendar. "Chris and Lexi opened. But yes, Jen's here. She works until—"

Charlie waved off the rest of her sentence. "That's good enough. No Stu today?"

"No," she confirmed. "He's not on until tomorrow morning, when he opens with Lexi."

"Is Jen on the floor, do you know?"

Ashley shrugged. "She should be, but honestly, I haven't seen her. Maybe she's in the back room with the resistance machines?"

"Client?" Charlie asked.

Ashley squinted back at the screen. "No one listed that I can see. Free floor time."

On her unstructured work time, then, the hour or so a day each trainer spent casually talking to clients about exercise form and fitness goals. Done well, these kinds of conversations led to clients joining fitness classes or signing up for private training. Some people were better at it than others. Serious and introverted, Jen struggled. She had the fitness creds but not the sales ability.

Stu, on the other hand, had no problem with chitchat or making a pitch. The trouble with Stu was, the pitches he made on the floor of the gym were usually for the vitamin supplements he sold at his second job. If he spent half as much time picking up personal training clients, he might not be facing termination. Stu, though, Charlie would have to deal with tomorrow.

"I'm stopping in my office for a sec, and then I have to head out for a meeting. Do me a favor, Ash. Could you block off some time on Jen's schedule later this morning—say, eleven, if possible? Then page us both with the appointment reminder, okay?"

"You got it." Ashley flashed another smile, her teeth dazzling white against her tanning bed complexion.

"Thanks." Charlie rapped his knuckles on the reception desk and went on his way down the corridor and into his office.

Before he could leave, he had to double-check his personal calendar to make sure his morning was free of appointments. While his Mac booted up, he rifled through a stack of envelopes on his desk—bills, invoices, estimates, product advertisements. Reviewing it all would have to wait.

The password prompt appeared as Charlie straightened the

envelopes on the side of his desk. As he prepared to enter his password, someone knocked. He hoped it wasn't Jen, mixed up about the time for her meeting with him.

He called out, "Come in!"

The door creaked open, and Lexi stuck her head into the office.

Charlie swiveled in his chair and smiled at her.

Lexi looked good. She usually wore her dark hair pulled back into a ponytail when on the floor, but today her hair was loose and wet, as if she had just come from the showers. Free of makeup, her skin was clear and dewy. At thirty-two, she was the age he'd been when he opened this gym. She was also the youngest woman he had dated in a long time. *The youngest of all the younger women*, he corrected himself. A man in his forties with an eye for women ten or more years younger, he was officially a cliché.

"Hey, gorgeous."

"Hey, yourself." Lexi closed the door behind her but stayed where she was. "You have a minute?"

"I have a minute. Just about. David called while I was in the car."

"David?"

"Yeah. He needs to talk to me about something, and I promised I'd meet him in a few. But I'll give you what time I can." Charlie rose from his chair and crossed his office to take Lexi in his arms. "You smell like chlorine."

"I swam laps on my break. I showered, though." She shrugged. "I guess the chlorine lingers."

"What happened to your usual run?"

"No run today," she said. "I'm not up to the high impact." She reached up, pulled his face to hers, and kissed him, stopping any more questions. When she offered him her tongue,

Charlie groaned and kissed her back. Kissing her almost made him forget his promise to David, or anything else for that matter. But then he remembered and he groaned again, this time with regret.

He pulled away and held Lexi by the hips at arm's length. "I can't do this now. I have to go. It's important."

"Far more important than me," Lexi said, an unfamiliar tone of reproach in her voice. He thought of her phone calls, the increasing frequency of their overnights, the way she claimed him at work, drew him into conversations with her as if only the two of them mattered. She was, he realized, so much more invested than he was. The truth hit him like a bus.

"Not so. He and I have the Celtics game tonight, remember? We're trying to make plans. How about you and I play squash at the end of your day to use up some of this pent-up energy?" he suggested. "I'll let you win."

"You never have to let me win. But no squash today. I don't have much energy at the moment." She brought her hand up to her mouth to cover a yawn.

It was Charlie's turn to raise an eyebrow, his in a question. "No energy? *You?* Come on, I find that hard to believe."

"Listen," Lexi began. "Charlie. I have to tell you something important. I tried to tell you last night at your place but I wimped out." She took a step backward, forcing Charlie's hands to drop to his sides.

"You're quitting. You can't quit." He made a move toward her and tried to reach for her again, but Lexi held up a hand to stop him in his tracks.

"No, not that." Lexi paused, took a breath, and then released it. "I'm pregnant."

Charlie's face froze as Lexi's words, their meaning, sank in. A baby. It crossed his mind to ask if it was his because what did he know about her, really? Was she being exclusive with him? They hadn't discussed seeing or not seeing other people at all; most of their time together had been spent in bed, having sex instead of deep discussions. But he couldn't ask. He would sound like an asshole. And, anyway, the minute the doubt entered his mind he dismissed it as ridiculous. Unless she had cloned herself, she didn't have time to be here at work, hanging out with him after hours, *and* involved with someone else. There weren't enough hours in the day.

"Are you—"

Lexi waved off his question. "Yes, I'm sure. I took a test. Two tests."

Charlie nodded. But this wasn't what he had wanted to ask, either. What he really wanted to know was, *Are you keeping the baby?* Again, he kept his mouth shut.

Lexi met his eyes and held them. "I've always wanted to have kids, you know," she said as if she had looked into his mind and found the question lingering in there, unasked. "I love kids, I'm good with them."

She was, Charlie had to admit that. She and Chris led the summer Active Kids programs, and she had a knack for engaging young ones in activities, reaching them on their level without being phony or condescending, a knack Charlie envied. He had no idea how to act around kids, didn't know what they liked, had no idea what they liked to talk about. Growing up as an only child, he'd never had to deal with younger siblings, and his own parents had always spoken to him as if he were an adult in small clothing. These days, the only kid he knew was David's daughter, Rennie, and he tended to talk to her as if she were a friend.

Lexi may have always wanted kids, but Charlie had never considered it. The same inherent flightiness that had kept him from settling down in the past for more than two or three years at a time didn't bode well for sustaining a relationship with a kid. An eighteen-year relationship, at least. And marriage—if marriage was what Lexi wanted to go along with the baby—seemed unwise to even contemplate. He was probably better alone. Probably she would be better off without him.

"You want to say anything?" Lexi asked, treading into his thoughts.

"I don't know what to say right now," he admitted.

"You could say it's not such a terrible thing. Or that you'll stick around." She shrugged. "At least you didn't ask if I was sure the baby was yours. Or what I planned to do about it. There is that."

Charlie's face grew warm. After a moment he said, "It's a surprise, that's all. This isn't the best place to talk about it, either."

"Then we'll talk tonight. At your place." Lexi reached up to the back of his neck, drew his face to hers, and kissed him again, lightly this time. Her lips were soft and lush, and he could imagine losing himself in her later, forgetting all this. But the baby was real, he reminded himself, a flesh-and-blood growing life. That would be very hard to forget about.

"Yeah, good idea," he agreed. "Let's talk tonight."

Lexi touched his cheek and left without another word, pulling the door closed behind her.

Charlie put his hand to the spot on his face where she had brushed him with her fingertips. The tenderness of her touch had surprised him. It was a side of her he hadn't seen before, a softer aspect of her personality that stood in stark contrast to her athleticism, her open sexuality.

He put his hand over his eyes and then ran it down his face, stopping to cover his mouth. He stood in his office and looked around him, took stock. He had come a long way, he'd made this business himself, out of nothing more than an idea and his own will to do it. He was responsible for a lot of people, their livelihoods.

Maybe I can do this, too, he thought as he stood alone in the quiet. *Be a father, be responsible for a child.*

A few minutes passed, and the dreamlike atmosphere Lexi had left in her wake lost its blurred edges. Charlie returned to the present moment. Another day at work. Everything needed doing right away, everything demanded his attention. *I have the appointment with Jen. I should call David first, though, and let him know I'm finally on my way. And we have the game tonight. And—oh, shit, Lexi thinks she's coming over tonight but I'm not going to be home.*

He cursed again, overwhelmed by the competing interests of all the tasks that lay before him. *David first*, he reminded himself. *He's waiting. And maybe when I'm done helping him, he can help me.*

Charlie took his phone out of his pocket and dialed David's number. Eight rings in, it became clear he wasn't going to pick up. Charlie left a voicemail.

"David, man, I'm in my office. Sorry, I'm running a little late. Something came up as soon as I got in, but I took care of it for now. I'm good to go, and I'll be there as soon as possible. Really, I'm on my way."

Charlie felt a blast of hot air as he opened the door and entered the small coffee shop. Diners turned to look at him. He had passed David's car, parked in the lot, on his way in, but he didn't see his friend's face among the crowd.

He stood at the cash register and waited for one of the busy waitresses to take a break from placing orders.

"I don't want to sit right now, thanks," he told the woman who walked toward him, menu and coffee pot in hand. "I'm looking for a friend. His car is just outside." He pointed out the window to the blue Toyota. "We were supposed to meet forty-five minutes ago, but I'm late. Was there anyone here earlier, waiting? Maybe he told you he'd be back in a few? He's shorter than I am." Charlie held a hand up to the level of his eyes. "Light brown hair."

"A solo guy?" the waitress asked and then shook her head. "These here are all my regulars. I'd remember a single, especially if he was a new face. Sorry."

David must have gone somewhere nearby to wait or to run an errand, maybe. Both the rain and wind had picked up in the last half hour, but he might have taken a walk if he was peeved about the delay. Charlie decided to grab a coffee to go and headed outside to look for him.

Outside, the wind off the water wasn't letting up. Rain blew sideways but Charlie kept going. He took a sip of coffee and looked up and down the shoreline. He noticed storefronts farther down the boardwalk; David might have ducked into any one of them. *Well, he should have just waited in the café or his car, and we wouldn't be in this situation.*

He knew he should probably take his own advice to wait, but he was too antsy to sit. Foolish or not, moving felt like progress, so he headed away from the car to walk the boardwalk.

The beach this early in the spring was a depressing place in need of a good cleanup. Winter storms had deposited all kinds of plastic crap and other trash at the high-tide line, and it would sit there until the weather improved and the cleaning crews were sent out. Not long ago, Lexi, horrified by the images of turtles and sea birds being choked by plastic netting on beaches, had suggested that Charlie stop selling plastic bottles of water and sports drinks at the gym and install bubblers instead. "Imagine if you have children someday," she'd said. "Don't you want to leave them a clean and healthy planet?"

The memory of that conversation stopped him in his tracks. That someday had arrived: he was about to become a father. What kind of parent could he be, he wondered, given the self-absorbed parents he'd had? Then again, David had done it, raised Rennie in his own way. David was a great dad despite his own imperfect role models.

He resumed walking, made it a few more feet, and then stopped. He looked back over his shoulder to the café. All he saw were cars on hard top. No David.

He finished the last mouthful of coffee, now cold, and flattened the paper cup. He folded it and tucked it into his jacket pocket. The row of shops wasn't that far ahead, and, determined, he pressed on, keeping his face down, letting the wind and rain mess his hair rather than batter his skin. After just a few more steps, the blurred outlines of the block of shops began to sharpen—weathered shingles, a rickety wooden fire escape, awnings flapping in the wind.

As he approached the shops, something else took clear shape as well. At first it looked like a large black sea bird perched on a fence post, its dark wings fluffed. As he got closer, he thought it might be a black trash bag, filling with air, aloft but tethered. But when he reached the post, he saw the object was actually a large, dark gray jacket puffed up with the wind. The air-filled sleeves were being blown around the rotting posts, a pair of sausage-like arms holding on for dear life.

He stopped and looked all around him, a 360-degree sweep, for the idiot who'd left this jacket behind on a day when the weather was brutal, the air biting. But he saw no one. He was the only sorry fool out there.

He couldn't waste his time worrying about a coatless stranger.

As he got closer to the few shops, their signs came into focus. A dollar store. A chain pharmacy. A local bank branch, small enough to house only an ATM terminal. Unless David had dropped into the pharmacy for a quick errand, it seemed increasingly unlikely he had come this way.

Charlie turned again to survey the area, this time facing the surf. He watched as the waves crashed over and over, attacking the shore and then receding. Where was David? Charlie began to feel the pointlessness of such a random and haphazard search, indeed of ever having left the agreed-upon meeting place at all. He should just return to his car or the café to wait.

He jammed his hands into his pockets, and as he did his fingers found the paper cup and also his BlackBerry, forgotten for the last several minutes. He cursed himself for being so stupid. He could try David's cell again.

Phone in hand, he unlocked the screen. He had missed a call from Lexi, along with several texts, all of them asking the same question in a variety of ways: *When will you be back?* He frowned and clicked through to voicemail: still nothing from David. He flexed his frozen fingers and prepared to make the call, but movement in his peripheral vision caught his eye. He looked up from the keyboard.

He was no longer alone on the beach, but the other intrepid soul wasn't David, not unless he had adopted a pack of dogs, large and small, since they'd last seen each other.

Squinting, Charlie saw that the dog walker was a woman, though she was slender and lanky enough to pass for a slight-framed young man. She was approaching from the far end of the shore. Charlie dropped his hand to his side and walked toward her, in the direction of the boardwalk and the flapping jacket. Two of the dogs broke off from the pack and bounded over to him.

Charlie froze; he had never been comfortable with dogs.

He needn't have worried. The dogs were uninterested in him. They stopped at the discarded jacket, pressing their noses into the pockets of the windbreaker to investigate.

"Bert! Ernie! Leave it!" The dog walker picked up her pace to a jog, her pack at her heels, and grabbed the errant hounds by their collars.

She was dressed appropriately for the weather, bundled into a water-repellant quilted jacket and Gore-Tex pants. She looked up at Charlie and apologized. "I hope these guys didn't scare you. They're more interested in that jacket than anything else."

"The jacket must smell more appealing, I guess."

"Probably it smells like the man who stopped to talk to these guys earlier. They liked him. I know it's his because he stopped to pat Jasper here"—she pointed to a shaggy, pale gold dog—"and got fur all over his sleeve. Jasper's a shedder," she added with a look at the dog.

Sure enough, Charlie noticed the sleeve was peppered with a few short, light hairs despite the wind.

"I talked to him a minute, but then I remembered I'd left my bag of dog toys at the car and had to head back. When we came back this way, he was gone but his jacket was hanging here."

"Weird thing to do. It's freezing."

"Uh-huh. Weird. Especially since he said he'd been waiting for a friend for a while, so he must have been pretty cold."

David, Charlie realized with a shiver, the first confirmation that he had been here. That he didn't recognize the simple jacket didn't mean much. David's workday clothes were generic and unremarkable. "I think he might have been waiting for me. You didn't happen to see which way he went?"

The dog walker shook her head. "Like I said, we left for the car. All I know is he was gone when we came back with the toys. Not much help, huh?"

David could be anywhere. Charlie looked again up and down the beach. No one. "No, no, it's good. Thanks for the information. I'll head back to the cars and wait."

"Can you call him?" She nodded at the phone still gripped in his hand.

"I tried when I got here and was about to call again when the dogs came over." Charlie smiled at her. "Thanks for the reminder."

"No problem. I hope you guys connect. He seemed a little preoccupied, but he was a nice guy, real nice to the dogs. And dogs can tell, you know? When people are jerks or not jerks?"

Charlie nodded, but he didn't really know dogs at all. He was anxious to stop talking and make the phone call.

As if sensing his impatience, the dog walker gave a couple of hand commands and rounded up her crew. "Good luck," she called over her shoulder as they all took off across the open sand.

Charlie watched the dogs and their handler trot away before he hit redial. Her story had left him feeling uneasy, though he wasn't sure why.

After a moment of dead air, the ringing began. "Pick up, pick up, pick up," he willed. When his outgoing call kicked once again to David's voicemail, he gulped down some acid that had churned up from his stomach. He didn't leave another message.

He looked again at the jacket tangled around the fence post. Maybe it wasn't David's. Maybe the dog walker had spoken to some other man. The uncertainty gave Charlie cause to check the pockets, didn't it? If he found no ID, he would return it to the post and leave, no harm, no foul.

As he debated, another gust blew under the coat and lifted it into the air before depositing it on the sand. He took that as an invitation to do something, and he crouched down next to the jacket and reached his hands into the pockets to explore. In the first one he found a watch, a vintage Panerai. He remembered the day David first showed it to him: the day of his graduation from business school. His father had presented him with it the night before, and David had still been incredulous the day after. "Maybe I finally did something right?"

In the right-hand pocket, Charlie found a keychain cobbled together from disparate components: a long leather wrist strap, a silver carabiner, a combination corkscrew and bottle opener serving as a fob, keys to a couple of deadbolt locks, and keys to a Camry that was right then sitting in a parking lot not far from where he squatted. David wouldn't walk away from these things willingly—not a jacket on a day like this, not the keys to his car, certainly not his watch—but if there had been some kind of crime involving his friend, these things would be gone too. Wouldn't they? What did it mean?

Charlie's brain couldn't make sense of the situation. It felt sluggish and dull. Maybe if he started moving again, looking again . . .

He shoved all the objects back into one pocket, rolled the jacket into a ball, and secured the package under his arm. The only place he hadn't looked was along the shoreline and the jetty. That was where he would go now.

He stood and started walking and the wind off the water hit him square in the face. It was okay, though, manageable. Without sun in the sky, the choppy sea ahead was murky, the color of lead, but the tide seemed to him to be receding, the waves much less furious than when he arrived. He kept going, making a sweep with his eyes as he walked, first left and then right, up and down the coast. He saw seaweed, broken shells, rope, and faded buoys, but no signs of life.

To his right, the coastline curved sharply inward, and he trudged a little farther through the heavy, wet sand to see his way around the dunes. There was no one in this direction, either, nothing much at all of note but another pile of trash a few feet ahead among silvered driftwood.

He didn't expect much but pressed on toward the pile of trash, which, he could now see, was not trash at all but clothes and shoes weighted down with a large piece of old wood. A belt had been coiled and tucked into the right shoe. The shoes were plain enough and practical enough to be just right for kitchen work.

The coffee Charlie had finished in a hurry threatened to travel up his esophagus as he dropped to his knees next to the clothes. It was cold on the sand, damp, but he didn't feel much. The wind howled in his ears.

Jules tapped out David's cell phone number again. She had to track him down; Rennie would be frantic until she had her diorama. This particular teacher was a hard-ass, one of the ones who stressed personal responsibility and advocated for less coddling. Perhaps she would accept the project a bit late if David explained his role in the mix-up, but Jules thought it best not to take the chance and find out. Her thumb hovered over the send button as she took a few seconds to will her husband to answer, adding a whispered "bastard" for the trouble his secrecy was causing now. She hit send.

Wherever David's phone was, it was ringing. Once, twice. Jules drummed the laminate desktop with her fingertips as she listened to ring after ring. "Oh for God's sake," she said as she disconnected.

The second her finger lifted from the button, the phone rang in her hand.

"David? Thank God."

"Jules?"

"Wait. Charlie? If you're looking for David, get in line. He's supposed to be here but he's not, and I've got a crisis brewing."

"Jules—"

"No, really. I have to hang up in case he calls, but I'll tell him you're—"

"Jules. Stop," Charlie interrupted. "I'm trying to reach *you*, not David. I know where David's supposed be. He's supposed to be with me, we planned to meet this morning."

"So he's at the gym?"

"No. No, he's not, and neither am I."

"Well, where are you two, then? You know what, never mind. Tell David Rennie left her homework in the car. He'll know what I mean. She needs it at school within the hour, and he can leave it at the front office." She sighed with exasperation. "On second thought, why am I making you the messenger? Put him on the phone and I'll tell him myself."

"Jules—

"Seriously. We've been trying to get hold of him for a while, Charlie."

Charlie sighed. "Me, too. I've been waiting for him, too."

"What? I don't—"

"He called and asked me to meet him for coffee, at the beach. Only I was late. But I'm here now, and his car's here, but he isn't. I thought you might have heard from him."

"I don't . . ." But Jules couldn't finish her thought. She dropped into the desk chair.

"Um, Jules? There's more," Charlie said, an edge of anxiety creeping into his voice.

No more, she thought. *This is already too much.* There was too much going wrong today, too much to write off as simply a bad day that an air-clearing conversation and a good night's sleep would cure. Jules heard Charlie repeating her name. Her brain registered this, tucked away the fact of him trying to speak to her.

On the other side of the room, a customer was arguing with

Florence. Florence was the queen of calm, one reason why Jules liked her on the counter on busy mornings, but today, the calmer Florence remained, the louder their customer grew. "I can't believe you won't wrap this in plastic like I'm asking you to."

Florence must have related the no plastic wrap/no plastic bag policy Jules had instituted for the warm flaky pastries so they wouldn't end up soggy by the time they reached their destination. "I don't care," the customer insisted now. "What happened to the customer is always right? I'm traveling with them and I need them covered with plastic."

A month ago, a day ago, Jules would have been angry enough to intervene, and David would have laid a hand on her arm and held her back from a confrontation. She would have been grateful. Even now, despite all he had been hiding from her, despite how confused she felt, she needed him here. He would make quick work of this woman; in the end, she would leave with the pastry packaged the way Jules preferred and be happy to do so. Had she told David this lately, that she needed him? That no matter what was going on, she needed him?

Not recently—maybe not ever. Jules was unaccustomed to leaning on others. For most of her life she had been the strong one, everyone's supporter. First, her mother's, as far back as adolescence, when her father left; Rennie's, especially now, as her daughter navigated the increasingly complicated social terrains of middle school; and she had been David's cheerleader as well, the person who grounded him and bucked him up when he worried or doubted himself. She didn't sink into despair herself; she didn't have time. But she did need him. And today, he was not here.

"Jules? Are you there?"

"I'm here," she answered, pulling herself together. "Tell me again. Tell me what you know."

Charlie ran through it all as Jules struggled to follow: David's car in the beach lot. The meeting Charlie had arrived late for. The dog walker who had seen him. The belongings left behind, the clothes.

"He was gone by the time I got here," Charlie finished. "I have all his things. But he's nowhere in sight." There was a pause, and then, "Why would he take off his clothes? It's freezing out here. It's been storming, you know? The waves are crashing."

His desperation thrummed across the lines between them. Jules looked up from the desk in time to see the problem customer grab her boxed pastries and leave in dramatic fashion, yanking the door shut behind her. In her wake, the tattered ends of the plastic sheeting flapped. Behind the ratty tarp, David's pet project looked dark and dead.

"Hold on, hold on a minute," she told Charlie, and she took the phone from her ear and held it on her lap. She wanted to take note of the moment. Something was happening, something . . . not good. Even if David turned up in a minute or an hour, it wouldn't matter. Things would never be the same. This she knew.

"Jules," Charlie persisted. "Should I wait for you here? You should see if you recognize the clothes. Should I call the cops?"

These were decisions she should make but she wished Charlie would tell her what to do instead. She closed her eyes and gripped the phone tighter. The endless stream of questions reminded her of her mother, her mother's rush of rhetorical questions once she found the letter her husband left in his wake: *Do you think he'll have second thoughts? Do you think he'll be back? He'll be back, won't he? Do you think this is some kind of mistake?*

Back then, Jules had had to call the doctor for a house visit and sedatives. In the weeks after, while her mother lay in bed, she had determined what groceries to buy and what meals to make, which bills were most urgent to pay with the limited amount of money they had in the bank and which could coast without being paid for a week or two, or even longer. She felt too tired now, too tired to do this again. Alone. "David," she said to herself, "David, I need you."

Too late. He was nowhere to be found.

"Jules?"

She could hear Charlie's voice even as she muffled the receiver in the floury folds of her apron. She opened her eyes to see Florence staring at her. Rachel, too, and Sandy, her eyes full of questions.

Jules returned the receiver to her ear. "Yes, Charlie. Call the police. And tell me again exactly where you are. I'll meet you there."

She disconnected and this time held the receiver over her heart. She could feel the muscle fluttering rapidly under her ribs, a wild bird in a tight cage. There it was, the feeling she had been refusing to recognize all morning as one strange thing after another revealed itself to her. This was fear. And she was alone with it.

April–June 2010

4

"And how did that make you feel, seeing her again after so long? What has it been, three years?"

Ah, a two-part question, her favorite kind. Not. Denise Healey crossed and uncrossed her legs at the knees, trying to get comfortable. It was a struggle every week, her legs a bit too short for this sofa with the deep seat. She was also buying some time as she decided which part to answer first. Therapists. How did this-that-the-other-thing make you feel, Denise?

God, sometimes she hated the questions, and sometimes she hated being here. But she also worried about stopping therapy; what if she slipped back into the muck of anger and depression that held her fixed in place after Matt left and after she quit the job she had loved but was no longer doing well? The threat of feeling stuck there again dogged her day and night. Movement of any kind seemed more productive, and at least therapy kept her putting one foot in front of the other.

She decided to answer Part B first. "Since April 2008, so almost exactly two years. That date is in your notes." She lifted her chin, motioning to the file folder on the coffee table between them.

Dr. Chamberlain smiled. "You like to be exact."

"Who doesn't?"

"Oh, many people don't, or can't. Some professions come

with a lot of gray area. Like therapy, as you can imagine. In other jobs, people cut corners. As in, good enough is good enough."

Denise shook her head. "In my line of work, I've found being exact is necessary, even if it might strike you as nitpicking. Anyway, dates are dates, and you asked."

"I did. I also asked how seeing the girl made you feel."

The girl. The daughter of a man whose disappearance she had investigated. An investigation that began with suspicion and ended with a body washing up on a north shore beach. The eventual determination: suicide.

Denise had seen the girl, now fourteen, a high school freshman, on Friday as she waited for her boys in the pick-up line at school. Still out of work, she filled her days with what she called "perfect mom" routines: hot breakfasts, homemade lunches, well-balanced dinners, and conversation around the table. Also, rides to and from the high school. Her boys balked a bit at these. A junior and a senior, they were too old for rides, they argued, and they looked stupid in front of their friends, and they wanted to take the bus anyway. Argue, argue, argue. But Denise insisted. *Come on*, she said. *All those years when I couldn't do these very things, couldn't be here in the morning to wake you up because I was working? Couldn't drive you to practice? All those years when you complained I wasn't like the other moms?* Tommy and Teddy had exchanged looks after she finished speaking and rolled their eyes. But they'd given in. They had been more tender boys since their dad moved out and filed for divorce, the final break in a marriage that had been, admittedly, crumbling for quite some time. Her boys, God love them, were still rather protective of her, as if they sensed her aloneness was still raw. Or her health still fragile.

"Denise? Time's almost up. Why don't you try to answer before we call it a day?"

Look at this, I'm all over the place again. This was her other beef with therapy: that nothing—no conversations, no thoughts—went in straight lines. Talk therapy was so inexact, the opposite of everything she valued. Ask a question about one moment in her day and before she knew it, she was crying about the death of her childhood pet turtle.

Denise nudged herself back on track: Okay, the girl. She would have started at the high school in September, out of Denise's purview in the middle school for the two years before this. Denise had only seen her a handful of times back in '08, and yet on Friday she had recognized her immediately. She had a good memory for faces, and it helped that the girl looked almost the same, except a little taller and more mature. And harder. Funny word to use to describe a kid, she thought, but hard was the right one. Her eyes were narrowed as if facing the world with wariness, her mouth set in a straight and determined line. She held her books tight against her chest as she shouldered her way through the crowd of students heading for the buses.

Denise wondered if she was still a crier. Looked like she was not, but boy, she had wept a lot two years earlier when Denise had grilled her mother about whether she might have had a hand in her husband's disappearance. At the time, Denise had grumbled to herself about snotty, privileged kids being allowed to derail her interviews. She hadn't meant to be overheard questioning—well, okay, *badgering*—the woman. She admitted to herself now that the girl had not been snotty at all, and that she'd been wrong to treat the family the way she had. But clothes and shoes folded neatly on a beach during what amounted to a nor'easter, and no sign of the man who was supposed to show up for a meeting he requested with his friend? It had all seemed weird and fishy to Denise. Like a set-up, at once too pat and too leading, as if someone had meant to direct everyone's attention to the clothes and shoes left at the water's edge. And anyway, it wouldn't have been the first time a wife and a friend had hooked up to off an unsuspecting husband, nor would it be the last.

Unfortunately for the wife and the friend, Denise's husband, Matt, had only days before confessed to cheating with a younger woman they both knew from the chipper recipe columns she wrote for the local newspaper, columns Matt had formerly ridiculed. Caught around the time of the man's disappearance, Matt had sworn he would give up Heather and asked for a second chance. He'd seemed contrite, so Denise had agreed. She'd been a good Irish Catholic wife, well drilled in the sanctity of her marriage vows. But the feelings of betrayal had persisted, flooding her personal thoughts and spilling over into her professional life. A case of bad timing, those two had found themselves in the crosshairs.

Are you two sleeping together? How long have you two been sleeping together? Are you sure we won't find a witness who has seen you two stepping out together on at least one occasion? Denise had thought if she chipped away, she might break one of them, and breaking the friend looked most likely. He, like the daughter, had been distraught, or doing a good job of pretending. The wife, though, had been silent, unreachable, which had only made Denise double down and prod harder.

Unfortunately, the girl had been on the stairs just outside the room, listening in on the questioning, and had let out an eardrum-piercing wail after Denise made these accusations. The mother had jumped out of her seat and gone ballistic, the family friend barely restraining her from doing Denise physical harm. Threatened with arrest, the woman had backed off, thrown Denise a dirty look, and followed her daughter up the stairs. "Just doing my job," Denise had told the family friend as she left the house for the first time. Not an apology. Lord no, not that. *Only doing my job.*

After two days of investigating, and with solid alibis and the banker's evidence of a large loan default in hand, she'd had to admit she was likely wrong in her initial assessment. The disappeared guy had lost his shirt in debt, and it was looking more and more like he'd drowned himself.

Her boss had reamed her a new one at that news, told her she had wasted valuable man hours on a pointless line of questions. They were this close, he'd said, holding his thumb and forefinger a millimeter apart, to being sued for harassment. The dead guy's father was some bigwig banker and might, if pushed, make a stink. Well, it had been a bad couple of weeks: the heroin overdose she'd gotten called to, the one with the two parents dead in the front seat of their minivan and their toddler crying in the back; the child rape; and the arsenal of illegally owned guns and bomb-making equipment found stockpiled in a local home by a child visiting for a weekly piano lesson. And then Matt, confessing he was not going to end things with Heather, that he was in love with her. The destruction people could wreak had been her best and only excuse.

We all understand the stress, her captain had told her, *but you've got to pull yourself together.* Okay, she'd agreed, and she had for a while; she really had tried to rediscover her zeal for her work and do her best. But not long after, Matt had moved out, and Denise, following months of little sleep and a whole lot of inner rage, had run out of gas at work and resigned, staunch in her decision even as her partner, Joe Canelli, urged her to consider taking an open-ended leave instead. No, she'd told him. She had to stay at home to keep her two boys close, help them through the separation, give them some semblance of a family. "I'll find something less . . . consuming to do with my life."

That had been the intention. The reality was, one morning she'd looked down and seen the days' worth of coffee stains on the sweatpants she hadn't changed out of, and then looked up to see her boys making their own breakfasts and making hers, too. So here she was now, eight months in, sitting on this couch that was definitely not made for shorter girls week after week, trying to get well while being reminded of all the pain she felt and had caused.

How did it feel to see Rennie Herron? Good question.

She cleared her throat. "I thought: Good. She's a survivor. That's good, right?"

Dr. Chamberlain gave her a funny look but didn't ask again. Yes, Denise understood she hadn't exactly answered the question, that an assessment of the girl wasn't the same as an assessment of her feelings, but she was done. Some thoughts she had to keep for herself. She clasped her hands together, set them on her lap, and waited for the clock to run out.

Tommy and Teddy had baseball practice after school, and Denise had well over an hour to kill between her weekly therapy appointment and picking them up. Today, she went to the school early to pass the time there. She could have returned home to catch up on laundry or made a grocery run, but so much of the last eight months had been about waiting—waiting for the minute hand to reach her allotted forty-five minutes of therapy, waiting to feel better, waiting for day to turn into night—that she now waited by default. There was little point in multitasking. Her days were long and wide open. She'd have nothing but time to do the grocery run later, bringing her two sweaty boys to help her shop. They'd clamor for salty snacks, but so what. Maybe she could get them to pick a vegetable as well.

Waiting and bargaining with teenage boys: her life in a nutshell. A surprisingly passive existence for a formerly hyper-engaged detective. *You are aggressively curious*, her boss used to say—a backhanded compliment if there ever was one—to which she would only shrug. Behind his back, though, she griped to her partner, "Why are ambitious, smart women always 'aggressive'? And how else should I do my job, if not with curiosity?"

In the car now, slowing down to take her place outside the school, she reminded herself that the detecting life was no longer her life for many reasons—her mental health and the well-being of others chief among them. She had once been proud of her dogged determination to solve crimes, and look what all that relentlessness had brought her: Divorce. Reprimands from her higher-ups. No, she was glad that go-get-'em attitude was a thing of the past. She was.

She arrived as the first dismissal bell sounded, but instead of pulling into the waiting line, she parallel parked across the street from the pick-up lane and turned off the car. Putting groceries back on her mind, she ran through some supper ideas. Maybe the boys would like a rotisserie chicken. As she rummaged at the bottom of her large handbag for a pen and her notepad to jot down a quick shopping list, the second bell sounded. She stopped mid-search, turned in her driver's seat, and watched the doors, waiting for them to be thrown open. Force of habit, she thought, that although her two wouldn't be in the crowd, she watched anyway.

Within seconds, the students began to flood out, coming through the doors in a trickle at first and then in one big wave. She saw a few of her sons' friends—squirming their way out of the crowd like puppies with too much pent-up energy—and smiled. Then something else caught her eye, and she sat up straighter and craned her neck. She barely registered the sound of the pen falling from her hand and hitting the console.

Her heart sped up with excitement. There she was, alone again, books clasped to her chest again, bringing up the rear of the exodus and not in any hurry to overtake or catch up to anyone. Physically, Rennie looked well enough, decent height and weight, decent posture for a teen. Her hair, shorter than it had been two years earlier, was clean and combed. She looked cared for. Better than just surviving. Denise ought to know what that looked like now that she herself had cleaned up after weeks and weeks of sweatpants and unwashed hair.

But there was that hard stare again, the lack of connection with the kids around her.

Denise sat back. She kept her eyes on the girl, watched her make progress through the crowd of kids getting into cars until she was one of only a few students who arrived at the crosswalk.

A walker. Odd. A bit of a mystery. She would have assumed Rennie was a bus student. The home Denise had visited to conduct the interviews and, later, to give updates was a few miles across town, on the edge of the town's conservation land. Another oddity, she thought, that she could recall it so vividly. A good-size house on one of the smaller lots on the street, the property had nevertheless offered a great deal of privacy in its backyard. Neighbors might not have noticed comings and goings, never mind a fight or an assault taking place on the grounds. She recalled her surreptitious look into the garden shed on the day of the disappearance—a not-quite-legit look at the time, but no one had stopped her as she scanned for things out of place, for spots or stains no matter how minuscule.

One of the last things her husband had told her before moving out, during the time they were still—she'd thought—in the limbo space of trying to repair their derailed relationship, was that she was beginning to approach everyone with suspicion. She had defended herself: "That's simply not true, not everyone."

He'd countered by listing examples. "I see you giving side-eye at the deli counter, for God's sake, like you're looking for a thumb on the scale. Spying through our window curtains whenever a strange car parks on the street. What, drug deals? And then there was that interrogation of your own sister when you thought she might be leaving the kids unsupervised on the days she had them at her house."

"Boy, that's a long list of grievances, Matt. I guess I'm just a bad person for being concerned."

"There's concerned, babe, and then there's suspicious. You probably even think I'm still doing something I shouldn't be."

Funny, she had wondered that; funnier still, he *had* been doing something again, she just hadn't found the evidence to prove it. His decision to leave her, when it came, had taken her by surprise—not because she couldn't believe it but because he had been one step ahead of her the whole way.

Matt had been offended by her suspicions. That was rich. Still, maybe she had let her skepticism spiral out of control. Years of confronting all the bad things humans did to other humans, day in and day out, could jade a person. Her superiors had said as much with their reprimand. And Denise was not so far up her own self-righteous ass that she couldn't admit that when more than one person told her the same thing, perhaps there was something there to examine. It was the old "where there's smoke, there's fire" principle that often guided her detective work.

Sometimes that principle had stood her in good stead, made her a sharp detective. She'd helped keep the communities she served safe through pre-emptive policing. She'd channeled her concern into effectiveness.

"There's concerned, babe, and then there's suspicious."

Denise stared out the windshield. Ahead, the girl was becoming indistinct as she walked farther away from the school. Maybe she could get back to her original intent and back to effectiveness. It would be a sign she was getting better, wouldn't it? Putting the mistakes of policing behind her and returning to the desire to help that had drawn her to her job in the first place? Wasn't that what her captain had meant when he'd urged her to get back on track?

She checked her watch. She still had over an hour before the boys would be done. Time enough to follow the girl and check up on her just this once to make sure she was staying away from harm or trouble. Denise reached for the key and started the car. Yes, there was something about that hard set to the girl's face that worried her. She put on her blinker, checked her sideview mirror, and pulled out into the street.

"We haven't talked much about the boys lately, Denise. Last time you mentioned them, they were well, but as I said, reactions to major change can often be delayed. How are they presenting? Are they adjusted to the post-divorce landscape?"

Another two-part question. Denise wanted to groan. This had been an otherwise uneventful, even boring, session. How do you feel today, Denise; what kinds of self-care have you practiced this week; any luck with the guided meditation tapes I gave you? No complaints; none, unless you count a quart of Brigham's chocolate chip ice cream as self-care; and no, no luck. Some longer answers to other questions ("I went to the movies with a girlfriend and it was nice to get out, blah, blah, blah"), but nothing too deep or revealing. Nothing about her one-sided encounter with the girl, certainly nothing about following her to the well-worn apartment building just off the center of downtown.

The best thing about what appeared to be the new home of the girl and her mother was that it gave the mom a two-minute walk to work, assuming she was still baking downtown, and the girl the chance to stretch her legs after a long day at school. Otherwise, wow, what a change from their former, spacious foursquare home the nondescript brick block of a building made. Denise had pulled to the curb as the girl put her key in the front door, and she'd watched for a few moments longer as, front door still wide open to anyone looking in off the streets, the girl checked the mailbox. Right then, her impulse had been to lean out her car window and call a caution to the teen to close the front door behind her, like she told her own boys to do on the rare occasions they came home to an empty house. "Safety first, lock yourselves in when I'm not here!" But she'd said nothing, hadn't given herself away.

She'd even held back from strolling past the bakery where she figured the mother still worked, though she had indulged in a quick drive-by. The place was still up and running. From the outside, it looked the same, although she noted the windows weren't as decorated as they'd been before. And the empty space next door that would have been the café was now a new business altogether: a bike sales and repair shop. There were bikes on the sidewalk outside the front door, bikes displayed in the windows. Life had gone on for other people.

"Denise?"

"Oh. The boys. They're still fine. Happy enough. Both of them go between the two homes without too much complaining. Tommy is the easier-going one. You know, Mr. Happy-Go-Lucky. Teddy misses me when he goes, but he really likes seeing his dad. He did his college applications earlier this year with Matt's help, and they really bonded over that. I guess we're lucky. Ticking along."

The therapist nodded. "And how about you and Matt?"

Denise uncrossed her legs, then crossed them again. She was uncomfortable talking about Matt, and for her, internal discomfort almost always led to physical discomfort. These kinds of conversations were when she felt the sofa was most punishing. "There is no me and Matt," she said. "There's Mom and Dad."

"All right then, how are Mom and Dad? You think the co-parenting is going well?"

"We don't talk enough to argue. And anyway, we've always made a point of not arguing in front of the kids."

She shifted again. Her two-sentence answer had consisted of a lie and then a truth. The truth was that they had always saved their disagreements for private moments. The lie? They had talked enough to argue that past weekend, Matt pulling her aside to ask if she was remaining locked on to the boys, to their activities, their well-being. "Are you backsliding? Ted says you seem distracted again."

"Grilling him, are we?" Instead of looking at Matt she had focused on the stairwell, waiting for the boys to appear at the top of the stairs with their bags.

"Noooo." He'd drawn the word out. "He asked Heather if she might take him to Staples for supplies for a social studies project. Somewhere in there, he mentioned that you keep forgetting to take him."

Fantastic. Heather as her Teddy's new confidant? *Shoot me now*, she had thought in the moment. And then, no. This was pure Matt, one-upping her. He was like those alpha dogs that circled until they spotted a weakness and then pinned their subjects to the ground with a paw to the throat.

She'd turned and glared at him. "Seriously, Matt. I haven't forgotten. Between school and sports and chores, we haven't had time. Tell Heather I said thanks for taking him."

"No need to snap at me, Dee. I'm checking to make sure you're all right. You know what you've been like. Just because they're relatively easy boys doesn't mean they don't need a hundred percent of your attention."

At times like that, with Matt pushing her every button, Denise could feel the pulse points in her neck beating a tattoo and her temples throbbing. The only thing that kept her from exploding at him was the thought that she couldn't—wouldn't—give him, Mr. Know-It-All-Holier-Than-Thou-Backstabbing-Cheater, the satisfaction of proving his allegations true. She knew the truth anyway, and so did the boys, and that was all that mattered. They had been her life, her entire life, this past year. Now that she could feel herself reviving, coming back to the self she used to be, that curious and dogged self, it was natural that she would be less involved in every aspect of the boys' lives and start to engage in her own again. To be honest, finding Rennie had seemed like a sign that it was time for her to turn the corner of self-pity and walk on the street of purpose again. She could keep an eye on the girl and continue to be a good mom. Hell, she *was* a good mom, doing it all on the home front during the week. Weekend Dad Matt could get right off his high horse. It wouldn't kill Heather to drive to Staples once.

But before she could slip and tell him where to go, she'd heard feet overhead and the boys had appeared on the stairs. Plastering on a smile, she told Matt, "Thanks for the reminder." And then she'd opened her arms wide for hugs as the kiddos met her down in the foyer.

She looked up from her lap to see the shrink's raised eyebrow. There was no need to discuss any of this with her, no need to make the woman skeptical of her progress or wonder about a new obsession. Besides, if she started to appear more engaged, like she was pulling it all together, maybe they could start talking about things that really mattered, like whether she seemed well enough to stop coming to these sessions.

"The boys are good, co-parenting is good. This week has been pretty good, actually. Sorry to be boring."

"I would say positive rather than boring. That's all positive news, Denise." The therapist gave a quick look at her desk clock.

"Time's about up today. Before you go, I'm going to assign you some homework."

Denise wanted to groan like her boys did at every mention of chores, but she didn't. "Okay, shoot."

"I'm really pleased you made some time for yourself and a friend this week, and I want you to build on that. Get out again. And please give the guided meditation a try, once a day every day this week. You pick the most relaxing time of day and then set aside twenty or thirty minutes to listen to the CDs and try the techniques. Think of it as 'Denise time'—you alone in peace and quiet. One week. We'll talk about how you made out at our next appointment. Deal?"

Denise thought she'd rather have her fingernails pulled out with her rusted pliers. But seven days would give her time to come up with a reason why meditation didn't work for her, maybe even time to invent an alternative that would please the therapist as much. A daily walk in the state park, maybe, or laps in the Y pool. So, wearing the same smile she saved for her most trying moments with Matt, she nodded. She hoped her enthusiasm was convincing.

"Deal," she said.

5

School traffic was always choked on Monday mornings. Kids moved at a slug's pace after the weekend, taking their time exiting their rides. Denise smiled to herself. Her tired two were slumped in the backseat, each doing his best gastropod impression. The struggle to get them out of bed that morning had been an epic symphony of snooze alarms and raised voices. Now, as she waited to enter the horseshoe drive, her foot on the brake, she glanced up at the rearview mirror and looked at them. "Almost there, guys."

Teddy only grunted in return, but he sat up straight and moved his pack from the floor to the seat. Tommy, slid halfway down the seatback, was engrossed in writing something in a notebook splayed out across his knees and didn't move.

"Tell me you're not doing homework at the last possible minute," Denise said.

"I'm not doing homework at the last possible minute," he said. "I'm making a list of things I need to do this week." But instead of continuing, he hastily shut the book and shoved it and the pen into his school bag. Then he too sat up straighter.

Denise raised an eyebrow. This was unlike her more laid-back son. Checklists and responsibilities and a focus on completing tasks? Oh well, maybe he was turning over a new leaf.

The car in front of her inched ahead and Denise followed suit, creeping up the street another car's length. When she stopped, she looked in the mirror again. The boys looked ready to hop out fast when she finally made it to the driveway, something the drivers behind her would thank her for. She looked beyond her boys at the cars behind, so many of them that the crossing guards were holding up the traffic trying to enter Main Street from the small side streets. It was nothing short of a miracle that a disgruntled driver didn't flip into road rage mode every morning. In her experience, most situations involving an impatient public were riots waiting to happen. Matt used to laugh at her pessimism, but she knew she was right. Order was always, *always* hanging on by a thread.

Before Denise turned her attention back to the movement in front of her, her eyes fell on the driver in the car immediately behind her. His was a familiar face, older but distinguished, attractive, with a full head of immaculately combed salt-and-pepper hair. He had crossed her path before—maybe here at school, maybe through work, she wasn't yet sure—so she ran his features through her mind. She was good with faces.

She tried to see the student in the car with this familiar-looking man, thinking that the second face might jog her memory, but he or she was in the backseat, like her boys were, and partially obscured by the driver.

As she stared and ran the man's features through her memory like she was running a plate, he looked straight at her, his lips set in a line, as if he were fed up. The loud honk he issued next confirmed that he was, in fact, peeved.

Denise looked ahead: The cars had moved again. She was holding up the line. But instead of moving, she looked again in the rearview mirror. She froze. She knew who he was.

"Mom."

"Mom."

"Mom, come on. Move! Mom, what are you looking at?"

Both boys twisted in their seats, trying to figure out what had captured their mother's attention.

"Nothing," she said, shaking off her stupor. She rolled the car forward and stopped at a prime place in the horseshoe. "Here we are." She tried to smile at the boys, but they met her cheer with sarcasm.

"Weird, Mom," Teddy said. "Brain fart."

"Yeah, I know, smart aleck. Wait until you're my age, all sorts of fun await." Using the mirror, she glanced behind her again. The car behind her had also reached the horseshoe and she saw its back door open. A young girl stepped out onto the sidewalk.

Teddy followed her gaze and nudged his brother. "It's your girlfriend. Mom's looking at her—the strange freshman girl. Look."

Tommy turned and then shrugged. "So?"

"So? Aren't you always talking to her?"

"No. Go blow yourself."

"Hey, hey, hey." Tommy's vulgarity snapped Denise out of her thoughts. "That's enough, you two. Do you know that girl?" she asked him.

"Not really," he mumbled, defensive, and before Denise could blink he had hopped out of the car.

Clearly, he did know her girl, and maybe Denise would get to the bottom of that, but not now. She looked over her shoulder at her firstborn, now following his brother out of the car.

"Teddy, stop calling people 'strange.' That's not the way I raised you."

He slid across the bench seat toward the open door. "Sorry, Mom."

"Apology accepted. I love you both!" she called after them, but Teddy slammed the door before either had acknowledged they had heard her.

Denise looked once more at the car immediately behind her, at the rest of the cars behind her. She had to move before she pissed people off. Her brain snapped into quick-thinking mode, and she knew exactly where she needed to go next. Not back home to read another few chapters of the book she had at her bedside or to try the ridiculous meditation exercises only long enough to make up a reason why they wouldn't work for her; not home to scrub her toilets, either. Not at all back home, where her brain and her mad investigative skills would atrophy, dry up, and wither like all the plants she had tried to grow, ever. No. Fuck all that.

She gave the distinguished man behind her one more look and pulled away from the curb.

"Nell, I'm out front. Can I get an all-clear to come up and see you?" Denise stood outside the building where she used to report to work, her cellphone pressed to her ear. She was pleased that her former partner had answered her call. If it had been anyone else picking up his phone, she would have disconnected immediately. But she used his nickname anyway; it was their code that this conversation needed to stay private.

He used hers back. "Dennis? You're *here*?" he hissed into the phone. Those two whispered words right there told her all she needed to know. There would be no going into the building unless she wanted a tongue-lashing from the higher-ups. "Not a good time."

"Shoot. I wanted to look at something on the database."

"Whoa. You're ballsy. Not happening today."

"Can you meet me out here, then? I need some help."

There was dead air on the line for a couple of seconds, followed by a muffled sound. Denise waited, and soon Joe was back with her. "I can leave for a few," he said. "Head to the coffee shop across—no, scratch that. Go down the block and wait for me at Peets. No one from here sets foot in that place. You're buying, Dennis," he added, and he hung up.

In the line at Peets, Denise remembered to check her wallet for cash. The five-dollar bill and change she had would pay for two small black coffees, so that was what she ordered when it was her turn at the register. Joe was going to have to like it or lump it.

She moved to the other end of the counter and watched the lone barista handle an espresso machine with so many levers and movable parts it looked like it belonged in Dr. Frankenstein's laboratory. Denise's two paper cups looked sad as they waited by the industrial drip machine, ignored in favor of the more complex brews with their yak's milk foam or whatever the young woman was pouring into ceramic cups the size of bird baths. Finally, in between a cappuccino and something called a flat white, the young woman took a minute to pour Denise's black coffees. Glancing at the Sharpie scribbles, she called, "Dennis?"

Denise raised her hand and the cups were placed on the counter in front of her. Just then a voice at her ear made her jump.

"Did you really order using your code name?"

She turned and there was Joe. "I did not," she answered, and she squinted at the writing on the cup. She held a cup out to Joe and he took it. "See? An 'e' on the end. She's just too busy to pay attention to details like that." She tilted her head. "How are you, Nell?"

"Good, good. Let's go sit somewhere at the back." He pointed to tables at the other end of the room, away from the windows that looked out over the sidewalk.

"Lead the way."

When they settled, Joe gave Denise a long once-over. "You're looking good."

Joe was one of her few work friends who continued to stay in touch, but she hadn't wanted him to see her in person during her lowest days. And then one day he'd come over anyway, under the pretext of bringing her some of his mother's homemade chicken and escarole soup. He hadn't remarked on her appearance, but he hadn't had to; Denise had seen the concern in his eyes.

"Ah, the days of lying in bed and neglecting to bathe are behind me."

"Seriously, we were worried about you, Dee-Dee."

"Yeah, yeah, I was worried about me, too. But. Onward and upward." She raised her cup.

Joe touched his cup to hers. "Cheers to that." He took a sip, swallowed. "So, what kind of help do you need?"

Denise set down her cup and ran a hand through her hair. "The disappeared guy, the drowner from the beach—"

"Whoa, whoa, whoa. That case was, like, Kryptonite for you."

"I know, but hear me out."

Joe made circles with his hand for her to continue.

"The daughter? Rennie? She's at my boys' high school now. I've been seeing her off and on when I get my kids."

"Ah yes, Renata Herron. Has she seen you seeing her?"

She wasn't surprised that Joe remembered the girl's full name. Some cases stayed with a person. This was one. She shook her head.

"Probably a good thing. Go on," he urged.

Denise took a second to decide what to say next. She didn't want to admit to Joe that she had followed the girl and invite a lecture, or worse. "She leaves the school on foot, so I assume they've moved in closer to town. Could they have lost the house? Did you ever hear anything?"

Joe nodded. "Makes sense, but no. Nothing."

"Anyway, this morning, a Mercedes pulled up behind me and

it was the girl with her grandfather—the drowner's shitty father, remember him?"

Joe gave a wry laugh. "Uh, yeah. 'I'm Paul Herron, the North Shore's Most Important Man.' How could I forget? I thought there was no love lost between him, his wife, and their daughter-in-law? Son and his parents were semi-estranged, the grandparents were upset they'd had only minimal contact with their granddaughter?"

Denise sat back in her seat. "Exactly. And now he's driving the girl to school on Monday morning in his fancy car."

"Huh." Joe set his cup on the table and proceeded to fiddle with it, tipping it back and forth. It annoyed Denise when he did this, but she knew he was thinking, so she said nothing.

"Okay," he said finally. "I admit it's a little weird after the passive-aggressive head games those two were pulling on the dead guy's wife. But maybe they all decided to bury the hatchet. Maybe they offered support and the wife accepted, for the sake of the kid." He looked at Denise looking at him. "I can see your wheels turning. What is it?"

Again, Denise wasn't ready to admit she knew where the mom and daughter lived, and that because of those low-rent digs it was unlikely the grandparents were providing cash support. Instead, she reminded Joe that they hadn't pegged Grandad as a champ in the emotional support department. "Remember how cold he was?" She shook her head. "And given the badmouthing—"

"Two years ago, remember?" Joe shrugged. "A lot can happen in two years."

"Granted. But given what we did see two years ago, this 180 in behavior, I don't know, it seems odd. And I don't like odd."

Joe nodded. He knew she didn't like odd. She knew he didn't either. She let him sit with the image of the girl, the grandfather, the Mercedes, the volley of insults they both remembered being lobbed at the wife on that morning two years earlier. Joe did the thing with his coffee cup again and caught it just before it tipped all the way over on its side.

"Good save," she said, "but knock it off. The next time the coffee's going to spill all over the place."

"Yes, Mom. Jeez, I can tell you've been hanging out with the boys a lot lately." Still, he stopped playing and set the cup to one side. "How are the boys?"

"They're good. Keeping busy with baseball practice at the moment, doing homework under duress. Not complaining too much that they're back and forth between homes."

"Leads me to my next question. How's that a-hole of an ex-husband of yours?"

"Hey, that's the father of my children you're talking about. He's *super* a-hole ex-husband to you, thank you very much."

That made Joe laugh. He had never much liked Matt.

"He's unchanged, Nell. Still telling me all the ways his approach to things is far superior to mine." Denise lifted her cup and drank the rest of her coffee in one long swig.

"And you?" Joe asked.

"Me? I'm okay. The boys keep me occupied."

Joe looked at her. "As does worrying about old, closed cases and kids you once crossed paths with, apparently."

"Touché. I know I have no business meddling. I should stick to carpools." Denise attempted a laugh, but when she looked at Joe, tears stung her eyes.

Joe reached across the table and covered her free hand with his. "Not what I was suggesting at all. My point was, enough of the small talk. You're here because you're concerned about this girl. I need to know what you're thinking if we're going to review those files."

"'We'? You mean—"

"Once a team, always a team. So spill it. What's your gut telling you?"

Relieved, Denise smiled, but with Joe offering help she owed him all the facts she knew. She got down to business. "My gut is telling me that something about the grandfather situation is off, Joe. You know I said I saw Rennie at school? Well, I followed her home the other day. And before you say anything"—she held up her hand—"I'm not a stalker. I'm concerned. Anyway, I followed her to a really run-down apartment building, where she let herself in. New home, probably. The bakery is right down the street, and if Julia Herron is still affiliated with the bakery, it makes sense they'd live there, especially if they lost the other home."

Joe nodded. "I'm with you so far."

"But here's my problem: Why? Today the girl is in the drop-off line in her grandfather's Mercedes but they live in a dump? Why live in a dump if he's so well off? Don't play devil's advocate with me and tell me Julia Herron might be perfectly happy where she is. No one wants to live in an old place like that with their kid, trust me. They live there because they have to."

"She was kind of proud, though," Joe mused. "I can see her not wanting his money. But true, she probably wouldn't want to deprive Rennie if she didn't have to. The question is, then, does she have to? You think Herron is doing something squirrelly?"

Denise shook her head. "I don't know. First his son kills himself, and all he and his wife talk about is their unreasonable daughter-in-law. And now he drives his granddaughter to school, but doesn't do anything about where she lives? It doesn't add up. And the girl . . . She looks so lost. Lost and hard. She's freaking fourteen years old, and she looks like she has the weight of the world on her."

Joe gave her a long look. "You feel responsible."

"I do." She shifted in her chair. "That case is where I started to screw up. I was horrible to Julia Herron right in front of her daughter, and I wasn't at all sympathetic to the girl's feelings. Her father was dead, for God's sake, and I couldn't get past my own problems. I don't know that I can do anything now, and maybe it's all in my imagination, but I'd like to try and make it up to that family."

Joe stared at her another few seconds, and then he looked at his watch. "I need to get back."

She started to stand as he pushed himself away from the small table, but he held up a hand. "You stay for a few minutes. Just in case. But here's what you're going to do later today. Email me with the list of things that are bothering you. A list of things you think we should look into. I can't look at anyone's bank records or any other shady stuff; this can't be official, you know that, so don't even ask. We stay within the data I can legally access. And I'll see what I can do. Use my personal email address," he reminded her.

Denise hadn't realized she had been holding her breath until she sighed with relief. "Thank you, Joe. For the help, and for taking me seriously. Others wouldn't, you know. I owe you."

"Yes, you do. I want a better coffee next time," he said. "You're a good cop, Dee-Dee." He leaned down and kissed her cheek. "Remember, email me your ideas and I'll be in touch."

Denise nodded, careful not to tip her head too far forward in case the tears pooling in her eyes overflowed. Tears of gratitude.

You're a good cop. In the last months of her marriage and her job, she had assumed she was losing her mind as everything around her spun out of control. The therapy had helped; with it, her days had grown less foggy and monochrome. Little by little, life had returned to full color. And now, along with the gold of sunlight and the red flash of her backyard cardinals and the bright blue of the sky that she once again noticed each time she walked to the mailbox, she knew her investigative instincts had also returned.

Perhaps she had not lost her mind but her way, like a confused bird flown off course. *Way* off course for a while, but no longer. Denise heard Joe's voice rattling around in her head again: *You're a good cop.* Maybe she still was, and her search for answers to all the unanswered questions would help right her way and the way of all the others affected by the drowning. Maybe she could help that happen. Maybe.

6

Energized by the meeting with Joe the day before and eager to get to work on the questions he'd requested, Denise called her therapist and left a voicemail to cancel her therapy appointment. The extra time spent at home would be more productive. She sat down at the computer after tidying the house and typed out every single question she could think of regarding Paul Herron, his daughter-in-law, and his granddaughter.

Joe, she wrote, *are there any records of domestics or altercations or even unpaid parking tickets—anything? As the head of a bank, was he ever charged with any kind of malpractice? Long shot, I know. The guy seems like a pillar-of-the-community type. But can you dig?*

Today I'm going to go into the bakery (no, really, I'm not *a stalker) to have a quick look around. Knowing where the wife and daughter now live, and knowing they're only minutes from the shop, my best guess is that the wife still works there. If* so, *how did that happen?*

I'll check into that on Friday when I head into court to check the public bankruptcy records. Is there a filing for the bakery? We know it's up and running, but the wife can't still own the place, right? With all that debt? Maybe it was bought out? New owner? Hmmmm. Can I track that down?

In the meantime, whatever you can find . . .

She was jazzed after hitting send. More jazzed when Joe

replied later with a simple OK. It wasn't important that she had no real theory yet of what was going on with this family; the story would likely come together once she'd gathered answers to her questions. Right now, the important thing for her was the return of her instinct, the resuming of productivity.

Yes, this was selfish. Having a purpose reintroduced excitement to her day and made her feel necessary. But more than that, this newfound usefulness could go a long way to help her make amends to this family. She could go groveling to Mrs. Herron, tell her she was sorry for piling on during her lowest moments, and explain that she had found out about her own husband's affair and it had tainted the way she looked at the drowning case; that things had only gone downhill for her from there. But the excuses weren't enough; mere apologies weren't enough. She'd gotten a bad vibe when she'd seen Paul Herron in her rearview mirror, and a lost vibe from his granddaughter all the times she'd walked out of school alone. Now she felt motivated to do something more than offer words. What the something more was—well, she didn't know that yet.

The phone rang when she was absorbed in these thoughts, and it jarred her back into the moment. A glance at the phone screen: "Restricted." This would be the therapist, then, calling to reschedule or perhaps to offer a phone-in session in place of the canceled one. Well, no. She couldn't spare the time; she needed to get on with her plan.

She had meant what she told Joe. She intended a visit to the bakery to scope out the current status of the business. She looked at her watch. She had a little over an hour before she needed to collect the boys. Enough time to fix herself up and drop in on the way to school. Out of the law enforcement look Julia Herron knew her by—blazer and wool slacks and bun at the nape of her neck—she would blend in as another suburban mom.

Most people didn't have the memory for faces she did, and it was often true that the smallest change in a face, like a pair of glasses, or hair up or hair down or hair covered, would render a person unrecognizable to casual acquaintances, especially in a fleeting glance. Some people barely looked up to notice those they came in contact with. This was what Denise was counting on—that Mrs. Herron wouldn't take her eyes off her work. If things played out differently, she would bail.

Satisfied with her plan, she went upstairs to prepare.

Standing across the street from the bakery, Denise observed her surroundings. There were the lackluster windows again, and she noticed, too, as she entered the crosswalk, some peeling paint on the door frame. A man in white pants, a white undershirt, and a white apron stood outside the front door, smoking down a cigarette. Getting closer, she could see that his shirt and pants were wrinkled, and both articles were on the gray side of white. Even his white apron wasn't crisp and clean but sagging and dotted with translucent, greasy patches.

As Denise approached, the man tossed his cigarette butt onto the sidewalk and ground the embers out with his heel. He walked back into the bakery just as Denise came up behind him, but instead of holding the door for her or letting her pass ahead of him, he let the door swing closed in her face. She was beginning to understand the general air of disinterest about the building.

Inside, the overall appearance was not much different than outside, clean enough but worn. The layout was the same as she remembered from her last visit during the active investigation of the disappearance, but it all looked tired, in need of a fresh coat of paint and some updated display cases. There was no sign of Julia Herron. If the rude guy was a new owner, even a new employee, then the interior's decline made sense, for he seemed unaware of customers, never mind their concerns. If someone else was the owner, that person probably cared even less, judging by the caliber of person they had hired.

She was not the only customer inside; two people stood in line ahead of her. Waiting her turn, she took a minute to scan the back of the place—the kitchen and prep area. The rude man seemed to be back there alone, and he had, she noticed, washed his hands after the cigarette. Points for basic hygiene. He was now drying them, but he paused with the towel in his hands to look around.

"Hey!" he called. "Where are you? This was my break time, not yours. You'd better not be off the floor!"

His voice was loud enough that the woman behind the counter stopped tying up the box in front of her and looked over her shoulder. She frowned and shook her head slightly before returning to her task.

"Hey!" the man called again, and this time he left the kitchen through a back door on some kind of mission.

The employee rolled her eyes.

Denise caught the woman's eye and gave her a sympathetic smile. "Kinda rude," she said in a low voice.

"If Tony ever learned manners," the clerk said as she rang up the order, "he forgot them pretty fast."

The other two customers laughed, but it was an uncomfortable sort of laugh. Denise could tell they were anxious to leave. If she hadn't been there for a single purpose, she too might have walked out the door.

As it turned out, the other two customers were together, and they left once they paid.

"What can I get for you?" the clerk asked.

Denise had been too busy scoping out the place to look at the choices in front of her. The cases were full of cupcakes, and the boys would think she'd lost her mind when she came home with a box of those. But they would eat them. "How about a dozen chocolate cupcakes," she answered. "Half with chocolate frosting, half with white."

Boxing those would take some time, she hoped. As the woman assembled a large box, Denise started chatting.

"Is Tony the new owner, then? I haven't been by here in years."

"Tony? Don't think so. He only bakes, as far as I know. The owner I wouldn't know if I tripped over him. I'm only on a couple of mornings a week, and I haven't been here that long."

"Julia Herron doesn't work here anymore?"

"Julia . . . oh, Jules? You do go way back with this place. She's still here, she bakes with Tony. That's who he's gone looking for. She went out back to sign for a delivery." The woman shrugged. "But he didn't ask me where she was, he yelled instead. Why should I clue him in?"

Why indeed. He was a jerk.

But more important was that Denise finally had her confirmation: Julia Herron was indeed still baking here. Rather than being satisfying, however, the news worried her. She was now the sole customer in the shop, and she felt exposed; what if Julia suddenly returned to the kitchen? She would like to get a look at her, but that would have to wait for another day. The information she'd already gathered would have to be enough for now.

"Say," she said with a look at her watch, "I have to get my kids at school, and I'm running a little behind. Do you mind not tying up the box? I can take it as is."

"Sure." She tucked in the front flap and handed the box over the counter. "That'll be—"

A pair of loud voices arguing interrupted her.

"Ugh, they're at it again. I don't know how much longer I can take this. That'll be thirty dollars, please."

Jesus, thirty bucks for a dozen cupcakes that she could buy for maybe ten bucks at Stop and Shop? At least digging in her wallet gave Denise a reason to turn her face away from the register and the back of the kitchen. The argument continued; the voices grew closer.

"You don't take a break when I take a break!"

"Tony, it's hardly a break to be out back signing for a flour delivery. Besides, my baking is all out of the oven."

Denise looked up from her purse as she handed two twenties in cash to the counter person. As she did, she saw Julia sweep past an irate Tony to reach for a clean apron. Her back to Denise, she tied this on and stepped over to the sink, where she proceeded to run water into a sink full of dishes.

Denise remembered Julia as being a handsome woman and she was still, but she looked thinner than Denise remembered, her arms wirier, her dark hair sprinkled with gray. Denise would have liked to observe more interaction between the two bakers, but she also didn't want to push her luck. When the woman behind the counter handed over a ten-dollar bill in change, she took it and made a hasty exit, the white bakery box tucked under her arm.

At home, the boys stuffed their faces with the chocolate cupcakes. They had already eaten two apiece, washed down with cold milk. Now two sticky hands hovered over the open box and then reached in for another round. Watching from the next room and in the middle of listening to a voicemail message, Denise was powerless to stop the carnage.

"As much as I understand that emergencies come up unexpectedly, I appreciate twenty-four hours' notice for—"

Denise clicked the cancel button and then erased Dr. Chamberlain's message for good measure. Next week's therapy appointment was already on the books, and right now she had work to do. She put the handset on the dining room table and went back into the kitchen.

"Mom, these are *sick*," Teddy told her.

He looked sick, his lips brown, his hands smeared with brown, and the front of his sweatshirt covered in sticky, brown crumbs.

"So sick that you went in for number three?" She whisked the box from the center of the kitchen table and put it up on top of the fridge. Not that height would stop any motivated teenager.

"He means sick in a good way," Tommy explained. "So much frosting." To make his point, he ran his finger over the top of the cupcake he was holding and let the big brown blob fall into his waiting, open mouth. "Did you know Heather is a vegan?" he asked Denise as he licked his fingers.

"Why would I know that?"

Tommy shrugged. "She writes about all kinds of food but she doesn't eat meat, or even butter, and she doesn't let us eat sugar when we're there. Dad either. Dad lost, like, twenty pounds because Heather told him sugar is poison and more addictive than heroin, and she made him stop eating it."

"Basically, you're poisoning us with these cupcakes," Teddy chimed in.

"According to Heather," Denise said. "If she feels so strongly about it, maybe she'll take you in and feed you tofu all day long. Doesn't that sound good?"

Tommy grinned, his mouth full of cake. "We're not leaving you for tofu, Mom. We want all the cupcakes."

"Nice to know all I need to do is bribe you." Denise walked over to her younger son and kissed the top of his head. Then she kissed Teddy's head for parity. "Go wash up now, you two. Then homework."

Alone in the kitchen, Denise pulled down the box of cupcakes, took one for herself, and sampled. A little too sweet for her taste, but the sugar gave her a much-needed jolt. Heather didn't know what she was missing.

A few bites in, the phone rang. Without thinking, she walked into the next room and answered without checking caller ID.

"Hello?" she said—then winced, realizing it might be Dr. Chamberlain again.

"You have a minute?"

"Joe." She breathed a sigh of relief and perked up. "Did you find something?"

"Maybe, maybe not. An inconsistency, though, in something Mr. Herron said. The guy otherwise checks out as your model wealthy citizen, who also happens to be a model driver."

"What inconsistency?" Denise could hear the shuffling of paper.

"I went back and looked at the notes of the family interviews because who has perfect recall of conversations that happened two years ago? I did remember the dad said he'd had a phone message from his son asking to talk later that day. Do you?"

In those interviews, Denise's mind had wandered from Matt back to David Herron's wife and best friend, her mind obsessed with adultery. "Remind me."

"The Herrons were at home the night before the disappearance, and on the morning of the disappearance, and neither of them knew anything except that their son left a phone message early in the morning, and that it wasn't noticed until closer to ten. He said the message was brief, nothing more than, 'Call me back when you can.' Certainly not urgent enough to cause worry or warrant a call back right away. We saw the phone records for that morning—one incoming and nothing outgoing—but we didn't actually listen to the message. It had been erased. The duration of that particular call matched the amount of time for leaving a brief voicemail, so we had to take Herron's word about the content."

"Okay, yes, it's coming back to me," Denise said.

"But then David Herron's mother went on a rant, blaming her daughter-in-law for being the kind of wife that would drive David to kill himself, saying—I quote from my notes— 'She nagged at David to keep us from seeing our granddaughter, and then she nagged at him to quit his good job to give her this foolish bakery business. She probably badgered him until he couldn't take it anymore.'"

"Right. There was no love lost. Which, I might add, is why seeing Herron with Rennie the other day made me so curious."

"Exactly. No one else had anything bad to say about the daughter-in-law except these two. In my opinion, that's garden-variety family dysfunction. But here's the thing that's a little off. After his wife's tirade, Mr. Herron says, 'Be quiet, Miriam. Julia had nothing to do with this. Nothing.' That's also direct from my notes. Keep in mind that until that point, he was pretty cool to the daughter-in-law, too. Not like his wife, but cool. Then, all of a sudden, he's so certain."

"What are you thinking?"

"What if Paul Herron was so adamant because he knew about the financial problems before we did? What if David left a more detailed message and he listened to it earlier rather than later that morning, as he told us? Or worse, what if he had been discussing the problems with his son for some time and knew about the debt? That would explain why he could sound so certain *before* the money issues were revealed to us that his daughter-in-law wasn't involved."

Denise thought about what Joe was suggesting. "Was he certain about something, or was he simply cutting off his wife's rant? One odd statement isn't much to go on, Joe."

"As I said, Dee-Dee, maybe it's nothing. But maybe it's something. We only have Herron's word that he didn't hear the message in time to make a difference. And we have no idea what they might have discussed at any other time. In any case, I didn't pick up on his word choice then because I had no reason to. It was clear the parents were truly shocked. Even now, it doesn't really matter if the guy got a whole slew of phone calls prior to the phone message. There was no foul play."

"Is that your way of telling me to back off?"

"Not at all. I wouldn't help you if I thought you should back off. I understand why you're doing this, I do. I mean, it doesn't matter legally. If he knew his son was distraught and he, say, hung up on him—well, it makes him a shitty person, but we can't arrest someone for being a jerk. Not that we intend to arrest anyone anyway, but you know what I mean."

"Yes, I know." Denise paused a second to process Joe's information. What he'd found in reviewing his notes was incredibly thin. *"Julia has nothing to do with this. Nothing."* Sharp-tongued comments made in interviews were never unusual in moments of high emotion, and these parents had just learned their son was missing, presumed dead. Joe was right, too, in saying that the older man being a jerk sucked, but it wasn't a crime. What, then, was she doing, raking all this up again—and why?

She absentmindedly stuck her finger into the buttercream of the half-eaten cupcake and brought it to her mouth, letting the sugar dissolve on her tongue. "So much frosting," Tommy had said earlier. Denise imagined Julia Herron getting up every morning, making all these cupcakes, whipping up the icing, piping it out in decorative swirls, all for a place she no longer owned but was somehow still tied to. What were those ties? Why didn't she go work elsewhere; why did she stay in a place with all those bad memories? And why was an estranged grandfather suddenly no longer estranged? Why, why, why? There were too many of those whys and not enough answers, Denise realized as she sucked the traces of frosting off her finger. But she also understood that even if no one was held accountable for a man's suicide, Julia had a right to know what had driven him to it, especially if it had anything to do with the man who was driving her daughter to and from school.

Joe's whisper shifted her out of her thoughts. "Dennis, I gotta go. It's getting hot in here."

He was no longer free to talk. "I hear you, Nell." Denise wasn't bothered. There was work to do. "I'll call you after I check those bankruptcy filings. Thanks for all this today. It was really helpful. Talk later."

7

First order of business: pour wine.

Denise took the very full glass to her sofa and settled in. She had a book, she had the television remotes at hand, she even had a notebook and pen in the event she wished to make notes about her dive into the bankruptcy records filed at the courthouse. But all things except the wine remained untouched. Drinking and thinking, she told herself.

Most of her Fridays went this way, creating distraction in the empty house with noise from the television or words from a page in the absence of the noise made by her two boys. They were with Matt, and she would be alone until Sunday. Wine helped; sipping gave her something to concentrate on and left her sleepy enough to forget the boys weren't in their rooms as she went upstairs to her own. She missed them when they were with Matt. The change from being a nuclear family of four to being this modern, fractured version had taken lots of adjustment.

"Nothing will change." She and Matt had looked their boys in the eyes and sworn this up and down, but for all the pep talks, their lives *had* changed, and in significant ways.

She shifted on the sofa. She knew that Julia Herron's altered circumstances were affecting the way she thought of her own, here in this empty house on a lonely Friday night. The woman's business was gone, her house was gone, her husband was gone.

Not gone in the way Denise's was, gone from her bed but at least still around to help; no, gone for good, and at his own hands. He had turned out to be a stranger.

When Denise married Matt, she had looked into a future full of work, home, children, all with someone she loved and thought she knew, much like Julia Herron probably had at the beginning of her relationship with her husband. Not once had Denise seen the possibility of divorce. In her twenties and even early thirties, she'd never even looked ahead to imagine disease or death, the one thing that would get them all in the end. *Maybe this is how humans cope with their doubts and uncertainties*, she thought. *They ignore them and plow ahead, blinders on. After all, if we looked ahead and saw a future of bad things, of loss and pain and death, how could we make attempts at happiness? Why would we bother?*

Denise shook her head. *Jesus. This is morose, even for me.*

She knew why she felt so low, and it wasn't only because of the absence in the house. The morning spent researching had been fruitless, bordering on a waste of time. She swapped her wineglass for the notebook and pen and thought about what she had learned—or rather, hadn't learned. There was no record of a bankruptcy filing made in Julia Herron's name or under the bakery's name. Nothing. Denise tapped the pen on her bottom lip and wondered what the lack of a court filing meant.

The doorbell broke the silence and Denise's concentration. She set pen and notebook down on the sofa next to her. Who would be stopping by, she thought, at the supper hour on a Friday night? She had a moment of panic, thinking it might be her therapist tracking her down at home for not returning messages. *No way*, she told herself as she stood and tiptoed to the front door. If she didn't like what she saw out the peephole, she would stay quiet and pretend the house was empty.

But it was Joe she saw, carrying a pizza box.

"What are you doing here?" Denise asked as she opened the door to him.

"Bringing you pizza, obviously. I thought we could talk about the case. Can I come in?"

"Please." As he walked by, the scent of garlic made her feel dizzy. "Tell me that's from Pinocchio."

"Do I know what you like?" Joe asked. He lifted the lid and showed her a selection of slices from her favorite hole-in-the-wall joint.

"Oh my God, their spinach and garlic pie." Her stomach growled noisily.

Joe laughed. "Good, you're hungry. I had no plans after work, and I thought you might have some beer in the house."

"I haven't had beer since Matt moved out. I only have wine." She pointed to her glass and the open bottle on the kitchen peninsula.

"I like wine," Joe said.

"You do? Why didn't I know this? Have a seat. We can eat in the living room if you want." Denise moved toward the kitchen to fetch plates, napkins, and an extra wine glass.

"You think you know everything about me, but you don't," Joe said, following behind her instead of sitting on the sofa. He set the pizza box on the counter, and she poured him a generous glass of wine to match her own. He lifted it. "Cheers."

Denise reached over to clink his outstretched glass.

"My father used to make wine in our basement when I was a kid," Joe said. "Sweet stuff. Not very good. But that didn't stop my brother and me from sneaking tastes whenever we could get away with it." He chuckled. "My taste has evolved since then." He looked at Denise, who was staring at the pizza, and laughed again. "Go ahead, dig in!"

For the next few minutes, they stood at the breakfast bar,

eating and chatting about TV shows and sports teams, but mostly about Denise's sons. Like her, Joe was divorced, although he and his ex-wife had had no children. He seemed to like kids, though, and she thought he was dating someone pretty seriously, or had been. A man like Joe could remarry, could still have a kid—or several, if his girlfriend was young enough and game enough. After all, a man's biological functions didn't run down like a woman's. It occurred to her in that moment that the same was true for Matt. Certainly Heather was young enough; was she, Denise wondered, anxious to give Matt more babies? And what about her ex? Was he anxious to have a round two?

Denise shuddered at the thought and pushed away her plate. Suddenly feeling full, she crumpled her napkin and tossed it on top of the remnant of pizza she'd left unfinished.

"What's wrong?" Joe asked.

"Other than being a loser who is jealous of her ex-husband's shiny, happy life? Ah." She fluttered a hand. "I get like this on Fridays when I miss the boys. Pay no attention." She topped off their glasses and led the way into the living room, where she curled up in the corner of the sofa.

Joe sat next to her. "Let's take your mind off Matt the Brat. What did you find out today in bankruptcy court?"

"Ugh. Nothing but dead ends. There was no bankruptcy petition filed for Mrs. Herron, or for the bakery as a corporation or LLC—nada. I was just brainstorming what to do next, where to look next, but I didn't get very far because you rang the doorbell and diverted my attention with pizza and vino."

Joe raised an eyebrow. "*You're* pushing the vino. Seriously, though, in the absence of court docs, what's next?"

Denise rested her head on the back of the couch. Truth was, she had no idea what to do next. Her mind was muddled from the alcohol and she felt sleepy. Why was she even thinking about

Matt, about Heather, or about Julia Herron, for that matter? She honestly couldn't remember. Perhaps if she rested her eyes for a minute.

"Dee-Dee? You're falling asleep."

"Mmm, I know. Feels good."

"You're starting to snore."

"Meh, that's too bad."

"I find it oddly attractive."

Denise gave a snort of laughter. "Yeah, about as attractive as my garlic breath."

"You could let me find out about that."

Denise opened her eyes and looked at him. "Okay, if you were trying to wake me up, mission accomplished."

"I'm serious. I like the snoring, and I'd probably like your garlic breath, too. Tossing all these ideas around with you recently, I've realized how much I've missed hanging with you."

Denise scrambled to sit upright. "Jesus, Nell. What about your girlfriend?"

"There is no girlfriend. And you can stop calling me 'Nell' for now, when it's just the two of us. Here, we can be Joe and Dee-Dee."

Joe and Dee-Dee, as in Joe and Dee-Dee the people and not Canelli and Healey the cops. After years of working together, they knew each other well, spoke in shorthand, joked and laughed together, and looked out for each other. That was what friends did, that was what good colleagues did, at least in her world. But it was also how romantic partners behaved. Why had she never looked at Joe this way?

She looked him over now. He had leaned toward her, a longing look in his eyes, but was keeping his distance. She had never noticed before that his shrewd eyes could go as soft and liquid brown as a besotted puppy's.

"Joe," she began, "there's a solid chance both of us will wake up in the morning and realize this is the wine talking. So maybe—"

A ringing phone cut her off.

"I should get that," she said, and she rose—carefully to make sure she had her equilibrium—and went to the kitchen, where she'd left her phone.

It was Matt.

"What's up?" she said into the phone.

Matt didn't waste time with small talk. "Why the hell don't you even know what your boys are up to?"

"What exactly *are* they up to, Matt? Porn, the occult, human sacrifice?"

In the background, Denise could hear Heather talking to Matt in soothing tones. "I am calm," he said in reply. Returning to Denise, his volume dropped but his tone remained upset. "I found a notebook in Tommy's backpack. And don't say a word, Dee, about snooping. Because if you had done this sooner, we wouldn't be this far down the road. Are you still there?" he asked when she offered no reply.

"I am. I'm waiting for you to tell me what's going on."

"Fine. So I find this notebook. The little shit's been lending money to kids in school. The notebook is a record of their names and how much they owe him. Here's the kicker, Dee. He makes them pay him back, with interest. Our kid is essentially a loan shark."

Denise's mouth dropped open.

"I swear to God, I should turn him into the school. He needs to be confronted with a can of whoop-ass—"

"Matt—"

"And some serious discipline. What the hell are you doing over there during the week?"

"Matt—"

"Are you back to lying in bed all day, Dee? Because I swear, if you're not locked onto these boys, I'm taking you back to court."

"No one's taking anyone to court, and I want you to shut up right now." Denise's back was to the living room, and she didn't notice that Joe had crossed the room to stand next to her until she felt his breath on her neck.

"What's going on?" he whispered.

Denise held up a finger. "And another thing," she said, returning to the phone call. "You're not turning anybody in to the authorities at school. The last thing you want is a sixteen-year-old hanging around your house all day, studying for the GED because he's been expelled from school. We're going to stay calm, here, Matt. You confiscated the book, yes?"

"Yes," he hissed.

"Good." Denise pressed her free hand into her temple, where a cluster headache was developing. "Try and return to normal for now, and we'll sit down with him on Sunday when I pick him up. We'll nip this in the bud, okay?"

"Okay, but I'm seriously pissed at you, Dee."

"*At me? Not Tommy?*" she wanted to ask. She could feel her blood pressure rising, but she wouldn't give her ex the satisfaction of seeing her lose her temper. Instead, she bit her tongue.

"Whatever, Matt. I'm hanging up, and we'll talk on Sunday." As she went to disconnect, however, a thought occurred to her and she paused. "But wait, there's something I don't understand about this," she said. "The kid doesn't have a job, I certainly don't give him an allowance. So where'd he get all this money to lend to his classmates?"

"How should I know where he got the money? Maybe he's into something even worse than—wait, hold on a sec." Denise could hear Heather speak in low, supplicating tones again, and then Matt as he said, "Oh for Christ's sake, babe," right before he came back on the call with her. "I know where he got the money. We'll talk on Sunday." He hung up.

Denise sighed and powered down her phone.

"That sounded intense," Joe said. "Kid trouble?"

"A bit," she told him, and she rubbed at her temple again—although, miraculously, the cluster pain had subsided as soon as Matt's voice had stopped shrieking in her ear. The wine haze was gone, too. *I'm sober*, she realized. *As sober as a church lady.*

"I should go," Joe said, but he made no move to go. By now they were both leaning against the counter, and his eyes were scanning her face. Puppy dog eyes again.

Ah, what the hell, Denise thought. *After the day I've had.*

Matt and the kids would be addressed on Sunday. The case, if there was anything there, could wait; she couldn't do much more digging until Monday anyway.

She reached out and put her hand on Joe's arm. "No. Stay."

"So that happened."

"I'm maintaining deniability, Nell."

"Not letting you off the hook, Dee-Dee. And I told you, it's not Nell. We're not hiding behind aliases anymore. Not after sex." He pulled her close and kissed the back of her neck.

Denise burrowed in closer. "Okay, Joe. Joseph. Better?"

"Better. But guess what? My real name is Giuseppe."

Denise turned her head, although she was spooned in so close to Joe that all she could see was his ear and its sideburn. "No way."

"And my brother Mike is Michelangelo."

"Now you are pulling my leg."

Joe ran his fingertips up and down along the curve of Denise's side and said, "I think I am most definitely *not* pulling your leg."

When she gave a contented sigh after a few seconds, he laughed a little.

"What's so funny?"

"Nothing's funny. I'm happy. Happy to make you happy. Happy to be here. I've wanted to be here for a good long while, Denise Healey."

Denise alerted a bit at that information. Was he expecting an equally earnest, soul-baring admission?

Honestly, she was glad for Joe's presence in her bed tonight. He was a fun, engaged, and, yes, sexy man. And Lord knew she had missed sex; it had been a while, a long while. And boy, he'd rung her bells tonight, oh yes he had. But the truth was, she hadn't fantasized about Joe. Ever. She had been married for most of their friendship, and her married fantasies had been confined to imagining what life would be like if Matt announced suddenly that he wanted to split the household chores right down the middle. No, she had never carried a torch for Joe. Nor had she thought of him as a potential provider of hot sex until he'd looked at her tonight with longing in those eyes.

Was she now supposed to fib to make him feel good? Did he expect that? Her younger self would have tried to make him happy, would have given him the answer he wanted to hear. "Oh, Joe, I've desired you for so long, you great big he-man." That had been her MO with Matt from the beginning, fawning over him, making sure *he* felt good, and then that pattern had lasted throughout their marriage until she'd realized she was giving, giving, giving and not getting much praise or acknowledgment, and definitely no equal consideration for her feelings or desires, in return. Some men constantly needed to hear how awesome they were, in bed and out; some women had been raised to fill that purpose. And when she had finally decided no more, Matt had labeled her grim and cynical. Everything was her fault, none of it was his. Then, as was typical of Matt, he had moved on to find someone who would pick up the fawning where she had left off.

As she rested in Joe's arms, Denise tried to tell if he was holding his breath, waiting for a response, but he seemed to be relaxed, content, his hand stroking her skin on and on as if he had all the time in the world, as if he had no purpose except to make her feel good in the moment. Maybe he wasn't expecting much more than that. Maybe she should try and do the same: relax.

"Joe."

"What's that, Denise?"

"I have to be honest." She pulled out of their spooning and turned onto her right side, facing him. "You are a superior kisser. And I'm glad to see you in a different light now, I am. I'm glad you're here."

"But?"

"But I never thought of you this way until you made eyes at me in the kitchen."

Joe looked at her another few seconds, then took her face in his hands and kissed her. "You're the best, Dee-Dee. I'm a lucky man. Now"—he kissed her again—"I'm starving. Are you hungry?"

Denise smiled. She had planned to make do with some toast for breakfast while she made lists about how she might proceed with learning more about Rennie Herron's current circumstances. "I could eat, but I need to do some work, too."

"Are you kicking me out?" Joe asked.

Denise thought about this. Did she want him to leave? "You could stay, and we could keep working together," she suggested.

"Let me cook breakfast, then. We can toss around ideas while I'm working in the kitchen."

"I suppose I have some food lying around," she said, and before she knew it Joe was sitting up and reaching for his jeans.

"Do you mind if I . . .?" He pointed to the door of her master bath.

"No, you go ahead. I have to find some clothes anyway."

As soon as Joe disappeared behind the bathroom door, Denise got out of bed and went to the closet for her robe, collecting clean clothes along the way. At the bedroom window she stopped and pulled open the curtains. It was getting lighter outside; the streetlights were off. In the early morning sky, she could make out a line of small black birds circling her neighbor's roof, swooping around and into and out of their chimney. Swallows, she thought they were, grazing on insects. And they were hungry. She watched for a while as she waited for the bathroom to be free, and their purposeful flight was so mesmerizing that Denise didn't hear Joe come up behind her until he was close enough to reach under her breasts and pull her close, to whisper in her ear, "Whatcha looking at?"

"The swarm of birds."

Joe lowered his head to be level with hers and rested his chin on her shoulder.

"Hey," she said. "I just thought of something."

"Yes?"

"If there's no record of bankruptcy—"

Joe laughed softly, leaned down, and kissed her neck. "I'm sorry but I thought you were about to tell me you're out of eggs. Okay, I'll bite. You just thought of something, and . . ."

"*And* . . . so what if there's no bankruptcy filing? We haven't necessarily hit a dead end. Assume the bakery was sold. Maybe the answer's there. Maybe I should find out who bought it."

"Well . . ." Joe cocked his head. "With ideas like that to follow up on, you're really going to need some breakfast."

The two boys entered the house like a pair of gangly labs coming in from a walk, jostling for space as they shook off their jackets, bags, and shoes.

"Hang it all up, you two," Denise said. "Kitchen table in thirty seconds. We haven't finished talking."

"Why do I have to listen to another lecture?" Teddy protested. "I didn't do anything."

"Okay, fine, you go get a jump on homework. And before you tell me homework's not important this close to graduation, I still want you studying something. Tommy"—Denise tapped the face of her watch and pointed in the direction of the kitchen—"you now have twenty-five seconds to meet me there."

She left the boys behind and made her way into the kitchen. She couldn't hear any more bickering behind her, just the sounds of cleaning up. Tommy knew better than to grumble after she had neatly pulled them all out of a grueling two hours of Matt lecturing him. Luckily, Matt had reined in at least some of his anger over the weekend and hadn't yelled as much as she had expected, but his heavy-handed expressions of disappointment had gone on and on. Denise had seen her son's eyebrows twitching as he held back from rolling his eyes, but he'd managed to restrain himself. She'd felt for him; she'd almost rolled her own eyes when Heather had piped in that she felt betrayed by his poor decision to use the money she had given him for a dangerous scheme instead of putting it into a standard savings account.

After enduring as much as she could, Denise had slapped her knees. "Well, I think that was really, really productive, and Tom's learned an important lesson. Just look at him."

All the adults had turned and seen a boy with his head hung in contrition. Denise knew him better. Maybe Matt did, too; he'd started to open his mouth again. But Denise had stood and held her hand out to Heather. "Thanks for opening your home to us," she'd said, and since neither Matt nor Heather knew what to make of Denise being pleasant, they'd both shaken her hand and hadn't said another word.

"Thanks, Mom," Tommy had said on his way to the car.

"Don't thank me yet. We still have some talking to do, me and you."

Now, Denise braced herself and detoured over to the bottle of wine she and Joe hadn't finished two nights before. She needed a drink, and she was grateful there was a good glassful left. *God made alcohol for a reason*, she thought, smiling to herself, as she poured.

As she took her first sip, Tommy clomped into the room and took his seat at the table. She looked at him looking down at his hands. Part of her felt that her son had learned his lesson after suffering through his father's long monologue. It was late, too, and they were hungry; sometimes it was best to parent after a good night's sleep. But no—she needed to insert her own parental wisdom.

She left the wineglass on the counter and went to sit next to her son. "Tommy."

Her tender tone seemed to surprise him, and he looked up. "Aren't you going to yell at me?"

Denise smiled. "Tom, do you remember my work? I mean, it feels like a lifetime ago to me, but it hasn't been that long since I was a cop."

He nodded.

Encouraged, she continued, "Part of that work was about making sure justice was served when people did something wrong. But another really big part of it was making sure people didn't screw up in the first place. My boss always said that was the best kind of policing, and I agreed. But that means being ten steps ahead of what's going on, and I think in that department, with you, your dad and I dropped the ball. Maybe you think the lecture went on too long . . ."

She paused to look at him. He smiled and nodded.

"And I would agree with you. But your dad wants to be sure, *I* want to be sure, that you get it. That you know what you did was wrong and you're going to stop."

"I will stop, Mom, I have, I swear, but I want to say some—"

Denise held up a hand. "Hear me out first. I want you to go to every single kid you gave money to and tell them they don't owe you a thing in return—not the money you lent, not the interest you charged."

"I already thought of that, Mom, and I will. But you and Dad have talked and talked, and you act like I'm one step away from joining the mob or something, and you haven't even once asked me why I did it! Why can't I try and explain first?"

Tommy was breathing hard and his voice held such an edge of anxiety that Denise pulled back and really looked at him. His cheeks had flushed bright red. The curse of his fair complexion: agitation made him blotchy.

"Of course you can speak."

"I had all this money from Heather. It was ridiculous, the amount of money she gave me for helping her move her sofa and stuff around dad's apartment. At school, someone asked me if I could give him lunch money, and he said he could pay me back with interest. He told some of his friends, and word started to get around. I didn't really see that I was doing anything different than a bank does. Or, like, a credit card. It wasn't as if I planned to knee-cap someone who couldn't pay me back. Most of the kids couldn't pay me any time soon anyway, the ones who have no money. Their parents aren't around, or if they are around, they aren't involved."

"Meaning?"

"Some are in jail or just gone. A couple are dead. I'm not trying to say I was being, like, a saint, but I really never meant to hurt anybody either."

Tom's face remained flushed, but he was breathing more evenly now. Denise thought of all the latchkey kids. The kids who roamed around town without supervision. The kids (like her own) of divorce, not intentionally neglected but falling under the radar as they traveled between homes. And he was right: a few of his classmates had a parent in jail. She ought to know; she'd had a hand in putting some of them there. And yes, some parents were dead, another thing she knew all too well.

As Denise sat quietly with Tommy, a memory popped into her mind. Of a school drop-off right after April vacation. Of seeing Rennie get out of her grandfather's car, of listening to Teddy tease his brother about his "girlfriend."

"Tommy, can I ask you something?"

"If you're not going to start lecturing me again."

Denise shook her head. "Just a question. Back in April we saw a girl get out of a car behind us in the school line. Remember? Teddy teased you because he'd seen you two talking?"

Tommy looked down at his hands again, which were folded now and resting on the kitchen table. "I remember."

"Okay. Did you lend money to that girl? Is that why you had been talking to her?"

After a beat, he said, "Yes."

Denise exhaled. It was like it used to be at work, her holding her breath while she waited for a witness to drop an important piece of information. She would hardly be aware of holding her breath until she released it and felt the relief of being right.

"One more question?" If Matt overheard this conversation, he would surely accuse her of getting off topic. Too bad. She needed to know. "Do you happen to know why she needed the money? Did she tell you?"

Tommy shook his head. "They don't always, and I don't ask."

"Okay."

"Okay, as in, that's it? I can go now?"

"You can go now. Up to do your homework like your brother. I'll call you when supper's ready."

He pushed his chair back, but he didn't rise immediately. "Do you know her, Mom? The girl you're asking about?"

"I do. I met her the day her father went missing. I worked that case."

"Oh."

Denise watched his face and saw he was turning something over in his mind. Boy, this kid was readable. He'd make a terrible cop. "What?" she asked.

"You're not going to get her in trouble, are you? For borrowing money? She's not a bad kid. She's not even strange, like Teddy thinks. She's—never mind. You'll think *I'm* strange." He stood and turned to go upstairs.

"No, I won't think you're strange. Finish your thought," Denise said to his back. "She's . . . what?"

Tommy stopped in the doorway and turned around. "Sad, Mom. She's just sad."

Denise nodded at her youngest. She was grateful to him for the information, but now she needed some time alone. And there was her wine, too, waiting for her across the room. "Okay, Tommy, thanks. Now off you go."

He didn't hesitate, and within seconds, Denise was alone. She got up and grabbed her glass, and then stood at the counter, taking large sips. Joe would be horrified. Still, she wanted to dull some of the effects of what she'd learned. It didn't please her that the sadness she'd felt radiating off Rennie was real, even if it confirmed her instincts. She may not have caused the sadness by storming into the Herron home two years ago with no regard for anyone's feelings, but she had compounded it.

One more time, she raised the wineglass to her lips—but just before she sipped, she remembered the vow she'd made to help Rennie and practically slapped her glass back down on the counter. This was no time to wallow in self-pity or dull her senses. Denise looked up at the clock. Her boys needed dinner; further investigation would have to wait until later. She would get to it, though, and get to it feeling sharp and focused. Denise smiled and brought the wine glass to the sink.

The last dinner dish dried and put away, Denise pulled the stapled copy of David Herron's case notes from the kitchen junk drawer where she kept her bills and other urgent mail. Technically, she shouldn't have these, but she had taken her notes when she left the job. The work was hers.

Joe's hunch about Paul Herron was based on thin evidence, but Denise was choosing to trust his instinct that the man knew more about his son's financial problems than he'd let on. That hypothesis gave her a starting point. What she needed now was stronger evidence, and she would find it, even if that meant she had to stay up all night reading and rereading these notes.

She started flipping through the stack in front of her, reacquainting herself with the sequence-of-events timeline she had created to map out the morning of April 20th, from its 2:00 a.m. start as Julia Herron woke for work, to the 911 call made by Charlie Gale. In between was the window of David Herron's disappearance: sometime after 8:00 a.m., after the man made a call to his friend and after he was spotted by a dog walker, and before 9:16 a.m., when Gale called the cops after showing up to find an empty car and the man's clothing. The timeline was cut and dried.

However, reading between the lines to spot something they had missed before wouldn't be so easy. Her gut had failed her the first time around with this case; or rather, she had mistaken a mind clouded by suspicion and indignation for one full of sharp insight, rendering every conclusion she came to that April suspect. She couldn't make the same error now.

Denise picked up the pen and tapped her lower lip. To get it right this time around, she would have to carry out the next task with as much care as she had given the timeline. Noting details, double-checking them, keeping a record, drawing unbiased conclusions based only on the evidence—all the steps she used to take to build a case.

She turned the notebook on her lap sideways and got to work, drawing five vertical lines, separating the blank page into six columns. Each column she labeled with the name of a primary witness; after hesitating briefly, she decided to count Paul and Miriam Herron as enough of a single entity to share a column. That done, she struck a horizontal line through the columns halfway down the page. In the top half of each, she jotted relevant information from each person's statements using the old case notes and interviews. In the bottom section, she wrote her impressions and noted any oddities that jumped out at her. Maybe with this detailed spreadsheet laid out, something would speak to her. Maybe there was nothing. It was a chance she would take.

After an hour of poring over statements, she had reread everything except the statement made by the bank's lending specialist two days after Herron's disappearance. She turned to it.

The young man's name was Daniel Fulke Hopper. She

remembered this because it was an unusual name that she had assumed was hyphenated; she had written it that way on the statement sheet. Hopper had corrected it when he signed, and the name had stuck with her.

In the interview, Hopper, flanked by the bank's president and legal counsel, had confirmed David Herron's financial troubles, explaining both the original terms and subsequent cancelation of the loan to Denise. The information he shared—that Herron's entire portfolio had been placed in "imminent rescind of loan and order of re-payment" status—had changed the focus of the investigation to likely suicide. The debt had been hefty. David hadn't paid off the first loan before taking out a second, and he'd also taken out a second mortgage on the house. Denise remembered whistling when she heard the figure and thinking for the first time of Julia, who had been kept in the dark about the debt. "So many secrets. Mr. Herron must have felt the walls closing in," she had concluded.

Hopper had gone on the defensive at this assessment. "The amount owed was certainly enough to cause Mr. Herron some worry, but other worried clients don't kill themselves. I don't see why we should feel at fault." He'd squirmed, though, as he said this, his body language belying his words.

The bank's president, perhaps noticing the younger man's discomfort, had presented a less conflicted message: "It may seem harsh to call in a loan, but the action is intended to keep a borrower from getting in much too deep. The policy protects all our customers, as well as the health of the bank."

Denise had raised an eyebrow at that but said nothing more.

Hopper had also given them information about the meeting scheduled that day with David: "They were supposed to come in at nine, but no one showed up," she had written.

Of course not, Denise thought to herself in the quiet of her kitchen. David Herron was likely drowning himself at nine o'clock. Those frigging bankers.

But something nagged at her. What? She stopped making notes for a minute and leaned back in her chair, fiddling her pen between her fingers about as expertly as she'd twirled a friend's baton in her youth. The pen slipped from her hand and flipped once or twice before falling down at her feet. As she was feeling around for it on the floor under her chair, the home phone rang.

She gave up on the pen and got up to answer, making a silent wish that it wasn't Matt with another bee or three in his bonnet over Tommy's screw-up.

"Dee-Dee."

"Joe. I'm so glad it's you. I thought it might be Matt."

"How'd it go at his place? Everyone calmed down?"

Denise turned and leaned against the wall. "It was no better and no worse than I expected. Tommy was glad to get out of there. Me, too, for that matter. I had to hold my tongue when Heather, Tommy's personal ATM, started going on about how she felt betrayed. That was a bit much."

"I'll bet," Joe said with a wry laugh. "Your boy okay? He's not destined for a life of crime, is he?"

"Ha! Doubtful. We'll all be watching him now. He claims he was helping kids whose parents are in jail—"

"Oh brother."

"Yes. In jail or dead, and there's my Tommy, doling out lunch money like he was a one-man benevolent aid society. But Joe . . . one of the kids he loaned money to was Rennie Herron."

"Huh." Joe went silent for a few seconds. "Another point of intersection."

"I know. There she is again, right in the middle. Anyway." She sighed. "I thought I'd have another look at the Herron case notes, but I'm not seeing anything there. Maybe because there is nothing to see. Am I grabbing at all these flimsy 'maybes' and 'what-ifs' for any reason other than I'm desperate to make myself feel better? If that's the case, then—"

"Hey, hey, none of that. You're reviewing this case for the facts, remember? Because you want to fill in the blanks of that day. Because there's a young girl who lost her father. Because, because, because. A million good reasons, Dee. And yeah, maybe getting at the truth will make you feel better. But why shouldn't you?"

"I don't know, Joe, I think I'm fried tonight."

"Then put away the work and get some sleep. I'll come over if you want. I can stay. Although maybe you wouldn't get any rest."

Despite her mood, Denise smiled. "That's a nice offer. If it weren't for the boys, I'd take you up on it."

"After all those lectures, Dee, they might not show their faces for the rest of the night. We might get lucky."

Denise prepared to turn him down again, but she stopped. Something he had just said was making the back of her neck tingle. "Wait. Can you repeat that?"

"What, about getting lucky? Only say the word."

"No, no. Sorry. What you said first. About the boys."

"They might not show their faces?"

"Yes! You said 'they.' I know what was bothering me. Hold on."

Denise rested the phone on the counter, ignoring Joe's "Wait, what?" and went to the kitchen table for the photocopied notes. Back at the counter, she ran her fingers through the text on each page until she saw what she was looking for in Daniel Hopper's statement. "They were supposed to come in at nine, but no one showed up."

They. Not he.

She hadn't pick up on this during the interview. She had zoned out by that point. But even if she hadn't, would she have noticed it? Sometimes people used the plural when they meant an individual. But maybe there had been more than one person planning to attend that meeting about the defaulted loan. She knew of at least one person who could clear up that mystery.

But before she reached out to Daniel Hopper, maybe this was a good time for a gut check.

She picked up the phone receiver and heard Joe whistling, killing time.

"Hey," she said. "Listen to this."

8

"Here's the thing," Denise began.

All day yesterday, she had practiced the pitch she was about to make to Dr. Chamberlain, and now that they'd gotten through the obligatory check-in, she dove right in. She wanted the issue out of the way before she discussed anything else on her mind or answered questions about her futile attempts at guided meditation.

"I want to take a break from our sessions for the next few weeks," she rushed on. "Summer vacation is right around the corner, and it will be Ted's last summer at home before college. Besides, Matt will have the boys for a couple of weeks straight at the beginning of July, and I'd like to be home with them as much as possible before and after. We might even have some time for spontaneous day trips. Or whatever."

She held up a finger. "Wait." As soon as the excuse left her mouth, she'd realized this wasn't quite what she wanted to say or do. Yes, the boys would be showered with attention this summer. That part of her request was true. And Joe, too, would have some of her time and energy. Maybe her feelings for him would turn out to be nothing more than gratitude for being the one person who still believed in her skills, or maybe she was simply sex-starved. But she wanted to see where, if anywhere, that relationship was going. Still, an hour out of a week wasn't going to derail any of these summer plans.

The truth was, she no longer wanted to answer questions about why she wanted to help Rennie Herron or how she was doing. If she had learned anything here in these sessions, it was the importance of examining herself and her feelings, and right now, her feeling was that she and therapy were done. The next phase of healing had to be much more active and productive than taking this seat on the sofa.

What she really needed was to find and speak to Daniel Hopper, but the effort was turning out to be harder than she had expected it would be. A few phone calls had informed her that Hopper had left his bank shortly after their interview. He'd split with his girlfriend around that time, too, and neither she nor his coworkers could say where he'd gone.

Denise bet Dr. Chamberlain knew better than to expect a say in this breakup. If Denise declared herself done, they would be done; there would be no need for her to channel the hardened demeanor Matt had affected when he announced their marriage was over. For a few moments she pictured herself standing in the doorway to the therapist's office, as Matt had stood in the doorway to their kitchen, hands shoved in pockets, stone-faced, shut down, declaring he was done. With luck, the therapist would refrain from throwing the object closest to hand, which for Denise had been a banana intended for a school lunch bag. She had hit Matt squarely in the chest with the fruit. Maybe if she *were* tempted to throw something, the therapist would reach for the tissue box; it was softer than her ubiquitous clipboard, that was for sure.

Denise smiled.

"You look happy, Denise. Can we pause in this moment and talk about what you are feeling?"

"Can you tell me how you are feeling, Denise?" It was a question for the beginning, the middle, and also the end. The question no longer annoyed her, and she smiled once more.

"Yes. Yes, it's time."

July–September 2010

9

"Dan, Dan, our wandering man!" a tattooed and pierced twentysomething belted out. "Running all over the world, our Dan."

The line cooks and dishwashers laughed, and the rhyming joker, the young woman who plated cold appetizers and salads, laughed hardest of all. For the first couple of weeks, Dan hadn't bothered learning her name—or anyone else's, for that matter—but he knew them all now. This girl had been especially persistent, always reminding him, "I have a name, you know, and it's not 'Excuse Me.'"

Mya. Her name was Mya.

In those months before arriving at the restaurant in Chicago, Dan had shown up for his work shifts and done his job without calling attention to himself. But the staff he had joined in the city was close-knit and chatty, and they'd started giving him, the new guy, a good-natured ribbing once it had spread around the kitchen how many times he'd moved in the last two years.

To Dan, underemployed and over-isolated for the past several months, the attention had made him feel like he was lit up in flashing neon. But he hadn't actually minded being singled out. A few months earlier, he wouldn't have made eye contact with a coworker, never mind joke with several of them, but he had felt vulnerable in the city, lonely for human contact after all the months of rejecting it. He'd gotten the Chicago gig a year and ten months after leaving his career and friends behind in Boston. While he had managed okay at being alone in all that time, he really wasn't suited for solitude, not like some of the introverts and rebels he had worked with during his travels. It took effort, keeping himself apart.

He had thought he would find anonymity in a large city. Instead, he was constantly refusing invitations for late-night beers after his shifts. This group had expectations. And now the rhyming couplet bestowed by Mya had made him one of the crew.

Dan stopped reviewing his checklist for the evening's private party. He looked around the room at the people smiling at the joke and at him, and he wondered what life would look like in a smaller place, working in a smaller job, a place where he wouldn't be tempted to have something more than work in his life.

"Excuse me," he said as he left the kitchen, the laughter growing fainter behind him.

The next day, he was on another bus, leaving another town.

Every time he'd taken off before, relief had washed over him as he hit the highway. Not so this time, as the bus pulled out of downtown; not so as the bus followed the twists and turns of southbound Lake Shore Drive and he watched the Loop skyline recede. This abrupt departure felt much more complicated. He had admired the kitchen staff, how they laughed and joked and got through some of the most grueling days with good humor. They were good people, and he regretted leaving them short staffed, especially without explanation.

As the bus closed in on the Indiana Dunes, Dan stared out at the bleak industrial landscape of Gary and hoped he had made the right decision to give in to the pull of his native New England. The tickets that would get him to Bar Harbor, Maine, were in the inner breast pocket of his jacket, and during the ride he let his fingers brush the glossy paper of the ticket envelope many times to make sure he hadn't lost track of it. The tourist destination he had chosen made sense as a place to land: familiar enough to banish the homesickness that made him vulnerable to offers of friendship, yet remote enough to offer solitude.

People talk about burning bridges. When Dan left Boston at the end of May 2008, he had decimated his entire life. Without a backward glance, he'd boarded a bus to go across the country with nothing more than a few belongings and enough money to tide him over until he found work. On the way, he'd spent time cooling his heels in a few characterless and interchangeable bus depots and slept on his share of unclean and uncomfortable benches, until finally the coach pulled into Phoenix. He had planned to go all the way to California, but what he'd seen of the monotonous emptiness of the desert as they approached the city had exuded calm.

Maybe if he had learned to tolerate the intense heat, he might have adjusted to life in the desert, but he hadn't. He'd left well before another summer rolled around.

After Phoenix came Albuquerque, a choice made without a second thought after being introduced to a cousin of a coworker, a guy on his way to New Mexico to work in a casino. Dan asked for a ride in exchange for gas money. Behind the wheel of his old Honda, the cousin revealed himself as a taciturn guy who suited Dan's disinterest in small talk just fine. They'd taken Route 66 most of the way, country music radio filling the car, talking only when one or the other needed to request a bathroom or food break or announce that it was time to gas up the tank.

Once in the city, after a few days and a few phone calls, Dan got hired at a restaurant popular year-round with skiers and golfers and those driving from the airport for Santa Fe or beyond. He started to pick up some side work, too. As a young boy he had worked alongside his father at home, learning from the older man how to fix appliances and do basic wiring and plumbing, so when the refrigerator at the restaurant went on the fritz, he fixed it. Pleased with the results, Dan's general manager spread the word, and soon Dan had as much extra work as he wanted.

Even though all the work had gotten him through a fall, a winter, and a spring full of vacationers, Albuquerque hadn't quite been perfect. Though there was steady work, the neighboring casinos that suckered folks into losing their money had reminded Dan too much of the bank he had worked at—their lending practices, the people who'd gotten burned, those who hadn't managed to recover, and his role in their tragedies—all the reasons he'd left Boston in the first place. So, in June, he'd packed his single duffel and moved north to Taos, taking the bus once again.

The air had been cooler up so high in the Sangre de Cristo mountains, and the evergreen trees packing the national park lands had given him some green, a relief after all the earth-toned, scrubby scenery he'd been surrounded by for the last year. The mountains had felt familiar as well, larger and taller versions of landscapes in Western Massachusetts, New Hampshire, Vermont. For the first time since setting out on the road, Dan had fought sporadic but compelling urges to return home. And although he'd reminded himself that his home and his life in it no longer existed, the longing had not subsided.

He'd done his best and stayed in Taos until March, but the urges had demanded a distraction, so he'd hopped on a bus to Chicago, which would now also be in his past.

As the bus blew through one state after another—through highways, toll plazas, and an occasional stop—Dan gave in to sleep, a relief. He was deeply tired, and he slept hard until the bus slowed. Stirring, he turned to look out the window.

He was home. They had crossed the New York state line and were approaching the Massachusetts Turnpike's ticket booths, decrepit structures where live humans still handed out paper tickets. Dan hadn't driven in months. As he looked out the window now, he recalled all the traffic tie-ups he and Stacy had waited in, how anxious and often angry he used to feel when the roads leaving Tanglewood became parking lots and he couldn't make good time getting back home. How that used to matter.

How that life used to matter, he thought as he took in all the familiar sights. There were the old-growth trees climbing uphill, the rotary and exit signs for Lenox and Lee and Stockbridge; there, too, was the outlet mall, tucked into the hills well off the exit ramp, the one that he used to fake-grumble about visiting when he and Stacy came out here for long weekends. His fiancée had loved to shop and shop and shop. Another pair of heels, of trainers for the gym. Another work suit, bathing suit, another winter coat; and what about this dress for the office Christmas party, or this one? That one, he would answer, pointing; or how about both? He shopped, too, for more and more stuff to bring back to their home in the city. Yes to a few more ties, to another couple of suits, and yes to the Bose speakers because the pair they currently used was not wireless.

Seeing it all after so long away, he felt detached, as if it had been another person living that life. His leaving had pissed Stacy off. He had tried to explain to her that he had to go so he wouldn't damage more lives, as he had at the bank. All she could say was, "You're a selfish bastard."

Well, yes, he had thought as he stood outside their condo and waited for the taxi that would take him to a friend's house. *Me being selfish is the whole point.*

He turned away from the window, settled back into his seat, and closed his eyes again.

The bus driver pulled off the road before reaching Bar Harbor and announced that they'd take thirty minutes at ML's Stopover Café in Ellsboro, about an hour away from their destination, for a bathroom break and a quick snack or meal.

Dan stretched his legs and followed several of his fellow passengers to the café to pass the thirty minutes. A handwritten sign taped to the glass of the front door caught his attention: "Help Wanted, Cook. Must Be Handy." Not for the first time, Dan was grateful that his mechanic father had made him help with so many projects. He'd said the skills he was teaching Dan would stand him in good stead, and they had. In the final days of Dan's bank job, the quiet in his office had given his mind too much time to ponder his role in his clients' problems. But as long as his hands were in almost constant motion, his mind stayed quiet.

It was also the old man who had insisted on college, who had urged his son to move up and out of their working-class background. But the two had clashed in his father's final years—ironically, over the very parts of Dan's life his father had encouraged him to aspire to.

"Tempting others to gamble with their life savings," he'd said, condemning Dan's work. "You're a glorified con man."

"You wanted me here," Dan had hurled back. "You pushed me into college, into getting this degree. According to you, this job was my opportunity to have a better life than you."

He'd expected his father to back down then, shake his head, walk away. Instead, he'd looked Dan in the eye and said, "You're right, I did. So tell me, have you made a better life than mine? Have you?"

For a while, Dan's answer had been yes. Yes, as he did his work, reviewing requests and securing loans large and really large for businesses deemed solvent enough and ready to stretch. Yes, as interest rates climbed and riskier financing options were floated. Yes, life was better, even in the wake of the bursting bubble, even as he got tough with his borrowers and changed terms, called in notes, rescinded and revised deals. Yes, because all of this kept his employer, and himself personally, afloat. Better than afloat: profitable.

His answer would be very different now. He was relieved to be out of that world. Only it was no longer possible to tell his father so.

From the doorway of ML's, he looked around him at the street, at the nearly full parking lot, and at the several cars heading out to the national park. Ellsboro seemed a steady place, a place where he could do good work, maybe live the better life that his father challenged him to live. At the very least it beat another hour on the smelly, cramped bus, he decided, and he walked inside.

While he waited for the line at the restroom door to shorten, he took a seat at the counter and ordered coffee and then, when the beverage's bitter aroma hit his nose and his stomach growled, a grilled cheese to go with it. He couldn't remember what he had last eaten, or when.

He salivated as he peered into the kitchen to see the woman who'd taken his order slap two slices of buttered bread on the hot grill, one of which she topped with a slab of white cheddar cut from a large wedge and then a few thin slices of a small red apple.

The bread was from a standard white loaf, but the sharp cheese and the tart apple made up for its plainness. Dan gobbled the sandwich down in a few bites, even as the molten cheese burned the roof of his mouth.

"Tastes like my grandmother's apple pie," he said. "She always served it with cheddar cheese."

"Ah, you're one of the select few who gets it," the woman said, smiling. "Some people order the grilled cheese and ask me to hold the apple, as if I didn't know what I was doing, combining the two. The sandwich is good, if I say so myself."

"Delicious," Dan agreed.

"I'm ML. My sandwich invention, my café." She looked past Dan, out the window.

"It looks like people are starting to head back to the bus. Let me get your check."

"I'll take a heat-up first, please. And I'm Dan. Dan Fulke."

"Good to meet you, Dan. Do you want a to-go cup?" When Dan shook his head, ML shrugged and topped off his mug. "So, you're not going all the way to the island?"

Dan took another sip and thought about his options. Mt. Desert was a destination by default, Acadia National Park a place he knew from years ago—a summer camping trip made with some college buddies. He'd always intended to return with Stacy, and when he saw the destination on promotional fliers lying around the Greyhound station, it had seemed like a good fit; he'd figured there would be ample work on the island for tourist season and maybe beyond.

But here was a job in Ellsboro. It was neither a booming metropolis nor a resort destination—even the nearest larger city, Bangor, about an hour away in the other direction, wasn't that—but the town was doing well enough to support a restaurant and gas stations, car and boat mechanics, entire businesses devoted to providing equipment for campers and hikers and kayakers on their way to rentals or summer homes.

Dan lifted his coffee mug and swiveled in his seat to look back out the window, beyond the handwritten sign. The others were lining up outside the bus door. He swiveled back to face ML. "You know, I think I've gone far enough. You're looking for a cook?"

She set the coffee pot back on its burner and nodded. "A few odd jobs, too, in addition to the cooking. You want work?"

Dan nodded. "I do. I have experience."

ML raised an eyebrow. "Really? Well, here's my situation, and you can tell me if you're still interested after hearing it. Norman, my regular full-time cook, moved south a couple of weeks ago to live with his daughter, right at the start of the busy season. I need the help—and fast. There's cooking and minor repairs. I could use someone to touch up the paint around the place every now and then. And I always need a driver, someone to pick up food in between deliveries. The cases can be heavy." She studied Dan closely.

He knew what he must look like to her, tired and pasty and with forty-eight hours' worth of beard. "I know machines, and, sure, I can drive. And lift. This past year I was in a big kitchen, doing a little of everything. Before that I worked in a couple of places out West, pitching in where I was needed. I'm handy. Dad was a mechanic. I can do pretty much any work you throw at me."

"That right?" ML lifted an eyebrow. "But look, I really need someone who will stay longer than a few months, and it sounds like you've been bouncing around. We're coming out of a tough patch, between the economy and my staff problems, and the last thing I need is to be looking for someone again in four or six months."

"I work hard. I'd like a chance," he said.

She tipped her head to the side and continued scrutinizing him. "Well then. I guess I'd be stupid to say no." She gestured with her chin to his coffee cup. "Want another refill? Coffee's free for employees."

"You mean I'm hired?"

ML nodded and smiled. "You work as hard as you say and we'll get along just fine."

"Thank you," Dan said. "Thank you." The relief he felt surprised him. "I think I'm all set with coffee. But maybe you can point me in the direction of a place to stay."

"I can do better than that. My friend Angela rents out efficiencies in a big house about a mile from here. Give me a few minutes to clear up from the rush and I'll take you to her place myself. You can get settled."

10

Settled, Dan thought to himself as he sat on his newly made bed and looked around the room at the plain pine dresser that now held his two pairs of jeans—faded blue and dark blue—and the few changes of underwear that he owned, and over at the kitchenette, which had been furnished by those who had come before him with mismatched cups and plates and spoons and a couple of flimsy, non-stick fry pans.

He suspected it might take longer to settle into being one worker in a core staff of three. ML had been talkative enough as she showed Dan around the kitchen, but the other member of the team, Willa, had been more curious. She had peppered him with questions as her hands worked a pile of biscuit dough: "Why do you want to work here?" "Where are you from?" "What was Chicago like?" "Why'd you leave Boston?" So many questions as she kept at the motions of shaping, cutting, placing biscuits on a baking tray, her hands having a life of their own.

He'd stayed vague in his answers, but he couldn't forever. Now he wondered, *Was it a mistake, stopping here?*

He rested his head against the wall behind his bed. The thin pillow Angela had provided offered little comfort but he settled in anyway. He was tired of looking around the small spartan room, tired of trying to make sense of where he found himself. He closed his eyes and tried to sleep.

"Dan."

He looked up from unpacking cans of tomatoes onto the stainless steel prep counter. He had returned a few minutes ago from an emergency supply run with several cases of tomatoes loaded into the way back of ML's old gunmetal gray Volvo. Even after four weeks, he couldn't get over how many cans she plowed through in a week and how her chili stood out from everyone else's lobster rolls.

"You've been here how long?" ML asked.

He paused, took a bandana from his back pocket, and wiped his forehead and the back of his neck. "Four weeks. Give or take."

"Perfect." She reached down, grabbed two aluminum stock pot lids from the nearby pot shelf, and handed them to him. "You haven't had the pleasure yet because I usually take care of this before I go home, but I'm ready to pass the torch," she told him. To Willa, she said, "I'm finally going to acquaint Dan with our dumpster protocol. It's about time."

Willa raised an eyebrow but didn't say a word.

"Right then, Dan, follow me."

He trailed her to the back door.

"You're going to do your first trash run at the end of the day. Willa can help you."

He thought he saw ML's mouth twitch, as if she wanted to smile. But as quickly as he registered this, her face resettled itself into a blank expression.

"That's fine," he said, "I can do it myself."

"Not today. Willa's going to help you."

Dan frowned. By the end of his first week, he had made it clear he preferred working alone and keeping to himself. While ML and Willa went about their days in what he assumed were their well-worn routines—ML talking to Willa about whatever issue was being discussed on the public radio station she switched on in the morning; Willa changing the radio to a music station later in the day to sing along to the top hits—he didn't join in. He answered their questions with little more than a word or two. He came to work and got his job done. If either woman thought he was too standoffish, they'd never said so, and he wondered why ML was insisting he work with Willa now.

Before he could ask her what she was up to, ML turned and walked toward the dumpster, housed out back behind a latched gate. He followed.

"Okay. Once I'm ready to close, I collect all the trash together and bring it outside. I suppose that sounds pretty straightforward," she said.

He nodded.

"But look what we have with us today." She pointed up at a hill a short distance away, where a group of large birds was lurking.

They were really large, the ugliest birds Dan had ever seen. "What are they, buzzards?"

"Buzzards," she confirmed. "Properly known around here as turkey vultures. They have those scaly red heads, so I guess they reminded someone of turkeys. Wicked pests. When you see them, always double check that you've closed the dumpster lids completely."

He nodded. "I bet they can make quite a mess."

"Nah. The real problem is the other animals that climb in the dumpster and hang around too long, feeding. That's when the buzzards swoop in. I've seen those birds grab a small raccoon and fly off with it."

"Raccoons? Really?"

"Raccoons and woodchucks. We sometimes get bears in here, too. We've never had rats, luckily."

He lifted the pot lids. "So what are these for?"

"You bang them together like cymbals before you go outside with the trash," ML explained. She took them from him and brought them together lightly, showing him what she meant. "Make as much noise as you can as you walk out there. You'll scare off all the critters and keep the vultures from diving at you while you work."

Dan looked once again at the birds lurking on the hill. "I suppose that'll work. I'll leave these here, then." He propped the lids next to the back door and followed ML back inside.

It was a busy morning and afternoon. Dan didn't think about the dumpster until four o'clock, when ML locked the front door and flipped the "Open" sign to "Closed." Once back in the kitchen, she poured herself a cup of coffee and settled herself on a stool at Willa's workbench. "All that's left for you two is to take care of the day's trash. Willa, you keep an eye on Dan."

"Sure," Willa said.

She and Dan collected the trash bags from the different work stations and brought their load to the back door.

"Here," ML offered, "let me hold the door for you." She left her seat to prop open the door, making it easier for Dan and Willa to move the bags outside. Once Dan had the bags lined up at the door, he reached for the pair of battered aluminum lids he had tucked away and began banging them together.

Behind him, Willa started laughing. "What are you . . ." But she couldn't get another word out before dissolving into laughter.

Dan stopped making noise and looked at her. "This isn't funny."

"Oh, but it is," she said as she caught her breath.

"This is exactly what ML told me to do, to keep the animals and the vultures away." Holding the pair of lids under one arm, he tossed the bags into the dumpster with his free hand. When he was done, he closed the dumpster tight and clanged the makeshift cymbals once more for good measure.

"Animals and vultures? God, ML, what tale did you tell him?" Willa's laughter wound down, and she wiped tears from her cheeks.

"I might have said something about raccoons and bears in the trash. Maybe a little something about dive-bombing vultures." ML tried to keep a straight face but failed, and within seconds Willa was laughing again.

"So wait a minute," Dan said. "There aren't any bears prowling or vultures flying off with raccoons?"

"Vultures flying off with—oh, God, no," Willa said. "That dumpster is as secure as Fort Knox. And anyway, it's still light outside. There's nothing hanging around out here."

"Look, Dan." ML pointed. The vultures hadn't moved from their lookout in the trees at the top of the hill. "I fibbed. I'm sorry."

He studied her for a moment. "You're not really sorry."

"No, I guess I'm not. I had to come up with some way to get you to relax around us."

"And this was it?"

"Call it an ice breaker."

Dan looked from ML to Willa, who was still dabbing tears of laughter from her eyes with a clean patch of her apron. She looked up, met his eyes, and smiled at him. He noticed there were well-established laugh wrinkles at the corners of her eyes, and he started to smile back. But he caught himself.

"I need to finish cleaning," he said.

The next morning, ML cornered Dan the minute he arrived. She had come in earlier than usual because Willa had phoned to say she would be running late. “Her boy, Josh, had a restless night, and she’s trying to give him a little more sleep,” ML told him. “I thought I’d get a jump on her prep work, but all my equipment decided this would be a good time to die on me.”

“*All* your equipment?” he asked, hanging his windbreaker on a hook screwed into the wall outside the bathroom door.

“Okay, that’s an exaggeration,” she answered. “Not everything is busted, but close enough. The fridge is leaking, and the food processor is spinning so slowly it’s mostly useless. Anyway, you promised you could fix things, so here’s your chance to shine.”

Within minutes, Dan had the door off one of the two smaller refrigerators and was removing the rubber seal, which had clearly weakened over time from much opening and closing along with the area’s sharp variations in temperature and corrosive salt air.

“When do you think I’ll be able to put the food back in here?” ML asked. All her fresh dairy products were crammed in with the small vats of condiments in the prep fridge.

“I’ll need to get a length of new seal first, so that means it’s out of commission until I can get to a hardware store.”

She groaned.

“I promise I’ll be first in line when they open,” he assured her.

“Well, I appreciate that. Now how about the Cuisinart?” She flipped the machine’s power switch. The motor squealed to life, and the blade began to spin around the bowl at less than half its usual pace. “If you think I’m in a bad mood, wait until you see Willa when I tell her this thing’s not working.”

“I can give it a look, but I’ll be honest, it doesn’t sound good. How old is this beast?” He turned off the machine and ran a hand over the clunky square base before unplugging it. “Ten years?”

“Fifteen. Well, maybe closer to twenty.”

Dan raised an eyebrow but kept his thoughts to himself as he took apart the housing to get at the motor and diagnose the problem. He sympathized with her. He wouldn't want to plunk down four hundred bucks for a new model fitted with a collection of plastic gears either, but he suspected she would have to, as this machine's long run seemed to be coming to its natural conclusion.

"All these machines going at once. Mercury sure is retrograde," ML muttered as she hovered, watching him work.

"I can't fix it, and no one else is going to be able to either," Dan confirmed. "I think it's had a good long life, and it's time you put the thing out of its misery, Mercury or no Mercury."

This news, on top of losing the fridge seal and being behind in her prep work, made ML scowl. "You can't rig it to work for the day?"

"There's no need to 'rig' it; it turns on and spins, even if it is slowed down. Willa can use it today if she can stand the noise. But she's not going to like it much." Dan shrugged. "When I said I could fix things, I didn't mean turning back time. I don't do miracles."

"Now, did I imply I wanted a miracle?"

He tightened the last screw on the housing and set down the screwdriver. "Yeah, you kind of did."

ML looked at him and a smile broke out over her face. "I guess I did. Least I can do for all your hard work is get you some coffee." She grabbed the carafe.

Dan reached for a mug and slid it across the stainless steel counter, and she poured.

"Thanks." He blew on the surface of the coffee before taking a sip. It was good and strong. Thank goodness the Bunn hadn't died. Yet.

After a few seconds, ML said, "Are you happy here, Dan?"

"If this is about yesterday—"

She held up a hand. "Hear me out first. I know I'm talkative.

All my life, people have been telling me this. When my ex told me, he said it like he was diagnosing me with a fatal disease." She chuckled. "Have you ever been married? Or, more to the point, have you ever been divorced?"

Instead of answering, Dan looked down into his mug. If he was going to share anything about his past with anyone, ML would be the one. She was easy, nonjudgmental. She liked everyone. But he thought he could be the first person to challenge her good nature once she learned he had worked for one of the banks that had a hand in the downturn that had threatened so many livelihoods, hers included. And she would never understand his role in a client's death.

"I get it," she said when he didn't answer. "You like your distance, and that's fine. We didn't want you to be a stranger is all; we wanted you to feel as if you could join in. But I see now that yesterday's prank went too far."

"It's not . . ." He stopped himself. There was no point protesting. ML was right. He did need the distance. "If it means anything, I'm not uncomfortable here."

"Not uncomfortable." ML smiled. "Well, that's something. Anyway, I should let you get back to it. Those appliances won't fix themselves."

She pushed herself away from the counter and headed to the pantry to collect flour and baking powder for the biscuits.

Dan heard something fall to the floor and ML cursing her own clumsiness.

Seconds later, she stood in the doorway of the pantry, her hands full of ingredients. "I'd wish for Willa to appear soon, except then one of us would have to tell her—oh, you're here." She looked beyond Dan, and Dan turned.

"One of you would have to tell me what?" Willa asked as she unzipped her hooded sweatshirt.

When ML didn't answer, Dan piped up, "The food processor isn't working properly. I tried to fix it but . . ."

Willa slid out of her sweatshirt and shrugged at her two coworkers. "It was only a matter of time, no big deal. Really, it's the least of my worries today. Here—" She walked over to ML and grabbed an apron on the way. "—let me take those." She put her arms out for the canisters ML was carrying. ML gave them up without a fuss.

"By the way," Willa said, "I had to bring Josh to work with me. He never really fell back to sleep. There was no point sending him to his day camp if I was going to get a call to come pick him up because he was having a meltdown. He's in the back booth with his books. He'll be quiet."

At the end of the lunch shift, as Dan was wiping down the last of his work surfaces and whistling tunelessly to himself, he heard a commotion in the dining room. Willa and ML were taking inventory of the pantry, so he poked his head through the service door to see what was happening. A young boy stood near the back booth. He was holding several books but several more were on the floor, scattered around his feet. "Mum!" he called.

"That sounds suspiciously like a problem," Willa said, jogging past Dan. She called over her shoulder to ML, "Let me see what's up with Josh and I'll be right back."

Dan returned to the griddle to scrub off some stubborn specks of burned cheese. A couple of minutes later, he heard the service door squeak and turned, expecting to see Willa; he was surprised to see her son there instead. The long-legged and slender build, the sandy hair, even the freckles across the bridge of his nose were very like his mother's.

Dan set down the steel wool. "Hi, there."

"Hi. I'm Josh. My mother told me you're Dan, and that you're afraid of turkey vultures. Are you really?" The boy let go of the door, and it swung shut with a whoosh behind him.

"I suppose I was, but not so much anymore."

"I won't tell anyone. Mum told me because she thought I'd like the joke ML played. Because it was a joke about birds," Josh explained. "I know a lot about Maine birds. Mom also says you probably know squat about birds. That's from diddly-squat, and diddly-squat means nothing."

"Then it probably seems silly to you that a grown-up would be afraid of a bird."

Josh came all the way into the kitchen and hopped onto a stool. "Yes. See, if you knew about vultures, you'd know there is nothing to be afraid of. They only go after dead animals. Road-kill. They'd rather find something to eat out on the highway. And even if they did like to hunt for live raccoons, it has to be really dark for them to be out."

"Your mom said."

"My mom knows almost as much as I do. I have a book you could borrow," Josh said. "*The Birds of Mount Desert Island.* It's out of print but I have a copy I bought from the library's book sale. I didn't think it was a good idea for the library to sell that book because a person might like to borrow it for bird watching. But our librarian says they have another copy. I guess it's okay not to have two copies, and I like having my own. Anyway, you could borrow it today and learn something. It's out there with Mum." He pointed toward the dining room.

Dan had no chance to reply, as the door swung open again. This time it was Willa.

"Hon, I thought you were going to the bathroom. You need to go back and sit with your books. Dan doesn't want to be interrupted." She turned to Dan. "Sorry. This guy promised me he would sit quietly and read while I finish up here. Right, Josh?"

"But I want to give Dan my book."

Puzzled, Willa looked from her son to Dan.

"He offered me his bird guide," Dan explained.

"Because Dan knows squat, like you said."

Willa blushed. "Josh—"

"If you take the book, Dan, we can talk about birds the next time I'm here. I think I'll be here next Thursday afternoon with Nana, right Mumma?" Josh looked up at Willa.

She nodded. "But Dan's working now, honey. Why don't you—"

"He can work and talk. I know I can. I do it all the time at school. And Norman used to work and talk, remember? He would wash dishes and tell me stories about the Navy and—"

"Joshua. Seriously. Stop. TMI."

He looked up at Dan. "That means too much information."

"Yes, I think I heard that somewhere. How about this," Dan said. "I can look at your bird guide once I'm finished for the day. Before I go home. Does that sound good?"

"That is a solid plan," Willa said. She put her hands on Josh's shoulders but he wriggled out.

"It's better if you borrow it. Maybe you can even go on a bird-watch with us someday. The island birding festival is coming up. I know you'd like it, and I could teach you a lot of things that aren't in the book."

Dan looked up and met Willa's eyes. She must have seen he had no idea what to say because she jumped in. "Dan's still getting used to the job, Joshie. He's got his own things to do. How about we play it by ear?"

"I hate that expression," Josh said, "because it usually means no. You just don't want to tell me no right away." His face flushed, two warm red spots appearing high on his cheekbones.

"You're right," Willa said. "I shouldn't have used that expression. I promise we'll talk about it at home."

Dan could tell the boy was still fighting back tears. "What your mom said is true. I am still adjusting to the job and living in Ellsboro."

Josh considered this. "Do you have friends here? I have one friend at my school, but I don't see him in the summer and sometimes he pretends he doesn't know me. You and I could be friends."

"You go on back to the booth so Dan and I can finish up," Willa said. "I'll talk to him about the birds, I promise."

Satisfied, Josh nodded and left his mother and Dan to close up the kitchen.

Willa went to the cupboard near her workbench and collected her large handbag. When she turned, she looked tired. "Sorry about that. Josh isn't always as quiet as I said, and I know you want your space."

"Willa, it's fine, I—"

The kitchen door swung open again, and Josh burst in. "Here's the book, Dan. You should read the sections on the water birds first. Mumma," he said, turning to Willa, "you promised you'd take me to see the egrets before it's too late. They'll be gone soon. We could go during the festival. Dan could come with us."

"Josh, I asked you to wait until—"

"But I couldn't wait."

Instead of succumbing to frustration as he had earlier, Josh remained calm. Dan saw this had an effect on Willa. Instead of shooing him away again, she smiled.

"Not even until we get home?"

Josh considered this. "No."

ML walked into the kitchen as Josh and Willa were facing off. "I came to see if you're ready to lock up. What did I walk into?"

Willa chuckled. "Josh at his most persuasive. He wants me to take a day off for the birding festival."

"Sure you can have a day off," ML said. "I can get someone

to lend a hand, maybe your mum could help out. I'll ask her. You name the day, and it's done."

Josh whooped. "Would you come, too, Dan? Please?"

Dan's answer didn't come readily. He knew it would be wise to say no to the invitation, but how was he supposed to say no to a kid who didn't take no for an answer? He looked to ML, but she just shrugged and looked at Josh, her face soft; her affection for the boy was clear.

"Your call," she said, eyes still on Josh. "If you're interested in going, you should. I can find help for a day, if that's what you're worried about."

Dan's worries were bigger than finding a kitchen substitute. He was worried about making promises he couldn't—shouldn't—keep. He hoped he wasn't making a mistake as he told Josh, "Sure. I'd like that."

11

A couple of weeks passed. Josh spent more afternoons in his booth at the café and used the time there to review the birding festival schedule and pick activities to participate in. After consulting with his mother and Dan, he chose a bird-watching boat ride and a sketching workshop. He remained adamant that before the organized events began, the three of them would take an early-morning hike into Pretty Marsh to see the roosting colony of snowy egrets.

Early morning was an understatement; they left before the sun rose. Standing in Willa's driveway, Dan loaded all the hiking essentials she had packed into the trunk of her car. He didn't comment on the size or weight of the large canvas tote bag, but it was heavy.

Before they left, Willa handed Josh a brand-new sketch book. "I thought you might like this for the workshop today."

"I do!" Josh exclaimed. "I love it. Thank you. Can I draw in it before the workshop, Mum?"

"You may."

He climbed into the backseat of the car and set the book on his lap. "Dan read about the cormorants, Mumma," he said. "He knows a lot but I bet he doesn't know everything. He doesn't know what they are really called—do you?" He leaned forward between the two front seats.

"You mean other than cormorants?" Dan shook his head. "Apparently not."

"Shags. We call them shags." Josh shifted to look at his mother. "Some people who don't live up here call them shit pokes, but that's the wrong name, isn't it, Mum? A shit poke is a green heron." He rolled his eyes. "Everyone knows that."

"Everyone meaning every old fisherman north of Portland—and Josh," Willa told Dan.

"I wish you hadn't put the bird guide at the bottom of the tote bag," he said, but he sat back in his seat anyway and cracked open his sketch book, flipping through the empty pages, occasionally stopping to stroke the heavy paper.

"Shit poke?" Dan said under his breath.

"It's a fact." Willa shrugged.

"Interesting. Do you know, until the other night I hadn't even heard the word 'cormorant'?"

Willa laughed. "Oh really? We couldn't tell."

"Hey Dan, do you have a picnic basket at your house?" Josh called from the backseat. "We don't have a picnic basket. Nana used to have one, she told me. But she put it in the trash when she moved because she has no closet space. Mum has a picnic *bag* instead."

"My canvas tote bag," Willa admitted to Dan. "It's a bone of contention."

"Which isn't really a bone at all," Josh said. "That's an expression."

"A strange expression," Dan said.

"I think so, too," Josh said. "Contention isn't like a mammal with bones. That's just silly. As silly as a picnic bag!" He burst out in laughter.

"Pretty silly, then," Willa said. "Anyway, we're getting close."

And they were. Dan could see the sign pointing into the parking area.

"Tell me again what we're going to see," Dan said to Josh as Willa pulled into a space at the end of the dirt drive.

As the boy described in detail the colony of cormorants living on the rocks at the coast, down to the amount of guano they produced in a day, Dan gathered up their belongings and Willa sprayed Josh's arms and neck with insect repellent.

Josh was still talking as they approached Pretty Marsh. Willa was ahead, leading the way. Dan readjusted the long tote bag straps over his shoulder, yielded his place in the hiking line to Josh, and brought up the rear.

"But what about the egrets?" Dan asked when Josh paused. "Or is it herons we're going to see?"

"Egrets. They find food differently than the cormorants. They live differently, too—at least the snowy egrets do, and that's what we're going to see today. They don't breed out here on the island. They come up from the south in the summer to look for food and to stay cooler. They roost together overnight in their colony, and that's called communal roosting, Dan."

"I remember reading that. The birds sleep together in trees," he said, "like lots of people sleeping in bunk beds in a cabin."

"Yes! When they wake up in the morning, they fly off to salt marshes and catch frogs in the mud. I hope they're still here—it's kind of late in the season. If we do find them, we can watch them fly off to hunt for food. If we could stay the whole day, we might even see them come home to the trees at night." He looked down at Dan's feet. "You know, those are really bad shoes for walking here. But I guess you don't have any boots? You should get some. Mum can tell you where to go, right, Mum?"

Willa turned to look at her son and she laughed. "Sure. If Dan wants boots."

"I'm sure he wants boots. Don't you, Dan? We shouldn't go on any more hikes in the woods and marshes until you have some. Mum calls mine Wellies but I don't know why. I think she got them at the Trading Post?" Josh looked up at Willa for confirmation.

"I did. And I call them Wellies because it's short for Wellington boots, named after a boot-wearing English duke. But Josh, let's focus on the birds for the next few minutes. We'll figure out if Dan wants boots later." Willa reached for his hand.

Dan looked at his feet, at the tracks his running shoes made in the beds of pine needles, at the mud and debris collecting in the treads. These were his only pair of shoes. The soles had good traction for the slippery kitchen floor, but out here the ventilated runners made no sense. He should think of getting a second pair, maybe hiking boots to add some substance to the life he had kept pared down up to now, his one-hat-one-jacket-one-pair-of-shoes life.

"Mumma." Josh broke out of the hand hold and turned.

"Yes, hon."

"How can I be the guide if you won't let me walk ahead? Guides are supposed to go first."

"Are they? What if Dan wanted to ask you a question, though? What if you were too far ahead to hear him?"

Josh looked from his mother to Dan, considering. "I didn't think of that. I should have because Dan doesn't really know anything. I guess I could walk in between you for a bit longer." He reached out and took his mother's hand again, catching it mid-swing. "You can ask me anything, Dan."

"I'll keep that in mind," Dan answered with a sideways glance at Willa.

She bit her lip to keep from laughing as they continued on.

Within minutes, Dan noticed the heavily wooded path was clearing and the dense trees had thinned, giving way to lower, wilder shrubs. Underfoot, the mud squelched.

"I think we're close," Josh said.

"It's certainly wetter than it was a few minutes ago," Dan said.

Willa looked pointedly at Dan's shoes and raised an eyebrow.

"But I'm not complaining," he added, smiling at Willa.

Before she could react, Josh tugged her arm. She bent down, and he whispered something in her ear.

When he finished, she drew back and looked at him. "That's a personal question," she said. "Come on, we only have a little further to go." She took his hand again and tried to move ahead.

Josh didn't budge.

Dan looked between the two and saw that Willa's face was flushed. "What's up?" he asked.

Willa looked off into the distance, her eyes trained on the trees or the clearing or nothing at all. Then she sighed. The sound came from way down deep, a mournful sound in the quiet morning.

"I asked Mum if you're married." Josh looked between his mother and Dan. "If you're not, you could be my mum's boyfriend. Then she wouldn't be a single mother. You're not married, are you, Dan?"

"No, Josh, I . . . No."

"Josh, please," Willa said.

Josh ignored her. "That's sad for you but good for us."

Willa held up her hand. "We can talk at lunch about friends and boyfriends and anything else that's worrying you, okay? For now, I think we should get moving or we'll miss the egrets. How much further do you think?"

The question seemed to work to get the boy back on track. He looked around and took stock of their surroundings, and then consulted the topographical map he had used to lead them that far. Dan could almost see his brain working behind his eyes as he began to convert coordinates on the map to an actual distance. "I think we're close, maybe a quarter of a mile."

"So about five minutes?"

"Or three or four minutes, if we walk fast. We can walk fast, right? I mean, we don't want to be late and miss the roosting."

"I can walk fast," Dan said. "Let's do this."

Josh, refocused, took his mother's hand again and started off. Dan gave them a little lead before following.

As Josh predicted, they reached their destination in no time. Dan took in the clearing and the boggy land. Behind them, in the direction of the ocean, the early-morning sky showed some blue broken up with low, patchy clouds. The further inland they were, the thicker the cloud cover. Some moisture had formed into dense clouds of fog that hugged the tree line and hovered over the inland pools of water. Rising out of the marsh were the trees Josh had told them to look for. They appeared dead, these stunted trunks of unidentifiable trees, weathered gray in places, rotted black in others. Here and there, they were dotted with ghostly white blobs. Dan blinked, and the white blotches began to take shape as gangly birds, heavy-bodied with exaggerated S-curve necks. It was an eerie sight.

"We're here. We shouldn't get any closer," Josh cautioned. "The egrets will wake up and leave soon anyway, but if we don't scare them, we can watch them for a while through the binos." He held out the glasses to Dan.

When Dan saw him shiver with excitement, he declined the binoculars and motioned for Josh to take the first look. Josh grinned and raised them to his eyes, holding his elbows parallel to the ground. Dan and Willa took a couple of steps back to give him room.

"You realize," she said as she kept an eye on Josh, "you may never get a turn with those."

"It's okay. This is still quite a sight even with the naked eye."

Willa nodded. "A little creepy, I think. From here, those

shaggy tufts on their heads look like white fright wigs," she added. "Like Einstein hair. Einstein birds."

"Can I get a little closer, Mumma?" Josh's voice interrupted, wafting back in a hissing whisper.

"A few more steps, hon, and that's it. Any further, and you'll be too close to the marshes."

"But I have my—"

"Even with your boots on," Willa answered. "And besides, aren't you supposed to be making as little noise as possible?"

Josh grumbled a bit but did as he was told, stopping next to a cluster of bog brush that seemed to be nature's last effort at shoring up the eroding dirt at the edge of an embankment.

"He likes to test the limits," Dan said.

"Always. He's curious. Sometimes too curious." Willa toed at the ground with her right foot, quickly making a divot. "I'm sorry about the matchmaking. He says whatever pops into his head."

"It's fine. He's a good kid, Willa."

"He is a good kid. Thank you. Sometimes in the day-to-day of dealing with school and camp, I need to be reminded."

Dan threw her a puzzled look. "But he's so smart."

Willa nodded. "He is, but the social aspect is a challenge. 'Socially awkward,' they say, because he'd rather be by himself than participate with the other kids. Somedays it feels like experts are coming at me from all directions with testing, ed plans, therapists. That all makes me forget to really look at him and appreciate how much fun he is. It didn't help that in the middle of all this, his dad left. Adam, my ex—well, he couldn't cope very well." She held her hands up in a time-out gesture. "But that's a story for another day."

Dan stared off into the stand of trees, not really focusing on the birds but not ignoring them either. As he stared into the marsh, his focus softened, blurring the birds' forms until it was hard to tell where the birds ended and the fog started. He, so guarded and so used to fending only for himself, probably wasn't the ideal person to talk to about an isolated kid.

A squeal of excitement shook the stillness that had enveloped Dan and Willa. "Mum! Mum, look!"

The grownups followed Josh's outstretched arm as it pointed to the sky. In the stunted trees, the egrets were rousing themselves, shaking off their lethargy. Feathers ruffled and fluffed as, one by one, the birds unfolded themselves and stretched, all enormous wing spans and ungainly movement, and then pushed off their branches or stumps and took flight, rearranging their awkward bodies into streamlined torpedoes as massive wings beat against the air and propelled them into the sky. Soon the trees were empty, the birds gone without a trace.

The humans left behind stood silently, still in awe.

"Wow." Dan broke the silence.

Josh pulled himself up to drier land using the branches of a bog shrub like they were lengths of tow rope. He scrambled to his mother's side. "I did some sketches while they were in the trees. But they flew away too fast for me to sketch them in flight. Can we come back another time?"

"Maybe," Willa said, and then she laughed at herself. "Sorry. I can do better than maybe. Yes, we can. At least, you and I can." She held out a hand for her son's sketchbook. "These drawings are beautiful, honey."

And they were. Dan looked over her shoulder to get a look. The boy was accomplished for someone so young.

"I decided to write a bird book about all the birds we see today, and I want to illustrate it myself. Especially birds in flight. Did you see the egrets fly off, Dan? That was cool! I didn't know it would be this cool!" Josh bounced on his toes, his excitement on display.

Dan smiled. "It *was* cool." And it was. All those birds, completely still and then not. A colony, as Josh called them, with a common purpose: to breed, to find food, to live; to fly to the next place to start the cycle all over again. It must be a hard life, he thought, although he imagined in flight the birds might be free from some of the hardscrabble routines they practiced in order to stay alive. Maybe for a few brief moments, anyway. He blinked at the strange sensation of tears burning his eyes as he watched Willa put her arm across her son's shoulders.

"If you pack up your sketchbook and pencils," she was telling him, "we can head back to the coast for the cormorants, and then off to the workshop." Josh nodded his agreement and began putting away his things.

"Sounds like a plan," Dan said, but he was slow to move, slow to turn and catch up as he watched Willa take Josh's hand and lead him back to the hiking path, back in the direction of the ocean.

For another moment Dan stalled, his eyes on the empty trees ahead of him, until Willa stopped and called his name.

"You coming?" she asked.

Dan lifted his hand in a sort of wave. "On my way."

He hustled to catch up.

After the sketching workshop, Willa spread out lunch across one of the picnic tables outside the visitors center. Josh ate quickly. Once he washed down his last bite with a swig of cold milk, he asked if he could go look at the park map posted on the tourist information board. "It's not far."

"You may, if you come back in a few minutes to help clean up," Willa said.

Josh agreed and darted off.

Willa reached for a second thermos. "This is tea, not milk. Yes or no?" she asked.

"Yes. Please."

"Good." And she poured. After, she leaned back and looked up at the sky. Some dark clouds were moving in. "Looks like rain. Maybe. We should head to the boat soon, see if they're still planning to go out."

"Yes," Dan said, but he didn't move. The day had been so relaxed and so easy that moving now might ruin that.

He lifted the cup to his lips and tasted. The tea was a pleasant temperature but the taste was awful. He made a face.

Willa laughed at him. "Chamomile's not your thing?"

"First time trying it. Sorry." He set the mug down.

"It's okay. People either love it or hate it. I don't drink caffeine past eight or nine in the morning, but we can try peppermint tea next time. You might like that better."

Dan looked up when Willa said "next time." Another hike, another warm drink, another day spent together outside work?

After spending more than two years untethered, Dan found Willa here, smiling at him, and Josh, eager for his company. For the first time, Dan wondered if he had spent enough time alone, if having friends and a life up here was within his reach. Maybe after all the months spent wandering from place to place, he had paid for his ambition and the mistake of calling in one loan too many.

"Willa, earlier, when Josh asked—"

"Mumma!"

Dan looked up at the sound of Josh's voice. He was over by the map, talking to a woman holding a notebook and pen. She seemed to be asking Josh questions. At her side was another woman carrying a large camera.

Dan looked at Willa. "A newspaper interview?"

"I think so." She got up from the picnic table, brushed off her lap, and walked over to her son.

Dan stayed put at first, but Josh called him over, too, so he went. When he reached the group, the woman with the notebook introduced herself. "I'm writing a story about the festival for the regional paper, and Josh was nice enough to tell me how much fun he's having. I wondered if it's okay to take a picture? Maybe of the three of you together?"

"Sure," Willa said, and she looked back at Dan. "Dan, would you . . ."

He waved her ahead. "You and Josh go. You don't need me in the shot."

But Josh grabbed them both by the hands. "You need to be in the picture, too, Dan! The reporter said she would send me a copy of the paper as a souvenir."

Within seconds, a few photos were taken, and the reporter thanked them before moving on to the next group of festival goers.

"This was mostly a great day," Josh said as they returned to the picnic table to pack up.

"Mostly?" Willa laughed.

"Well, I have a little worry. Mumma, can a lie be little, or are lies always big?"

Willa stopped short. "Did you tell the reporter something that wasn't right?"

Josh shook his head. "She was the one who said something that wasn't right. When I pointed and showed her who I was with, she asked me if she could talk to my mom and dad about taking pictures. I thought I should tell her that Dan's my friend, not my dad, but then I didn't want to make her feel bad. Sometimes people don't like it when I correct them all the time. The kids at school don't."

Willa didn't answer immediately, but her neck reddened as she looked from Josh to Dan.

"I know it's not true, Mumma. But I wasn't telling a lie on purpose."

"I understand. You didn't want to embarrass her."

Josh thought about that and then turned to Dan. "Are you angry?"

Dan shook his head. "I'm not angry. There's no reason to be."

Willa handed her son some paper trash. "Could you go put this in the recycling for me? Then we'll head down to the boat."

"Sure." Josh skipped off to the bins.

Willa turned to Dan when Josh was out of earshot. "This is Josh being Josh. But he interrupted you. You were going to say something?"

Dan smiled but he felt a shiver of unease disrupt the steady hope he'd felt earlier, like a random blip in an otherwise regular heartbeat. "It was nothing. Really," he added when she gave him a puzzled look. "I can't remember what I was going to say. But"—he looked up at the gray clouds overhead—"we should get moving. I think you might have been right about the rain."

Dan poured the eggshell finish paint into the tray. ML had sent him to the hardware store with instructions to come back with a shade of off-white paint for the café's dining room walls. A shade, she specified, without muddiness. Dan, long used to her creative descriptions, had understood "muddy" to mean whites that had their brightness dulled with a smidgeon of black, brown, or green. But what had complicated his mission was her other requirement: the paint needed to be bought from the cast-off shelf, the place for paint colors that had been mixed and then rejected. These cans were always half price, and ML liked nothing more than saving dough. But finding something usable there was a crap shoot. There was often a good reason why colors ended up on those shelves.

After some poking around, however, he had lucked out, finding enough cans of a neutral shade called Buttermilk Pie to get the job done.

Now, back at the café, he slapped a few wide swaths on one of the prepped walls as a test, then took a step back to judge the effect. The long holiday weekend had been full of spectacular weather, and today's end-of-the-day sunlight flooding in through the front windows picked up the hint of yellow in the white, making the dining room glow. A glowing space was good, he decided—not at all muddy. He paused to put on gloves and twist his roller onto an extension pole, then began to make his way around the room.

A few minutes in, the telephone interrupted Dan's work. Most likely ML checking up on his progress. It was only a matter of time before her curiosity got the better of her. His boss was the only person who thought she was easygoing. *The rest of us know better*, Dan thought with a shake of his head, but he smiled anyway as he carefully set down the extension pole, peeled off his gloves, and answered the call.

"Relax, ML, I promise I am hard at work, and you'll be able to open in the morning," he said in mock exasperation. But instead of ML's husky voice, a young boy's laughter reacted to Dan's words.

"It's not ML, Dan. It's *me*. Josh!"

"Josh! This is a surprise."

"You don't mind, do you? Mum didn't think it was a good idea to call you while you were painting. But I told her you would want to know I got my copy of the newspaper, the one with our picture in it!"

Two weeks had passed since the birdwatching festival in Acadia, but the reporter had kept her word. "That's great. I'll have to see it sometime."

"Can you come over now?"

In the background, Dan heard Willa say, "He's painting, Josh, remember? We can always bring it into the café tomorrow. You have no school because of the holiday."

"Okay, Mum, but maybe he wants to come over right now."

Dan leaned back against the wait station and listened to the discussion between mother and son going on without him. The boy was never shy about declaring what outcomes he wanted and when he wanted them. He'd willed himself right into Dan's life.

He jumped into the conversation. "Josh, your mom's right. I can't stop now because all the paint is out, and it's kind of a mess here. I need time to clean up. But maybe I can swing by on my way home, if it's not too late. Why don't you put your mom on, and I'll check with her?"

Reluctantly, Josh handed over the phone.

"Sorry for all our back and forth there," Willa apologized. "You must be in the thick of it."

"I am. But I told Josh I might be able to stop by after I finish the second coat and clean up. I shouldn't be late; I'm close to being done. And I won't stay for long."

"Oh. Well, sure."

"Sorry, I should have asked if it was okay first."

"No, no. It's good," she insisted. "I think Josh won't be able to sleep until you see the photo."

"Okay, then. Tell him I'll be there as soon as I can. He can relax."

Willa laughed. "That horse has left the barn. You should see him right now. Dancing. Twirling. Jumping on the sofa."

"I can imagine. Hey, I should finish this job if I'm going to see that photo any time soon."

"Of course. I'll let you go."

Dan hung up, gloved up again, and returned to his equipment.

The first coat was up. *Nice work*, Dan thought, as he looked over the walls. But the longer he looked, the more something about the paint job nagged at his eye. Then he spotted the problem: he had missed covering over a narrow strip of the old paint up near the joint of the wall and ceiling. He shook his head and lifted the roller back to the wall.

He was just finishing his last stroke when the telephone rang again. He smiled. If it was Josh checking his progress, he could tell him he was halfway done.

This time, he didn't bother taking care to stow the unwieldy equipment—just removed his gloves and took the extension pole with him.

He picked up. "Perfect timing. I am officially finished with the first coat. Not long now."

There was a pause on the other end before an unfamiliar female voice broke it. "Good evening. Am I speaking to Daniel Hopper?"

Dan froze. Daniel Hopper, not Daniel Fulke. He heard the woman repeat her question, once, twice, but her voice sounded distant and distorted, as if she were underwater. Or he was, his head fully submerged.

"No." He managed to push out the one word, but it was a struggle.

"No? This isn't Daniel Hopper? Then may I speak to him, please?" she asked, and this time he heard her clearly. He wasn't drowning after all. He sucked in some air.

"No. I mean, there's no one here by that name," he said, and he hung up.

After a second or two, he took the receiver back off the cradle and set the thing down on the desktop. For once, he was grateful for ML's old push-button phone, her frugality. *A cordless phone? I'd only lose track of it. And why would I want an answering machine or a voicemail service? Who needs to reach this place after hours?* The noise coming from the receiver, alerting him it was off the hook, grew insistent, annoying, but he cared more about the caller reaching a busy signal if she tried the number again.

He stumbled to a booth and sat on the edge of the bench seat, his feet on the drop-cloth he had placed carefully on the floor. He covered his face with his hands. Someone knew where Daniel Hopper had gone and who he had become.

Back in Boston, his full name—Daniel Fulke Hopper—had become a burden. Bad guys always seemed to have three names, and his had caught traction in the newspapers for a few weeks, associated with loan defaults and suicide. He'd dropped "Hopper" and started using his middle name, his mother's maiden name, as his last name instead.

It had only taken only a few weeks after leaving the city to get used to his truncated name. Other reminders of his past had taken much longer to overcome. Until he moved this far north, he had often detected something familiar in the profile of some woman he passed in a store or at one of the restaurants where he worked, which never failed to make him stop breathing for a couple of beats. Fear paralyzed him, the noise of the crowds around him receded, until all he could hear was the blood throbbing in his ears. Then the woman he thought he knew would excuse herself to reach past him for a can off the store shelf or smile up at her waiter as she paid her bill, and with her full face turned in his direction, it was enough to tell: No, not her—older. Or younger, or thinner, or happier. *Not her, not her, not her,* he would repeat to himself. Not Mrs. Herron. That was good. She hadn't followed him.

One of the last times he had seen her—the widowed wife, Julia Herron—she had been sitting in front of him in his old office, a stunned look on her face as she processed what his boss, a senior vice president, was telling her. Dan had played second chair to his boss that day, nodding as the older man explained to the widow that while the bank was sorry for her loss, they were responsible neither for her husband's death nor the fact he had left her carrying crushing debt. Suicide was terrible, but this *choice*—and Dan's boss paused after the word—as well as her signatures on the documents, meant he had left her holding the responsibility for repayment of his very large building loan. How could the bank have known he was keeping financial secrets from his wife? Anyway, she'd had ample opportunity to be more curious about her business. During the entire spiel, Dan had just kept nodding, balancing sober banker face with empathetic banker face, trying to mirror his boss.

It had been his job, then, to escort the stunned woman out of the offices, and he had done so, solicitous, showing the way with an outstretched hand, holding doors for her. At the front entry, he'd made the mistake of touching her arm as he ushered her out to the sidewalk.

"Take your fucking hand off me," she had said.

He'd held up both his hands in surrender. "We are only trying to help."

"Like you helped my husband?" she asked. Her accompanying laugh was full of acid. "He might have walked into the ocean alone, but you pushed him every step of the way. You killed him after taking advantage of him, Mr. Hopper, you and your goddamned predatory bank. And I know exactly what you are trying to do now: getting every last penny you think you're entitled to. You're no help; you're a parasite, is what you are."

Back upstairs in his office, it had taken Dan every ounce of resolve to keep from packing up his briefcase and leaving.

He hadn't, not then. However, by the time he'd gotten home

later that day to the tasteful and expensively appointed house he shared with Stacy, the tickle of shame he'd felt after the meeting had become an uncomfortable itch. A hair shirt.

A little over a month after that encounter, he had taken only his essentials and walked away from everything else. Nothing he'd owned, nothing he and Stacy had owned together, had been worth the price of a man's life. Maybe by denying himself a full life, he would stop hearing "Mr. Hopper" in the widow's angry voice, repeating itself over and over on a loop, reminding him of who he was and what he'd done.

Who could have found him after all this time, after all his crisscrossing the country, after dropping his last name? And why now?

"Of course it would be now," Dan said aloud in the messy dining room. At some point in the last few weeks, he had allowed himself to believe he had paid for his mistakes with almost two and a half years of his life. But leaving a job, meting out some half-assed self-punishment, was not the same thing as taking responsibility for his mistakes. He saw that now.

It took effort, but Dan sat up straight. The first thing he saw was the phone receiver across the room. The buzzing had stopped. He forced himself to his feet and over to the receiver. As he reached for the smooth plastic, he noticed that in spite of taking care to keep his hands clean, a drop of paint had seeped in and dried in the folds of a knuckle. Buttermilk Pie. Dan shook his head. He'd really looked forward to joking about the color's name with ML in the morning. She would smile at the food name, something homey and appropriate for a place dedicated to good home-style cooking. He had looked forward to seeing her face light up when she took in the effect of the clean, crisp walls and all the furniture back where it belonged.

Dan hung up the receiver and then, after a couple of seconds, picked it up again. With a fresh line, he dialed in the code number for retrieving information about the last logged incoming call. If this most recent one came from a blocked or unlisted number, he'd get nothing. If it came from a cell phone, he'd get nothing. And if it wasn't the most recent call, if someone else had called the café while the line was out of service, the record of the earlier call would be gone. But maybe he would get lucky. He picked up a pen from the repurposed juice can near the cash register just in case.

A few seconds later, surprised by his luck, Dan had a suburban Boston telephone number written down on one of ML's order pads. He pressed the disconnect button and released it quickly for a clear line. And then he called the person who had called him.

"Hello," he said when the woman with the brusque alto voice answered. "This is Daniel Hopper. I understand you are looking for me."

Dan stared at the freshly painted wall across the room, the phone pressed to his ear. The woman who had tracked him down in Ellsboro was the police detective, Denise Healey, who had been present during the interview he gave days after the suicide—not his former employer, not Julia Herron, and not a lawyer hired by Julia Herron, as he'd thought it might be. That was a surprise. It was a bigger surprise to learn that the detective had found him by accident only the other day, in the online version of the article Josh had been so excited to see in print.

"I have been googling you for months, and then earlier this week I got a hit. A photo of you in a north Maine paper," she said. "Dan Fulke, Ellsboro, Maine. I recognized 'Fulke' as the middle name you gave me on your signed statement. With that and your location, the rest was easy. Listen . . . I need to ask you a question about that statement. Can I read you something from it, and maybe you can clarify your meaning for me? When you told me about the missed meeting at your bank, you said 'they,' as in 'they were due to come in that morning.' I didn't pick up on it at the time. Was someone supposed to join Mr. Herron at the meeting? Who did you mean?"

"His father was coming, too," he said. "We thought so, anyway. We'd been expecting them both at the bank for the meeting."

"The older Mr. Herron never said anything to us about being involved in the meeting with his son. You're certain he was expected?"

"Yes. He's an acquaintance of my boss—I mean, my former boss. When David Herron called the day before and said his father would be coming to the meeting as well and that he might be willing to help with the loan, my boss agreed that we could postpone the default process until we heard their plans. But maybe he didn't tell you because he changed his mind."

"About coming to the meeting?"

"Yes—and about helping in general. David Herron called us early that morning and said his father was refusing to come into the bank and refusing to give him cash. But he begged me to wait, just a bit. He thought he could change his father's mind, said he had someone else to talk to—I mean, he was all over the place. We couldn't rely on his promises. Paul Herron did write us a check in the end, though. Too late to help his son, but he did bail out his daughter-in-law."

"Wait. Time out. He wrote you a check? To pay off the debt?"

"Yes, about a month later. Paid it off in full. Up to that moment, we understood there would be a filing of bankruptcy."

There was a long pause before Healey spoke again. "I'm sorry, but you were actually there? You know this firsthand?" she asked.

Firsthand? Dan recalled the day the VP in charge of commercial lending visited his office with news. "Julia Herron has secured representation for her bankruptcy filing. That was fast. Means this situation will start to wind down now, as quickly as the courts allow. For your part, don't talk to her anymore."

He had only talked to her one time before—the time when she had been so angry. So he'd told his boss, "Fine by me." For God's sake, he hadn't wanted to see her again, to feel her anger again. But the next day, she had shown up, as if discussing her had drawn her to the bank. She'd caught Dan unawares outside his building, just as he was returning from lunch. He'd had no choice but to bring her to his office to avoid a scene in the lobby.

As soon as they entered his office, she'd slapped a piece of paper on his desk. "Here you go," she'd said, staring him down. Dan remembered how the light from the overhead fixture had caught golden sparks in the dark brown of her irises. He'd looked from her eyes down to the piece of paper. A check, a large one, for the balance of the loan. He couldn't make sense of it.

"My father-in-law is buying out my debt," she'd said. "He asked me to have the lawyer send you the check and I told him that's what I'd do. But I lied. I wanted to look you in the eye." She'd shaken her head then. "Don't think I'm not full of rage at my husband; I am. I. Am. So. Angry. But you"—she'd pointed straight at his chest—"you might have fixed this. Stopped giving David money sooner, maybe, or negotiated a way for him to pay you what he owed. You could have done something. But you wanted to protect your bank more than you wanted my husband to succeed. So, there you go." She'd nodded at the check between them, by then under his fingertips. "Consider it protected."

"Mr. Hopper?"

Denise Healey's voice snapped Dan back to the present.

"Yes. Actually, Mrs. Herron brought the check to me, so yes, I know it firsthand. It was a big deal for the bank. The check meant we could close the books without going through the court, something that could have taken a long time. It was a big deal for Mrs. Herron, too. Every piece of the bakery would have been liquidated in a bankruptcy, right? Not necessarily the case if the loan was paid off. Assuming she didn't sell, she could keep it up and running."

Dan waited for a response or another question, but all he heard was silence.

"You still there?"

"I'm still here. Processing all this." After another brief pause, Healey said, "Okay. Let me confirm. We go back to April 2008. David Herron tells you his father is willing to meet and help with the loan, but at the last minute, Paul Herron declines to do that. David Herron kills himself. A few weeks later, his father pays off the loan. Am I good on the facts so far?"

"Yes. That's what I know."

"The bank gets paid, Julia Herron skirts bankruptcy, the bakery stays open. Paul Herron saves the day. Except he could have done it all a month earlier and maybe saved his son's life."

Until that moment, Dan hadn't wondered why the detective was asking new questions two years after the case had closed with a ruling of suicide. He should have, but he had been too relieved that the person on the other end of the phone wasn't Mrs. Herron or an attorney hoping to revive all the old accusations, and he'd wanted to be helpful to the family after being unhelpful for so long. But once he heard this cynicism in the woman's voice, he asked, "Are you charging Paul Herron with something after all this time?"

"Ha! Charge him with what? As my former partner says, he didn't actually kill his son, and we can't charge him for being a bad human. No, that's not why I called you. But hey, you've been very helpful, and I've kept you long enough. Thank you for your time, Mr. Hopper."

Before she could hang up, Dan called, "Wait!" He listened for the sound of the call disconnecting. When he heard no click, he continued, "I don't understand. If you can't charge anyone, how is what I told you helpful?"

Healey sighed loudly, as if she were anxious to end the call and annoyed by his persistence.

"Please," he said. "I'd like to know what I'm helping with."

Healey sighed again, but this time she sounded resigned. "All right. I'll start by telling you what I knew before I called you. Julia Herron no longer owns the bakery. There's a new owner, but some of the people who work at the bakery don't know who that is. Mrs. Herron still works there, but as a paid employee, one of two full-time bakers. Until I spoke to you, I had no idea who that new owner might be."

"You think it's Paul Herron because of the check?"

"I think it's Paul Herron because of the check. Do I know for sure he now owns the place and made his daughter-in-law a salaried employee? No. But I will find out. Now, I should really go and do just that."

Dan couldn't let her hang up, not yet. "Please," he said. "Why? Why are you doing all this if it won't matter?"

"Oh, it will matter. I think Herron should own some responsibility for refusing to go to that meeting on the day his son died, and that might happen now, thanks to you. As to why . . . Well, here's the deal, Mr. . . . Dan. I'm not even a cop anymore, all right? I quit because I screwed up those first few days of finding out what happened to Herron. I pissed off his wife, I made his kid cry. I see the daughter, Rennie, at my son's school now, and you know what? She's miserable. She's a reminder of everything I did wrong that April. I'm doing this because I live with so much guilt myself. I don't know if I can make up for the lousy way I did my job, but I'm going to try." With that, Healey hung up.

Several seconds behind her, Dan hung up the phone. He stayed rooted where he was, though, thinking about everything she had said. For nearly two and a half years, he had also been tormented by the lousy way he had chosen to do *his* job. Like Healey, he'd harmed this family. Like her, he felt he owed them something. Until today, he'd thought he had paid, and paid dearly, by giving up everything that mattered to him. But he'd been deluding himself. The fact remained that a man was dead and other lives had been permanently altered. His sacrifice hadn't helped the people he'd harmed. Or healed his own guilt, in the end.

September 2010

12

The noise woke him up, the incessant, harsh calling of the crows. It was early, just after three o'clock. Exhausted after the long day, Dan had fallen asleep some hours before, sitting up on his bed, still dressed in his painting clothes, spattered jeans and T-shirt damp with perspiration. Now, as he tried to straighten up, he heard a series of clicks in his neck and felt pins and needles teasing his lower back.

Though his body kept protesting, he sat up anyway, managed to swing his leaden legs over the side of the bed and to stretch out some of the kinks as he walked to his open window.

"*Rr-aaah*, rr-aaah, rr-aaah, rr-aaah." Something had set off the birds, and they called, raspy and high-pitched, from the tops of the trees out back. Hands propped on the sill, Dan looked out into the dark morning, trying to see beyond the parking lot. He had once gone walking back there in the daylight, and he knew there were several large, messy nests arranged in the tallest branches of whatever those overgrown trees were. If the birds were speaking to each other, Dan wished they would run out of things to say.

"Jesus, shut up," he whispered into the great, dark void and he pulled down the window, hard, making his point.

But closing the window didn't help much. The bird chatter and calls were only muffled, and the room was instantly stuffy.

Dan's head felt heavy. He was groggy enough to wonder if he had dreamed the last several hours, if maybe everything that was in his head right now was the product of REM sleep. But no, no dream. It had all happened. The painting. The phone call. The long conversation with Denise Healey.

Not long after he hung up with her, he'd finished the second coat of paint and rearranged the furniture. After that, he'd called Willa and asked her to apologize to Josh. "I won't make it tonight. This job is taking longer than I expected." A lie, but Healey's phone call had put him off balance and he'd needed time alone to think.

Willa had been very understanding. "It's fine. Josh can bring the paper into work tomorrow."

"Sure," Dan had said. "Tomorrow." But this had been another lie; tomorrow, she and Josh would be at the café, but he would be gone.

Standing in the middle of his small room, Dan thought of his last day at the bank. Sitting speechless at his desk, in shock at the sum on the check Julia Herron had slapped down in front of him—not because it was astronomical but because it was headed for the bank's bottom line and eventually his own pocket; the profits of someone's suffering. He had tried to offset this thought with another, more positive one—that at least Mrs. Herron would keep her business, something good to come out of the mess. But that thought hadn't been enough to distract him from how he'd benefited from his callous treatment of David Herron, and feelings of guilt had kept him anchored at his desk for the rest of the morning, staring into space, unable to work. He'd sat on through lunch and then through a scheduled meeting he should have attended. He'd sat and let the doubts and the shame creep in. And at four o'clock, he'd packed up his briefcase and left it all—the work, the life, even the money—for good.

Now it turned out that Mrs. Herron hadn't kept the business, that it was likely her father-in-law had usurped it. There was no bright side in the wake of all his failings, not even a glimmer. Dan wished he'd left the job sooner, or, better yet, that he'd never worked there at all. He wished so many things, and of course wishing was pointless. Past actions couldn't be changed, and they couldn't be expunged simply because he decided to try.

He left his spot at the window and went to the dresser, rooted around for a pair of clean socks, grabbed these and his sneakers, and sat down on the edge of the bed. His large duffel bag was close at hand, under the bed. Setting his things down, he bent over and pulled the empty and flattened bag from its storage place. Unused for all these months, it had collected dust bunnies. One or two floated into the air when he plopped the bag onto his lap and unzipped the flap.

Dan looked into the bag's black, empty inside and recalled the heft of the full bag slung over his shoulder, all the hours he'd put in on buses, everything he'd rejected along the way. Aimlessly, he started picking at the clumps of dust still stuck to the bag; he ran his thumbnail up and down the teeth of the zipper, approximating the sound the zip made each time he pulled it closed and hit the road, just another loner on the move.

Halfway to Bangor, Dan's eyelids and limbs began to feel heavy. His joints ached; his skin felt hot to the touch. By the time the bus reached the outskirts of the city, he was shivering and he knew he needed a room, not another bus connection.

It took all his effort to get up out of the seat when the bus reached the airport stop. He got off. The short walk to a cluster of cheap to mid-range hotels felt like walking toward the finish line of a marathon, but he made it. Once he checked into the cheapest available room, he hung the "do not disturb" sign and fell into bed to ride out the fever.

He spent the next few fitful days with the covers either pulled up around his shoulders or kicked down to the foot of the bed. Occasionally, he braved shaky legs to stumble to the bathroom, where he guzzled water straight from the tap. And in between were the dreams. Vivid ones. The ghostly egrets perched in the trees; the wind shaking their feather tufts when they took flight; the birds in flight, a line of them flying in circles above his head, dizzying him when he looked up. Below the circle, Dan spun with them until he was nauseated. Even then he couldn't stop looking at their beating wings, their bodies moving forward like missiles. They reminded Dan of Josh—his attempts at friendship, his sheer persistence.

After the birds, Josh visited his dreams, ones in which Dan was like his own father, showing the boy how to rewire a lamp or change out the plumbing under a sink or paint the walls for ML—all the skills his father had talked him through way back when. His father had possessed a lot of patience; maybe Dan was full of the same quiet deliberateness of effort. Although, he felt he gave up too easily. He knew he did.

In another dream, there was Josh again, his face red with frustration as he sat in a booth at ML's with a newspaper opened to a photo of himself with Dan and Willa. "Where are you?" he cried. "Why didn't you come? What did I do wrong?" When Dan put out his hand to comfort the boy, his reach fell short and Josh evaporated. Taking his place under Dan's hand was Julia Herron. "Take your fucking hand off me," she said, and Dan recoiled from her as if he'd touched a live wire. He rose above the scene this time, flying circles like the birds had. Those were the heavy front doors of his old workplace they stood in front of, the marble tiles of that building's lobby that they stood on. Her face was full of disgust; his, confusion. *Why doesn't she like me?* He opened his mouth to protest. "I am only doing my job. I am only making my living. I am only trying to live my life." As if he were underwater, his speech slowed, the vowels emerged muffled and flat. Could she understand him? "Please," he said. He reached out again but her arm disappeared, and this time when he drew his hand back, he held a glossy, blue-black feather.

When he looked up from the prize in his hands, Julia Herron was far away, a crow heading to the sun, unreachable.

In the hotel bed, under its scratchy blanket and perspiration-soaked sheets, Dan lifted a hand to his hot face. His eyes were closed, the lashes wet. These tears were the flu. They were the dream. No, they were regret.

13

"Tommy. Tom."

Denise tried to get her younger son's attention as they approached the school, but he was wearing earbuds and listening to loud music on his brand-new iPod—another gift from Matt and Heather in a summer full of Matt giving shiny objects, this one marking the start of Tommy's last year of high school. "Bribe," Denise had pronounced the iPod, until Joe suggested she should remember who her boy preferred spending time with, reminding her, "All the gifts in the world don't seem to change the fact that Tommy seems happiest with less 'stuff' and more time with you."

It was true, her son did prefer her house to his dad's, more so now that Teddy had moved into his college dorm. "I swear, all Dad and Heather talk about is their elliptical machine and their workouts," Tommy had told her more than once. At least the gifts he received were no longer oversize cash payments for help around the house, and Denise thanked God for that small favor. She was sure son number two had amassed quite a large sum of money before she and Matt had shut him down.

That brouhaha had subsided, as she had known it would once Matt's privacy was threatened. As she'd told Joe in the wake of the family discussion, "Matt loves to throw his weight around, but it was clear he didn't want a mopey high school senior ruining the groove in the love shack."

"The love shack." Joe had smiled at her. "What's this place, then?" He had made a broad sweep with his hand.

"A den of iniquity," she'd answered. "A part-time den of iniquity. The rest of the time"—she reached for the belt on his jeans, started working the buckle with her fingers—"it's home to one very straitlaced suburban mom."

Joe had helped her by removing his shirt, then hers. "Straitlaced? Tell me this mom wears glasses and her hair up in a bun. Because I find that very hot."

"You're living the fantasy," she'd whispered into his mouth before kissing him.

She smiled now, the attempt at getting Tommy's attention forgotten as she thought of the surprise of Joe—the second good thing in her life after her kids, and the one good thing in her life that belonged to her exclusively.

She hoped to be able to add work to that list soon. The summer, spent searching for and finding Daniel Hopper, had whetted her appetite for gainful employment. She hadn't told Joe yet, but she was working a job lead: an open position on a team specializing in corporate investigations. If hired, she would be starting on a bottom rung of their company ladder, but a rung gave her a foothold. She didn't mind starting over if the research work scratched her itch to investigate.

Lost in thought, she almost missed the turn onto Main Street. For once she was glad for the slow-moving cars and even for the iPod and Tommy's absorption in it. As she slowed for her left turn, she looked out the corner of her eye at her son, who was bobbing his head in time with the tinny, insistent beat she could hear pouring from the earbuds. To get his attention, she rapped him on the arm with her knuckles like she was knocking on a door.

"Hey," he objected as he lifted the earbuds away from his probably damaged eardrums.

"Start packing up. And leave your iPod in the car. You know the rules. It'll be in your room when you get home. Speaking of getting home"—she said as she made another left to pull into the drive—"you know I can't pick you up today. I have that first-round interview later. How about I swing by the grocery store on my way home? If the company likes me, we'll celebrate with a nice dinner, okay? Maybe ice cream for dessert?"

"No Joe?"

She shook her head. "Not for dinner. I may talk to him later tonight, though. Does that bother you?"

Tommy considered her question and then said, "No, Joe's all right."

She smiled. "I think so, too."

"And what if they don't like you? Are you going to be okay?"

She sensed a hint of the worry both Tommy and Teddy had carried following the worst months of her depression. She thought she would be okay now, but really, who knew what might sideline a person, and when? But to Tommy she said, "I'll be fine, promise. If they don't like me, we'll skip dinner and go straight to the quart of Brigham's chocolate chip."

He grinned. "Good. I'd rather have the ice cream anyway."

"Wise guy. You do your homework while you wait for me to get home. No phone, no computer, and no TV until after it's done. And no fooling around."

"What are you talking about?"

"You heard me. No monkey business. Of any kind."

"Yeah, yeah," he said under his breath.

When Denise pulled up to the curb, Tommy jumped out and threw her a back-of-the-hand wave without turning around. His usual smile was restored to his face by the time he greeted his group of friends. A few more months, that was all she had to get him through before he, like his brother, would be out in the world. She sighed and inched ahead with the flow of traffic exiting the horseshoe.

As Denise drummed on the steering wheel with her thumbs and waited, she looked around her at the traffic. There, heading down Main Street, was the large dark Mercedes she recognized as Mr. Herron's.

She felt the old pull of concern for Rennie, this time seasoned with a small amount of guilt. Once the summer vacation had rolled around, her unofficial monitoring of David Herron's daughter had paused. When she wasn't hanging with Joe and enjoying the strange but nice turn their relationship had taken or hard at work getting Teddy packed up for college, her time had been spent tracking down Daniel Hopper.

When the Mercedes stopped at the light, the passenger door of the sedan opened and Rennie jumped out. As the girl skirted stopped cars to reach the school lawn, Herron pulled over to the curb, got out of the driver's side door, and stood there. But, all he saw was what Denise saw: his granddaughter getting swallowed up by the crowd of young people mingling outside the school, enjoying their last few minutes of freedom and fresh air before class started.

The car behind Denise gave a loud honk, and she realized she'd missed the traffic moving forward a few car lengths. She inched up, then glanced back at Mr. Herron again. He remained parked, standing outside his door, his hip brushing up against the mirror. If he were watching to make sure his granddaughter got into the building, he must be frustrated. There was no way to tell. But the man's continued presence seemed like fate—not that she believed in such a thing. What she did believe in, however, was her intuition, and that was telling her to check him out. Instead of exiting straight for home, she turned left and left again and pulled up behind him.

"Mr. Herron, isn't it?" she said, leaving her car, her hand outstretched to shake his. "How are you?"

Herron turned at the greeting but didn't offer his hand in return. "I'm sorry, I can't place you. You are?"

"It's been a while. Denise Healey. Detective Healey. I worked your son's disappearance." Denise watched his face, and he frowned. Yes, he remembered now, remembered not liking her questions. He was also confused; Denise could read that in his eyes.

He opened his mouth to speak but paused. "I don't understand," he said after a few seconds. "What do you need to talk to me about? Are there some new . . . discoveries, or . . ."

"Oh no, sir. This is completely coincidental. I just dropped off my son, looked over, and saw you and your granddaughter. Thought I'd say hello. How is Rennie?"

"She is very well," he said. "You say your son is in school here? You must live in town."

"He is. A senior. And I do, not too far from here actually." Denise turned her head and looked back over her shoulder in the general direction of nowhere special. Let him think she lived close enough to see him all the time.

"Rennie got out of the car in a hurry this morning," she continued. "Kids. My son does that too, jumps out before the car has stopped moving. Sometimes they act without thinking, especially these first few days back, when everything is so chaotic. Speaking of which, I hope you all had a nice summer? The weather was decent."

Herron narrowed his eyes. She'd made it clear she was observing him with his grandchild, and now his earlier confusion gave way to caginess. "Is there a point to these questions, Detective?"

Denise laughed a light laugh. "Oh no, making conversation, that's all. And it's not 'Detective' anymore. I'm in the middle of changing jobs—careers, really. After years of policing, I'm moving into private investigation, go figure." Behind her back she crossed her fingers and hoped she wasn't jinxing herself by pretending to be hired before it was a done deal. "Looking into fraud and all kinds of deceptions. Should be interesting."

If she had blinked, Denise would have missed the flicker of worry in Herron's eyes, as if he wasn't sure if she were talking about her new job or something else altogether.

She had rattled him, but only briefly. Within seconds, he composed himself.

"Investigations need people who can be discreet and rational," he said, "and I seem to remember you're the police officer who didn't keep her cool when speaking to my family in those days after my son's . . . disappearance."

"You remember correctly."

There was another flicker in his eyes—surprise this time. He must have expected defensiveness.

"For the record," she added, "I'm sorry about that. While it was my job to ask difficult questions at difficult times, I should have been more sensitive. I hope I've learned from that experience." She smiled. "You know, it's funny what owning responsibility will do for a person. Take me, for example. Owning responsibility for the way I acted has prompted me to look back over that entire case. Your son, his wife, Rennie—they deserve that kind of review." She dipped her head. "You have a good day, now." She started for her car.

"Ms. Healey."

She turned around.

"But it's not your job anymore, is it? Reviewing the case, asking difficult questions at difficult times?"

Denise smiled at him. He had scored a point or two in their volley. But he had not taken the game. Not at all. "Oh, you know what they say about old habits. Have a good day," she repeated, her smile grown bigger, and she went for her car for real this time.

Well, now, she thought, watching as Mr. Herron got into his luxury car and drove off. *That was interesting.*

14

Sun streamed in through the large windows and reflected off the metal-and-glass surfaces of the bakery's display cases and counters, temporarily blinding Jules. For over two years now, she and Tony Montanara had been engaged in a daily standoff over who would lower the front window shades against the full afternoon sun. Being blinded by the glare wasn't the worst of it. Amplified by all the glass, the sunlight softened the buttercream icing on the cupcakes in the display case, and by the afternoon the painstakingly piped-on decorative peaks and swirls slumped. Jules had once suggested that the person within reach of the shades at the moment the sun began beating in should draw them, but Tony wouldn't be persuaded.

Her father-in-law had coaxed Tony out of semi-retirement from a nearby, long-established bakery for his expertise at running what Paul called "a tight ship." Since then, Tony had applied his previous bakery's success with streamlining production to operations at the Welcome Home, and in his world, his expertise didn't include drawing blinds. This role was beneath him.

It was not, however, beneath Jules or the afternoon counter help, all females, and all of whom he bossed around. Tony was an unabashed misogynist who was convinced his anatomy disqualified him from carrying out menial tasks. If Jules wanted the blinds lowered, and if she wanted to avoid a lecture about melted frosting, she knew to suck up her frustration with Tony and resign herself to doing the task.

On this Tuesday afternoon, she walked to the window without comment, passing Tony as he tinkered with the vent he had taken apart and tried to fix the week before. The man was cheap. He hated using a repair service, calling outside help a waste of good money—which Jules didn't get, considering it wasn't *his* money. But his unskilled repair efforts made problems worse. She suspected he had reassembled the parts incorrectly the previous week or had forgotten to put a vital piece back in altogether because the vent hadn't worked properly since. As she watched him, sweat beaded up on his forehead and the back of his neck. Between that and the sight of his stubby, meaty fingers fumbling with the filters, Jules had to look away.

At the window, she pulled on the chain until the shade rolled all the way down. Through the small gap between shade and window frame, Jules could see the sun's light bouncing off metal light poles and signposts, car windshields, and silver front-end bumpers. It was a beautiful day, but the reflected light seared her retinas, making the people standing at the bus stop look like black silhouettes. She blinked to try to adjust her eyesight.

Behind her, Tony hollered, "Whaddaya waiting for, Christmas? Back to work!"

Tony had a bunch of motivational one-liners like this in his repertoire: "Cupcakes don't get baked by themselves." "You're as slow as molasses in January." "Daydreaming is all right for poets." If there was anyone less likely than Tony to know what poets did or didn't do, Jules hadn't met them. She ignored him and stayed at the front window, now shading her eyes with her hand. Peeking out, she could see another world going on beyond her own, one she wished to escape to. She sighed and dropped her shoulders.

Just as she was preparing to turn back to the counter and her work, the outlines of two figures across the street caught her eye. Her eyesight was still impaired, and she blinked until the shape of one began to reveal some female curves, dressed in baggy trousers that might have been chef issue—Mai, she assumed, out in front of her restaurant. Next to her stood a male figure, but he wasn't tall enough to be Mai's partner, Leo. Where Leo was lanky and slightly bowlegged from standing on his feet in the kitchen for years, this man's shape revealed a less active life, from a slight paunch to a backside that didn't quite fill the seat of his pants. A common middle aged type. David's type. Jules heard a familiar buzzing in her ears as a building anger made her heart race. She hadn't yet made it through a day without being reminded of David, meaning she hadn't yet made it through a day without feeling near-murderous rage.

She hadn't anticipated such anger on the day she trudged through heavy, damp sand to reach Charlie, who, as shell-shocked as she was, held David's watch in one hand and a gray jacket in the other. The day had been cold, and Jules had shivered as a persistent wind blew into her. She'd listened as Charlie spoke but struggled to understand what he was telling her, repeating over and over, "This makes no sense," and interrupting the flow of his narrative. The policeman who had arrived on the boardwalk minutes before her had cleared his throat and asked her to refrain for a minute while he took Charlie's statement of the events of the morning.

As Charlie spoke, another officer, all business in a fitted blazer, had left the unit fanned out across the beach and approached them. In her hands was a plastic bag holding a pair of shoes: wet, sandy, but identifiable as David's. When Jules saw these, she'd reached for Charlie, but she'd lost her footing and fallen against him; she'd felt him encircle her with his arms to lift her up, his knuckles grinding into her spine. Then she'd broken down, knowing in that moment that David was gone.

The shock and grief had lasted less than forty-eight full hours. It had changed to incredulity as Jules learned about the events that had led to David's disappearance: The second mortgage and the huge building loans. How he had started to beg the bank for more money, how he'd ended up begging them for more time. She'd learned about that one when the bank's chief loan officer called their home number just after breakfast on day two to void David's request for a loan extension because he had not shown up for their scheduled meeting. Not that his presence would have mattered. When she'd asked to speak to the bank president for some clarity about what was going on, the underling had told her, "There are no more extensions—there's no more money. It's the same thing I've told your husband for weeks now, only he won't take no for an answer."

The exchange had left her humiliated but also, for the first time, aware of the circumstances David had put them in. She finally knew why the plastic tarp hung frayed and opaque with wear, why the contractor had walked away from the job site, why he had argued with David on the street, out of earshot. Why, in particular, David had been testy and secretive and dismissive of her offers of help. Why he had misrepresented her to their staff, and why he'd hidden everything he told them from her. By the end of that second day, she had cycled past grief to outposts of shame and mortification before arriving finally at anger. And there she had stayed since, with Tony her daily reminder of how much her life and her work had changed because of David's bad judgment and deceit. If she ever longed for her husband, for how he had once listened, or for the feel of the length of his body on hers, all she had to do was look at Tony and any tenderness she felt hardened.

"Come on!" Tony said, a sneer in his voice.

Jules jumped. He had crept up behind her, his mouth was close to her ear.

"The cupcakes won't take themselves out of the oven."

She clenched her hands into fists. She knew if she didn't get some air right then, she might actually punch Tony. Instead of swinging, she turned and hissed, "You get them. I need some fresh air," and then she pushed through the front door and stepped onto the sidewalk, letting the door swing shut behind her.

Now what? she asked herself. In that moment, she understood why people smoked. Cigarettes probably had been invented by someone who needed her hands safely occupied to keep from strangling another person.

Across the street, Mai was alone now, sweeping the sidewalk of the cigarette butts and cast-off candy wrappers that accumulated there every day. With no David to sweep obsessively in front of the bakery anymore, Paul now paid a guy with a leaf blower to come a couple of times a week to clear the sidewalk and back lot. In between his visits, the storefront looked like crap. David would have hated that.

Stop it, she told herself.

As Jules stood a moment longer, considering her next move, Mai looked up from her task, smiled, and waved. "Come say hi!"

Jules nodded. The pleasure of talking with a civilized human being might eclipse her foul mood. The lights changed, and she took a step into the crosswalk. Behind her, the bells on the bakery door jingled wildly. She turned to the noise and froze with one foot in the street and one still on the curb.

Tony stood in the doorway. "The timer is ringing!"

She stared at him. "You're kidding, right? You passed the timer to come out here and get me to turn it off? I said I was taking a break."

"And I said the cupcakes need to come out of the oven. You want burned cake, that's on you. Explain it to the customers. Explain it to your father-in-law."

"You're serious?"

Tony didn't bother replying. He went back inside, pulling the door closed behind him.

As Jules stared after him, she heard the walk signal begin to peal its warning that she had missed her chance to cross. She could wait for the next light and hope Tony was bluffing.

What was she thinking? Tony never bluffed.

"I'm sorry," she called back to Mai. "An emergency. Later?"

"Sure," Mai returned. "Any time."

Jules raised a hand, gave a thumbs-up. Feeling defeated, it was all she could muster.

"Stupid man," she said under her breath as she headed to the bakery's front door.

There were some bright spots that made this arrangement tolerable, she reminded herself as she went back inside. Among all the horrible surprises she'd received in the wake of David's death, some good had emerged. Unexpectedly, she had developed a better relationship with Paul and Miriam. Not perfect, but better. With David gone, the depth and breadth of his financial missteps revealed, she had faced certain bankruptcy. Instead, her in-laws had stepped in to bail her out. It had taken her by surprise when Paul had asked to meet before she gave the go-ahead to her lawyer to file the court paperwork. "You don't want the financial implications of bankruptcy dogging you for years," he had said when she sat down with him, "and I have a proposition."

Telling her he was looking for a way to keep active in smart investment opportunities, he'd handed her a big check that would allow her to pay off the debt David had accrued, saying he wanted to buy into the business. There were conditions, he said, words that set off alarm bells, but Jules had agreed to listen. What he'd proposed was this: He would install himself as managing business partner, with full rights to make decisions about daily operations, the first being the shift to baking cupcakes. He would wall off the adjacent storefront, which was the largest driver of the debt, and sell the space. There would be no café. And Jules would need to put her large house on the market to begin to address the second mortgage that had been propping up the bakery's operations for years, another nasty surprise. "You've never actually made much profit," her father-in-law had told her, "but that will change." He'd then told her about Tony, a man he'd assured her would help the bakery transition from making quality pastries and good bread to churning out trendy cupcakes. Weekend visits from his granddaughter rounded out his list of conditions.

Amid so much instability and ground down by feelings of betrayal, Jules had accepted.

Her new reality was now a full week of work. All five weekdays were spent working alongside the tyrant, from early morning to midafternoon, and on the weekends she worked alone for a few hours in the late afternoons, mixing together cheaper ingredients than she liked to use to make batters and icings and fillings to prep for use during the week. All seven days, she worked for an hourly wage—generous enough, but it still amounted to less per week than she and David had paid Sandy.

Her salary was the only point she had argued. "We did better by Sandy," she'd said.

"Yes," Paul had reminded her, "and look where that got you. It's belt-tightening time.

"But don't worry. I'll match what you make and set that aside in an account that you can eventually combine with any savings you put aside to buy me out. You'll be an owner again one day."

By accepting his plan, Jules could begin to claw her way back to something like a normal life for herself and, more importantly, for Rennie. Propping up the partnership was the understanding that everyone in the family was pulling together to provide Rennie the stability and routines she needed. And the arrangement was working. Rennie spent weekends with her grandparents—most recently the holiday long weekend—and Paul did the school drop-off at the start of each week. It seemed as if old grievances were being repaired. Jules reminded herself of their progress when Tony was at his most trying.

She hustled over to the ovens and turned off the buzzing timer. She shook her head. This example of Tony's pigheadedness made her resolve to talk to Paul about the work environment. She would ask him to set aside some time this weekend to discuss boundaries and other ways to make the kitchen run better. With Rennie there, he would be in a more receptive mood. Maybe she could even convince him to let Tony go and allow her to hire someone else. She thought of the old days, working with Sandy; she was now established at one of the bigger artisan bread bakeries and was, by all accounts, happy, but maybe she could be lured back.

Jules started pulling cupcake pans out of the oven and laying them on her bench to cool. When they were all out, she went to close the oven door and it slipped from her grip and banged shut, dislodging the vent cover Tony had attached only a few minutes earlier. The metal rectangle clattered to the floor, and Tony shot her a dirty look from across the room as she picked it up and tried to secure it back in place.

She reached up and flipped the power switch. The fan screeched to life and then died, and then the cover fell off again.

"We really need to call a professional," she said. "It's not working properly."

"What did you do to that thing?" Tony pushed his way over. "I had that fixed."

"Tony, the cover was barely attached, and that's only the beginning of the problem. I'm calling the service number." She started for the phone.

"They'll charge a fortune. I'll look at it again after I finish what I'm doing." He gave a dismissive wave and returned to his work.

Jules wasn't about to let him have another go. He would likely turn it into a fire hazard if it wasn't already. She shuddered and picked up the cordless on the way back to her bench. "How about I call Charlie?"

Tony never argued about calling Charlie, since he offered his help for free. With any luck, he might have time to stop over later that day. Or if not, then tomorrow morning, before he headed to his gym. Charlie was handier than Tony, almost as good with the equipment as David used to be, and he didn't mind pitching in.

"I'm always here for you, Jules," he had told her in the days following the disappearance. If she tolerated the arrangement with her in-laws, she truly welcomed the continued contact with Charlie. He was present and steady. "You'd give me the support I needed if something happened to Lexi. David would have, too."

Jules couldn't tell Charlie that she would never again be sure of David's ability to help in a crisis. After all, he had given up on his own miserable situation and left his mess to others to sort out. But Charlie continued to blame himself for not reaching David at the coffee shop in time to talk him out of his despair. Why would she burden Charlie even more with her own cynicism? She kept her mouth shut and accepted the help.

Charlie didn't answer. Jules left a message. If he showed up today, great. If not, maybe she could figure out how to disable the circuit breaker to the vent. Then Tony could tinker to his heart's content without burning the place to the ground.

After reviewing the class curriculum and the quiz and test schedules, the computer lab teacher set aside the last fifteen minutes of class for quiet keyboarding practice—busy work for a warm afternoon after a long weekend. As long as Ms. Murray saw fingers flying across the keys, she was satisfied that everyone was logging their practice time. While many of the kids used the time to do what was expected of them, others sneaked looks at books hidden on their laps or did homework, and more than a few instant-messaged friends who were in other classes or study periods.

The way Rennie figured, sending rapid-fire messages to her best friend, Gigi, did constitute keyboard practice, and it was the best way for them to stay in touch. Rennie didn't have a computer at home. It was an expense, her mother said after they moved to the dingy downtown apartment and their old desktop died, they could no longer afford. But she got an hour in almost every day at the public library, and on weekends she had unlimited time on her grandfather's computer. And there was also this small amount of time in computer lab when her schedule meshed with Gigi's and they could chat for a few minutes, despite Gigi being a few hours away in Northampton.

The girls had messaged back and forth since the day near the end of eighth grade that Gigi found out her parents were divorcing and she and her sisters would be moving out of the town where she had grown up to be closer to extended family. They were packed and gone before that summer was in full swing.

Gigi said Rennie was lucky that when she moved, she at least got to stay in town, but Rennie didn't feel lucky. Her mother worked too much, and her only friend was miles away. She missed her dad—the way he read to her, listened to her, knew when she needed an ice cream, knew exactly the right thing to say; she missed their old life as a family and regretted that she hadn't been able to apologize to him for being a brat on the morning he drove off and never returned. The guilt was heavy. If she had been better, less mouthy, less demanding, would he have come home that day instead of . . . well, instead of what he did? She had no one to ask. There was no one to confide in that she felt that her dad's suicide was her fault. Her mother was hardly home, and besides, she didn't want to talk about Rennie's feelings. "The past is the past and we'll only look forward," she'd said over and over, and she was true to her word. They no longer talked about her dad at all, none of the bad stuff and none of the good memories, either, as if that were the key to moving on.

It didn't help that many of the kids she used to call her friends now acted as if she had a contagious disease. Since the day the story of her father's suicide was printed in the newspaper, many had stopped talking to her. Other kids, ones who'd never liked her all that much to begin with, were outright hostile. They called him loser and coward and embezzler, confusing his inability to pay back the money he borrowed for the bakery with stealing money from the bakery.

To this day, those kids were still ignorant and mean. And on the days when Rennie needed someone to walk home with, someone to give her courage out on the sidewalks, where most of the taunting happened, there was no one. Long-distance support couldn't give her a hug or sit on her bed for hours, giggling over silly things.

Gigi had been begging Rennie to visit since she moved, and Rennie had promised she would. Some days, it was only the idea of visiting Northampton that kept her going. The problem was finding money for a ticket. They had no money, or that's what her mother always said. "No, I can't replace the computer because I have no money"; "No to the UGGs, I'm sorry." But she longed to be away from this place where nothing happened and no one liked her, this place full of reminders of a life that had ended and wasn't coming back. As the last minutes of class ticked away, she wrote to Gigi, "I will visit. Soon! Still trying to get bus money."

U come to see me? Squee! :D <3<3<3

Will make j say yes

Yay! My mom can ask her if it helps.

Cool! Maybe! Oops murray says time to shut down.

Stinx, talk l8r?

U know it l8r xoxo

Rennie quickly logged out and cleared the computer's browser history. She glanced at the clock. The bell would ring in a minute, and after dismissal she'd have three minutes to get to study hall. If she ran from this class, she could stop at her locker and get the books and supplies she needed for organizing her subject binders during the free period. If there were time after that, she would use it to make solid travel plans.

Still, the ticket's cost: the problem she couldn't solve. Rennie began biting her thumbnail. At the end of the previous year, Rennie had thought she'd found a way to get the money she needed. There was an older boy in school who other kids whispered about as someone who loaned cash to all the poor kids. It had taken her days, but she'd worked up the courage to ask him for help. She had barely finished the request when he'd handed over forty bucks. It had seemed so easy, the ticket she wanted to buy within reach. But she'd had the money less than two days when he'd stopped by her locker again to tell her that when she was able to pay him back, she would not only owe him the forty but also another four dollars in interest.

"Interest?" Her face had burned with embarrassment. If she could have afforded to pay him back with interest, she wouldn't have needed to borrow money in the first place. Then there was the added shame of being stupid enough to fall into the same kind of deal that had gotten her father in trouble.

The next time the kid approached her she'd been ready for him, waving the bills in his face. She was down to a dollar and forty-nine cents to her name, but she didn't care. There was no way she was going into debt—although according to the kid, she already was.

"Thanks. You still owe me the four bucks, but you can pay me any time," he'd said, smiling, as if he were unaware of how angry she was.

"I didn't even have this money for forty-eight hours," she'd snapped.

The boy had shrugged. "That's the way loans work."

As if she didn't already know that.

Fast-forward these few months, she was still short the four dollars needed to repay the interest and was no closer to purchasing a bus ticket. She had vowed to babysit, but so far, she had no clients. Even Charlie and Lexi wouldn't hire her. No one wanted a fourteen-year-old babysitter with no experience.

Well, then, if she couldn't earn the money for a bus ticket, she would think of another way. Maybe Gramps and Grandma would give her cash for both her birthday and Christmas instead of clothes. She could start dropping hints next weekend, telling her grandfather she wanted to start putting money into a savings account or investing in stock. He loved that sort of stuff. On the other hand, once she told him she was interested in banking, he would surely ask for updates about how her money was growing. Or "compounding," as he liked to say. However, when he found out she planned to spend it on a trip to visit a friend, he wouldn't be pleased. When Gramps wasn't lecturing about savings or the stock market, he had a lot to say about people who made bad money decisions.

The bell rang. Rennie gathered her things in seconds and followed the crowd out into the hall. As she made her way to her locker, she heard someone call her name, and she turned. No, it couldn't be.

"Hey," Tom Healey said, catching up to her.

"I still don't have your money," Rennie said. Out of nervous habit, she brought her thumb to her mouth again and started chewing the cuticle. Since he had stopped hounding her, she'd assumed he had forgotten and she was safe.

"You shouldn't do that," the boy said, and he pointed at her thumb in her mouth.

Rennie backed away from him and frowned. "What do you care, anyway?"

He smiled. "I care about a lot of things."

"Jerk." The word fell out of her mouth, and, though she shocked herself with her boldness, she didn't apologize.

Instead of being offended, he laughed out loud. His loud bark caught the attention of one of the teachers monitoring the hall.

"Mr. Healey, you are supposed to be moving on to your next class."

"Yes, sir." To Rennie, he whispered, "Which way are you going? Let's walk."

Rennie balked.

"Please. I need to talk to you." He reached for her arm.

Rennie dodged his grasp. "I'll go, but don't touch me."

He put up his hands in surrender. "Hey, it's cool. I only want to get away from Pritchard in a hurry. Lead the way."

"Whatever." Rennie started walking, but as soon as they rounded the corner at the end of the hall, she stopped. "Well? What is it?"

"My parents found out I was lending money," Tom said, "and they made me stop. My mom told me I needed to forgive all the outstanding loans, so that's what I'm here to tell you. You don't owe me the interest anymore. And I can give you the forty bucks back, too, no strings attached." He pulled two twenties from his pocket.

Rennie hesitated.

"I'm serious, they're yours," he urged.

The warning bell rang just then. Rennie had thirty seconds to get to her class and zero time to detour to her locker first. But she didn't care. The news had been worth it; she was one step closer to Gigi. She took the money from Tom and hitched her backpack high on her shoulder. "Thanks."

"Yeah, no problem," Tom said. "What will you do with the money?"

Rennie started to hand the money back. "If telling you is part of the deal, then—"

"It isn't." Tom tucked his hands in his pockets. "Please. Take it. I was just making conversation because all this feels awkward."

Rennie gave a little nod. "I'm not doing anything stupid with it. I need the money for a ticket to go visit a friend."

"Oh, cool. Something fun. You deserve it. With everything you've gone through—you know, with your dad and—"

"I've got to go." Rennie turned and walked away, determined not to give Tom Healey the satisfaction of seeing her red face or the tears pooling in her eyes.

"The back of your shirt," Jules said, pointing. "You got into some flour."

"Huh?" Charlie turned his head and tried to look over his shoulder. "Where?"

"Down here, silly," she said, and she brushed away a white stripe at the middle of his back. "The stuff is everywhere, even where you think it wouldn't be. Clothing covered with flour is my occupational hazard." She pulled a stool out from under her worktable. "Sit. How about a cup of coffee?"

Without waiting for an answer, she circled around him and walked away. In her wake, Charlie smelled vanilla.

He did as he was told and sat, although the wooden stool was uncomfortable. He had been crouching even more uncomfortably while standing on a small ladder under the bakery's vent hood, and stretching now would be better than sitting. But there was coffee on offer, and a chance to talk to Jules for a bit before he hit the road. He would stretch as soon as he got to work.

Maybe the discomfort had little to do with the stool, he thought, left on his own to look around. It continued to be difficult to come into the bakery kitchen. He still expected to see David at the cash register or coming out of the storeroom and felt the jolt of disappointment when he saw the buffoonish baker that Paul had hired instead. Tony. The guy strutted around like he was king or a god, even though he was too stocky and unfit to be even remotely godlike. Gods didn't often find themselves out of breath after lifting a bucket of cake frosting.

Even worse, Tony was a boor who thought he knew everything about everything. His quick "fix" of the vent had included reassembling some parts in the wrong sequence, tossing out an essential piece of the motor, and pinching and damaging a wire. Jules had been smart to disable the breaker to the vent yesterday afternoon; if not for her, the whole place might have gone up in flames. The best Charlie had been able do was disassemble the fan and disconnect and cap the crimped wiring. As he waited for the cup of coffee, he looked through his wallet for a business card. Jules needed a professional fix. Once he had the right phone number, he set down the wallet and reached in his back pocket for his phone. Unlike Tony, he knew when a job was beyond him.

"All set. My vent guy will be over tomorrow morning," he said when Jules reappeared.

"You're the best." She handed him a paper cup fitted with a travel lid and protective sleeve. "In case you need to drink and run."

"Thanks. I can stay for a bit. Sit down with me?"

Tony walked up as Jules pulled out a second stool for herself. "Heh. Coffee break?"

"Yes, Tony, coffee break," she said, her eyes tracking him as he approached the table. "Consider this our thank-you to Charlie. Nice of him to come over this morning and look at the vent for free, isn't it?"

Charlie lifted the cup to his lips to hide a smile. Idiot, he thought, prowling around them like an alpha male. On a whim, he stood and stretched, towering over Tony. "Needed that after crouching for the past hour." He clapped Tony on the back. "Call me the next time you get the urge to take anything apart, okay fella?"

"Ha-ha . . . okay, fella," Tony said, but his laugh was hollow. "Since it's break time, I'll be outside having a cigarette."

As soon as he disappeared out the back door, Charlie took his seat again, looked at Jules, and dissolved into laughter.

She smiled back but shook her head. "Now imagine working with him every day. I dare you."

"What a blowhard. How much longer before you can send him packing?"

Jules shrugged. "I think maybe this time next year? Eighteen months, maybe? I should be in a position to pay off the loan by then. Then I can ditch the cupcakes and get back to making some decent pastry. And no more Tony. Yay," she added, but there was no cheer in her voice.

Charlie reached for her hand and squeezed it.

"I'm fine," she said. "Tired of him"—she tipped her chin at the back door—"and tired of all of this, sometimes. But yes, it's good to see the end of the road. And really, Paul's kept us up and running, and I suppose he didn't have to. I'm only feeling . . . I don't know. Pressure?" She turned her head and looked out the window. "Pressure to turn things around and get us out of this mess as soon as possible."

"You know." Charlie rubbed his thumb across the palm of her hand, feeling her calluses, watching her fingers contract reflexively around his. "We've come a long way since . . . since that April morning. Every day, we get up, we take one more step forward, even when it's hard. Don't forget that."

She nodded.

"Now that you're so close to the end of this arrangement, it makes sense you're impatient. But it'll happen. Try to take it easy on yourself, if you can."

Jules closed her eyes, and Charlie felt her relax a little. He'd done a lot of handholding, literal and figurative, in the past two years. Not that he minded; staying connected to Jules mattered to him. He couldn't risk losing more of the people he thought of as his family.

In that moment of quiet, as Jules rested and he sipped his coffee, he saw himself back on the beach, felt his heart race as he took in the hectic scene: a German shepherd jumping from the back of a cop car, that female cop leaving the shoreline with a plastic bag pinched between her forefinger and thumb, the bright blue gloves she was wearing the only spot of color in the dreary day. So much came back to him: the steady hum of the ocean, the shouts of the searchers at work, the dog's barks when he alerted; inside him, feelings of fatigue, despair, and confusion; and then the wind, too, constant and unrelenting. And the questions, a hail of them: "Can you take me through your morning from six o'clock on?" "Do you know why your friend set up this meeting with you?" "Any disagreements between you two recently?" "Do you know if he had disagreements with anyone?" "Was there anything in the phone call—noises in the background, voices—anything that seemed out of place?" "What was Mr. Herron's tone?"

"Do you have to ask all these questions right now? You're wasting time! Please stop and find my husband!" Jules had growled in frustration and took off in the direction of the water.

The detective paused only a moment. "Sir? Anything you remember from the call?"

"You've got to excuse me," Charlie had said, going after her.

Jules had made it as far as the strip mall before Charlie caught up to her in front of the Rite-Aid. She kept her back turned to him.

"Whatever you're about to say," she said, "I don't want to hear it. We need to find him. I might kill him for scaring us like this, but we need to find him."

"Jules." Charlie had reached then for her hand. "It's best if we stay put. David will turn up."

But he hadn't.

Clues had turned up in the days and weeks that followed. The dog walker who had spoken to both men had come forward and proven helpful. Her encounter with David had backed up Charlie's account and offered clues to David's state of mind. Once the bank officials contacted Jules and added their information about the finances, David's state of mind had been clearer. And then some body parts had washed up on shore, and they'd been identified as David's through DNA matching.

With discovery upon discovery, Charlie had been flattened by his guilt. How much of this could he have stopped if he had made it to the beach on time? What if he had been a better friend, the kind of friend that David might have confided in from the start? How had he not seen signs of a problem?

"Because he chose to mislead you," Lexi had answered him back then.

At the time, Lexi's voice had startled him. Charlie hadn't realized he was worrying the same questions aloud over and over, hadn't even remembered she was there with him. Then, he'd been unwilling to place all the blame on David, had still been upset with himself, and Lexi, too. *Those minutes you held me up in my office? I can never get them back.*

But no. He'd stopped himself from thinking those things, he'd buried the resentment to focus instead on his responsibilities. That was his daughter in there, he had thought with a look at Lexi's newly swelling belly, and the best thing he could do going forward was exactly what David had failed to do. He could and would stay present. For Lexi and the baby. For Rennie and Jules.

Charlie returned to the present and patted Jules's hand gently.

Her eyes opened. "Oh. I think I nodded off for a couple of minutes. I'm so embarrassed." She brought her hands to her cheeks.

"Don't be. You're tired. Fact of life these days, for all of us."

"Seriously, that was rude," she said. "How are Lexi and the baby? Lark's teething still keeping you up at night?"

"Nah, both girls are great," Charlie said as he looked down into his coffee cup, fiddling with the travel lid, avoiding Jules's eyes. He was ashamed to admit that, despite his promises, he saw so little of his family that on some days he only saw Lark in the mornings, and even then only long enough to pass her off to the sitter as he and Lexi left for work. Lately, Lexi had begun to push back at his time away from home, especially when that time was spent in Jules's company. Like this morning.

"Hey," he said with a look at his watch, "I should go. Work beckons." He stood. "Tell the vent guy to yell at Tony a little bit. Guy deserves it." He took a step away, then backtracked, leaned down, and kissed Jules on the cheek. "I haven't forgotten about hanging those bookshelves for Rennie. I'll call you and set up a time to come over. Maybe this Sunday would work?"

"Rennie will be thrilled to see you. She'll be at Paul and Miriam's until Sunday afternoon. If you come then, you can stay for supper."

"Sunday it is."

Jules stood and stretched. "We'd love Lexi and Lark, too."

Charlie nodded. "Thanks. I'll tell Lex."

She studied him. "Are you sure you're getting enough rest yourself? Really, Rennie and I can tackle the shelves."

She was standing close enough that he could smell her vanilla scent again. He lingered, enjoyed it a bit longer. "You smell good," he said. "You always do. Vanilla."

She gave him a crooked smile. "Funny that you'd notice."

"I notice." He started to return the smile but then the back door opened and slammed shut, hard, as Tony came in from his smoke break, and they both took a step backward, putting some space between them.

"I'll confirm Sunday as soon as possible," Charlie said, his face warm.

Jules nodded, and he strode to the front door and pushed his way outside.

The fall air felt cool and refreshing on his face after the close heat of the bakery, and Charlie stopped to take a deep breath before heading to his car. The kitchen's spell of warmth and close air and hushed conversation made with heads leaned in broke the minute he inhaled, although he imagined he could still smell the vanilla. "You smell good." Had he actually said that? Yes, the words had tumbled from a mouth operating without its usual filter, revealing a state of mind that he was trying to ignore. Jules had smiled, though. A little. Maybe she'd been pleased—or maybe confused. They had been interrupted before whatever was going on between them became clear. What was clear, however, was how sharp Lexi's instincts were. She wanted him to make some space between himself and Jules, and he knew he should.

Charlie sighed, guilt piling on top of guilt, as he climbed into his car. When the door closed behind him, those guilty thoughts filled the space around him. Failing David when he needed help the most, trying to take David's place in Jules's life as he neglected his own family, not loving Lexi enough. Not loving her at all, really. Charlie knew if David had not died, had not plunged himself into the ocean that day, he would not have asked Lexi to marry him once, let alone the half-dozen times he had. She would have been the mother of his child always, but the affair itself would have sputtered and died, like every other relationship he'd ever fallen into had eventually sputtered and died.

But he had to try and sustain his relationship with Lexi, now more than ever because there was Lark. With her, there was no more walking away, not even when the scent of vanilla stayed with him and made him want to bury his face in Jules's hair and breathe her in. He had to be a good father, a responsible parent with and partner to Lexi, a support for Rennie when she needed it, and only—*only*—Jules's friend. He had to remain fucking focused.

With that clear, he looked in his side mirror and pulled out into traffic to make his way to work.

It had been a brisk day at the bakery, but business dwindled in the late afternoon. In preparation for closing, Jules enlisted the counter staff, two high school girls, in wiping down the display case glass while she tackled the trays of leftovers. The few cupcakes that remained unsold were tucked into plastic clamshell boxes and refrigerated, ready for tomorrow's day-old shelf. Tony's early calculation of receipts showed that it had been a profitable morning, and he gloated. But once he no longer had the math to obsess over, he focused on micromanaging the young women, pointing out smudges on the glass and crumbs left behind on the shelves.

"Girls, you're too slow. Did your mothers teach you nothing?"

As Jules turned from packing up food to cleaning up the last few utensils left in the sink, she opened up the tap full blast and hoped it would drown out his nagging. On average, the high school help tolerated six months of Tony's temper, just long enough to learn a few marketable skills—running the cash register, making small talk with customers—before finding another job and jumping. Jules always gave the ones who quit a glowing reference for their next employers. Part of her feared lawsuits down the road. Even the most incompetent lawyer could argue this was a hostile workplace. When Jules tried explaining this to Tony, he dismissed part-time employees as easily replaced. "You'd rather pamper them? Wake up. They have no real stake in this shop," he said, "and we might as well make them work hard while they are here."

Although she knew better, Jules tried to make him see her point. "It doesn't hurt to be nice to the kids. I find we get more loyalty from people if they feel valued rather than exploited."

"And that's how come all your people stayed when the bakery was failing, huh?"

In almost every conversation, Tony circled back to some aspect of her failure.

Rachel had jumped ship quickly, but Sandy hadn't wanted to leave. Likewise Florence. However, the recession had hit hard. They'd needed reliable hours, lots of them. At the time, Jules hadn't been sure she would be able to offer steady work again. Besides, Paul had wanted to take things in a different direction: part-time workers. To him, the high school students were ideal. There was an endless supply looking for summer or after-school work, and he could pay them less and not have to offer health insurance. So Jules had bitten her tongue and tried to be grateful for the staff she was given.

Jules also tried to turn a deaf ear to Tony's nagging most days, but today she couldn't. She turned off the taps. "Do you have to raise your voice to get your point across?"

Tony stopped mid-tirade and turned his angry eyes in her direction. "What did you say?"

"I said, do you have to be so loud? I think the girls can hear you just fine." Emboldened, she continued. "And if we had a customer in here right now, I'd be embarrassed." She looked at the girls. "Jess, Izzy, why don't you call it a day? The cases look ready enough for the morning. Bring me your timecards. I'll sign you out for the full hour."

"Thanks, Jules!" The two young women couldn't remove their aprons fast enough. As Izzy led the way to the back rooms, she kicked something lying on the floor near the baker's bench, and it skidded across the tiles until it was stopped by the back wall. When she caught up to the object, she retrieved it and held it up to Jules. "Someone's wallet," she said.

Jules walked over and took it. "Oh. It's Charlie's. Thanks, I'll make sure he gets it. Now, timecards," she reminded them.

On the other side of the display case, Tony shook with suppressed rage. Jules avoided looking at him and concentrated instead on the timecards, writing in the date and time, certifying both with her initials. When she was done, the girls grabbed their purses from pegs bolted onto the kitchen wall and darted out the back door. Jules wagered with herself whether one or both of the girls would fail to return for her next shift. She guessed it was likely.

Tony pointed his finger at Jules. "You. Have no right."

"I have every right," she challenged. "They work for me, too, and I don't want them treated the way you treat them. Maybe Paul should sort this one out."

Tony rocked a second on the balls of his feet and then stormed across the bakery until he was standing uncomfortably close. "Fine, you talk to him about this." He raised his finger once again. "He'll set you straight about who works for who here, okay? So, yeah, you go ahead and ask him, see what he says."

"Get your finger out of my face," Jules said, more calmly than she felt. Tony was a small man, but hefty, and he had adrenaline working for him. And what did he mean about setting her straight about who worked for whom?

Before she could ask, the sleigh bells on the front door jangled. It was a last-minute customer.

"Shoot," the woman said. "You're closing."

Jules appreciated the diversion. "Not quite," she said. "Some things have been put away, but I can get you anything you'd like."

Behind her, Tony balled up his apron and hissed, "I'm leaving. You clean up and lock up."

Without a look over her shoulder, she said, "You go right ahead and leave. I'm fine here without you."

A guttural noise issued from Tony's throat. Jules hoped he wasn't having a stroke, but if he did it was his own fault, getting so worked up.

"Now," she said to her customer. "What can I get for you?"

15

Jules opened the front door of the gym and walked into the noisy, brightly lit lobby. A few young women milled around the juice and smoothie bar, towels in hand, wiping sweat from necks and foreheads. Several more women streamed down the stairs from the spin class studio. They, too, were damp with exertion. Jules sidestepped the crowds and walked toward the reception desk.

"Mrs. Herron! Hi!" Ashley, the front desk clerk, greeted her warmly.

"Hi, Ashley. It sure is busy in here."

"It is. Back-to-back spin classes, both booked solid. Did you want class information?" She reached for a photocopy of the class schedule.

"Oh." Jules shook her head. "No, I'm not ready for classes yet. I'm here to return this to Charlie." She reached into her handbag and pulled out his wallet. "He came by the bakery earlier and left this behind. Is he around?"

"Gosh, he was at the other gym earlier, but I think he's back by now, maybe with a client." Ashley focused her attention on the computer monitor and called up a staff calendar. "Yes, he's in the squash courts. I'd take it for you, but I have nowhere to secure it. Lexi's in the office, though. Want me to call her?"

"That would be great," Jules said, trying to sound positive, although she found Lexi difficult to talk to. The two women had nothing in common besides motherhood and Charlie, and Lexi seemed disinclined to chat with Jules about either. *Oh well*, Jules thought as Ashley slipped away from her post, *all I need to do is say hello, hand over the wallet, and leave.*

Jules turned her back to the computer terminal and looked out over the main floor of the gym, where some people lifted weights and others chatted with each other over the high-energy music pulsing from large speakers. Charlie had built something good here, she thought, a useful place for his clients.

Jules remembered the goals she and David had set for the bakery as they sat together all those years ago and made plans. They would create a place for people to find comfort in small, homey ways—in a brownie served up with a glass of milk, or in a muffin still warm from the oven to be enjoyed with the Sunday paper, or in a couple of slices of oatmeal bread for the lunchbox peanut butter sandwich. Those goals felt so naive now, far removed from Paul's cynical marketing efforts. It dawned on her, as she stood in this industrious place full of fatigued-but-happy-looking people that she hated—*hated*—going to work.

"Jules?"

Lost in her thoughts, Jules startled at Lexi's voice. "Lexi. I was daydreaming, sorry. It's been a long day and—"

"For me, too. So, what can I do for you?"

"Well, here," she said, and she held out Charlie's wallet. "Charlie left this behind at the bakery this morning."

"Stopping in to sneak some sweets, was he?" Lexi shook her head. "I keep carbs out of the house for good reason." She lifted the wallet from Jules's hand. Even her forearms were lean and toned, Jules noticed. Maybe the carb warden was onto something.

"Don't worry," she said. "He didn't buy anything. He came by to work on the motor of our vent this morning, although he couldn't fix it. Tony threw away an essential part of the motor when he was tinkering, which is why the vent stopped working in the first place." *So much for a quick in and out.* What was it about Lexi that made her babble on and on? "Anyway, Charlie must have put his wallet down at some point. One of my staff found it on the floor this afternoon."

Lexi stared at the wallet in her hand. "Sounds like a waste of a trip, since he couldn't fix anything after all."

"True. But he was helpful anyway. I wouldn't have gotten to the bottom of the problem on my own, and using his repair person will save us wait time and a few bucks."

Lexi continued to look at the wallet.

"Okay. I've got to run. Please tell Charlie thanks again. Hope we see you and the baby sometime soon. Rennie always asks—"

"I'll tell him. Thanks for driving this over." She slipped the wallet into the pocket of her track pants and disappeared back behind the desk and into her office.

From her seat at the computer, Ashley shot Jules a look and shrugged. "It's always super busy this time of day. Sorry."

"No worries." Jules smiled and tapped the reception desk with her fingers. "Thanks for your help."

Jules had almost made it to her car when she heard her name being called again.

"Jules!"

She stopped and looked behind her. Lexi. She turned and let the younger woman catch up to her. Long-legged and moving with purpose, she reached her in no time.

Jules gave her a puzzled look. "What's up?"

Lexi reached out and put her hand on Jules's upper arm. She smiled, but her eyes held no warmth. "This is a bit awkward," she began, "but I'm just going to come out and say what I need to say. I hope you'll understand where I'm coming from."

"I'll do my best."

"Charlie is a busy guy. Two gyms. Loads of employees. A family. His own family, I should add."

"Lexi—"

"Hear me out, please. He hasn't been home with Lark a lot lately, and she is growing up so fast. So, I want to talk to you, woman to woman—mom to mom, really—about something Charlie has a hard time bringing up with you." She looked Jules squarely in the eyes. "He's embarrassed to tell you that he hopes you'll stop calling and asking him for help. He feels like he can't say no to you, even when it's a drag on him. I figured I'd talk to you on his behalf. You know what that's like, wanting to protect the person you love, keeping them from taking on too much so they don't, well, burn out?"

"*You know what that's like.*" That was a low blow. Jules said, "I think you're having this discussion with the wrong person. Charlie *offers* to help. And, woman to woman, I have to go home now, so if you'll . . ." She shook her arm free of Lexi's hold and continued to her car.

"Naturally he offers," Lexi called after her. "He thinks you're helpless. Piece of advice, Jules. Stand on your own two feet. It's time. You get on with your life and let us get on with ours."

Jules stopped and turned. She took a few steps back in Lexi's direction. "Guess what? That's what I've been doing for the past two years, Lexi—getting on with my life, whether I like it or not. If you have issues with how your husband—sorry, partner—spends his time? As I said earlier, take it up with him. I didn't ask for any of this."

Before Lexi could get in another word, Jules walked away. Her heart raced, the heat of anger rising in her chest, but she knew she had to keep it together until she was in her car and out of the parking lot. Losing her cool in front of this woman was unthinkable. Lexi, Tony—she couldn't let bullies get a rise out of her.

As this day came to an end, two things were clear. She needed to speak to Paul and make her case for letting Tony go, and she would have to cancel the plans she'd made with Charlie for that weekend. No more assistance, no feeding him dinner as thanks, no pretending to get along with Lexi. David had put her livelihood in jeopardy, but she didn't have to remain shell-shocked and helpless, yielding to Paul's executive decisions and relying on Charlie's handouts. Intending to be hurtful, Lexi had instead done her a favor.

"I can take charge; I'm ready." The declaration made Jules smile, until she remembered her day, her year, her life. She remained in debt, working a job that gave her little satisfaction. And now her circle would be shrinking. What, exactly, was she in charge of?

Rennie had been home from school for only a couple of hours before she started unzipping her duffel bag to start packing. It was only Wednesday, but she was already looking forward to spending the upcoming weekend at her grandparents' house. As she tugged at the zipper tab, it jammed. She pulled harder, and a few stitches along the side seam popped open.

She was still trying to work the zipper open when she heard her mother's key in the front door. She returned her mother's greeting with a subdued "hi" from her room.

It was the same every day. First, her mother dropped her keys into a glass bowl placed on a small table near the front door. Then she flipped through the day's mail, if there was any. And finally, she made it down the hall to Rennie's bedroom. Rennie's keys were meant to go in the bowl, too, but Rennie walked right past, her keys in hand or in her pocket. "Try harder to remember," her mother said. "That way we won't have to hunt for your key ring every single morning."

It wasn't forgetfulness. Rennie actively resisted the habit. The idea of having a regular place for her keys in this depressing apartment, having any kind of routine here at all, made her feel defiant; she wouldn't settle in here. Her mother might have accepted this as home, might go through the motions of a day here—keys, mail, a knock on Rennie's door, supper, rinse and repeat—as if she were content, but this wasn't Rennie's home, and it never would be.

Her door cracked open a few inches, enough for her mom to stick her head in, despite the fact that Rennie had asked her over and over to knock first. She didn't bother complaining, though. What was the point? Her mom didn't listen.

"Hi, Mom."

"Hey, Rennie. How was school?" From the door, she squinted at the bag on Rennie's lap. "Packing for the weekend already?"

Rennie nodded. "It's no big deal. I had some time."

Her mother looked curious but didn't ask any more questions. "Okay. Let me go wash up and put supper on. I'll call you when it's on the table. Soup-and-sandwich night."

"Great."

"Tomato soup okay? If not, I—"

"I don't care," Rennie snapped. Right away, she felt guilty. "It's fine. Tomato's fine."

Her mother nodded her head once and retreated, closing the door behind her.

More canned soup. Fluffy white bread for the sandwiches. Rennie knew she was acting like a brat again, but supper could be depressing. The previous year, they'd started picking up bags of staple foods at the weekly food pantry and walking home with plastic shopping bags filled with half gallons of milk and jars of peanut butter, rice pilaf mix, and spongy-soft loaves of bread. The bags knocked against their calves as they walked home. Her mother hated the bread most of all, grumbled as she walked that the slices would be squashed together and misshapen by the time they got home, and reminded Rennie that it couldn't compare with the crusty loaves she used to make before Grandpa decided to reopen as a cupcake bakery. Her mother hated the bread, but she took it. It was free.

Rennie worried a loose thread at her bag's now gaping seam. After a year of shuttling back and forth like this, the bag wouldn't last much longer. It showed the wear of carting shoes and clothes and a pile of textbooks to and from her grandparents' house every weekend. Rennie thought of the red Jansport bag trimmed in leather that she had begged her mother for the year before last. That bag had been built to last. But her mother had stood firm and nixed the expensive brand, insisting instead on this generic version from Target. No logo, no cool hidden pockets. When Rennie complained, she'd gotten a frank lecture about what they could no longer afford.

"Things are different now," her mother had said, her mouth in a fixed frown.

Rennie, although only twelve at the time, had not been oblivious. Her father was gone; they had no money; yes, their lives were different. But rather than giving her a lecture, Rennie had wanted her mother to hold her, maybe to cry with her, to miss her dad along with her. Rennie wanted her dad back and for their life to go back to the way it was. As they pushed the shopping cart up and down the aisles with purpose, Rennie had felt each cheap school supply as a rebuke: "It's your fault your father's gone. Your fault things are so difficult now."

More than anything, more than any stupid, expensive school supplies, she had wanted to be forgiven for driving her dad away.

But she couldn't tell her mom about the argument or her mom would hate her as much as she hated herself.

Rennie looked around her, from the fraying duffel to the cheap curtains. Her bedroom in the apartment was a dimly lit space with only one window, and that was shaded by a tree growing too close to the building. And the room was small. Rennie had gotten to keep only a few furnishings from her old bedroom in their big house. There was no room for her large dresser, or the converted sea chest where she had kept board games, or the pair of armchairs that she and a friend could collapse into after a long day at school. Everything she couldn't keep had been sold.

"Your fault," Rennie said aloud. "Yours."

"Rennie! Supper's ready!"

Her mom's voice broke into her thoughts, but she stayed on her bed for a few more seconds. She looked through the one window in her small bedroom at the side yard and, beyond that, the rear parking lot. She needed to get away from here, even for a few days. Over supper, she would bring up her idea of visiting Gigi. With Tom Healey's forty dollars, she had the money; all she needed from her mom was a yes to the travel part. She would promise to do all the chores at home for the next decade, if only her mother would agree to let her go.

"Rennie, come on! Soup's getting cold!"

"Coming!" she called back. Full of purpose now, she jumped off her bed and got moving.

"Mom." The one word broke the silence that had descended over dinner.

Her mom looked up and blinked—startled, maybe, to find she wasn't alone—and set down her soup spoon. "I'm sorry honey, I was about a million miles away. It was that kind of a day at work."

"I talked to Gigi today. Well, not really talked. I IM'd her from computer lab."

"During school hours?"

"Yes. In computer lab. So Gigi was telling me—"

"But you're supposed to be practicing computer skills in lab, right?"

"Mom, instant messaging *is* practice. The teacher doesn't care what we do during class time as long as we're practicing keyboard skills. But that's not even the point. Gigi was telling me—"

"*I* care what you spend your time on, even if the teacher doesn't. I want you to come out of high school with good skills and a good education. And good grades."

The conversation wasn't going the way Rennie had hoped. Her mother was maddening—one minute tuned out, the next riding her about grades. "My grades are fine. I'm trying to tell you about Gigi. She has her own bedroom now and a second bed. She wants me to come and visit."

"Well, that's nice." Her mom took one more bite of her sandwich and set the last small piece of crust on her plate. She wiped her fingers on a napkin and then stood to start clearing her dishes. "Would you like some more soup before I clean up?"

"No, I'm finished." Rennie stood and dropped her spoon into the bowl. The action made more of a mess than she intended.

Her mother turned around and took in the splatters of red dotting the tablecloth. "What is that all about?"

"Nothing, nothing. I didn't mean to do that, the spoon slipped." But she *was* frustrated, tired of having her attempts at getting her mother's attention ignored. Maybe the spoon drop had been more of a fling than a slip.

Her mother seemed to be thinking the same thing. She hovered closer to the table, her attention going from the soiled tablecloth to Rennie's face, as if scanning both for clues. "I was listening to you. Gigi wants you to come and visit. What am I missing?"

Instead of answering, Rennie sat back down and crossed her arms at her middle.

"Rennie, sweetheart, I work all day with a man who wants me to guess the meaning of every cryptic thing he says. It's exhausting. If you have something to say, spit it out."

Rennie stared. *Spit it out.* As if it were so easy to do that, so easy to talk to a mom who was overworked and unhappy. As if her mother wasn't just going to shoot down her ideas anyway. Rennie felt angry that she would have to explain how she'd gotten the ticket money and then grovel for permission when she knew the answer would be no. At the same time, she felt guilty for wanting to do something fun when her mom was so miserable. A thought flashed through her brain in that moment of silence as her mother waited for her to speak: *Dad did this to us. This is all Dad's fault.*

Immediately, she felt pressure on her chest, a weight pressing down. She tried to breathe, but breathing was almost impossible. How often had she eavesdropped on one of her mother's conversations with Uncle Charlie about the huge financial mess her father had gotten them into? Every time her mother raged in those months after her dad left, Rennie had wanted to crash out of her hiding place into the middle of her mother's conversation and yell, "Don't say that! He loved us! It's my fault he's gone. Mine. If I hadn't been terrible to him, he would have stayed and fixed things."

But then, as now, she couldn't say a word.

Her mother sighed. "It's like pulling teeth, Rennie. Look. I have to call your grandfather and talk to him about Tony. Clear your dishes and go finish your packing and your homework. Take the tablecloth with you. Put it right into the hamper with the whites."

She turned away and rummaged in a drawer for a clean tablecloth. Rennie had been dismissed.

Jules tried to lift her mug of tea to her lips, but her hands were shaking. She had convinced herself it would only take a few words from her to persuade Paul to oust Tony to make the work atmosphere safer and that she could manage the baking by herself. But a few minutes into the conversation, her confidence had taken a hit. Paul had said he didn't want to talk in specifics on the phone and suggested instead a family dinner the following evening.

"You and I can chat after dinner," he'd said. "If Rennie likes, she can start her weekend with us a day early. I'll collect her from school tomorrow. Have her bring her weekend bag. And we'll invite Charlie, too," he added, "with his family. I can't remember the last time we were all together. Miriam will love this."

Jules doubted Miriam would be pleased with last-minute dinner plans on a Thursday, but she had felt powerless to object to Paul's suggestions. He'd promised they would talk. Wasn't that enough? Oddly, it wasn't, and as soon as she hung up the phone, she wondered how it had happened that she'd lost control of the discussion, how she had allowed Paul to take charge and turn dinner into the evening's highlight, reducing her concerns to an afterthought.

Jules set the mug down and absentmindedly began to play with the edge of the fresh tablecloth, folding the hemmed edge over and over with her fingers and thumb. There was no real reason to worry, she told herself. "I'll tell him what's going on in the shop, and he'll believe me," she said aloud in the quiet kitchen. "Deep breath. You've got this."

Yes, I've got this, she thought as she stood and went to rinse out the dregs of her tea. Paul would listen to her. There was no real reason to worry.

16

"So, yeah, anyway, it's only Thursday morning, and you'll be gone to work already. Lexi and I are about to go in, too, but I wanted to touch base about the weekend. Like I said the other day, I'm totally up for handyman duty. And dinner."

Charlie stopped talking and caught his breath. He had been rambling on nonstop, using way too many words just to confirm he would be over on Sunday to mount the shelves in Rennie's bedroom. This should have been a simple enough voicemail, but he was struggling to wind it up before Lexi came downstairs and caught him on the phone.

"So call back to confirm, leave a message if I don't answer. I'll call you back. Uh, bye. Talk soon. Yeah, bye."

He hung up and set down his phone. His palms were damp. He shook his head and picked up a napkin from the basket placed at the center of the kitchen table. "What am I, thirteen?" he muttered as he dried his hands.

"Who were you talking to?"

Charlie looked over his shoulder and saw Lexi paused in the doorway, her gym shoes in her hand, her feet bare.

"What?"

"Who. Were. You. Talking. To? I heard your voice as I was coming downstairs."

She padded into the kitchen and sat next to him at the table. She held her shoes on her lap and started loosening the laces. It bugged him that she never spent the thirty seconds to untie her laces before removing her shoes.

"Lark's playing in the crib, thank goodness. Tell me that was not the sitter on the phone, canceling." Her fingers tugged at the double knots.

"Oh. No, I was leaving a voicemail."

"For?" Lexi stared him down.

Openness. It was her big ask since she sat him down a few months ago, two years after David's drowning, and told him he was spending too much time with his dead friend's widow and daughter. To appease Lexi after that discussion, he had agreed to run all the chores and odd jobs he did for Jules by her. And he had; well, for the most part he had. Some things, like yesterday's vent fix, took up so little of his time that they hardly seemed worth mentioning. But there was no point in keeping any of the jobs secret; he understood this. Lexi smelled evasion like it was last week's trash. And yet sometimes he evaded anyway.

"Uh, it was a message for Jules."

Lexi stopped loosening her laces and rolled her eyes. "What does she want now?"

"You remember. I offered to help hang some bookshelves for Rennie. I thought this Sunday would work." Lexi liked Rennie just fine. Throwing her name in the conversation was calculated. Maybe, just maybe, Lex would drop her focus on Jules, like a dog finished with a toy.

"You can tell her you're too busy, you know."

"Lex, I can find a few minutes. I get it over with this weekend, then that'll be it."

"Until the next time." Lexi lost interest in the shoes and set them on the floor. She stood and walked to the sink, where she grabbed a clean glass from the drying rack and filled it with water from the tap.

"Hey, how about a smoothie before we head out?" Charlie asked.

Lexi wrinkled her nose. "Pass me my vitamins, will you?" As she asked, she lifted her arms over her head and stretched, lifting the water glass up high without spilling a drop. Her shirt rode up her flat stomach. The promise of sex always entered these moments of conflict, Lexi using her tanned skin and toned muscles to remind him of what he had at home and what he left behind every time he drove to Jules's place. She would throw him crumbs like these if he behaved. The hell of it was that he found her body so desirable still, even as he was being manipulated. Or was it conditioned? "Good boy, Charlie. Good boy." The person he most loathed after these encounters was himself.

Charlie tried not to sigh as he stood and brought the bottle of vitamins to Lexi at the sink. She finished stretching and took the bottle from him.

"What's on your plate today?" he asked.

She waved him off and popped a pill. After a swig of water she said, "Don't change the subject."

"Come on, Lex, I—"

Over on the kitchen table Charlie's phone rang.

"Tell her you decided you can't help," Lexi warned. "I mean it."

"You don't know that it's Jules." Charlie grabbed the phone. "See?" he said, waving it at her. "It's Paul Herron."

Lexi relaxed and showed a hint of a smile. Even though he had described his miserable childhood to her, she loved his wealthy parents, and she loved their oldest and best friends, the Herrons, too.

"Hey, Uncle Paul. Yeah, we're doing great. Lark is excellent, running around here like the Tasmanian Devil and learning new words every day." Charlie smiled, as he always did when people asked after his daughter. "Yes, I agree, she's a bright one. How's Aunt Miriam?"

From her spot resting against the counter, Lexi snapped her fingers to get his attention and mouthed, "What does he want?"

Charlie held up one finger, pulled out a chair from the table, and sat down again. "Good, good. That's great. She's keeping busy, then? Awesome. So, what can I do for you, Paul? Lexi and I are about to head out the door for work. Yeah, I know, always working. The gyms are busier than ever, and that's not a bad problem to have, these days." He paused, listening. "Dinner tonight? It's short notice for a sitter. Oh, bring the baby?"

He turned to look at Lexi. She smiled and nodded. Charlie could practically read her mind: *Face time with Miriam; what will I wear?* Miriam liked Lexi, too, although she insisted on calling her by her full name: "Alexa carries herself well, so positive and strong!"

"Yes, we'd love to," he told Paul. "What's that? Oh. Sure. Great. Sounds like a fun evening. We'll see you between six and six thirty, then. Love to Miriam. Bye."

Lexi set down her water glass and clapped her hands together. "Well, great! I'll wear my black wrap dress. It's been ages since I've been anywhere without yoga pants. Now, if you cancel the weekend plans with Jules, my day will officially be made." She grinned, triumphant. Charlie didn't respond, and Lexi narrowed her eyes at him. "What?"

"Uh, Jules will be at dinner, too."

"You're kidding me." Lexi dropped back against the counter.

"Why would I kid you? Paul thought it would be good for us all to get together. They're planning a barbecue in the yard. While it's still warm enough. Rennie's excited for us to bring Lark."

Lexi shook her head. Charlie could see she was conflicted. If she agreed to go, they would spend an evening with Jules. If she balked, she would miss an evening with Miriam. She was so transparent; the struggle over which to choose played out on her face.

"Let's just go," he said. "It'll be a couple of hours."

She stared at him, affectless, and this began to piss him off.

"You know you don't want to miss huddling in a corner with Miriam, whispering with her like you're a couple of middle school girls."

"Sometimes you're a real jerk, Charlie. Call Paul back and tell him we can't make it," she said. "I'm sick, Lark's sick. Anything, I don't care."

"You're the one who was eager to go."

"I changed my mind." Lexi's voice was firm—and louder than either of them expected.

Down the hall, Lark began to cry. Until now, she had been playing contentedly in her crib. They both looked in the direction of the baby's room.

"See what you did?" Lexi said, but she didn't budge from her place.

Her lower back now rested against the drawer pull. *That has to hurt*, Charlie thought. "Well, I'm not going to listen to her cry." He stood and started for the hallway.

"I don't think you get to decide that," Lexi said, stopping him in his tracks.

"I can't decide to check on her? She's my daughter."

"And all of a sudden you want to start acting like her dad?"

This was going nowhere good. Charlie took a deep breath. "Look," he said, softening his tone. "We can talk more on the way to work. For now, let me get her settled again, all right? For the sitter? She'll be here any minute." He started to move toward the hallway.

Lexi pushed away from the counter and cut him off. "Uh-uh. I'll do it. *You* stay right here."

She pushed past him, and as she went by, Charlie saw the shape of the drawer pull imprinted on the skin of her back, a red, angry-looking stripe above the waistband of her yoga pants. He winced. He and Lexi had been out of sync and bickering like this for a while, and the arguments always circled back to Jules. In between them, there was always Jules.

Lexi returned to the kitchen holding Lark close to her. Already a tall girl, their toddler had her long legs wrapped around her mother's torso, her head tucked under her chin. She looked over at her father with big, shining eyes, her cheeks bright red from the exertion of crying. With her there, he wouldn't continue to argue, and Lexi knew that. He never got involved with dumb women.

"No more tears, Larkie, okay?" He reached out a hand and smoothed her fine hair away from her face.

Lexi twisted her body so Lark was just out of Charlie's reach.

"Lex."

She looked him square in the eyes. "I've decided. I want to stay home tonight, the three of us. If you'd rather spend your family time with people who aren't even related to you, and are practically strangers to me, that's your decision."

"Strangers?"

"What? That's not true?" Lexi hoisted Lark higher on her hip. "Jules is a stranger to me. I barely know her. She never speaks to me unless she has to. She only confides in you and asks you for favors. Maybe the woman could learn how to hang her own shelves. Or at least hire someone. She's using you, Charlie. You feel too responsible for David's death to see it."

The words stung. He had confided his feelings of responsibility to her in a low moment, after a Coast Guard rescue mission had failed to turn up any sign of David's body.

"But I was late for our meeting, Lex," he had sobbed into

his hands. "If I had gotten to the coffee shop sooner, maybe he wouldn't have done this."

"People who want to kill themselves will always find a way," she had said.

Maybe she had been trying to relieve him of his burden. But it had also been a harsh thing to say, dismissive and cold. Lexi had a wide streak of cold in her and little patience for people who might struggle. Being a hard-ass made her a great trainer but sometimes a difficult human being. The truth was, he had been late, and he did feel responsible. He wanted her to understand what this meant to him, that while he had been kissing her in his office and learning he was about to become a father, he had failed to keep a promise, and his friend had given up and taken his life.

He looked at mother and daughter now. Lexi continued challenging him with her cold eyes, but Lark had calmed in her mother's arms. What tenderness Lexi possessed she gave to Lark, and that was good. Charlie didn't want their daughter disturbed by their arguing. He had lived in a state of constant anxiety as a child, and it was important to him to keep the peace.

"It's not just the guilt, Lex," he answered, trying to stay calm. "I made a pact with my best friend years ago, and now his wife needs me. Jules is in a tough spot."

"It's been over two years of the same tough spots. Jesus."

"Hey, we go to dinner, we make nice. Miriam will show you her newest antique or rope you into one of her charity events, and you'll have a good time. Come on. Two hours."

"Okay, fine. Two hours of my cooperation. But in exchange for that, I ask that you forget about the bookshelves and whatever else. Stay away from Jules and Rennie for, say, six months. Concentrate on us, on your own daughter. Let Jules get on with her life."

Charlie stood still. In the silence, he heard the clock ticking.

He looked around him at the familiar kitchen. The sink was full of dirty dishes. The tray of the high chair was littered with Cheerios left over from breakfast. Lark was wearing only one sock; where was the other?

Lexi stood still, too, Lark on her hip, and waited. "Well?"

Charlie lifted his hands at his sides. "It's a couple of bookshelves for a girl who lost her father."

"Yeah, I didn't think so. You're so blind, Charlie. Not just about Jules, but about yourself."

"We've got to go to work," Charlie reminded her. "How about this? We can talk later, when we've both had some time to think."

"So *I* can think, you mean, and change my mind. How about this?" Lexi's voice was unnaturally chipper, matching the false, broad smile she put on for her daughter's benefit. "I'll give you some time to think about the conversation we've had. Six weeks of it. I have that much vacation time on the books. Lark, tell Daddy that Mommy just decided we might go visit Nana tonight."

"Wait. You're leaving?"

"Leaving? Who's leaving? Lark and I might like a vacation, that's all. Right, sweetie?" She bounced Lark on her hip. "What do we say to Daddy, Lark? What do we say when we go on vacation?"

"Bye-bye, Daddy." The child brought the flat of her palm to her face and puckered. She flicked her hand and sent a kiss flying through the air. "Blow kiss."

Charlie pretended to catch it. He grasped the kiss in his fist and held it against his heart. He looked once more at Lexi, pleading, and she looked back with steel in her eyes.

"Bye-bye, Daddy," Lark said again. She blew more kisses as Lexi took her down the hall and back to her room.

When they were out of sight, Charlie opened his fist, but instead of a kiss there, he saw nothing.

"Well, this is going to be a nice evening," Paul said with a smile at the group gathered on the patio: his wife, his granddaughter, and Charlie.

Charlie thought branding the evening "nice" at this point was overly optimistic. He was already well into his first beer and had barely said a word since he walked in. Rennie was chewing at her cuticles. And Miriam seemed locked up inside herself, maybe nursing a grievance. She liked being fawned over, and Lexi turned the flattery on high in her presence, but here Charlie was, alone, bringing only his made-up story that Lark was ill and Lexi had opted to stay home with her.

He wished Jules would hurry up and show. She would be the bright spot tonight.

Paul set a platter of grilled salmon on the long teak table. Now that the fish was finished, he focused his attention on the quiet group, clapping his hands together, making a show of checking his watch. "Julia should be here any minute. We'll need place settings," he announced to everyone and no one in particular.

Charlie swigged the last large gulp of his beer and then walked over to get another bottle from the aluminum tub filled with ice and drinks. He tossed his empty into the recycling bin as he passed.

"Charles, I wish you'd let me give you a glass." Miriam started for the kitchen but Charlie held up a hand.

"Bottle's fine," he said as he twisted off the cap.

"Something's burning, Gramps," Rennie said, pointing.

Paul turned. Flames were licking up from the grate, engulfing a portobello mushroom.

"I think I used too much olive oil." He returned to the grill to flip the mushrooms. "Miriam," he said over his shoulder, "can you put some foil over the fish while I keep an eye on these?"

"It's the balsamic vinegar," Miriam said as she headed into the kitchen for the roll of foil.

"I'm sorry?"

"Catching on fire, Paul. The sugar in the vinegar. I told you to brush it on after the mushrooms were cooked."

"You did, my dear," Paul said to Miriam's back. He looked over at Charlie and shrugged. "She's usually right."

Charlie nodded and then started in on peeling the label off his beer.

Paul speared the mushrooms with his long fork and set them onto a fresh platter. "Now we can eat as soon as Julia arrives."

Miriam walked back out through the French doors with the aluminum foil roll. "She's the one who wanted an early night. You did tell her to come right after work, didn't you?"

"Yes, dear, I did." Paul walked the mushrooms over to the table. "Cover this one, too. We'll keep everything warm."

As Miriam crimped a sheet of foil around the fish, she turned her attention to Rennie. "Your mother didn't say anything about running late, did she?"

Rennie shook her head.

"Then what's keeping her?" she asked Paul.

"Traffic, maybe," he said. "Or a problem at work. She'll be along."

Miriam clicked her tongue. "It's starting to get cool out here, and the rest of us would appreciate some warm food. Rennie dear, go get the plates and silver from the counter. Napkins, too. We'll get started on the table at least."

Charlie watched as Rennie obeyed her grandmother without a word, bringing her thumbnail to her mouth as she slipped around the outdoor dining table to go inside. Miriam's criticism bothered her, plain to see. Miriam used to make David this nervous, too, one of the reasons why, in later years, he did his best to avoid his parents.

"Aunt Miriam, can you chill about Jules already? I wouldn't have agreed to come over if I thought you'd be sniping at her before she even arrived. We've all had long days." The atmosphere was getting to Charlie, as was the smoke from the burning vinegar. Or oil. Whichever. He stood and sauntered over to the untended grill and dropped its lid down to smother the flames.

"Charlie, Miriam," Paul began, trying to head off an argument.

But his caution was unnecessary. Miriam closed her eyes and lifted her chin. When she opened her eyes again, she had hit some kind of reset. A smile plastered on her face, she said, "Excuse me a minute," and then slipped back into the house, passing Rennie in the doorway.

Rennie's arms were laden with a stack of plates, napkins, and cutlery. "I think I hear my mom driving up."

Charlie trained an ear and, like Rennie, heard the distinctive rattling of Jules's failing muffler growing louder as she drove up to the house. He had offered to take the car to be fixed, offered the use of his own temporarily while she was without a car, but she wouldn't have it.

Charlie watched Jules park her car behind his. "Call me any time," he had said in the days and weeks after David disappeared, and he had meant it. Plumbing fixes, painting the living room and kitchen in her dingy apartment, putting an extra deadbolt on her door—he had been happy to take care of these. The odd jobs had been just as much about him and managing his own loss as they'd been about helping Jules and Rennie mitigate theirs. "Handouts," Lexi had called his offers to help. Jules, proud, had practically called them the same thing, more like Lexi on this point than either woman would have imagined possible. All he wanted was to be useful, and yet Jules's muffler continued to hang on by a thread and his girlfriend had left him, taking their kid with her. What bullshit.

Charlie's eyes felt heavy, perhaps a result of the beer or the pollen in the air or the tears he had shed earlier watching Lark get bundled into her car seat. He had hoped the evening would distract him from his worries, but he only felt surly. The sight of Jules unloading bags from her car, her face relaxed and unguarded, lifted his spirits for a few moments, until he remembered how little he mattered to anyone right now.

He forced himself to rally. "Hey, Ren," he said, "sit here with me and give your mom that comfy chair. She's been on her feet all day." He gestured to the empty space next to him on the wrought iron bench, its seat softened only a little by a thick cushion.

Rennie got up from the padded wicker chair and joined him. Charlie put his arm across her shoulder and drew her close. "I've missed you," he said.

"Me, too. Uncle Charlie, I wanted to talk . . ."

But at that moment, the side gate rattled, and Charlie saw that Jules was struggling with the complicated latch, laden down as she was by the two shopping bags she was holding.

Charlie took his arm from Rennie's shoulder and stood. "Let me get those," he said, and in a few long strides he met Jules and took the bags from her hands.

"Wine in this one, seltzer in the other," she said as, with her hands free, she went back and properly latched the gate. "I should get them in the fridge." She offered to take back one of the sacks but Charlie moved them out of her reach.

"I've got them. I'll go see where Miriam wants to put it all."

Jules rolled her eyes but followed him across the lawn. They both stopped at the bench for Jules to plant a kiss on Rennie's head. "Mmm, did you shower here after school? You smell like expensive shampoo," she said, and she ruffled Rennie's hair for good measure.

"How was work?" Rennie asked.

"It was work," Jules said.

"Julia!" Paul called from across the patio. Jules lifted a hand in greeting and walked toward him. "Did you have a good day?" he asked.

She nodded and offered him her cheek when she reached him. "We're still on for talking after supper?"

"We are."

Charlie turned and caught her eye. "Talking?"

Jules smiled. "Bakery stuff. Sorry I didn't put out a memo," she teased. "Now, where is the munchkin? I'm dying to see how big she's grown since I saw her last."

Charlie recalled his daughter's face looking over Lexi's shoulder yesterday as she was carried back to bed, saying, "Bye-bye, Daddy." She was gone now, Lexi was gone, only over the border in New Hampshire, but it might as well be a million miles away.

"She's actually sick. Running a fever. Lex kept her home." He kept on going into the kitchen. Jules followed.

"Julia. There you are."

"Hi, Miriam. Sorry I'm running late. I stopped for wine and sparkling water. Can Charlie put them in the fridge?"

"Why, yes, he may. But I already have both."

"And now you have more," Charlie said, and he sidestepped Jules to get around the vast island plunked down in the center of the kitchen. He found an empty shelf in the refrigerator, unpacked the warm bottles, and laid them flat to chill.

"You two catch up. I'll see if Paul needs any more help. He already burned one part of the meal. I'm not sure he can handle the rest on his own." With that, Miriam left.

Charlie shook his head, then grabbed a beer from the stash in the fridge and held it out to Jules. "Bet you need this. Or would you rather have wine?"

Jules shook her head. "I need to be on my toes in this house. I'll stick with water for now."

Charlie nodded and set the beer bottle down on the island to rummage again in the fridge. He bypassed Jules's generic seltzer water for the Perrier. "Might as well have Miriam's expensive stuff." He busied himself with locating a glass and filling it with ice.

"Other than a sick baby, is everything good?"

"Yeah, sure," Charlie said as he opened the Perrier bottle. "You?"

"Me? Work is a bear, and I'm not quite sure how much Rennie likes school this year . . . Hey, that's enough." Jules put her hand on his arm to stop his pour. The head of seltzer rose and overflowed the rim of the water glass.

"Geez. Daydreaming. Sorry."

"Don't worry." Jules reached for the paper towel roll. She tore off a few sheets and blotted the puddle until the counter was fairly dry. "I know how it is when you have a sick kid."

Charlie popped the cap from his third beer, took a sip, and stared out the window. He considered telling Jules the truth, but he remained silent and the confessional moment passed.

"You know, Rennie hoped to see them. She loves Lark, and I think she wanted to talk to you guys again about babysitting. I know Lexi isn't big on leaving Lark with anyone, and Rennie's only fourteen, but she's a responsible fourteen."

Lexi, Lark. Lexi, Lark. Charlie shook his head. "Not gonna let this one go, are you?"

"Sorry, I didn't mean . . ."

Charlie exhaled. "*I'm* sorry. I'm just tired. Tired of saying no to Rennie, for one. I'd love to hire her, but Lexi isn't on the same page. I can fix appliances. I can install bookshelves. But there are some things, especially where Lexi's concerned, that I can't make happen." Parched, Charlie chugged some beer and then set the bottle down.

Jules walked over and stood next to him, placing her hands alongside his on the cool marble surface.

"Please don't worry about it. It's not your job to solve all my problems."

Today, Jules smelled like sugar, burned sugar. Different than vanilla but still sweet. Charlie shifted his weight and stepped away from Miriam's massive showpiece of an island, stepped away from Jules.

"We should get back outside and help Rennie set the table before Miriam comes storming in here, wondering why we're making her dinner get cold."

"Charlie—"

"Come on, Jules. Dinner."

17

Everyone but Jules had moved inside. Dinner had wrapped up quickly once they had all gathered to eat; conversation had chugged along but felt stilted and polite. When the plates were empty, talk had petered out. Charlie and Rennie now worked side by side at the sink, washing and drying Miriam's dishes, while Miriam put them away. From her seat on the patio, Jules watched the three of them, all hand and arm motions, Miriam occasionally stepping this way or that to reach cupboards and shelves.

Paul wasn't a part of the tableau; he was waiting for her in his study.

She, meanwhile, was stalling.

A few minutes earlier, as an unusually quiet Charlie stood to collect dirty plates, Jules had cleared her throat and addressed her father-in-law. "It's late, it's a school night, so can we . . ."

"Ah, yes," Paul had said. "We'll talk in my study. No one else needs to be bothered with work matters."

The concern for privacy had struck Jules as odd, coming from a man who routinely asked about cash receipts and customer counts in front of anybody and everybody. She'd looked at him with curiosity. He'd smiled and changed the subject.

"I'll go wash up, and meet you inside in, say, five minutes?"

"Sure," she had agreed, but here she sat ten minutes later,

watching the others work and wondering why this summons to his office had prompted such a feeling of dread. She was missing some information, something that Paul understood but she did not, she was sure of it.

Before David's car and phone had been found at the beach, before his trail of lies and deceptions had unfurled, before she'd finally learned the truth in such an abrupt and painful way, she had missed many facts. Or rather, she had seen the facts but had assembled them in the wrong way, in a way that made sense according to a world where David told the truth. Since then, she'd sworn to herself that she would be more shrewd, and Paul's words set off warning bells. Work disagreements. A private discussion that they would have in a room that was the essence of Paul's domain, decorated with leather and books, everything smelling faintly of tobacco. What facts was she missing now?

Jules looked into the kitchen again. Miriam had disappeared. Rennie was drying her hands on the front of her jeans while Charlie sprayed and wiped down the counter. They appeared to be talking. Whatever problems he had tonight, at least he was giving Rennie his attention. Jules sighed. She was cold now, and she slipped her arms into the sleeves of the cardigan she had thrown over her shoulders earlier in the evening. September days could be as humid as July weather, but the nights always cooled way down. It was time to go in, so she did.

Paul lit a cigar. He took a puff and relaxed back into his chair. "Not supposed to have these things in the house," he said, and he smiled.

Jules made no comment. This kind of information, casually dropped into conversation, had always confounded her about her husband's family. There was a deliberateness in the way each individual conspired to keep information from one or all of the rest. David used to laugh along with her when she pointed out examples of the poor communication. He'd claimed he was different. He was not.

"Before I go up to bed, I change and wash in the washroom down here to get rid of the smoke smell. Brush my teeth, too." Paul winked at Jules. "Don't tell."

Because heaven forbid someone tell the truth. Jules had not had the easiest or most advantageous upbringing, but she and her mother had at least communicated with each other. Paul's and Miriam's dysfunction had always exhausted her; today, it angered her as well. David was raised in this atmosphere, polluted by it. Paul's wink would never make that right.

"Don't tell? You're not a child, Paul. Wouldn't it be simpler to say to Miriam, 'I'm having a cigar, now leave me alone'?"

"You think if I tell Miriam the truth, she'll leave me alone to enjoy my cigar? You really are an optimist, Julia." He shifted the cigar to the corner of his mouth and spoke around it. "The bakery, then. You have a grievance of some sort?"

Jules frowned. "I wouldn't call it a grievance, no. I want to talk to you about Tony, and the way he talks to the counter staff. You know there's a high turnover."

Paul nodded.

"It's because he yells at them. Berates them. That kind of treatment doesn't make them work harder. It only makes them quit."

Paul stared at her as if this was all very interesting but not earth-shattering.

Jules shifted and described to him the most recent episode in Tony's rantings. "And I could find former employees who would tell you he's mistreated them, too," she finished. "I don't want to see this spiral out of control, where someone's filing a harassment lawsuit. That's not the kind of workplace I want. I didn't think that's what you want, either."

"No one wants that. I'll speak to him and get his side of the story. You have to understand, he's a passionate person and—"

"He's a bully," Jules corrected. "That's the only side of the story."

"He's a passionate person, and he wants things done right. But I'll talk to him. Now, that was easy." Paul held the cigar between thumb and forefinger and smiled. "We're glad to have Rennie for the extra night. Thank you for that. We love having her here."

Jules ignored the subject change. "Actually, I'm not quite done."

"With?"

"Tony."

"This is sounding more and more like a grievance to me." He motioned with his hand for Jules to continue. She watched a curl of smoke weave around the swift movement of his finger as she collected her thoughts.

"The girls he yelled at today? I hand-signed their timecards and sent them home a few minutes early to get them out of Tony's way. He got in my face then, and it was threatening. Why do we need to hold on to a hothead?"

Paul shifted and crossed his legs. He puffed at his cigar a bit. The sweet smoke hung in the air. "You know he owned another place for years?"

Jules nodded. She had heard the broad strokes of the story a million times, and apparently, she was about to hear it again.

"He sold that place to his son and daughter-in-law and thought he'd retire. Well, he didn't like retirement, and he also didn't want to go to work for his son."

"So he came to work for you instead. I know. What does that have to do with anything?"

Paul set down the cigar on the rim of a pristinely clean ashtray that he probably had to wash to maintain his ridiculous charade.

She had never seen him lift a dinner dish in all the years she had known him. She watched as the cigar's lit end burned red-orange for a few seconds, but without oxygen being drawn in, the glowing embers quickly turned ashy gray, the smoke from a curl to a wisp. "It has to do with understanding Tony's role. You see, after he decided to go back to work, he also realized he was the kind of guy who didn't want to work for anybody, not really."

"But . . . but he works for you, so . . ." Jules stopped. Tony's words, yelled at her in the heat of their argument, came back to her: *You ask your father-in-law who works for who.* She had difficulty drawing a breath, but she tried. "When I sent the girls home, Tony told me I had no right to do that. He told me I should talk to you about who works for whom. What did he mean?"

Paul looked at his hands. He was uncomfortable.

"I'm serious," Jules pressed. "I want to know."

"Okay." Paul tented his fingers. "My bank handled his money and his loans for years. His mortgage, his business financing. I've known Tony for a long time. He was a reliable customer. When I gave you the money and started managing the place, I asked Tony if he wanted to come out of retirement. I needed a baker."

"You had a baker. Me."

"But you had no one helping you, remember?"

Jules nodded. "Sure. I let everyone go because the bakery's future was uncertain."

"There you go. I solved the problem."

It had been a godsend, Jules remembered, to have someone swoop in and solve all her problems. At the time, she'd been reeling from David's betrayal and drowning in debt. Her face softened as she recalled the relief she'd felt when Paul arrived with his solutions.

He must have seen this on her face. He lowered his voice, almost crooned, "It was the right thing to do, helping you. Helping my granddaughter." He smiled.

Jules nodded. "You solved the problem. But still, that doesn't explain what Tony was talking about. 'Who works for who,' those were his words. I'm under the impression we both work for you. That you agreed you'd let me pay you back for your investment in the bakery. That once I paid you, I'd be the owner again and you'd step aside."

"You can still buy me out, Julia."

"But?"

"But you told me you trusted me to make decisions."

Jules tensed. "And?"

Paul turned his head to the side and lifted his chin, as if working out a kink in his neck. After a few seconds he looked Jules in the eye. "I wouldn't have invested all my own capital in the business. That would have been foolish. Tony invested with me. He's part owner."

Jules clasped her hands together on her lap and dug her nails into her palms to keep herself from screaming. But she felt like it. "He's part owner," she repeated.

"Well, technically majority owner—51 percent. He drives a hard bargain, and he had ready cash from his own buyout. We pooled the money and paid off the debt. I did manage to make some stipulations. For my 49 percent share, I manage the finances and make the financial decisions. That leaves him to run the floor without interference. We stay out of each other's way."

Jules pushed her nails deeper into the fleshy pads of her palms. She wouldn't let Paul see her lose her cool. Every word, every action from this point on had to be in aid of making a swift and clean exit from this house. For the past two years, she had endured Miriam and her subtler but still present jabs, all for the sake of her daughter, but she had felt kindly toward Paul because she'd believed his biggest flaw was being allergic to confrontation. She had underestimated him.

"I work for you both?"

"Technically, yes."

"And technically more for him than for you?"

Paul waved this off. "What's a couple of percentage points? When you're ready, you'll pay me back and you'll be a part owner again, like you were with David."

Jules smiled although it hurt every muscle in her face and neck to do so. "Wow. Part owner again."

"Yes! Exactly!" Paul said, relief relaxing his shoulders. He sounded almost gleeful. "We saved the bakery, we're giving you back a thriving business."

"Part owner again," Jules repeated. "Of a thriving cupcake bakery, no less. Yes, I'm so lucky. First time around, I was part owner with a reckless liar. Now I'll be part owner with a misogynistic hothead. Lucky, lucky me." She pushed herself out of the plush armchair and walked to the office door. Once there, she turned. "One more thing: I quit."

Paul narrowed his eyes. "You're overreacting. It's a good arrangement, and I was trying to do the right thing. For you, for Rennie. Look." He got up to follow Jules to the door. His chair scraped the oak floorboards as he scrambled to get out from behind his desk. "I'll talk to Tony. You're right, he shouldn't yell. Once he's on board, you and I can start talking about the timeline for the transfer."

Jules stopped. "The transfer?"

"Yes. Of my shares to you."

He was nervous now, probably wondering if she would retaliate by restricting his access to Rennie. And maybe that would have to happen. She would decide that later. For now, she only wanted to be gone from this house. She shook her head, but she was surprised by how calm she now felt. Before she reached for the doorknob, she looked her father-in-law up and down, from his perfectly coiffed hair to his sockless feet in their pristine mint green boat shoes. Mint green. What a sad, sad man, saddled with two bullies—one at work and the other at home—and bad taste in shoes. He was smaller than she'd ever realized, his eyes almost at her level.

"I told you: I quit. And good luck," she said. "You'll need it."

With the dishes done, Rennie hung out with Charlie on the patio and helped him build a fire in the enormous pit. He was letting her do most of the work, nodding his approval at every stage instead of jumping in to show her how it was done. She had watched her dad build contained fires in the fireplace for years and had paid close attention when he'd explained how best to light the logs, so she knew what to do. Unlike Charlie, however, her dad had kept the actual work to himself, promising he would let her try her hand at it someday.

"Humor me," he'd said when she'd accused him of treating her like she was still a baby. "I don't think you're a baby, I promise. It's more that you're growing up so fast. Sometimes I'd like you to be my little girl a little longer." He had tried to hug her after he said this, but she'd only pulled away and sulked some more. She had been horrible to him for a couple of years, not only on that last day when she'd stormed off and left him in the car outside of school.

"Here, why don't you give this a try."

Rennie looked up from the logs in the fire pit. Charlie passed her the spark lighter and a twist of newspaper. "Light it, touch it to the small branches, and then drop the paper in."

"I know. Dad showed me a million times."

When the fire caught, Charlie sat back and smiled. "Nice work."

Rennie nodded. She was pleased he was impressed with her

skills. But she would give anything to have her father here praising her instead, to have a chance to say she was sorry for all the times she was mean to him, for all the hugs she refused to return.

Within minutes, the blaze was full and strong, its flames leaping and the wood crackling with spitting sparks.

"Time for the grate," Charlie said, and he replaced the mesh chimney that would contain the fire.

With everything in place, they moved away from the pit and returned to the wrought iron bench. Rennie leaned into Charlie's arm. He lifted it and pulled her close.

It was weird not having anything to do but sit. Doing dinner chores, listening to the adults' conversation, however boring, washing dishes, lighting the fire—these kept her mind from wandering, like it did now, back to her dad.

There was a period in that first year when she'd refused to believe her father was dead, even after they had proof. She'd slipped up once and told her mother she believed he had been hurt, was maybe suffering amnesia and couldn't find his way home. After that, Rennie wasn't allowed to watch soap operas with her Nana Jean anymore, the ones her nana loved where men named Stone or Brock woke from comas and couldn't remember their real lives. Or their wives. Or their daughters. But life wasn't like the shows. No stranger had shown up in any hospital in any of the surrounding towns, although she'd scanned newspapers when she could. Eventually, it had been impossible to ignore DNA evidence, even when she'd tried. When they'd gotten the box of ashes in the mail, her mother had begun speaking of her dad in the past tense, and then not at all, and Rennie could no longer hold onto even the slimmest soap opera hope. She'd had to come face to face with facts: her dad was gone, and she had driven him away.

Uncle Charlie shifted a bit, and Rennie looked up at his face. The burden of carrying this guilt alone was heavy, and Charlie was strong. Tonight, though, he felt far away. He stared beyond the fire into the darkness. Probably he was thinking of his sick daughter at home; he had his own problems. Still, he had always told her she could talk to him about anything.

"Uncle Charlie," she began.

"Yeah, sweetheart?"

As she opened her mouth to tell him her secret, their peaceful moment was interrupted by loud voices. Rennie pulled away from Charlie and sat up to see her mother exiting the house quickly, followed by her grandfather.

"Rennie?" she called.

"We're over here, Mom."

Charlie stood. "What's going on?"

Her mom ignored the question. She walked across the patio and tapped Rennie on the shoulder. "I need you to collect your things, sweetie. Homework, books, anything else you have stored here—anything from toothbrush to mittens. I know it sounds silly, but you should get everything you can. We're going home now, and you might not be back for a while."

Rennie frowned at her mother but got up from her seat and started toward the house, passing her grandfather, who had followed her mother onto the patio at a slow, resigned pace.

"I wish you would calm down and sit so we can continue our discussion," her grandfather said.

Rennie paused at the door to watch.

Her mom didn't answer and didn't turn to face him. Instead, she retrieved her large handbag from a patio chair, rummaged inside until she found her car keys, and slung the bag over her shoulder.

Grandma, invisible for the last half hour, magically appeared from wherever she had been hiding. "What on earth are you all worked up over?"

"Nothing, Miriam," Jules said. "You're both mistaken. I'm as calm as calm can be. Rennie, get going," she called. "I'll wait for you in the car. Night, Charlie."

Charlie half stood from his seat. "Wait, what—?"

Her mom shook her head. "This isn't the best time. I'll call you. Rennie, I said move!"

Rennie moved. Upstairs, she shoved her schoolwork into her duffel bag, and all the clothes from the dresser and closet into the extra suitcase she kept under the bed. She cleared out the bathroom next—her lip gloss, toothpaste, even the tampons she hadn't yet tried but kept hidden in a cupboard.

Back in the bedroom, she cast one more look around. There, on the pillow, was her special nightgown, folded neatly after breakfast by her grandmother. Grandma had a sharp tongue sometimes, but she had a kind side, too. Not a cuddly kind, but the little things she did when Rennie stayed over, from buying Rennie's favorite shampoo to leaving this nightgown laid out with care on the pillow sham, were kind in their own way.

Rennie picked up the nightie and stroked the embroidered chain of pink and red flowers circling the neck and cuffs. It was a hand-me-down, and her grandmother had taken great care to point out the needlework and the silk thread. "My mother stitched those flowers. It took her days and days," she said. "I always thought I would have a daughter to give it to, but passing it on to my granddaughter is just as special." She also told Rennie she was allowed to take it home with her and wear it whenever she wanted. "It's yours now. Only please don't let your mother toss it in the washing machine." Rennie had always taken good care of it, keeping it away from the laundry basket and washing it by hand as her grandmother had instructed.

She sat down on the bed and chewed on the cuticle of her barely healed thumb. What did her mother mean, she might not be back for a while? Days? Weeks? Or never again? She thought of day after day spent between school and the drab apartment, and she hoped whatever her mother and grandfather had fought about would blow over.

As she was thinking, there was a light tap on her door. Rennie took her thumb from her mouth and hid her hands under the nightgown. "Come in."

The door opened, revealing both grandparents standing there.

"We're checking to make sure you're ready to go," Gramps said.

Rennie nodded. "What's happening?"

"You're going home," Gramps answered with a sad smile.

"I mean the fight."

Gramps shook his head. "It's between me and your mother, and we'll get it sorted out." When Rennie didn't budge, he said, "Come on, now, you need to do what your mother asked. She's waiting."

Her grandmother came and sat next to her on the bed. She took the nightgown from Rennie and began folding it back into a neat square. "Rennie, you're perfectly welcome to stay until your mother calms down." She placed the nightgown on her lap.

Rennie saw a smear of blood near the collar. Her thumb had bled on it. She hoped her grandmother wouldn't notice.

"Miriam. The situation is bad enough without you butting in."

Rennie looked at her grandfather. She had never heard him speak that way to Grandma.

Grandma set the nightgown on the bed and stood. "I want her to know she's always welcome here."

"She knows that. Now, Rennie. Off you go. Your mother is waiting."

Rennie stood, collected her duffel and suitcase, and headed for the bedroom door, passing both grandparents on the way. When neither of them reached out to hug her or offer to help her, tears stung her eyes. *Keep going, keep going, keep going*, she willed herself. Halfway down the stairs she remembered the nightgown, left behind on the bed. She couldn't go back to get it; if she looked at her grandparents again, she would burst into tears and never stop crying. Maybe leaving it meant she would be back for another overnight stay. Or maybe it meant she would never see it again.

"What was that all about?" Rennie asked as she opened the back door of the car and threw her bags onto the backseat.

"Get in and we'll talk," her mother said.

She did as she was told. Once in the passenger's seat she said, "Okay?"

Her mom turned the key in the ignition. "Give me a second. I've got to get away from this house." She backed out of the driveway and into the quiet street. After driving half a block, she pulled the car onto the shoulder of the road and cut the engine. She kept her hands on the steering wheel but looked over at Rennie. "Listen, I know your Gramps has helped us out since your dad died—"

"Am I never going to see them again?"

"Rennie, please. Let me finish? By helping us out, I mean that he paid the bank what your dad owed and bought the bakery back for us, but also as an investment for him."

"But that's good, right?"

"I thought so. He's been telling me all along that when I saved enough, I could pay him back."

Impatient, Rennie said, "So? What's the problem?"

"The problem." Her mother took her hands from the steering wheel and folded them in her lap. "The problem is, he didn't tell me the whole truth. And the whole truth is, Gramps doesn't own the entire bakery; he only owns half. The other half is owned by Tony. I asked to meet with your grandfather tonight to tell him that Tony is horrible to the girls who work at the bakery. It's not right, and I asked your grandfather to let him go. That's when he told me the truth—that Tony is co-owner of the bakery, and when I buy out your grandfather, I'll end up with Tony as a partner. I told him no way, there's no way I can continue working with Tony." She looked beyond Rennie, out into the darkening night. "So I quit."

"You can't quit, Mom! Can't you buy out Tony and be partners with Gramps?"

"Trust me, little one, if the situation were that simple—"

"Don't call me little!" Rennie snapped. "I'm not a stupid baby. And so what if Gramps didn't tell you everything? He kept Dad's business going. He was trying to help."

Her mother pinched the bridge of her nose. "Listen. Obviously, I don't feel you're stupid or a baby. I'm sharing some real, grown-up problems with you here, complicated problems. Yes, your gramps helped us. Those were bad days, back when we almost lost the bakery. But he made me believe Tony was just another baker. He shouldn't have done that." She reached for Rennie's hand. "You don't need to worry about anything. We'll be fine. I can work for someone else. You've been through a lot in the past couple of years, but you don't have to worry. I've got this."

Rennie pulled away, leaving her mother's hands reaching out between them, empty. "You don't understand," she said.

"What don't I understand?"

"You sit here and complain that Gramps didn't keep the bakery in the family, and then you turn around and walk away from it yourself. That's bullshit, Mom. Bullshit."

"Listen, it's not—"

"No, *you* listen. You think this is your chance to erase Dad for good because you're so mad at him. Go ahead, then, quit. But if you don't care about something Dad built, I don't care about coming home with you. I'd rather stay with Gramps and Grandma." Rennie reached for the door handle and pulled. She scrambled out and made her way around the back of the car for her bags. When she saw her mother open her door and start to follow, she jogged away, making straight for the lit-up house.

Charlie made his way to the end of the Herrons' driveway after Jules pulled away and expected to see taillights diminishing in the distance. Instead, he found her parked on the side of the road. She hadn't made it very far. He approached the car. Even if she didn't want to talk now, he wanted to make sure she and Rennie were okay.

He was halfway to the car when the passenger door flew open. He stopped and watched Rennie hop out and then yank her bags out of the backseat. The car's interior light illuminated Jules's face, capturing the moment when confusion turned to despair as she realized Rennie was leaving and not returning. Within seconds, she recovered and got out of the car, too, also leaving her door open, the bubble light casting a weird shadow on the ground.

As Rennie passed Charlie, she clocked his presence but she moved on past him, her arm brushing his. He reached out and caught her sleeve. She yanked it from his grip, but it was enough to slow her.

"Rennie," he said. "Talk to me for a minute."

"Leave me alone. I'm going back in the house, where people actually care about me."

"Come on. I care about you, and I know your mom does. Can we go back to the car and talk to her together?" He looked beyond Rennie. Jules had stopped giving chase when she saw Rennie skid to a stop.

"No! I'm not talking to people who don't listen!" Rennie

yelled. She walked off, rounded the brick wall that curved in at the foot of the driveway, and headed toward the house.

As Rennie's determined footsteps grew fainter, Charlie rubbed a hand over his eyes. Between being ignorant of what had just happened and his many trips to the beer cooler, his mind and muscles were sluggish and slow to react. He pulled himself together and walked the rest of the way to Jules, who was still standing a few paces behind the car. Both doors were still as mother and daughter had left them, spread wide like the two wings of a bird ready for takeoff.

"Hey," he said.

Only then did she seem to notice him.

"I'm going to let Rennie be for the night, as much as I want to storm the place and drag her home," Jules said. "I'm too tired. Does that make me the worst mother in the world?"

"They'll take care of her. She'll be fine."

Jules nodded and then sighed. It made a lonely noise out on the quiet, unlit road. She got back in the car then, pulled the door shut after her, and stared out the front window as if she were considering driving straight off a cliff. Charlie circled around to the passenger side, then dipped his head into the car and looked across at Jules's profile.

"Mind if I . . ." He slid into the passenger's seat and pulled the door shut behind him. The interior light extinguished, and they sat in the pitch black.

"I'm playing catch-up," Charlie said into the darkness. "You might have noticed I had too much to drink tonight."

"Yeah, I did." Her voice was soft, gentler than he expected after the evening that had transpired.

"You want to tell me what happened? Rennie was pretty upset." His eyes were adjusting to the dark; he saw Jules nod.

"Yes, she was."

"Fourteen. Man." He shook his head. "I remember thinking I knew everything at fourteen."

Jules laughed wryly. "Then we get old and we figure out we don't know anything. We never did." She sighed. "I've been a fool. Again."

Her features were now clear to him and he saw her grimace as if she had bitten into a hard, sour apple. He lifted his hand to reach for hers and then stopped, unable to read what she needed. His left hand hovered over the console between them for a second longer and then he brought it to rest on the cool plastic handle of the emergency brake. "I'm not much help," he said. "I feel . . . stupid, and maybe still a bit inebriated."

Jules smiled a little. "Those two people will do that to you. Drive you to drink." She tipped her head in the direction of the house.

Charlie smiled back. "Truth."

"Hey. I quit my job tonight."

Charlie sat back. "You did what?"

"Quit my job."

He turned his body to face her. "Why? What happened?"

"Can we not talk about it right now? I need to stop thinking about Paul and Miriam. I need . . . a plan."

"A plan?"

"For Rennie. For the rest of my life."

"Okay. How about you make plans after a good night's sleep? You look tired."

"Yeah, well, you don't look so hot either."

Jules looked Charlie up and down. He felt seedy under her scrutiny, in need of a good hot shower and a shave.

"You can't drive home," she said.

"Probably not." He waved off her concern. "It's fine. Miriam will let me stay if I ask nicely."

"If you'd rather, I can give you a ride to your place. You can come back for your car in the morning, right? Lexi can drop you on the way to work or something."

Lexi. Lark. Where were they right now? Was Lexi sitting in her mother's knickknack-filled living room, bitching to her parents about the attention Charlie was paying to a dead man's wife? Was Lark sleeping or crying herself to sleep? Or had she been distracted by her grandparents, not giving her father a second thought?

"Sound good?" Jules asked. She had her hand on the key in the ignition, ready to go, waiting for his answer. When it didn't come, she asked, "You okay?"

"Drunk. Tired. Old? But yeah, fine," he said. "And sure, you can drive me home."

Jules, satisfied with his answer, turned the key. "Buckle up."

As soon as she shifted into drive and eased the car into the narrow road, he put his head back and closed his eyes.

"Here we are," Jules said, and Charlie stirred. He opened his eyes just as she rounded the corner and pulled into his driveway. The house was dark. He had forgotten to leave a light on.

"Looks like everyone got to bed early. That's good," Jules said as she switched on the map light. "I bet Lark will be as right as rain after a good night's sleep."

"I'm sure she will. Twenty-four-hour thing or something," Charlie muttered. He looked away from the bright light and fumbled in his pockets for his keys. He made contact with his wallet first; he pulled it out, set it down on the seat, and then reached in again to grope for the key ring. Finally, he hooked the ring and pulled it out, but once he did, he just stared at it as if he didn't understand what to do with it.

"Are you going to be able to see at the front door?" Jules asked. "I can shine my headlights, only I don't want to wake anyone."

He continued staring at his keys, not moving.

"Charlie? I think the beer's catching up with you."

He looked at her, confused. "What? Oh yeah." He rubbed his eyes. "Nah, it's fine. I'll find the door without the light." He opened the car door and swung his legs out.

"Wait a sec."

Charlie turned.

Jules picked up his wallet from the seat and handed it to him. "You're having problems keeping track of this thing."

Charlie took the wallet but looked puzzled. "What do you mean?"

"You left it at the bakery earlier this week, remember?"

"I didn't," he said.

She rapped him on the arm with the back of her hand. "Sure you did. You left it behind after calling the HVAC guy. I brought it to the gym later in the day."

He drew a blank. "I remember the day and the repair, I remember the phone call, but I swear to God, Jules, I don't remember you swinging by the gym with my wallet. I'm either drunker than I thought or I'm losing my mind."

"You don't remember because I didn't see you. You were with a client. I left the wallet with Lexi. She told me she would give it to you, and she did, right? I mean, you have it." She tapped the wallet with her index finger.

Charlie looked away from her face and down at the object in his hands and ran a thumb across the darkened leather. After Jules's visit to the gym, Lexi would have been certain that for every single meeting with Jules he had told her about, there were several more that he hadn't. She had slipped it back to him without a word, keeping the exchange with Jules a secret. Tit for tat, as his mother liked to say each time she had a meaningless fling following one of his father's infidelities.

How had he and Lexi arrived here, then, constantly one-upping each other? After a childhood of being in the middle of his parents' dysfunction, Charlie had vowed that if he ever settled down, family life in his own home would be different: he wouldn't fight, he wouldn't play the games his parents did, and his child wouldn't be a victim of the games, either. And yet he and Lexi had created a toxic atmosphere—not communicating directly, nursing resentments, and turning their daughter into both witness and pawn.

"Shit, shit, shit."

"Charlie? What is it?"

He shook his head and stirred again to leave the car.

"No," she said, and she reached for his arm to stop him. "You need to tell me what's going on."

Charlie pulled the passenger door shut and turned in his seat to face her. "What's going on? Okay. There's no one home. She left me, Jules. Lexi took Lark this morning and left."

"I can't believe it," Jules said.

Charlie laughed bitterly. "Oh, believe it. They're both gone." After a few moments of silence, he added, "I should have stayed at Paul and Miriam's. I really don't want to go into an empty house."

Jules took her hand from his arm and pulled the keys from the ignition. "Come on. I'll go in with you. You could use a couple of aspirin and some coffee. I'll put on a pot. Things might seem easier to deal with when you're sobered up."

"Nah, you have your own stuff. You should go."

"Where? To my own empty home? I'm in no hurry to do that either. Besides, you've been listening to me for years. A pot of coffee and a sympathetic ear are the least I can offer."

18

The sky lightened, and Rennie opened her eyes. Waking surprised her; she hadn't been able to fall asleep for what seemed like hours, with the arguments she'd overheard and participated in playing over and over in her mind. The thing that had settled her eventually was pushing the memories aside and concentrating on what she would do once the new day arrived. At least, she thought as she stretched out her legs and arms as much as she could in the cramped backseat of Charlie's parked car, at least she was rested enough to remember the plan she had made for the day.

She sat up, pushing off the pieces of clothing she'd pulled out of her duffel bag to keep her from freezing in Uncle Charlie's car. Last night, she'd waited until he and her mother drove off, and then she'd climbed in. Other than being cold, the car had been a perfect place to spend the night. Her mother had probably thought she was safe and sound in the guest bedroom in the big house; her grandparents would have assumed she had been whisked home by her mom. The time away from all of them had given her the opportunity to think, really think, about how screwed up her family was. And that was when she'd gotten the idea—a way to make herself feel better and everyone close to her a little bit worse. She would get herself on that bus to Northampton today, whatever it took, and put some distance between herself and her family. By the time they knew she was missing, she would be safe at Gigi's house, with people who cared about her. With that decided, she had finally been able to relax and sleep.

She swung her legs over the side of the seat and put her feet on the floor. She shivered. Her skin felt clammy, oily; the clothes she'd slept in were limp. She had to pee, and her only option was going behind the bushes in her grandparents' garden. In normal circumstances, she would think peeing outdoors was gross. But the walk to the bus that would take her into the city would be a long one, and she couldn't make it without going first.

Motivated, she stuffed all her belongings back into the duffel that now rested at her feet. The larger suitcase she would leave behind. She wouldn't need much until she got to Gigi's, and her friend would have clothes to share.

After checking to make sure the forty dollars Tom had returned to her were still in her pants pocket, she grabbed her bag, quietly opened the car door, and closed it just as quietly behind her.

The venetian blinds weren't closed all the way and the early-morning sun shone through the gaps. Jules stirred with the light but didn't open her eyes. She was exhausted. The good news was, she had nowhere to go: no work waiting for her, no child to bring to school. If she could drift back to sleep, maybe she could spend a few more hours in bed. When had this opportunity last presented itself?

She nudged at her mind until it quieted down, but the quiet was short-lived. Nearby, something was buzzing, insistent, like a swarm of bees. Bees terrified her. Irrational, she knew. She wasn't allergic. But her heart raced every time they hovered, attracted to sweetness, to perfume, to perspiration, to her food.

She stirred again, lifted her arm to shade her face with a hand. She opened her eyes, and what she saw was not her bedroom. It was a living room, but again, not her own. She'd been sleeping on a strange sofa.

The buzzing in the background continued, and so did her confusion. It felt as if she'd been drinking, except she hadn't; that much she remembered. Completely sober, she had driven Charlie home. They had talked, she and Charlie, late into the night. Talking. Charlie. Jules groaned, braced her hands on the cushions, and shifted.

Another voice moaned as she moved. The sound came from behind her, and she turned in its direction. Charlie, sleeping, wedged into the corner of the sofa.

As she watched him, the events of the evening came back to her. He had been drunk. She had ushered him inside his home and filled him up with very strong, bitter coffee. Their dirty mugs were on the coffee table still, the contents of hers largely untouched. She had lost track of the hour as Charlie rambled, talking about Lexi's line in the sand mostly—a line he had crossed. He called her ultimatums arbitrary, although he'd stumbled on his words and added a syllable.

"Her rules are so ar-bi-tra-ra-ry," he had said. "Wait, that doesn't sound right."

Jules hadn't corrected him. Soon enough, he'd forgotten about the word and moved on.

"Plus: 'Stay at home or help your friend. You choose the latter, and I'm outta here.'" He'd taken a loud slurp of coffee after that. "How is that a choice?"

Jules knew Charlie wasn't looking for an answer, and she'd let him sit with his question. She'd let him sit with his tears, too, when they came. Charlie had cried as he described watching Lark wave good-bye from her car seat in the back of the Audi, saying, "It's no life for a kid, being played between two parents. I should know."

It had taken an hour or so, but finally, Charlie had sobered up. "That's enough about me," he'd said. "I'm sick of listening to myself. Tell me, did you really quit your job?"

"I really did. Paul lied to me. It's impossible to go back after that. But it's not just the lies. The Welcome Home isn't the place we built anymore. I've been working my ass off for a place that doesn't mean anything to me—a place I can't believe in anymore." Jules paused. "On second thought, Paul did me a favor, just not the one he planned."

"Do you hate him?"

"Part of me thinks it's pointless to hate Paul for being Paul. I mean, I've known who he is for a long time."

"Not Paul. David."

Jules and Charlie hadn't talked about David in a long time. Months. The question had caught her off guard. After a few seconds, Jules shook her head. "Angry? Yes. At myself and him. But hate? I don't think I do."

Charlie leaned his head back against the sofa. "Mostly I miss him. He was my best friend. I wanted to be a good friend to him that last day, too. I tried, but I came up short. I've spent a lot of time feeling guilty about that, but I never admit how pissed off I am with him. And I am. I can't believe he did what he did, to all of us."

Jules reached for Charlie's hand and squeezed. "I know."

They had smiled at each other, sad smiles, and continued to sit quietly, the mugs of coffee long forgotten, the hour ignored, until Jules broke the silence.

"Sometimes I ask myself, 'How could he leave us? How could he leave Rennie? It makes no sense. What was he thinking?' Or I obsess, 'What happened to the man I married?' As if that man wasn't always afraid or constantly seeking approval or weak. But I knew the man I married, Charlie. David was all of those things, and I loved him even with his faults. If I'm honest, what he did wasn't surprising. It was horrible, but no real shock."

"Remember how David would roll his eyes at me after every breakup, telling me I should settle down and stay in a relationship?" Charlie shook his head. "Well, look who stayed."

"You did stay. You've been a great friend. And you were a good friend to David, don't you think any differently."

She had rested her head against the back of Charlie's sofa then, his hand still clasped in hers, and felt the desire to sleep wash over her. She could relax here; she was comfortable with him. Two friends, they had said all these things to each other without judgment. They were probably the only two people in the world who could understand what each was going through, she had thought as her brain slowed down for the night. What each felt because of their loss, the inevitability and yet the horror of David's act.

Then another thought had teased her tired mind, and she'd fought sleep to call it up. Something Charlie needed to hear.

"Rennie," she'd said.

"What about her?" Charlie had asked.

"I think she must wonder if her father cared about her at all. And if I do now. Don't let that be you, with Lark," she had whispered. "Don't let her think you didn't care enough to fight for her."

Now—all these hours later and with the sun climbing steadily in the sky—Jules watched Charlie sleep. The buzzing she had thought was a swarm of bees was his steady, rhythmic snoring. After the one moan he made when she'd moved, he had fallen right back into it.

Jules moved slowly to the edge of the couch, preparing to

stand without disturbing Charlie again. It was time to take her own advice and give Rennie her attention. First, though, she needed the bathroom, and another pot of coffee wouldn't hurt.

As she rose, her knees crackled, loud cellophane noises in the still living room.

"Jules."

She turned and met Charlie's eyes.

"You're here," he said. His eyes were open enough that she could see his surprise. Also his pleasure.

She smiled at him. "I am."

19

The day was humid, the air stagnant. Dan reached into the back pocket of his jeans for the bandana he had tucked in there that morning, but it was gone, perhaps lost on the Boston city bus or the larger coach he'd taken from Bangor earlier in the day. He was not surprised he was losing track of things. Since the bout of flu, he hadn't been at the top of his game.

Making do, he swiped his shirt sleeve across his forehead and hoped he didn't look too ragged. The flu had lasted four days and left him drained, thin, and scattered, but also determined to make a stop in this place before he boarded the next bus to god knew where. That Julia Herron had appeared to him in his fever dreams felt like a sign he shouldn't ignore; he had to take responsibility for his actions and apologize, something he should have done years ago.

He hoisted his bag up on his shoulder and opened the bakery door, setting off bells hanging from the doorknob. Inside, though, the place was empty—no customers, no staff, and barely any food in the cases. No one came running to help him, either.

"Hello?" he called once and then again, the second time louder.

A man's voice rang out from somewhere in the back. "Will someone go find out who's making the damn racket out front? That door was supposed to be locked!"

Within seconds, a frazzled young woman came to the counter, tying on an apron as she approached. "Sorry, sorry," she said. "We're closing early today and I didn't hear you from out back. We're having some problems with the baking, so I'm not even sure I can help you."

"I'm not looking for food anyway," Dan said. "I wanted to see Mrs. Herron?"

The girl gave him a puzzled look.

"Julia Herron. Your baker?"

"I knew who you meant. She . . . well, she's the reason why we're closing early. She didn't come in to bake today. I guess she quit."

"She quit?"

The young woman shrugged. "Guess so. No one really tells me anything. Do you want to talk to Tony, the other baker? Only, he's super angry today. You might want to come back tomorrow. Unless we don't open tomorrow. Do you want to talk to him now? Sir?"

Dan understood he needed to answer but he couldn't speak. Mrs. Herron's absence stunned him. He hadn't imagined this possibility, that the opportunity to apologize and the possibility of forgiveness would be lost to him. If only he had left Bangor a day earlier, if he hadn't traipsed around the country for months avoiding responsibility, if he hadn't left Boston after quitting the bank but had instead stayed to apologize. If, if, if . . . so many ifs, and now all opportunity was gone.

He shook his head and left.

Outside, the wall of humidity hit him again. He felt as immobile as the thick, still air around him, but he had to move, he had to go, and so, without better options, he headed back to the bus stop.

The bench inside the bus shelter was nothing more than a sheet of metal. The plexiglass walls held in the heat, and there was another man inside smoking some kind of brown cigarette, but Dan was too tired to care, his hopeful mood drained. He sat in the hot box, dropped his duffel on the pavement at his feet, gave it a kick with his heel, and slid it under the bench. Ignoring the other man and the foul smoke, he rested his head against the plexiglass wall and closed his eyes.

Minutes passed. He gave himself over to the heat and his fatigue, and he dozed. He heard a rushing in his ears that may have been the traffic whizzing by but sounded like churning water. The world behind his eyelids soon became the gray and gray and gray of concrete and stainless steel, of damp sand and sea and fog. He was standing on a shoreline, not imagining how cold the water would be but rather the weight of it and the relief of it all as that weight blanketed him and swallowed him whole.

"Buddy."

Dan felt his shoulder being shaken and he opened his eyes.

The man sitting next to him was looking at him. "If you're waiting for the bus, here it is."

Dan leaned forward and saw the city bus approaching. Yes, he could go back to South Station. It was movement, anyway. "Oh, thanks." He stood.

When the bus reached the stop, he got on.

"Joe," Denise whispered into her phone. She had planned to wait until she was parked at home in her driveway before calling him with the news, but she was too excited.

"Dee-Dee. I love it when you call me unexpectedly. But why are we whispering?"

Denise tucked her phone between her ear and shoulder and put both hands on the steering wheel to make the sharp left onto her street. "I don't know why because I should be shouting from the rooftops. I got a job!"

"You got what?"

"I didn't want to tell you I was interviewing this week in case it was a flop. But it wasn't! The first round was on Tuesday, and they called me back for a second time today. It's a PI firm, corporate investigations. Investigations, Joe! I'm back in the game!"

"Hey, second interview and they offered it to you on the spot? Way to go!"

"Uh-huh. Said no one else even came close, and they wanted to grab me up before someone else did." Denise slowed down to turn into her driveway. She pulled the car up close to the garage and put it in park. She was in no hurry to leave the car; she was savoring the moment.

"Smart people. I like them already. Seriously, Dee-Dee. I am so proud of you. You are going to be a great private eye."

"I believe I will be. Hey, do you feel like celebrating tonight? You, me, and the male child? I stopped at the store on the way home and bought a couple of steaks. Big ones. They'll feed three of us."

"You think Tom won't mind? Your boy might want to celebrate with you alone."

"Tommy likes you. And whether he'll say it or not, he likes that I have a life outside him and his brother. Besides, we celebrated round one together earlier this week. I want to include you tonight. What do you say?"

"I'll say yes, on one condition—you let me bring the wine. A new job calls for something more special than pizza red."

"You got it."

"Fantastic. Now, it's back to work for me, but I really am very happy for you. I . . . I love you, Denise Healey."

At those words, Denise relaxed against her seat back. *This. This*, she thought. Someone loved her again. And not just someone, *Joe*. Joe loved her. She hadn't yet put her feelings for him into words, but he was the person she wanted to share her news, her worries, her life with. "Thank you for believing in me," she said. "I love you, too."

Without waiting for his response, she disconnected the call. She wanted to own this moment, enjoy it. After she dropped the phone into her handbag, she pinched her forearm. Real. She was real; this wasn't a dream. And she was happy.

After a few more quiet moments in the car, she grabbed the shopping bag from the passenger seat and headed for the front door.

With a smile on her face, she went into her house—and almost immediately, she snapped out of her buoyant mood. The atmosphere inside the house felt charged, as if she'd left a computer on and whirring all morning. The front door had been locked, just as she'd left it; the windows were closed tight. She recognized nothing out of the ordinary, and yet the hair on her arms stood up. Years of relying on her instincts had left her certain someone was, or had been, in her home.

From its place in her handbag, her telephone buzzed. She crouched down to dig it out of the purse. Joe again. She answered in a whisper. "Hello?"

"Why are we whispering again?" Joe asked.

"It felt like someone might have been in the house, but never mind. I'm imagining things." She paused and listened. It was true: no noises, nothing. She walked from the kitchen to the living room and then to the bottom of the stairs. There was nothing out of place.

"I can send someone over."

"No, no, it's fine. What's up? You don't need to congratulate me again."

"Weird thing. Right after we disconnected, a call came into the station from Julia Herron. Rennie never made it to school. No one knows where she is."

"Wait, what? Are they thinking runaway, or . . ." Denise didn't want to finish the sentence.

"Runaway, maybe. Probably. There was some kind of disagreement last night between Julia and her in-laws. Rennie was upset by it and argued with her mom, told her she was staying with her grandparents for the night. But she never went back in their house, so I suppose the grandparents assumed she went home with her mother. Looks like she slept in a car on the grandparents' property, and now she's gone."

"That doesn't sound good."

"Look, I didn't want to ruin your evening with this, but you've been so concerned about this girl and I obviously have a history with the family, so I said I'd help look. I probably won't make it for dinner."

"Last thing you should worry about, okay? Jesus, Joe. Where could she be?"

"We're on it, Dee. Gotta run now. I'll keep you posted."

Before Denise could say another thing, he hung up.

Denise felt such a pang, as if she were living the anguish of the young girl. She had witnessed a disagreement between her mother and grandfather, but over what? Had Rennie learned what she herself had—that her grandfather had ignored his son's pleas for help? That would be enough to make both mother and daughter angry. But surely that bombshell would have made Rennie more likely to go home with her mother, not argue with her mother as well. The disagreement had been about something else, but what? And where was she now?

As Denise's mind turned over all these questions, a thud overhead startled her. There *was* someone in the house, in Tommy's room. Which was the last place to look for anything to steal but a collection of dirty socks and empty chip bags. She checked the time on her phone. School was still in session. She set down her cell and walked to the bottom of the staircase. "Tom? Is that you?"

She heard the bedroom door open with a clatter, and her son appeared at the top of the stairs.

"Mom? What are you doing home?"

"No, no, no—*I* get to ask that question. You should be in school for another, oh, twenty-five minutes. What gives?"

"I only had a study period at the end of the day."

"And you just left?"

"Sure. No one cares senior year. No one takes attendance. Hardly, anyway."

"It's week two of the school year, and most of you are still pulling together college applications. I'm sure someone cares if you skip. I know I do."

"Sorry, Mom. I'll text you next time."

Denise frowned.

"I mean, there won't be a next time." Tommy hopped down the stairs, taking two risers at a time. Before Denise could grill him some more, he asked, "How'd the job interview go?"

"I got the job. I planned to celebrate tonight, but that may be on hold."

"Why?"

"There seems to be an epidemic of skipping school."

"Huh?"

Denise shook her head and went back into the kitchen.

Tommy followed. "I don't get it."

"Skipping school has something to do with canceling our celebration tonight." She walked over to the shopping bag and started pulling items out of it. She handed the steak and some other perishables to Tommy and pointed to the fridge.

"You're not canceling to punish me, are you? This steak looks really good. What's this?" he asked, scrutinizing a bunch of greenery she'd just handed him.

"Rosemary. Fridge, please. And no, this isn't about you. Joe got a potential runaway and he may not be able to get away from work. Unlike you, though, she never showed up at school."

"She?" Tommy asked.

"Rennie Herron."

"Really?"

The tone in his voice made Denise stop unpacking to look at him.

He turned away. "Where does this go?" His back still to her, he held up a small glass jar.

"Mustard? You can leave it on the counter for now."

Instead of doing that, though, he started rummaging through the fridge, lining up all the jars of condiments and relishes and stopping to read each label, as if suddenly fascinated by the lists of ingredients.

"Tom?"

"Yeah, Mom?"

"Do you by any chance know where Rennie is? If you do, or if you think you have some information that would help Joe find her, now would be a good time to say so. I'm sure her mother's frantic. She's lost her husband already. We can't let her lose her daughter, too."

Tommy backed out of the fridge. His face was very pale. "I don't know where she is exactly. I talked to her yesterday, like you told me to, and I gave her the loan money back. She said she wanted to visit a friend and she needed a ticket. But I didn't think she meant right away, or—"

"Bus or train?"

"What?"

"Where is her friend? Would it be a bus ticket or a train ticket?" Denise moved past him to pick up her cell phone.

"She didn't say, Mom, I'm sorry."

Denise stopped dialing to squeeze her son's shoulder. "It's

okay—this is a good start. Thank you." She hit send and when she heard Joe pick up, she said, "Hold on one second." She turned her attention back to Tommy. "Now listen carefully because I will never, ever say something like this again. I am very glad you decided to skip last period today."

Dan checked his watch. They had hit traffic driving into the city, and it was now late afternoon, which meant his choice of destination cities would be limited. Not that he cared where he landed, as long as it wasn't this city or anywhere close by.

The waiting area was overcrowded. Dozens of people were packed into the room. A large group of travelers clustered around the departures board, some standing with bags slung over shoulders while many more sat on the floor, using their bags as makeshift chairs. One or two paced, but most had eyes peeled on the display. Dan looked at it as he shouldered his way through the crowd and saw the reason for the sea of defeated expressions: delayed, delayed, delayed. Every departure delayed.

"What's going on?" he asked a man who was pacing back and forth, a cell phone gripped in his hand.

"The police are searching the bus bays for some kidnapped kid. They won't let the buses go until she's found."

"No, man," a young man sitting on his backpack interrupted. "It's a runaway. They told me up at the ticket desk that they found the kid. Buses'll be moving soon."

He was right. Shortly after he spoke, some of the status updates began to change from delayed to departing, eliciting everything from cheers to groans of relief from the crowd. Several people got up and headed to their buses, creating a different kind of chaos in the waiting area. Dan backed up and let the crowd pass him—and stepped right into another person's path, a woman who was clearly in a hurry. She brushed by him, her arm grazing his, and turned only a fraction to call out, "Sorry!" in Dan's direction before continuing on.

He continued to watch her back as she pushed through the lines to get somewhere. His glimpse was fleeting; she soon disappeared behind the waves of travelers. He wouldn't have even bothered looking up if not for the apology, and the voice.

There was a time when Dan had thought he saw Julia Herron in some women he caught glimpses of at a distance. There was the woman with the same hair, the one with an identical frown, and another with the same squared shoulders, prepped for a fight. None had turned out to be her. Likely, this rushing woman wasn't either. Likely, she just looked familiar because Julia Herron had been on his mind all day. He had hoped he was done with the false sightings, but no. In that moment, he understood: that woman, that family, that job, and his failings would probably haunt him forever.

In a daze, he reached down at his feet for his duffel bag and realized it was not there. It was not on his back, either. And then he remembered shoving it under the bus stop bench. He hadn't picked it up again. It didn't matter; he owned nothing important, nothing of value. If someone found it, they would either take it for a suspicious package or simply take it, and they were welcome to it if they could use his clothes or the bag itself. He traveled better unencumbered anyway.

Jules hadn't run in years, but she was running now. *Please let us reach the bus in time*, she thought. *Please*. Detective Canelli had a head start. Once she'd given him Gigi's address, he had assured her that he would notify the bus line and delay departure of the Northampton bus. He was on his way, he'd said. He would reach the terminal first; he would find Rennie.

Maybe, Jules thought, not quite able to trust that this would all work out well. If Rennie were this motivated to leave town, she might find a way to slip through the detective's fingers. What was to prevent her from getting on another bus and disappearing to a place where she knew no one?

Stop, Jules said to herself as she sucked in air. She refused to go down that rabbit hole. She ran on.

This is what happens, it crossed her mind, *when a person thinks she can finally relax. When she thinks she has one thing behind her and time ahead to figure out the future.*

That had been her this morning, drinking coffee with Charlie, willing time to stop as she leaned her head back against his chest and listened to his heartbeat. They had nothing but time. They shared a laugh about the scene with Paul the night before, about Jules quitting her job. For many hours, none of it had been funny, and then suddenly it was, and they had both dissolved in laughter. Paul was an ass, Miriam had a stick up her ass, Tony was an asshole. Grumplestiltskin could stamp his foot and split himself in two, for all they cared. Oh, they had laughed and laughed at that. It didn't matter that they'd slept uncomfortably and very little or that Charlie had a hangover headache or that neither of them had brushed their teeth.

It was the first time in years that Jules had felt carefree. Years. Even before David's disappearance and the money troubles, even before David was laser-focused on opening the café, she and David had always lived with some level of stress. The friction between her husband and his parents, raising a child, being responsible for the livelihoods of others—there had always been something. To sit with Charlie and make fun of their horrible circumstances—one jobless, the other without his family—had been cathartic. It should not have been. There was nothing wonderful about your partner leaving and taking your kid, nothing enjoyable about being poor and out of work. But cathartic it was.

Jules reached the end of a corridor and turned a corner, bumping into people as she passed. One man looked at her funny. She apologized but she didn't stop to let him chew her out. She didn't care, not really. She was in a goddamned hurry.

Charlie was off parking the car now. Or, maybe he had found a spot and was on her heels. He had insisted on driving her into the city, had urged her to "Go, go!" as he illegally pulled into the taxi stand area outside. "I'll find you both inside. Go!" His superhero cape was back on, her need once again showing.

How ephemeral their joy had been. Charlie had just circled his arms around her; she had just closed her eyes. Then his phone had sounded, its ring ripping through the still room like an air horn, interrupting the peace that had followed their laughter. Charlie was Rennie's emergency contact, number one of two. *Call him first if you can't reach me*, she had noted on the school contact form, *the Herrons second*. The school administration had followed instructions, and thank goodness. Thank goodness she'd been with Charlie when he got the call.

He had answered but quickly handed her the phone. *Rennie never made it to school. Is she at home?* Jules had had to explain why she didn't know her daughter's whereabouts. "She spent the night with her grandparents. I'll call them. Maybe she's there."

Charlie had offered to call Paul and Miriam for her. "I have to talk to them about my car anyway, I can casually ask after Rennie," he added. "No need to spin them up, too." She had been so relieved. She didn't want Paul to learn of the disappearance and fault her parenting. Or worse. She had listened to Charlie bluff his way through the phone call. "Have you heard from Jules today? How's Rennie?" Heard Paul's raised voice in reply, "We haven't had a word from them since you all drove off last night."

Not a word, you bet your ass, she thought first. Her second thought was, *Paul thinks Rennie left with me, but I know she didn't. So where the hell is my daughter?*

That question had been answered when Detective Canelli called her. "We might have a lead," he had said, and then asked about a friend she might have talked about visiting.

"Gigi," Jules had said. "She lives in Northampton."

"The bus, then," the detective had said. "I'm on my way to South Station bus terminal. I'll meet you there."

Preoccupied with these memories, Jules's heel landed on something shiny—a wet patch, a sliver of cellophane, something—and she went down on one knee, the lower part of her leg extending out to the side at an angle, torqued. No one stopped. Damn city, a place where no one made eye contact either. She used a hand to help herself back to her feet. Her knee hurt like blazes, but nothing felt broken. A sprain, maybe. She would have to press on.

Slowed down, she looked at the signs above her head and knew she was close to the bus terminal. The waiting room was just ahead; the bus bays couldn't be too far. She limped on.

As she drew closer to the bus bays, there, right there, ahead of her and flanked by a uniformed police officer and Detective Canelli; there, not yet seeing Jules; there was Rennie. Jules eased to a halt, favoring her knee, and her body flooded with a relief so overpowering she felt woozy with it. Jules felt her injured leg buckle but before she fell to the floor again, strong arms grabbed her from behind and a voice she recognized whispered in her ear, "I've got you."

Charlie. He had caught up. Again, in the nick of time. Tears burned in Jules's eyes. Maybe she would have to talk to him about this—his impulses, hers. It would be a difficult conversation. But now there was only energy for Rennie. Rennie, standing several feet away outside a big, idling coach. Rennie, crying and nodding as the female officer spoke to her. Rennie, who looked up and across the terminal for no reason except maybe she felt something in the air change, felt her mother close.

"Mom!"

Jules shook free of Charlie's capable hands and, without a glance back, limped straight to her child, the girl who needed her.

The buses could wait; Dan wanted some fresh air. He made his way outside. It was still warm, but the humidity paled in comparison to the oppressive room he had just escaped. This close to the water, he felt a gentle breeze, and he walked into it, jaywalking across the street to head to Fort Point Channel. Ahead he could see some green space, a park. Farther on, across the water, planes were taking off, a reminder that people were going places, that he should be, too. He glanced down at his watch again. It wasn't that late. Buses would be leaving well into the evening, and the park, with its benches wrapping around the water's edge, was calling.

Dan walked over to the closest one and took a seat. Beyond his feet, harbor water lapped at the embankment. The waves were small, only ripples. Further out, the surface was almost placid. Ducks floated close to the edge, and Dan felt lulled by their bobbing and by the sound of the water licking land. He closed his eyes as he had earlier, outside the bakery. As it had then, the rest felt so good. Rested, he could hit the road again; he might go anywhere. South this time. South with the birds. Asheville. A coastal island. Florida. Someplace new where no one knew his past; a fresh start, just like Phoenix, Albuquerque, Taos, Chicago, and Ellsboro had all been fresh starts.

While Dan had been working out West, his father had died back here in the suburbs; he'd lived and died in the same town he'd grown up in. He'd woken one morning with his chest full of fluid, at least that's what Dan had learned from the small-town lawyer who had drafted the old man's will years earlier, after Dan's mother died. The lawyer had tracked him down after finding a postcard tucked into a drawer along with a copy of the will, his workplace address written on the back and nothing else. Dan had sent the postcard with its photo of pueblo dwellings from Taos—no, Albuquerque—so at least his father would know he was out in the world still, alive still. Stubborn, his father had never reached out.

Dan imagined his father dying, his heart pumping poorly, liquid rattling in his chest, his lungs unable to draw breath. A drowning of sorts, the lawyer had said. A cruel death, Dan thought, for a man who'd lived near the water all his life and loved to swim. With his eyes closed now, Dan saw his father trying to teach him to love the water, too. There he was, treading water in a large pool, his chin barely above the surface, as his young son shivered out on the lip, arms hugging his naked chest and afraid to go in. Every few seconds his father would dip deeper, take some chlorinated water in his mouth, and spit it out. When he could speak, he said to young Dan, "Have you made a better life than mine? Have you?" No, that wasn't right. He had said that later, years later, during the argument that would estrange them.

Dan concentrated again and his father reappeared. Yes. What he said from the pool was, "Come on in. The water is warm today. Come. Swim with me." But the little shivering boy shook his head no. He was afraid of the water covering his head. "Look," his father said, "I go under." He dropped below the surface and after a few seconds he shot back up like a rocket, hair wet, water streaming down his face. "Then I come back up. That's buoyancy. I am safe because I float. You'll be safe, too." To prove his point, he went under once more.

When the man in the water came up again, he was no longer

Dan's father. He was a different man, a sadder one. Dan was no longer a little boy but grown, a suit-wearing man standing on the sand and watching as the swimmer went under one more time, bubbles rising to the surface in his wake. And then . . . nothing.

"Sir."

Dan stirred.

"Sir, you can't sleep here."

For the second time that afternoon, Dan felt a hand on his shoulder, a firm nudge. He opened his eyes to see a policeman in uniform looking down at him, blocking the sun from his face.

"Was I asleep?" he asked.

"You were, and I need you to move along now." His warning issued, the cop moved from the immediate area, although he continued to monitor Dan's progress from several feet away.

Slowly Dan straightened up. He checked his watch. It was four o'clock. The nap had left him in an odd mood—confused, unclear. Across the grass, the cop gave him an encouraging nod. "Where should I go?" he wanted to ask the officer. Instead, he gave the man a wave and started walking as if he had direction and purpose.

For a short while, he had made himself believe he might have those. He'd imagined all sorts of things. A life working at the café. A life with Willa, maybe; maybe even parenting Josh. But all the time people had been welcoming to him, he had held everything back, denying himself, denying them. He told himself they wouldn't have wanted what he could offer anyway; he had always been so limited.

As he walked along the water's edge and farther away from the buses, he struggled to recollect the details of his dream but could only call up a fragment. Something about water. His father. A boy—himself, the boy who wasn't safe, wasn't buoyant, wasn't resilient. He wouldn't float, then or now; he'd known this forever, it seemed. And still the water drew him, and still he walked closer to it.

20

Early on Saturday morning, Denise called Paul Herron, identified herself, and said, "We need to talk about what you did."

She finally had all the facts she needed to confront the man. Joe, fired up on adrenaline, had called her after bringing Julia and Rennie Herron home from South Station. Speaking fast, he'd filled in the missing pieces.

"Rennie said there was a big fight on Thursday night. Her grandfather had been lying about ownership of the bakery. They found out that even if Julia had the money to buy him out, she was never going to own the place outright. Julia quit her job on the spot. Rennie was pissed at her grandfather for lying. But she was also angry with her mother for quitting. That felt to Rennie like a betrayal of her father."

Denise had groaned.

"It gets worse," he'd said. "Rennie also told us she yelled at her father on the way to school on the day he killed himself. She had been upset with him for being distant, and the last thing she said to him was she hated him. Rennie's felt guilty all this time. She thought he gave up because of what she said. But she hasn't been able to tell anybody; she thought her mother would blame her, too."

All this explained the look Denise had seen on Rennie's face the first time she saw her at the high school, and the air of sadness Tommy had said followed her around. The girl's guilt and grief weighed on Denise. "Maybe if I had figured it out sooner—"

"Stop it right now. You knew something was off, and you kept digging. You figured out what Tom knew, and you gave us the lead we needed to find Rennie. You did good, Denise. And don't forget, you still know some things about Paul Herron that no one else does."

She did, that was true, and she'd decided it was time to use her advantage.

Not surprisingly, Herron rejected what she proposed. "I am hanging up on you, Ms. Healey, and your empty accusations."

The trouble with people who thought they could get away with horrible behavior was that they always doubled down on the denials. But Denise was unmoved by Herron, his ego.

"Empty? Then you won't mind me talking to your daughter-in-law. Or your wife. Or how about this: I can share all the facts I know with a contact at the *Boston Globe*."

The article was a bluff. Rennie had been through enough and Denise would do everything she could to keep her from being hurt any more. But she *would* talk to his wife and his daughter-in-law if he refused to meet. She would hurt Herron where she could. That was a promise.

Herron's silence, coupled with the fact that he did not hang up, told her he had taken her measure and decided she would be true to her word. She raised a fist in the air when he agreed to meet her at nine that morning on the beach where his son had ended his life.

Joe drove her. He wouldn't hear of her going alone.

"You know where I'll be," she had protested. "And Herron's simply a bankrupt human, not a stone-cold murderer."

"He's a cornered, bankrupt, stone-cold human. I think you shouldn't go alone."

They left a half hour later and, running early, stopped for coffee at the Dunkin' Donuts drive-thru on the rotary. Denise quietly sipped her coffee as Joe drove the last leg of the trip.

"Are you worrying about the meeting? You can run anything by me, if you want."

Denise shook her head. "I keep thinking how this was David Herron's last drive. The last things he saw are the things we see. The rotary. The bridge. The clam and lobster shack. It was a lousy day, but maybe he saw all these things and had some hope because he thought his friend would be coming. He probably didn't know it would be his last drive. Or do you think he knew, Joe, deep down?"

"From the evidence we have? I'd say, no, he had no plans to kill himself. But when nothing worked out, he became desperate. Desperate people do all sorts of rash things."

"That makes sense, I guess. But this beach was so out of the way for both Herron and Charlie Gale. Why meet out here?"

"I think it was as simple as this: there would be little chance of running into someone he knew out here. He was a man who kept secrets, he wouldn't want to be seen. Why? You're thinking he had suicide as, what, a back-up plan?"

"I don't know what I'm thinking, to be honest. It's more that he's on my mind now, probably because I didn't give his state of mind a hell of a lot of thought back then. Being out here is a reminder of a lot of things."

Joe set his coffee cup in the cup holder and squeezed Denise's hand. "You've more than made up for anything you did or didn't do. You helped head off a disaster with Rennie yesterday. And this, today, confronting the old man? Above and beyond. I wish you could see how awesome you are. I say this with love, Dee-Dee. Maybe . . ." Joe slowed down the car and signaled a right turn. Ahead, Denise saw the signs for beach parking.

"Maybe?" she prompted.

"Maybe it's time to forgive yourself."

Denise turned away from Joe and surveyed the beach lot. Empty, except for their car. Joe had pulled into a space close to the sand line, as far as possible from the café where they had found David Herron's abandoned Camry. The air was still, and the early-morning sun was dappling the water, making the surface sparkle. So much had changed since that stormy day in April, herself included. But maybe not as much as she'd like. Perhaps this confrontation with Paul Herron would settle some of her remaining guilt, give her a small amount of closure.

She *had* helped Rennie, that was true. She'd spotted trouble on that girl's face a mile away. She could tell herself this, and Joe could tell her this, and yet . . . And yet. In 2008, she had failed the girl and her mother. Could she envision that failure becoming a little less burdensome? With time, could she forgive herself? That would be the advice she'd give Rennie if she spoke to her. *Maybe you made a mistake that day in the car, on the way to school. But you didn't cause your father's death. And you need to try to be good to yourself*

Denise turned back to Joe. "Maybe."

After a few minutes, Herron's Mercedes nosed into the parking lot slowly, like a hearse. He pulled into a spot close to the entrance but didn't step out of the vehicle right away. Wanting to take charge of the meeting, Denise got out of the car. Coffee cup in hand, she leaned down and met Joe's eyes. "Wish me luck," she said, and without waiting for a response, she straightened up, stepped out onto the sand-strewn hardtop, and headed for the weathered walkway that led through the dunes to the shoreline.

When she reached the walkway, she stopped and looked in Herron's direction. "Mr. Herron! I'm over here."

Paul Herron glared at her, the only acknowledgment that he'd seen her, and he took a few extra seconds to button his blazer, maybe anticipating a stiffer breeze off the water, or maybe stalling.

He's only delaying the inevitable, Denise thought. She was ready for him.

"I thought we might be civilized and discuss things over a cup of coffee inside," he said as he approached.

"As you can see, I'm all set," Denise replied. Buying him a cup when she was at Dunkin' Donuts had never occurred to her. "Let's walk down to the water."

Joe wouldn't be pleased to lose sight of her; if she knew her partner, he'd try to follow at a distance. Comforted by that thought, she walked on, staying a few steps ahead of Herron.

"This plan of yours, walking me down here, is blatant intimidation," he called after her.

Denise smiled to herself but didn't stop until she reached the approximate point where she had found David Herron's shoes and clothing. There, she stopped and turned back to Paul. "Intimidation?"

"Please. Taking me to the place where my son drowned? Well, I'm sorry, but I won't be intimidated, not by you or by any information you claim to have. Or by this place. It means nothing to me."

"You've never come here before today? Not to pay your respects, or even to remember your son? Huh."

"Don't you think you can judge me or how I choose to remember my son. My wife and I have all the memories that matter. There's nothing of David here. It's only a beach. Thousands of people have come and gone since he died."

Denise took a sip of coffee. Cool by now but a handy prop, useful for slowing things down. She looked over Herron's shoulder and spotted Joe in the distance, leaning forward on the boardwalk railing, pretending to look out over the ocean.

Herron grew impatient. "Why don't you tell me what you came to tell me? I don't have all day."

"Okay, sure. I think today is a good day for you to pay your daughter-in-law what you spent for your share of the bakery. Let her walk away."

Herron scowled. "She's already walked away. She quit. And why is my money suddenly your business? You know nothing about my business. Now, if that's all—"

Denise shook her head. "There's more. First, you're wrong, thinking I'm ignorant. I know all about the argument you and Julia had the other night. I know your daughter-in-law quit, and I know why. Second—I know about the meeting David set up for the day of his death. The one he invited you to attend with him. The one you ultimately blew off."

Herron was silent but he didn't flinch.

"How do you think your son felt, sir, standing here in that storm, looking across at all this water." Denise swept her arm in an arc. "Knowing—*knowing*—his father couldn't be bothered to lift a finger. You changed your mind about attending that meeting at the last minute."

"I didn't—"

"You did. It's been confirmed by one of the bankers who agreed to David's request for a meeting on the condition that you would be there. They were under the impression that you had a plan to help. The bank VP, he was an old friend of yours. They were otherwise losing patience with your son."

"As they should. He borrowed what he could not pay back, and then he wanted some sort of good faith arrangement." Herron shook his head. "I would have helped him if he'd met my conditions."

"Which were?"

"That he tell his wife what he'd done. That we hold a family meeting and decide together how to manage the debt." Herron scoffed. "But he didn't want Julia to find out, and instead, David did what he always did, Ms. Healey. Just like he did when he was ten and ran away with his best friend to avoid punishment for stealing things out of the neighbor's yard. And like he did when he was thirty-odd years old, giving us the silent treatment because he didn't want to answer difficult questions about his foolish plans to open a bakery. My wife always blamed Julia for the cold shoulder, but ignoring difficult things was a hundred percent David. This time, I wasn't going to let him run away from what he needed to face up to. I wasn't going to that meeting to bail him out until he brought every last detail of his fiasco out in the open."

"Well, I'd say that backfired."

Herron didn't say a word. He wasn't going to give in easily and admit his culpability, but neither was Denise going to give up easily. In her mind she pictured Rennie, months and months of her hard, unhappy face. How she had dissolved into tears when she'd seen her mother hobbling toward her. Joe had described the reunion so well, Denise had practically smelled the bus exhaust. She kept going.

"Okay, you drew a line in the sand over the meeting. But a month or so later, you wrote a large check to cover the debt your daughter-in-law had inherited. Why was that? Doing something out of the goodness of your heart?"

"Why is that so hard to believe?" Herron shook his head. "Julia and my granddaughter needed to keep going. If Julia held onto the bakery, Rennie's life would be safe and stable. It was the right thing, keeping the bakery open. My son couldn't seem to do that, but I was in a position to make it happen."

"It wasn't guilt money?"

Herron remained silent but Denise saw in his eyes the

calculating look of someone considering his next move. The slight turn of his head, the shoulder adjustment, the rearrangement of his facial features back into his default expression: disdain. "This conversation has turned into a waste of time. At my age, that means something. If you'll excuse me."

Denise let Herron walk away as she continued to look out over the calm ocean. Even the gulls were peaceful—some hanging out on the rocks, some strolling the sand parallel to the water instead of flying circles and screeching and dive bombing. It was a pretty day, and yet she couldn't forget the gray skies and dull, damp sand of that April. She heard the confusion in the voices of two people not comprehending that a husband, a friend was missing and probably dead.

Denise trained her eyes back on Herron's retreating figure. He was making slow progress through the mounds of shifting sand. Bare feet would have been more efficient than his loafers. From his lookout on the boardwalk, Joe gestured "What's up?" with his hands, and she shrugged in return. What came next? Did she let Herron go or did she continue to press for some kind of justice? Rennie was home with her mother now, and it seemed they were finally beginning the long process of healing together. Maybe that was the outcome Denise should be happy for. But Denise couldn't get Dan Hopper's statement out of her mind. Paul Herron had known his son was desperate. He'd known. And he'd done nothing.

"Mr. Herron."

He wasn't so far away that he couldn't hear her, and he turned.

"Do you ever give a thought to him?" Denise moved closer. "To what he must have been going through, here, when all his options ran out? For someone who claims to love his granddaughter, you don't seem to spend much time thinking about what losing her father has done to her."

"I think about my granddaughter all the time."

"Good. That's good to hear. Because here's what you're going to do. I'll let you pretend that you paid off the bakery debt and made the investment out of the goodness of your heart. In return, you're going to write Julia a big check. The amount you paid to erase the debt and any other money you owe her. You know why? Yes, because it's the right thing, but also because if you don't, I will go to her and tell her everything I know. Right now, she's angry, and she may keep you from your granddaughter for a while. But if she knows the entire truth, what you did to David, you'll probably never see Rennie again." Denise could hear the steel in her own voice. "I let that family down once before. Don't make the mistake of underestimating me now. You will lose. You have until tomorrow."

Without another word, she walked past him, toward Joe. Behind her, she thought she heard Herron call, "We've lost our son. We won't lose our granddaughter, too," but she didn't stop. The man had made his choices.

As Denise reached the edge of the sand, she looked up at Joe and he stepped away from the railing. He held out his hand, and she walked toward it.

21

In the small second bedroom, Rennie slept on. It was Monday; she should have been at school, but mother and daughter had spent all weekend talking and crying and both were exhausted. The previous day, when Jules had suggested a day off from school, Rennie had breathed a sigh of relief and said, "I hate it there anyway." This declaration had sparked a whole new conversation and more tears, but without the distraction of work and the daily tensions it brought, Jules had nothing but time to focus on what her child was telling her.

How much she had missed, she thought as she listened to Rennie describe her burdens, everything from the argument she'd had with her father on the day of his death to Jules's distance and the hole Gigi had left when she'd moved. "The kids here treat me like I'm damaged or have a contagious disease, and I needed to see a friend who cares about me," she explained. "I'm sorry, Mom, but I couldn't talk to you and I had no one else."

The reproach wounded Jules, but she knew it was true. While thinking she was capable and strong and a model of facing hard times head-on, she had come across as dismissive and uncaring and wrapped up in her own world of pain. The guilt of this might cripple her if she let it. *But I won't*, she had thought as she wiped tears from her cheeks and Rennie's.

"We're going to change this, Rennie. I promise." When Rennie looked at her, skeptical, Jules smiled and reached for her hand. "From now on, everything that happens, we make happen together, in agreement. We'll be together, like this," she said, and she held up the fist made of their entwined hands. "We can do anything. We can move schools; we can move altogether. Anywhere."

The idea of moving excited Rennie. "Could we really move? Maybe out near Gigi?"

"We could really move," Jules had assured her. "Why not out near Gigi? The schools in some of the college towns should be good, right? Northampton is a busy area, and I'll bet I can find work. Why not?"

With her daughter now fast asleep in the next room, Jules poured another cup of coffee and drummed her fingertips on the kitchen table. The word *move* ran through her mind and began to match the rhythm of her tapping. Move, move, move, move. The beat reminded her of a gallop, of riding off into the sunset. She smiled. *We could do it; we could pack up and move for a real fresh start.* Here, there would always be reminders of difficult times, starting with the bakery, which was practically right across the street. David was part of them and always would be, but he was also part of a past that wasn't coming back, no matter how hard she tried.

Her smile faded. All the ties to that old life were broken or breaking, like those to her in-laws. And the ones that were not exactly breaking were transforming. She thought of Charlie. Only three days ago, she'd woken up on his couch, blissfully unaware of all that was about to unfold with Rennie. She'd just been a woman hanging out with a man, one she liked for himself instead of for the history and the need between them. They had sipped their coffee in silence, and even after the mugs were empty and set aside, they'd continued sitting and resting together, Charlie with his back to the armrest, pulling her close, fitting her against his chest. Jules had felt his hand brush her hair, drawing her growing-out bangs away from her face, and then his fingers flit down to her chin to tip her cheek toward him. She'd felt his lips warm at her temple, and it had stirred desire, a feeling she'd thought was no longer available to her. The rush had been a wonderful surprise. And then the call from the school had brought reality crashing in.

She hadn't returned the dozen phone calls Charlie had made to her since then. She wasn't sure why.

The sound of Rennie's bedroom door creaking open nudged her out of her thoughts. Maybe she could find a nice small house to rent if they moved, a simple place that wasn't so poorly constructed. "Rennie? Come here a sec. I have an idea I want to run by you."

Rennie entered the kitchen, stifling a yawn.

"How about a drive out to Northampton today? We can be on the road as soon as you're ready."

"You mean to see Gigi?"

"Yes, but also to get the lay of the land—neighborhoods, apartments, schools. A scouting trip, to see if it's the place for us. If you're still interested in moving?"

Rennie skipped from her spot in the doorway and threw her arms around her mother's neck.

"I'll take that as a yes," Jules said, laughing. *My God, that feels good*, she thought to herself—the hug and the laughter and making her child smile. "Okay, scoot."

"I've been thinking of something, too . . ." Rennie let go of Jules and drew back a little. "I thought maybe we could have a memorial for Dad. I don't know, we could scatter his ashes somewhere. I know you don't like to talk about him much, but maybe it would be good for us to remember the nice things and also say good-bye?"

Jules, surprised, didn't answer right away.

"Never mind," Rennie said hastily. "We don't have to."

The ashes were returned to her after she had agreed to the remains being cremated; she'd forgotten about them, but Rennie hadn't. Now she remembered they were in a sturdy cardboard box somewhere at the back of her closet. She took in her daughter, looking younger than her years in a worn pair of Hello Kitty pajamas. Rennie seemed so raw, so vulnerable, so overwhelmed. The urge to protect her from the cold hard truths of David's death lived in every molecule of Jules's body. But the decision she had made to keep Rennie and herself moving forward without confronting the suicide hadn't made them better. A week ago, a few days ago, Jules might have said no and put an end to any discussion. Today, she had to trust Rennie knew best what she needed.

"You know what? I think that's a good idea," she said. "And maybe we can talk more about it in the car, make an actual plan. I want to know how you'd like to do this."

Rennie looked lighter when she said, "Thanks, Mom!" before heading off to shower.

With Rennie in the bathroom, Jules turned to her coffee. A few sips in, the front doorbell buzzed. No one ever just dropped in, and she hoped it wasn't Paul, looking for a confrontation. Jules walked to the intercom near her front door. "Who is it?"

"It's Fleet Feet Couriers," a male voice responded. "I have a delivery for Julia Herron. You need to sign."

Probably something from her in-laws; with luck, only something Rennie had left behind rather than a legal hassle that might ruin her day. She pressed the button to speak. "I'll be right down."

When she let herself back into the apartment, she was holding a couriered manila envelope. It was light, not heavy as she would expect if Paul were launching some kind of campaign to keep her tethered to him and to the bakery. Still, she wasn't ready to look at anything he sent, and she was struggling to shove the oversize envelope into her already full junk drawer when Rennie emerged from the bathroom, fresh from the shower, her hair in a towel.

"I heard the buzzer. What came?"

"Mail I don't want to deal with." Exasperated, Jules yanked the envelope back out and tossed it on the kitchen table.

Rennie walked over and looked at the return address. "Gramps. What could it be?" She ran a finger over the embossed label.

"Don't know, and maybe I don't want to know. If you're done in the bathroom, I'll go brush my teeth."

"Mom."

Jules paused.

"Remember when I was little, and I would cry about having a ton of homework? I never knew where to begin. You and dad would tell me to pick the thing I most did not want to do and do it first. 'Get it out of the way and it won't be hanging over your head.'"

Jules laughed. "My own words coming back to bite me."

"I want us to have a good time today. If you don't open the envelope, I'm afraid you'll be preoccupied. We won't have a good time if you're not in the moment."

Jules looked at her daughter. She was growing up—no longer that little girl, still worried but also wise. Jules had many regrets from the past couple of years. The biggest was being so lost in her own grind that she hadn't ever stopped to enjoy and marvel at her daughter's transformation. But that time had passed; there was no do-over. These mistakes were part of her, her scars; all she could do now was make different choices going forward. Rennie was right. The mystery of the unopened mail would preoccupy her all day, and she wanted to focus on her child.

"Here goes nothing," she said.

She tackled Paul's envelope. There couldn't be more than a slip of paper inside, she thought as she ran her thumb under the sealed flap. Inside, she found a check. When she looked at its face, she fumbled for a chair at the table, pulled it out, and sat down hard.

"Oh my God."

"What?" Rennie plucked the check from her mother's fingers. "Seriously, what's this? Are we rich?"

The sum was hefty—not enough to make them rich by a rich person's standards, but more money than Jules had seen in a long time.

"It says on the Post-it, 'salary and buy-out,'" Rennie said. "What does he mean?"

"This money is the amount your grandfather paid to clear the bakery loan. His half. Plus the salary he owed me." Jules thought of Paul penning this brief explanation and shoving the check in the envelope—washing his hands of her, her claims to the space. If she wanted, she could push for more. But she wouldn't continue to chain herself to him—or to her anger. The check was freedom, the ability to steer her own life. But there was someone else to consult first. It mattered what Rennie wanted. Needed.

"What do you say, Rennie? Do we accept this? Or do we stay and fight for the bakery?"

Rennie looked thoughtful. "I don't know. At first, it felt like we were being disrespectful to Dad. The bakery was so much a part of our family. But it wasn't the best part, not at the end, anyway. For me, the best part of Dad can be here." She laid a hand over her heart.

Jules set down the check and touched Rennie's arm. "Okay, then. If you can be ready in five, I can, too."

Rennie nodded and headed to her room to collect what she needed for the drive. Jules sat for a minute longer, surrounded by the possibility laid out in front of her.

Possibility after so much bleakness. How strange. How unexpected and wonderful and confusing and strange. Well, she thought, rising, there would be time to think about all that later. Today, now, there was a future to plan. A car that needed gas for a long drive. A daughter to hold close.

October 2010

22

Charlie tapped the brakes on his new sedan, slowing the car as he approached the center of town. He had traded in his now impractical 500-Class BMW for this sensible Subaru Legacy. The all-wheel drive and roomy backseat made up for relinquishing the nimble ride. The "dad car," Lexi called it. "Was the Forester too flashy for you?" she had asked when he first drove up to her door in the new car, half amused and half pleased to see that he had succumbed to something so sedate for driving Lark from her home to his.

Lexi had returned to their shared home from her mother's after only ten days away, but now, after a month of her being back in town, they were officially separated, complete with a mediated separation agreement and parenting plan. In the talks, Charlie had agreed to giving Lexi the second gym outright and adding a daycare program to both locations. That deal would please clients and also mean that Lark wouldn't have to be away from either parent when they worked.

In many ways their relationship was stronger now, post-separation, than it had been when they'd lived together. Healthier. His frustrations and Lexi's resentments had subsided, and pragmatism had taken their place.

For Lexi, this was a resurgence of her level-headedness. She'd had a chance to think, she told him in her first week back. "I think we push each other's buttons. The drama was exciting at times, but drama isn't love. I want better and you should, too."

Charlie had also had time to think while Lexi was gone, and he'd agreed. It was time for change. The seesawing between excitement and aggravation was not good for anyone. He couldn't kick the loneliness, though. What he had thought about most in Lexi's absence was his fear: fear of being kept from Lark; of having no one who cared about him; of being as alone as he had been as a young boy. And the loneliness had continued to dog him even after she'd returned.

He had lived with this all his life. David's friendship had filled the void; so had his series of short but intense relationships with women. A pattern of holding onto people for no reason other than fear could be considered a pathology, an action he might keep repeating because he didn't know any other way, his shrink had told him. It still surprised him that he had sought out a soft-spoken male therapist in Cambridge while Lexi was still at her mother's, but he was glad he had. Being a good father meant doing more than buying a safe car, and he wanted his head screwed on straight for the challenges ahead. Dr. Marsh prompted him to think beyond the moment, and his advice paid off. When Lexi said this to him about pushing buttons and wanting better, he didn't simply react. He thought about what she was saying. It was true, he concluded, that they would be better off apart.

And so, two weeks ago, with his blessing, Lexi had found a new place to live and moved out of the guest room, and a week ago they'd put their shared house on the market. Charlie was still looking around for his own place to live, but for now, Lark would live with him on weekends in the familiar old house with its cavernous great room. He was on his way to collect her now but was making a short detour into the center of town to Jules and Rennie's place.

Today would be the first time he had seen Jules since the day that started with them waking up together on his couch and ended with him watching Jules and Rennie climb into a police detective's car. A few days after, Jules had taken Rennie out to the Pioneer Valley to visit the friend Rennie had been running to, and what was supposed to be a few days' trip had turned into a permanent move. They had never returned. He only knew this much because Jules had sent one postcard from downtown Northampton. "Three days with Gigi's fam, few more days in an Airbnb, finally found a place to rent in Easthampton!"

Charlie didn't know what shocked him more: learning that Jules was moving, or the fact that she had sent only one card and never bothered to call. After that, he had assumed she was severing all ties with the past. And then, out of the blue, she'd called him the other day to let him know she and Rennie would be local for a few hours to pack up "the shitty downtown apartment."

"Can you swing by?" she'd asked. "Rennie and I want to ask you something, and in person would be best."

So here he was, driving, nearing the apartment building, hoping he'd find an open parking spot close to her place. The traffic here could be brutal. Lexi might say he was once again at Jules's beck and call—if she still said stuff like that, which she didn't.

But in his last visit to the therapist, he'd wondered the same thing aloud: "Maybe I shouldn't be so available. Maybe I need to protect myself."

"Tell me what you mean," Dr. Marsh had said.

"Here's the thing. We had this one night together," Charlie said, "just the two of us. We spent a night together, nothing sexual, and yet when I woke up and saw her next to me, I had this sensation of seeing all the broken pieces of our lives shifting right before my eyes, rearranging into a whole new picture. And instead of looking odd—Me and Jules? Come on— the picture made sense. I felt like I was seeing the future. You know, together. And then the stuff with Rennie went down. And Jules left. She left and I got one postcard."

"I'll call you," Jules had said over her shoulder as she and Rennie were ushered to the cop's car. And then she hadn't.

What went wrong, what went wrong, he would ask himself over and over in the week that followed, from the moment he walked into an empty house after work until he lost the battle to stay away from the open and available bottles of liquor. Then, as he'd dozed in front of the television one fuzzy-headed night, he'd thought he heard David's voice and the mix of sympathy and regret it always held when he was about to deliver what he knew would be an unpopular observation: "What do I always tell you, Charlie? Slow down. It's not the worst thing in the world to be by yourself for a while."

"That was the night I decided to find a shrink," he'd told Dr. Marsh. "Not because of the voices but because of how I was coping. The alcohol. Although I realize I might sound out of control. Hearing voices."

Dr. Marsh shook his head. "Not at all. Not if this is something that your friend would say to you. Is it?"

"More or less. He'd get on my case about my relationships. He thought I jumped into things too quickly, moving from one to the next without a break."

"Did you ever talk to him about what we discussed a few weeks back? That you have felt afraid of being alone?"

Charlie shrugged. "Maybe he knew. He knew what my folks were like. He was there. But no, we never had that kind of talk."

"I see. After you heard David's voice that night, did you answer him? Did you tell him what you told me about your future, for example, and seeing Jules in it?"

"You mean, did I talk back to someone who wasn't there?

No." He snorted. "Besides, it's not like I'd be comfortable talking to my best friend, real or imaginary, about the feelings I have for his wife."

"Understood. I imagine you miss your friend a lot. Was it comforting to hear him speak to you the way he used to, even if it was only in your imagination? Even if he was getting on your case as usual?"

"Comforting? I guess it was, in a weird way. But it was also hard because it made me wish he was back for real, that he hadn't killed himself. There are days when I'd give anything to have him lecturing me again instead of gone. But if he hadn't killed himself, I—"

Charlie stopped abruptly. Something had occurred to him.

"Do you want to finish that thought?"

The rest of the thought wasn't so easy to say aloud without feeling like a terrible friend. If David hadn't killed himself, there would have been no moment of waking up to see Jules next to him, no peaceful hours spent together, enjoying each other's company doing nothing very special. Drinking coffee. Smiling at each other. The awful thing that made loving Jules possible, and that offered him a glimmer of possibility that she might love him back, was the hard, cold fact of David's death.

"I was going to repeat that I couldn't have talked to him about loving his wife. But that's not right. The fact is, there would have been nothing to talk about."

"You mean if David hadn't died, there would be no possibility of a romantic relationship with Jules?"

"When I hear you say it, it sounds as if I like benefiting from my friend's death."

"I don't think you like this situation at all. In fact, your feelings trouble you a lot, don't they? You see an impossible choice between loyalty to a friend and a future with a woman you care about. A couple of minutes ago, you said, 'Maybe I should protect myself.' Protect yourself from what? Making a choice between friendship and love and living with the consequences?"

Charlie hadn't answered. He had been afraid to open his mouth in case all that came out was a loud wail.

Even now, as he replayed that conversation, he felt overwhelmed by the burden of the consequences, so much so that he lost track of his progress through town and overshot Jules's apartment building. Fortunately, the usually busy street was empty of traffic and he was able to make a wide U-turn to circle back.

He did a double take when he noticed the Welcome Home Bakery on his left. He had forgotten how close Jules had lived to her job, and he wondered if she had been tempted to stop back in since quitting. Taking his eyes off the road for a second, he tried to see in through the front window for signs of activity, but he was too far away and moving too fast. Had she seen or talked to Paul since their argument? Miriam? Charlie hadn't cared to be in touch since he grabbed his car from their driveway, and they hadn't reached out either. Just as well. He doubted the Herrons were embarrassed or even contrite, and he remained disgusted by their behavior toward Jules.

These thoughts distracted him, and again he almost forgot to pull over, but this time he caught himself before passing the apartment building by. He found a space easily, paid the parking meter, and went up to the front door.

"Uncle Charlie!" Rennie dropped a pile of white towels she was carrying onto the hallway floor and rushed over to him. Her exuberant hug was such a contrast to the mood that had settled over him that he laughed out loud. Charlie couldn't remember the last time she had looked so happy. Or healthy.

"Nice tan," he said.

"I joined a hiking club at school. We're outside a lot. I even got some new shoes." Rennie took a step back and lifted a foot to show off the low-cut boots.

"Impressive. Speaking as someone whose only hike these days is a climb on the StairMaster."

"Mom even comes with me sometimes. Although she's paranoid about ticks." Rennie rolled her eyes.

"I hear you talking about me." Jules's voice came from the direction of the living room. A second later, she stepped into the doorway. "Who wouldn't be paranoid about ticks? Hey, Charlie." She smiled at him but didn't come any closer. Her arms were full of paperback and hardcover books. "Rennie, can you take these from me and put them next to my handbag in the kitchen? They need to go to the library on our way out of town."

"Sure." Rennie picked up the dropped towels first and then took the stack of books from her mother. "Should I finish packing up the linen closet before I, you know?"

"Yes. Good girl. I need a few minutes with Charlie. Come back to talk to us when you're done."

After Rennie left, Charlie looked around at all the disarray.

"I know it doesn't look like it, but we're almost packed." Jules laughed.

"Can I help?" he asked.

She shook her head. "We've got a system. Most of our things are being donated. There's a truck coming soon, and we'll be ready for the pickup." She checked her watch. "I think."

"I can help. I'd like to."

"I know you would, but you're just as busy. Come on." She pointed into the small living room. "We can sit while we still have the chairs."

"Rennie really looks great," Charlie said as he lifted some boxes off a chair and sat.

"Doesn't she? She loves her new school. It's smaller and the kids are kinder. We spend a lot of time together outside of school. And believe it or not, the hiking has been a positive outlet. In fact, Rennie's hiking is kind of a catalyst for the plans she wants to talk to you about today."

"Plans?"

Jules nodded. "Ordinarily I'd let her come right out and ask you, but I think it's a good idea for me to prepare you first. She's asked me if we can scatter David's ashes up on Mt. Tom, near our new place. In the spring. Her club goes up there a lot and she loves it." She furrowed her brow. "See? I knew you'd need some time to process this."

It was true. Charlie was struggling to take in this news. "I guess I didn't know there were . . . I mean, the body, yes, but not . . ." *Ashes*. Twice, he couldn't get the word out.

"The state lab gave me a choice a while back. It was either cremation or a burial, and, well, I chose. They've been in a box in the back of a closet all this time."

Charlie shook his head as if that would clear it.

"I'm sorry." Jules's voice was soft. "Rennie's request took me by surprise, too. At first, I didn't understand why it was so important to her, but I get it now. She needs a good-bye, and we settled on the mountain in the spring. David and a mountain hike." Jules shook her head. "Who knows what he might have preferred, but I'll bet he'd like knowing Rennie will be able to visit him often."

Charlie wondered about the look on his face because Jules rushed to add, "If you don't want to take part, be non-committal when she asks. I'll smooth it over when the time comes."

"No, no. That's not—I mean, you were right. This is a big surprise." But as he sat with Rennie's idea of a good-bye, it began to grow on him. Over the past few years, David's absence had taken up as much space as his living presence. He had remained with them in the way humans live with heavy cement stanchions or brick walls. Stumbling blocks. Barriers. What would it be like if David as impediment disappeared with a proper good-bye and the landscape opened? Charlie's eyes teared up.

Jules noticed and reached out her hand to cover his. "Hey, hey. I've had more time to get used to this, but I understand what this is for you. I do. Good-bye means letting some things go and accepting others." She sighed. "Rennie needs that good-bye. We all do. David made mistakes, we made mistakes. If there's one thing I've learned, it's how easy it is to make mistakes and how quickly they can seem insurmountable. And how much we all need forgiveness."

Charlie thought of Jules carrying so much anger, of Rennie carrying so much guilt. David suffering because of his. All this time he too had been wallowing in guilt, trying to make up for it in all the wrong ways—attempting to be everything to everyone and in doing so failing to be anything of consequence to anyone. He thought, too, of the hurt he had brought with him today, the pain of loving people who seemed to leave him so easily, and he felt foolish. So self-centered. There would be time to talk about what, if anything, existed between him and Jules. But this wasn't that time. This time was for Rennie, for healing. There was so much to heal, after all.

A noise escaped him, something between a moan and a sob. Jules squeezed his hand.

Charlie and Jules sat like this, holding hands, until floorboards squeaked in the hallway and Charlie turned toward the noise. Rennie stood in the entry to the living room. He smiled at her. She and Jules may have moved, their futures may be uncertain, but they were part of his life right now, and that was good enough for the moment.

"I'm finished packing," she said.

"I hear you have big plans," Charlie said.

"Did you invite him, Mom?"

Jules shook her head. "I gave him a heads up that you would be asking him to join us on a hike in Easthampton. The invitation is up to you. I'm going to . . ." Jules motioned toward the kitchen and left.

"Uncle Charlie, I had this idea . . . I wanted to know . . . but maybe . . ." Rennie hesitated, as if unsure how best to begin.

"My advice is jump right in and ask," Charlie said gently. "I want to hear anything you have to say."

Looking relieved, Rennie blurted out her plans for an informal memorial to her father that would end with leaving his ashes up on Mt. Tom. "It's really pretty up there. I hike up a lot, and if he's up there, I can talk to him. I'd like that. I mean, this is all the way in April, on the anniversary, so you don't have to decide now."

"Of course I'll come."

Rennie threw her arms around him. "Thank you!"

"I hate to bust this up." Jules appeared in the hallway again. "But the donation truck has arrived. Rennie, you should make sure everything that's going back with us is out of the way. These guys mean business."

"I'll load my things in the car. Bye, Uncle Charlie. I hope I can see you before April."

"Me, too, kiddo. I'll be out when I can. You can take me on a hike, I hope?"

"Deal!" she said before darting off to collect her things.

"Not so bad, right?" Jules asked.

Charlie smiled. "Almost painless. Anyway, I should go. Lark's waiting."

"That's all going well?"

"Pretty well, thanks. Very civilized. And . . . I'm seeing a shrink."

"Well, I . . . Wow. That's big. Is it helping? Sorry, not saying I think you need help, but you know what I mean."

"I do. And it is. There's been a lot to deal with. Seems there was a need."

Jules nodded. "I'm . . . happy for you."

"Thanks. Now, I should go before I'm in the way."

Jules walked him to the building lobby. Beyond the front door, the Goodwill truck idled. Men removed dollies and moving pads for Jules's large pieces. Across the street and down the block stood the Welcome Home, its sign invoking a certain comforting experience for customers and memories of a different time.

"Hey," Charlie said. "I wondered." He pointed to the storefront. "Did curiosity get the better of you? Did you go in for one last look around after quitting?"

Jules drew her eyebrows together. "You didn't hear?"

Charlie shook his head. "I don't talk to the Herrons at the moment."

"Oh my gosh. I heard this from my friend Mai at the restaurant across the street. Tony's shoddy electrical work sparked a fire after all, can you believe it? According to Mai, it wasn't a big fire, and it was put out quickly. But burned wiring, scorched walls, and a melted vent hood were enough for Paul and Tony to close the place. No word if they're reopening."

"That's—that's terrible, but completely predictable." Charlie shook his head. "We *did* tell Tony he'd burn the place down if he kept at it with the lousy repairs."

"It's not funny, I suppose," Jules said after a moment. "Someone might have been hurt."

"But it's sort of funny. Or it's sort of karma. Or both. Except, wait, you must be concerned about your share of the place." Charlie ducked his head. "I'm sorry."

"No need to be. Paul gave me a check weeks ago. I'm officially out."

His eyes widened. "You talked to him?"

"Well, no. Only the check, not even a note. And that was out of the blue. He must have had an attack of conscience. Who knows?"

"Who knows?" Charlie echoed. "Okay, really going now. Tell Rennie I'll talk to her soon. And Jules . . . you look great, too. Keep taking good care of yourself." He turned and started through the door.

"Hey."

He pivoted.

Jules stepped toward him and reached for him. She drew his face close to hers and kissed him lightly, surprising him. She was always surprising him.

"Good-bye, Charlie. You take care of yourself, too."

23

"Here I am. Back." Denise dropped her handbag on the floor next to the familiar sofa and sat down. It had been a while. Four months of highs and lows and changes—some she welcomed, others she did not.

If Dr. Chamberlain was surprised to see her back after quitting therapy in June, she didn't show it. "It's good to see you, Denise. I hope you and your boys have been well?"

"Yes, the boys are doing fine. Teddy's started his first year of college, and he'll be home for Thanksgiving. Tommy is working on his college applications and he'll fly the nest soon. I started a new job a few weeks ago, and I love it. And I, well . . . I'm in a relationship, with an old friend. He's been joining in on some family things, and the boys are getting used to the idea that I'm dating."

"New job, new relationship, quality time with your boys—that's everything you hoped for when we ended our sessions."

"Yes. Yes, it is."

"And yet you're back."

Yes. Yes, she was. Denise looked around the familiar room. The small potted succulent, the non-controversial books on gardening and masterworks of art, the white noise machine: nothing had moved. Even the box of tissues, the high-quality kind with the lotion somehow baked into the paper, was in its place on the glass top of the coffee table, full as always, the top tissue pulled out a few inches, easy to grab.

Denise shook her head. "Remember how angry I was when I first showed up here?"

Dr. Chamberlain nodded. "I do."

Denise smiled. "I didn't want to be here, talking about my anger. I wanted a magic cure to get me out of bed and moving again. But you showed me that anger was at the bottom of my inability to get out of bed. You really helped me. I don't think I told you that when I left in June. I bet I didn't sound grateful. But I was. Am."

"Not telling me something. Hmm. You remind me . . ." Dr. Chamberlain picked up Denise's file from the coffee table and flipped through page after page of session notes until her finger landed on one place in particular. "Ah. Here. Shortly before we suspended therapy, you had started to tell me about seeing the young daughter of the man who committed suicide. You felt the breakdown of your marriage had contributed to your failure in that case."

"Rennie. Yes, I did tell you that."

Dr. Chamberlain put her finger on a line in the typed notes. "And then I asked you how it felt, seeing her."

"You did."

"And you didn't answer. Well, you answered, but the answer didn't address your feelings. You said you were glad she was a survivor." Dr. Chamberlain closed the file and set it down. "*You* look well. Your boys are well. You have found love again. And yet you're back. I find myself wondering why. I find myself wondering if this has anything to do with your seeing Rennie. What do you think?"

Denise thought she should feel better, that's what she thought. She had made Paul Herron pay, and she had expected that to make her feel elated; finally, some justice for the girl. And part of her *was* elated. In fact, she had been so overjoyed when she received proof from Herron that he'd sent a check to Julia, she'd called Joe at work to share the good news.

"Hey, great news. I'll bring the champagne. But listen, Dee-Dee," he'd said, "I might be a little late. Boston called. They have a drowner off Fort Point. No ID, looks like a suicide. There's no sign of trauma, and one of their patrol cops thinks he spoke to the guy on Friday afternoon for sleeping in the park. He was probably homeless, it could have been an accident. Still, they asked for our help. I'm pulling together a list of recent missing persons. Won't take too long, I think. We'll celebrate when I get there. You did good!"

Denise hadn't moved after Joe hung up. The news of this latest lost soul taking his life had reminded her of David Herron's last minutes, and this had overshadowed her happiness. Maybe she'd done some good, sure. And yet tragedy never ended; it kept coming. This thought made her by turns frustrated, disillusioned, deflated, and far more miserable than she'd anticipated.

What had her remedy really changed? She had wondered this as she sat there, the telephone clutched close to her heart. If her goal was to compensate Julia Herron, then sure, this was a win. Paul Herron had paid up, Julia had recouped part of the money her husband had lost. In reality, though, a well-off man had been only mildly inconvenienced. One man remained dead. A daughter's loss couldn't be reversed.

The months of therapy, hard work done to manage her anger and deal with her depression, now felt like a Band-Aid on a mortal wound, an inadequate solution to a wide and deep vein of unwillingness to accept that so much of life was out of her control. She couldn't make Matt love her once he had stopped. She couldn't make criminals stop harming the vulnerable. She sure as hell couldn't make Paul Herron bear the weight of his selfish disregard for his son's plight. Even now, she couldn't admit out loud that she could only do her best and that sometimes her best was not good enough, not nearly.

"I think . . ." But she couldn't get another word out. She felt as if an elephant was sitting on her chest; she couldn't breathe, couldn't speak. There were tears in her eyes, burning tears. She blinked, and they fell down her face. When she blinked again, the box of tissues was on her lap. She took one and then another and held both over her leaking eyes.

She didn't know how long she cried without talking, but it felt like hours. Finally, the tears began to subside. She wiped the last of the wet from her cheeks and blew her nose. "I'm sorry for blubbering like this," she said. To her ears, her voice sounded nasal and thick. She could hardly breathe through her nose.

"You never have to apologize for crying," Dr. Chamberlain said. "This is not a place of judgment."

"Ha! You might take that back, the more we talk."

"No, Denise, I won't. Here, mistakes, fears, or long-held behaviors that no longer work can safely come out of the shadows and into the light. Once we can see what you're struggling with, we can work on helping you understand yourself and, possibly, changing the way you move forward. It's my job, like investigating is yours."

"No offense, but trying to change someone is a sucker's game."

Dr. Chamberlain smiled. "No offense taken. Anyway, I wouldn't be changing you. *You* would be changing you. If that's what you feel you want?"

Was it? What she really wanted was to change Paul Herron into someone who was truly sorry for what he'd done, so sorry that he would take responsibility for those actions by owning up to them rather than paying up to avoid being outed. She also wanted to erase Rennie's sadness, and to give Julia her husband back. But she was only human.

"Do you believe in God?" she asked.

The question made Dr. Chamberlain sit back in her chair. "I am not religious, no. But many of my patients are. I see that faith gives them great comfort at times. Are you having a crisis with God?"

Denise gave her a sad smile. "I think I'm having a crisis with being human."

"Ah. I see. We worked on the anger before. And the depression. But this is deeper. Maybe at the root of it all? Your human limitations?"

"Maybe," Denise whispered. "Maybe I'd like to stop being so hard on myself."

"You *are* hard on yourself."

"If I fail to get the outcome I tried for, shouldn't I be hard on myself?"

"Do you want to continue to feel the burden of trying to be perfect?"

Denise thought about this. What would it feel like, she wondered, to give up that futile pursuit? Naked, maybe. As vulnerable as an infant coming into the world. She had so many worries, so many outcomes that she couldn't control. What if her boys grew away from her? What if Joe stopped loving her, as Matt had? If her new employer canned her sorry ass because she was getting older and slower and couldn't fit in? Maybe the planet would burn and they'd all die sooner than she wanted and, oh God, how could she go on, knowing she couldn't stop any of that even as she tried and tried and tried her best for the best results? It could be frightening to let go.

But what if it was freeing instead?

Tears welled again in Denise's eyes, but they weren't as fiercely hot this time. She shook her head. "I don't. No."

Dr. Chamberlain smiled. "Then let's get to work."

April 2011

24

The weather was beautiful, cool and breezy but free of rain, and the landscape inside the park lay ahead of her in crayon-box simplicity. Sky blue. Sunshine yellow. Grass green. April could be so iffy; Jules was thankful they had sun and not storms. It would have been too hard to say a second cold, raw good-bye to David.

She had invited a few friends to gather outside the welcome center of the state park where they would scatter the ashes. Gigi's family had arrived first, and Jules waved to Karyn, who had stopped in the parking lot to roll down the sleeves of her younger daughter's sweater. Gigi bounded ahead, calling out for Rennie.

"She's sitting at a picnic table behind the main building," Jules said, pointing back at the welcome center. "I think she might be feeling a little nervous about speaking in front of everyone, and she'd love to see you."

"Cool," Gigi said, and headed off to find her friend. After a few steps, though, she stopped and backtracked to throw her arms around Jules. "Thank you for moving here."

The force of the hug and Gigi's earnestness made Jules laugh with happiness, and she kissed her daughter's best friend on the top of her head. Her hair was warm from the sun and smelled of lemons. "Go on now, scoot. You give Rennie a hug just like that, and she'll be fine today."

Jules watched as Gigi took off for real this time.

"We're all thankful."

Jules turned toward the voice. Karyn reached for her and pulled her close. Jules was still in awe that their friendship had grown so deep so quickly. Once only acquaintances, the two women now met or spoke on the phone at least once a week, no matter how busy life was, and gave each other personal as well as professional support. Karyn had nudged Jules to apply for a job opening posted by a neighbor of her parents, and now Jules was working again.

"Lady, it wasn't me," she'd protested when Jules tried to credit her for the hire. "It was all you. You came out on top because you were the best candidate. Berat's lucky to have you. The job was made for you."

Karyn was right: the job as manager of a shared community kitchen was made for her. She remembered the interview day and how nervous she had been after being out of work for so many months. But Berat had put her at ease almost immediately as he shared his vision for a complex that would include the community kitchen, a coworking office space, an open studio for artists and artisans, and, in an adjacent outbuilding, a do-it-yourself auto repair garage. Where he was an idea person, he'd told her, Jules knew kitchens and production, and she understood a food entrepreneur's needs. Berat had needed this expertise. They complemented one another, and it felt good to be valued again as a partner in meaningful work.

The sound of tires on gravel interrupted their embrace, and the women broke apart to see Berat pull into the lot and park. When Jules had mentioned David's memorial and ash scattering in passing, he'd asked if he might come to support her. "I think we are friends now, as well as colleagues, yes?"

Jules had told him he was welcome but had half expected he

might change his mind at the last minute. Yet here he was, walking over to greet them.

Karyn touched Jules on the arm to get her attention. "I'll go check on the girls."

"You don't need to leave."

"Oh, visit with your guest," Karyn said over her shoulder.

When Berat reached her, he kissed her on both cheeks. "I am honored you have let me be part of this day—a day of endings, but also beginnings."

Of endings and beginnings. Jules nodded. "It means a lot that you're here."

Berat smiled. "I'll go say hello to Karyn while you prepare."

A light wind picked up. Jules buttoned the long cardigan she was wearing and started to turn back for the head of the hiking trail, where her friends were milling about, but she stopped when she saw a familiar face across the parking lot.

Charlie had seen her, too, and he raised a hand in greeting. He looked handsome and relaxed, a different man from their last visit months earlier. The changes in his life had been new then, and he had looked tired. Since then, she thought, juggling work with co-parenting must have grown more routine, less hectic.

She returned his wave, and he ambled over.

"Hi, you," she said, trying to sound casual although she felt shy. She had kissed Charlie twice in the last year, but because they hadn't discussed those kisses and where they might lead, there remained an awkwardness between them. Now, Jules wondered if too much time had passed without their speaking for them to recover.

"Hello back." Charlie solved some of the awkwardness by enveloping her in a hug. His arms felt as strong as ever. There was something so reliable about Charlie, something that always made her feel safe, although that very feeling of safety gave her pause.

While she certainly cared for him, his impulse to take over and hers to let him felt too easy.

After he let her go, he looked around. "I think I know everyone here today," he said, "except for that guy." He gestured in Berat's direction.

"My new boss. Berat. I'll introduce you. He's nice, you'll like him." Jules took Charlie by the arm, but he resisted.

"Let me see you for a few. Then we'll meet your friend."

"Boss."

"Boss-friend. He kissed you."

"Both cheeks. He's Turkish, that's what they do."

Charlie raised an eyebrow and Jules swatted his arm.

"Remember, this is Rennie's day," she said.

"Where is our girl, anyway?"

"Practicing her speech in the picnic area. She wants to do this service all by herself, but she's had a small attack of nerves. Gigi's with her. She'll be okay in a few minutes." She smiled at him. "She'll be glad you're here."

"Three years, Jules. I wouldn't be anywhere else." After a pause, he asked, "The Herrons? Here, or not here?"

"Not. I can't bring myself to call or email yet. But they aren't reaching out to us either. Rennie had the final say. She thought her father wouldn't want them here, and she's probably right. So, no. It's regrettable, but it's reality."

Charlie looked at her for a few seconds and then gave her another big hug. Someday she would have to work out what place he would have in her future; she would have to examine her feelings. But it seemed too soon right now. They had been through so much, so much in these last three years. Life had seemed dark and unmoving at times, chaotic and overwhelming at others. Maybe one day the way forward would be clear. Or maybe they would wait out the desire they felt for one another and realize it arose from the need they had to keep David alive, or their resistance to accepting he was gone. Jules just didn't know. For now, not knowing would have to be okay.

She clung to Charlie for a moment longer, long enough to spot two unexpected faces over his shoulder: a man and a teenage boy, walking over from the parking lot. The man, Joe Canelli, had been the first on the scene to find Rennie at South Station. Tom Healey, the boy, was Rennie's acquaintance from school who'd given Joe the tip about where to find her daughter.

"Can you excuse me?" She released her hold on Charlie and gave him a little nudge. "Go find Rennie. Or introduce yourself to Berat. I'll be right back."

Jules crossed onto the grass and made her way to the pair. Canelli was pointing up at the mountain, showing Tom some landmarks.

"Detective Canelli. Tom. This is a nice surprise. I know Rennie's kept in touch with you, Tom, but she didn't tell me you were driving out today. It's so thoughtful. Welcome."

"Mrs. Herron," Canelli said. "You really don't mind us showing up? Tom wanted to be here. I'm the chauffeur."

"Could I go say hi to Rennie, do you think?" Tom asked. "I . . . We miss her at school."

Jules noticed Tom's blush as he said this, and it was her first inkling that the young man might be, or might hope to be, more than a friend. Her daughter, growing up, having a first boyfriend. A milestone David would miss.

Oh, David. Jules experienced a wave of the gutting grief she had tried to hold at bay since first arriving at the beach to find a dog sniffing for traces of her husband's presence. For a long time, anger at her husband's recklessness and cowardice had made a strong buffer against this pain. But now, without the wall of anger around her, sadness could sneak in—at understandable moments, like today's memorial, but also in unexpected ones. Sometimes she would stand in the quiet of the community kitchen before the workday began and it suddenly reminded her of early morning baking in the days when she waited for her husband to arrive, days when she saw their future together so clearly. Jules knew longer stretches of peace now; she no longer tormented herself with unanswerable questions about David's motives or the strength and ultimately weakness of his love for her. But grief was part of her now. It had changed her. She would move, changed, into a changed future.

"Mrs. Herron?"

"Oh, sorry Tom. See the man in the puffy jacket? He's heading over to Rennie, too. Follow him. And Tom?" she added as he started off. "Would you tell Rennie everyone is here, and we should start our walk into the park in the next five minutes or so?"

"Sure!" Tom dashed off.

Jules returned her attention to Canelli. "It was really nice of you to come. I don't think I can thank you and Tom enough for helping to bring Rennie home."

"I, for one, like happy endings. But the boy and I can't take all the credit." Canelli paused, and it seemed to Jules as if he was weighing what to say next. She waited, and finally he made up his mind and continued, "Tom's mother and I are good friends. She's the one who had the hunch her son might know something, and that instinct prompted her to press Tom for any info he might have."

"I wish she had come today so I could thank her myself, but maybe you could pass my thanks along?"

"I will. Denise will be happy to hear that. She's felt . . . responsible."

Denise, she thought. *Denise Healey*. The name rang a bell for her but she couldn't think why.

"We both wish we could go back to '08 and change some of the things we did," Joe continued. "You know how that is. She's glad she helped this time around."

"Change some of what things? I don't—"

"Mom!" Rennie called before she could finish. "I'm ready. Is it time?"

She turned to see her daughter, flanked by her two friends, moving toward her with purpose. Maybe because she had just been talking to the police detective who had both worked David's case and found her child, or maybe it was something familiar about the determined set of Tom Healey's mouth, but in that moment, Jules was transported back to the morning of David's disappearance, watching a female detective walk toward her with evidence bags.

The woman had dogged Jules for days with her questions and presumption of guilt. "We both wish," Joe Canelli had said, referring to David's investigation. Was that policewoman Tom's mother? Denise Healey—yes, that must be her.

She turned back to confirm with Canelli, but he had slipped off somewhere. Later; she would talk to him later. There was a service to get on with. She straightened her shoulders and called back to her daughter, "Yes, it's time."

Jules and Rennie led the way down the Bray Loop Trail, an easy path into the state park. Rennie wanted to scatter some of her father's ashes in her favorite spot at the top of the mountain, and she would later, alone with Jules. With their friends, they'd decided, they would make this easier walk to find another peaceful spot.

Tom Healey seemed tentative around Rennie now that the trek was underway, and he stayed a couple of steps behind her and Jules. Berat walked behind with Karyn, Gigi, and Gigi's sister, the younger girl skipping on the trail. Charlie, walking alone, brought up the rear. Joe Canelli remained nowhere to be seen. Jules didn't mind his absence. It was unsettling enough to be reminded how many times in recent history her family had needed the intervention of the police. Now there was the coincidence to process that Tom's mother was the detective who had grilled her so aggressively three years ago, if it *was* a coincidence that their lives had collided once again.

Jules put the question out of her mind. She had promised Rennie she would be present today, and she would keep that promise.

She focused instead on her surroundings, their progress. In no time, they passed Bray Pond and walked into denser woods, where damp pine needles and last fall's decaying leaves littered the trail. Chipmunks approached their feet and ran away in frenzied, serpentine paths, never quite working up the courage to cross in front of the humans, but bold enough to show that they would not be scared off. The terrain opened up ahead into a clearing of state reservation land. Maybe where they were now, still among the thick growth, was a good spot to leave some ashes.

Rennie had slowed her pace and was walking now in silent unison with Tom. If this was a relationship that would, or had, become important, Jules would have to consider building some kind of bridge to his mother, thank her for helping with Rennie, and forgive her, too, for her past mistakes.

Jules thought of all the mistakes that had been made, from David's terrible ones to Denise's, Joe's, Charlie's, her own. For the first time in years, she thought of Daniel Hopper, how he had presented cold dispassion when in the company of his boss but looked haunted when she'd met with him on his own that last time. He had looked so young, a boy playing at a big desk, when she'd passed him her father-in-law's check. He had also made mistakes, and maybe he, too, had regrets. She wouldn't know; she didn't really care to know. But she no longer wished him ill.

Among the trees, Jules released her bitterness, her disappointments. People screwed up. Bad things happened. But sometimes they didn't. And that would have to be enough.

She came to a halt at the edge of the tree line. When she inhaled the fresh spring air, she recognized the orange scent of the plentiful white pine trees. Year after year, David had selected one of these stout, long-needled pines for their Christmas tree. Jules always argued that she preferred the tall, slender balsams, but when she did, he pulled her close and whispered in her ear that their house would smell like oranges. "Think of it, Jules. Oranges, for a whole month." His whisper had made the word *oranges* the sexiest word in the English language, and she could not, did not, resist. She remembered a lifetime of running her hand over his skin, of kisses, the love they'd shared when they made their daughter, the heat that had once existed between them. Yes, she had loved him. It was best to remember that and to remember David like that.

Here, she decided. *Here under this tree; this is where we should lay him to rest.*

"I think this is it," she said to everyone now gathered around, stopped because she had stopped. "The place."

Rennie nodded, then stepped in front of the closest white pine. Everyone fell into a semi-circle around her.

"I've been feeling nervous about expressing my feelings for my dad out loud. A friend"—Rennie stopped and looked at Tom, who blushed again—"said all I had to do, if I wanted, was to say the really important words. One of my teachers helped me find the poem I brought to read, and I was going to read it all. But now I realize I only need to read you the first two lines. The important words. The poem is called 'Lost.'"

She looked at Jules, who gave her an encouraging nod.

"'Stand still,'" Rennie recited, her voice quavering but clear. "'The trees ahead and bushes beside you are not lost. Wherever you are is called here.'"

The words brought tears to Jules's eyes. She felt someone move between her and Rennie. Charlie. He drew both of them close. She felt him tremble and understood he was crying, too. For a minute, maybe longer, they stood together. Then Rennie reached into the pocket of her jacket and took out a small drawstring pouch.

"Mom?" she asked, handing her the small bag of ashes.

"You want me to?"

Rennie nodded and showed her mother her shaking hands. "I'm too . . ."

Jules wasn't much calmer, and she fumbled with the ribbon ties for what felt like a very long time before finally managing to loosen the gathered mouth of the small sack. As she worked it open, she felt the wind pick up and blow across the clearing. She looked over the field. The tender new grasses shook; the branches, heavy with needles, rustled. She turned her back to the breeze as she began to tip the contents of the pouch onto the soil and matter at the base of the pine tree.

Right as she shook the ashes free, the wind gusted, whipping the now-empty bag from her fingers. Lightened, it somersaulted mid-air, once, twice, before landing at her feet. Some heavy ashes fell, too, but the lighter fragments were picked up by the wind. Time seemed to stop as Jules watched the dust get carried upward in an undulating wave, watched as the wave contracted and then expanded again. Someone behind her drew in their breath as the wind died out but the cloud of dust continued to hang and hover in front of them. She took two steps back, afraid the particles were about to rain down on her, but then the wind gusted again, taking the dust cloud up and out on the tail end of it.

For a few seconds, each particle glowed in the strong sunlight. They rose in its brilliance. Then, with one last rush of air, some of David's body flew out and out beyond them all.

Everything would be different from now on, the future all unknowable. Not the one Jules had seen so clearly on the day she met David in the library, or on the day they married, or even as recently as the day they got tipsy toasting the future of their small bakery. The entire world had shifted and would continue shifting, in ways no one could anticipate. But with change came possibility. While she couldn't know what her possibility would look like, she did know she would keep looking for it, everywhere.

And no matter what else happened, part of her past and David's remained: this girl at her side who would go on for whatever time she was given. Born, dead, reborn. Change, change, and change again. And so on. That had always been the story.

He checks his watch and panics when he sees his naked wrist. Then he remembers the watch is in his jacket pocket, the graduation gift from his father not lost but tucked away, to protect it. He looks up into the sky and notices now that sometime in the last few minutes, the rain stopped altogether, but he makes no move to put the watch back on. There is, he decides, little point. He knows he has been here, waiting, much too long. He knows Charlie will not show. He is truly alone with his problems, this much is clear. And fitting. He alone caused the problems, and he alone must solve them.

As he often does when he lies awake, he tries to pinpoint the moment on the timeline when he might have pulled the plug on the expansion to escape relatively unscathed. Almost immediately, he was in much too deep with the debt, his house and business collateral damage of an economy that had its own plans for him and others like him. But how could he stop when lenders were giving him money like it was a collection of cheap trinkets thrown from a Mardi Gras float?

As the wind blows his hair forward and swells up under the hem of his jacket, he sees himself later today, turning all his keys over to stern bank officials. He sees himself begging for work somewhere, his wife and daughter without a home, all of them stripped of everything. He sees Jules never ever respecting or trusting him again, and the thought of losing these two gifts is too much to bear.

Why couldn't he have been nicer to her this morning? Why had he been so cruel?

A huge sob builds in his chest until the pressure is so great he cries out in anguish. His wails are carried away on a gust of wind and disappear, and he feels no better with the release.

Try again, think of happy times, *he wills himself, and he closes his eyes.*

There she is, Jules, looking up from the pile of books at her feet on the floor of the public library. He's just met her but she feels familiar to him, as if he's known her forever.

Now there she is in bed, about to be his wife, tipsy on the Champagne they just toasted each other with, her legs open, her sex exposed, glistening with wetness.

There she is in white, a dazzling white to match her dazzling white smile, his bride, waiting for him. On their honeymoon, rising up from a swim in the sea, water running down over her golden skin. Legs split apart, Rennie emerging. Little Rennie: red and white, blood and mucus.

And then they were three. Everything that he had lacked in his own upbringing he gave her: unconditional love, freedom to explore, encouragement. He parented with intent; he was good at it. Or so he thought, anyway, until days like today, when he knew he had failed her, too—had failed to keep her world secure.

"I'm sorry," he says aloud. To everyone.

Jane Ward

His gut hurts. He is tired of standing, waiting, and he leans his back against a piling. It feels good to rest, and he slides down until he is sitting. He is one with the fence now. He can still see the parking lot from this new vantage point, but it is less likely that anyone will notice him. Not that it matters; no one is looking for him.

The sand feels cold and damp through the seat of his pants, but he doesn't much care. It has been a long morning, a long twenty-four hours. It has been a long six months of anxiety and sleeplessness, and sitting here on the sand, his back supported, his muscles and mind yield to the fatigue that has been nipping at his heels. His head feels heavy with worry and regret. There's little point carrying these now, though, and if Charlie is not coming, he will need a clear head for making decisions on his own.

Never a meditator, he nevertheless tries deep breaths, thinking about the breathing and nothing else. In through the nose, expanding the chest, pressing down with the diaphragm, expelling the air through his mouth. In, out. In, out.

The rhythm lulls him. In, out. Echoed in the sound of the surf advancing and retreating on the shoreline. In, out.

He opens his eyes wide and forces himself not to blink as the sharp wind brings tears that stream down his cheeks. He sits still for several minutes, letting the wind batter him. He is cold, and he hates the cold, but cold is something to feel, so he feels it. It makes sense to feel uncomfortable, to ache. The jacket is a barrier to the extreme weather, so he stands again, removes it, tosses it at the fence railing, where it just barely catches and holds. He lifts his arms out at his sides and imagines wings, being lifted like a glider or a bird—pretend play like he used to engage in as a boy running through the woods with Charlie.

The wind hits his damp chest and the clammy skin at the back of his neck, and it is both painful and exhilarating. He closes his eyes and sees it all, the good and the bad. He wishes he could have the good back and make the bad better, but he is only a man. The tears he cries now come from sadness and not the wind. He is only a man.

A new, rushing noise fills his ears, growing steadier and more insistent. He feels something rush past, and he opens his eyes once more. A large bird, pewter colored under the dull sky, pushes by, large wings beating, pressing down on the air to make progress. He follows it with his eyes until it lands on long legs at the water's edge. Curious, he leaves his spot, leaves all thought of his jacket and his friend and his morning behind, and moves closer. His knees and lower back are stiff from the cold and the worry, but he advances despite the discomfort until he is close enough to make out the graceful lines of the bird's long neck, its awkward shoulders, and it legs, absurdly delicate under its large, long body.

He stops. The bird wades into the surf and backtracks as a wave breaks on the incoming tide. It lifts ungainly wings and pushes off again, moves a few feet up the beach. He walks behind to see what will happen next. The bird homes in on something in the water and, gingerly, wades in again.

He looks down at his own feet—his work shoes, the heavy Vibram soles that have kept him rooted to such a slippery world—and he wonders what it would be like to be free of all the weight, to walk gingerly away and toward at the same time.

The air is cracked by another strong flap of heavy wings, and his bird takes off for the end of the rock jetty curving ahead into the deeper ocean.

He reaches for his laces. He sheds his shoes. Lighter now, he decides to follow.

Acknowledgments

Everyone who touched drafts of this book helped to make it better. At the 2014 Yale Writers' Conference, novelist Sybil Baker asked questions of the initial pages that challenged me to change direction. A.M. Monzione also read early pages and told me to keep going. Charlie Watts helped give a late messy draft a tighter structure. This book found the best home at She Writes Press, and I thank these wonderful sisters in letters: Brooke Warner, Publisher; Julie Metz, Art Director; Samantha Strom, Editorial Project Manager; Krissa Lagos, Copyeditor; and Laura Matthews, Proofreader.

Caitlin Hamilton and Rick Summie felt like my personal cheerleaders, the most enthusiastic and professional publicity team I could ask for. Joanna Broussard applied her bountiful creativity to my website redesign and produced something truly beautiful.

Preston Browning's retreat at Wellspring House in Ashfield, Massachusetts, gave me five uninterrupted writing days near the beginning of the project, and there the book grew by leaps and bounds. The atmosphere of fellowship created by Steve Kettmann and Sarah Ringler at Wellstone Center in the Redwoods outside of Santa Cruz, California, offered me a soft landing back into the United States and proved to be the best place to begin revising the final draft. The bulk of the work, however, happened between 2015 and 2018 in Nyon, Switzerland, where my days consisted largely of long dog walks around town and the countryside, and holing up on the Rue de Rive to write.

Thanks to Ellen Weeren for creating a supportive online writing community at A Reason to Write. Gail Randall Aspinwall, I wouldn't have made it through the slog without our FaceTimes and your last-minute help with editing. Terry Repak, thanks for talking writing with me on several long walks around Geneva and Nyon. Thanks also to Joan Santacroce for her willingness to add beta reader to her big sister resume; to Bennett Ward, someone always up for vintage steam train rides and steam punk festivals; and to John Ward who makes my work possible by letting me be me.

An illustrated children's book called *Cry of the Benu Bird* by C. Shana Greger (©1996, Houghton Mifflin Harcourt) introduced me to the brilliant rising of the Benu, Egyptian mythology's Phoenix, the bird that dies over and over, exploding into flame only to be reborn for a new generation. I thank Shana for allowing me to use a selection from her book as this book's epigraph.

The two lines of poetry that Rennie reads at the end of the book are the opening lines of David Wagoner's poem, "Lost" (from *Traveling Light*, ©1999, University of Illinois Press).

For the sticklers in the audience: I took some liberties with the geography around both Mt. Desert Island in Maine and Mt. Tom in Easthampton, Massachusetts; I took liberties with bus routes; and yes, I made up the town of Ellsboro altogether.

Finally, thank you to readers everywhere who continue to love—and learn from—all kinds of stories. It was difficult to write about suicide and anger and guilt, but maybe the notions of forgiveness and possibility will linger with you and lift you as they do lift me. For anyone who needs help, I wish you strength to make one call to the National Suicide Prevention Lifeline at 1-800-273-TALK (8255).

About the Author

Photo credit: Jason Grow

Jane Alessandrini Ward is the author of *Hunger* (Forge 2001) and *The Mosaic Artist.* She graduated from Simmons College with a degree in English literature and began working almost immediately in the food and hospitality industry: private events planner with Creative Gourmets in Boston, planner of corporate parties at The 95th Restaurant in Chicago, and weekend baker at Quebrada Bakery in Arlington, Massachusetts. She has been a contributing writer for the online regional and seasonal food magazine *Local In Season* and a blogger and occasional host of cooking videos for MPN Online, an internet recipe resource affiliated with several newspapers across the country. Although a Massachusetts native, Jane recently settled in Chicago after returning to the US from Switzerland.

SELECTED TITLES FROM SHE WRITES PRESS

She Writes Press is an independent publishing company founded to serve women writers everywhere. Visit us at www.shewritespress.com.

Magic Flute by Patricia Minger. $16.95, 978-1-63152-093-8. When a car accident puts an end to ambitious flutist Liz Morgan's dreams, she returns to her childhood hometown in Wales in an effort to reinvent her path.

Again and Again by Ellen Bravo. $16.95, 978-1-63152-939-9. When the man who raped her roommate in college becomes a Senate candidate, women's rights leader Deborah Borenstein must make a choice—one that could determine control of the Senate, the course of a friendship, and the fate of a marriage.

Center Ring by Nicole Waggoner. $17.95, 978-1-63152-034-1. When a startling confession rattles a group of tightly knit women to its core, the friends are left analyzing their own roads not taken and the vastly different choices they've made in life and love.

The Trumpet Lesson by Dianne Romain. $16.95, 978-1-63152-598-8. Fascinated by a young woman's performance of "The Lost Child" in Guanajuato's central plaza, painfully shy expat Callie Quinn asks the woman for a trumpet lesson—and ends up confronting her longing to know her own lost child, the biracial daughter she gave up for adoption more than thirty years ago.

Profound and Perfect Things by Maribel Garcia. $16.95, 978-1-63152-541-4. When Isa, a closeted lesbian with conservative Mexican parents, has a one-night stand that results in an unwanted pregnancy, her sister, Cristina adopts the baby—but twelve years later, Isa, who regrets giving up her child, threatens to spill the secret of her daughter's true parentage.

A Drop in the Ocean: A Novel by Jenni Ogden. $16.95, 978-1-63152-026-6. When middle-aged Anna Fergusson's research lab is abruptly closed, she flees Boston to an island on Australia's Great Barrier Reef—where, amongst the seabirds, nesting turtles, and eccentric islanders, she finds a family and learns some bittersweet lessons about love.